New Worlds

Brian W. Aldiss
John Clute
Storm Constantine
Matthew Dickens
Paul Di Filippo
J. D. Gresham
Simon Ings
Ian McDonald
Michael Moorcock
Kim Newman
Charles Stross
Jay Summers

Edited by David Garnett

New Worlds 1

Edited by David Garnett

Consultant Editor: Michael Moorcock

VGSF

First published in Great Britain 1991 by VGSF,
an imprint of Victor Gollancz Ltd
14 Henrietta Street, London WC2E 8QJ

With thanks to Michael Moorcock, Richard Evans and Ian Craig.

New Worlds is a Registered Trade Mark of Michael Moorcock
New Worlds Vol. 62 No. 217

A catalogue record for this book is available from the
British Library

ISBN 0 575 05134 5

Printed and bound in Great Britain by
Mackays of Chatham plc, Chatham, Kent

Contents

The first is for
Frances
For everything

Introduction

My first *New Worlds* editorials of the mid-sixties roughly coincided with the Beatles' first Number One, the assassination of Kennedy, the stepping-up of US bombing in Vietnam, Johnson's backing of civil rights and Medicare legislation, the rise of Black Power, the Arab–Israeli conflict, the death of Winston Churchill, the founding of the Kenyan republic, the rise of modern feminism. The only event of the decade which science fiction predicted with any accuracy was the moon landing of 1969. It is probably fair to say that for most of us this was also the least relevant event.

Certainly our sixties optimism was invested pretty thoroughly in what the Beatles represented both economically and artistically. Here were artists taking charge of their own destinies, whose work improved with almost every record, who were trying to develop an ethic to go with their power. Considerable power was still in new hands; the flow of wealth was moving steadily from capital to labour. The power was diverse, mostly benign and hugely inexpert. Within a few years the experts would move in to take over the free-wheeling pop corporations and discover the common denominators enabling them to produce a creative package whose progress they could predict.

During those brief years when power was distributed rather more widely than it is today, it had seemed that the old vices were mocked into oblivion and an age of virtuous experiment proclaimed. When the power was sucked back so greedily, so ruthlessly and so rapidly it caught most of us unawares; it seemed some moral Black Hole had formed overnight. We hardly knew what was happening to us. Through this period I think some writers lost confidence while others found unwholesome comfort in that return to old standards. Only in some visionary fiction was there any really coherent response to social change. If you examined the fiction receiving the greatest approval in, say, the *Sunday Times*, you usually discovered nothing more than a debased vocabulary, borrowed subject matter, a compendia of the century's received ideas.

For people frustrated by the banality and low levels of aspiration of the 'mainstream' it was hard to find alternatives, in English at least.

Those of us no longer entertained by the kind of fantasies, sf or otherwise, which filled the bestseller charts, were mostly looking elsewhere and still not finding much. The corporations providing us with bland sf bestsellers as well as bland social fiction and bland mysteries are usually the same offering us bland movies, bland records, bland TV shows. They frequently also produce our news-papers and magazines, which are distributed through wholesaling and retailing monopolies who decide what should or should not sell in the majority of our newsagents and bookshops. This means that small-circulation magazines – even anthologies of original stories published by major firms – can rarely get the distribution which would make them available to their maximum potential audiences and perhaps allow them to exist on something above a break-even level. The chances of a new, idiosyncratic writer being published by one of the corporations also get worse. The monopolies exist to maintain their own power and to extend it where they can. By gobbling up their competition as thoroughly as they have done in the past few years they are, if nothing else, reducing our choices and are certainly anathema to any kind of creative innovation. If eventually these monsters tend to collapse under their own weight it's no great comfort for the reader looking for something a bit more interesting or the writers who often go unpublished while the process is taking place. The few independents, who emerge to meet the demand, struggle to supply their audiences until the corporate people see there's a market to exploit and make an offer for their independence they can rarely afford to refuse. Only a few manage to continue and it is almost never easy. It feels to me a bit like the fifties.

The majority of us around the so-called underground movement of the sixties were not pie-in-the-sky hippie dreamers or sharp operators in Regency-cut jackets. The publications and the bands I associated with at least were moved not by dope smoke but by frustration with the awful inheritance of the fifties, the oppressive smugness of the previous generation, the grey choice of lamb or mutton, tweed or flannel, Amis or Braine. Most of our available literary models had the manners and opinions of the same seedy misfits in mackintoshes you saw hanging around outside radio shops or dirty bookshops. Pictures from Kingsley Amis's recent memoirs could be of some interminable office outing, of geeky chaps and strangely dressed ladies talking naughty and reaching spasmodically towards their reassuring, importantly mixed tipple while their reported conversation has the same unheroic heartiness, the identical embit-tered self-referring whine, of a million passed-over Prufrocks. Any reader wishing to get an idea of the awful predictability,

boastful pomposity, beery philistinism and unbearable depressive-
ness of the late fifties and early sixties would do well to read Amis's
exemplary book. Thirty years on, too little has changed. Even the
names are frequently the same.

Having, by the mid-sixties, at last escaped the bar-room philoso-
phies, the unremarkable ambitions of the Angry Young Men, we
became a little euphoric I suppose and thought our choices would
naturally continue to expand. Many of us thought you had only to
publish new ideas and original work for people automatically to
prefer them. It seemed public taste was improving and that popular
art was rising to higher and higher standards, making genuinely
original progress in various directions. The political climate seemed
to be improving, too ...

The seventies had something to do with our discovery that good
taste was not universal but that bad taste was. Sadly the corporations
discovered the same fact. Scarcely before the Sex Pistols had time
to make their first angry response to all this disappointment, they
were ruthlessly used by a young corporate challenger in his own bid
for power. Within a year, the Pistols went from being the authentic
expression of artistic and political frustration to a mere fashion
statement. Punk had become not a revolution but a safety valve.
Suckered again.

The present resurgence in good literary sf, both in short stories
and novels, has its origins chiefly in the semi-professional magazines
which, with *Interzone*, kept things going during the bad years of the
eighties. The resurgence owes much to editor-publishers like Chris
Reed, whose *Back Brain Recluse (BBR)* can now, like *Interzone*, be
ordered through newsagents. These magazines encouraged several
of the people published here and have supported a growing
movement of young writers in England and America.

Literary science fiction remains largely ignored by reviewers who
will still announce that J. G. Ballard or Kurt Vonnegut books are too
good to be sf, in spite of the writers' own claims that they are nothing
less. TV critics will still tell us, without a flicker of *déjà vu*, that literary
sf is more about inner space than outer space and proceed to air
the same extraordinary prejudices they have been airing for years,
based chiefly on the inability or unwillingness to learn an unfamiliar
vocabulary, a failure to detect irony, and a presumption that the
writers are primitives or *näifs*. When this kind of sf goes to the
reviewer eagerly awaiting the next David Eddings bestseller it is
frequently met with straightforward hostility.

The received wisdom from such people (including the grumpy
Amis who somehow felt sf, like jazz, had let him down) was that the
'New Wave' was nothing more than a series of airy experiments in

style, of grotesque self-indulgence and an unhealthy obsession with sex. I have seen these opinions regurgitated, always unexamined, for more than a quarter of a century and they are especially wearying since any glance at the evidence immediately contradicts them. Novels which first appeared in *New Worlds* included *The Crystal World* by Ballard, *Camp Concentration* by Disch, *Bug Jack Barron* by Spinrad, *An Age* by Aldiss and *Bill, the Galactic Hero* by Harrison. They might have been dissimilar, but they certainly weren't insubstantial. The same can be said for the bulk of the fiction published in *New Worlds,* the majority of which was republished elsewhere and continues to be republished (a representative anthology, *New Worlds,* Fontana, 1983, also contains a complete bibliography of issues). But if a myth can resist the evidence so thoroughly, it's probably no surprise that literary sf is still regarded with uneasy suspicion by Star Trek enthusiasts and by people who think of Malcolm Bradbury as both the mouthpiece and master of modern fiction.

Even if Philip K. Dick was right, after all, and *Total Recall* was his posthumous experience of corporate rape ('*We Can Remember It for You Wholesale*' with its tongue torn out), for me the nineties is a period quite as interesting as the sixties, producing a wealth of confidently maturing writers. The sixties was for some of us a marvellous high, a Golden Age. I said so while it was happening and I enjoyed it to the full, but once it was over there seemed no point in trying to re-create it. The times were, indeed, a-changing . . .

However, the same idealism, the same creative energy, the same anger, frustration and enthusiasm which produced the seminal work of the sixties is now producing the liveliest writing of the nineties. These particular times offer a great deal of optimism for those of us who want to embrace, enjoy and employ change. Even before it became a professional magazine in 1946 *New Worlds* always embraced and celebrated social, scientific and cultural change, changes in the way we thought and used language, fundamental changes in perception and art that represented those changes.

Because it was clear that so many talented new writers were emerging through the new magazines and slightly more visible original anthologies like Holdstock and Evans's *Other Edens* or Garnett's *Zenith,* and because none of these publications was getting the kind of support and distribution they deserved, I approached David Garnett to see if he would like to take over the editorship of *New Worlds.* Richard Evans, always a champion of literary sf, agreed that Gollancz (still one of the very few independents in publishing) would publish it and Ian Craig was eager to design it.

David Garnett seemed an ideal person to put his own mark on *NW* while continuing the tradition of publishing substantial work which characterised the best *NW* stories even before E. J.Carnell published Ballard's *The Drowned World* and *The Terminal Beach*.

The majority of *New Worlds* stories, whether they were series like Disch's *334*, Aldiss's *Acid Head Wars* or Ballard's *The Atrocity Exhibition*, novellas like Sladek's *Masterson and the Clerks*, elegies like M. John Harrison's *Running Down*, experimental sequences like Zoline's *The Heat Death of the Universe* and Jones's *The Eye of the Lens* (many of which were, so to speak, pre-post-modern . . .), were strong on content and style and tended to look at character and relationships with what can only be called a moral eye.

The *NW* writers, raised in the years when the information explosion made it impossible for anyone but the most socially isolated to ignore the world and the sins against the human spirit being perpetrated in the name of our old and honourable icons, questioned our traditional enlightenment remedies for the world's ills, values which writers like Heinlein, Clarke and even Wells had carried into the distant future and the depths of space.

Much of this kind of science fiction became, never deliberately, a rather clever means of escaping the uncomfortable realities of the present. At its simplest it creates a never-never land where big men do big things with big machines to grotesque enemies, or young women discover the joys of caring for sentient teddy bears.

The sf blockbuster has become as familiar as the bestselling spy story or any other commercially successful power fantasy which proclaims, to me at any rate, the dull despair of the barely enfranchised. But some writers in the tradition, say, of Wylie and Orwell and Dick used their fascination with the marvellous and new to tell sharp and often moving parables of the human condition. Joanna Russ, Harlan Ellison, Kit Reed, Frits Leiber, Gene Wolfe, Mary Gentle, Lewis Shiner, Charles Harness, Lucius Shepard, Gwyneth Jones, Terry Bisson, William Gibson, Pat Cadigan, Colin Greenland, Lisa Tuttle, Christopher Evans, Garry Kilworth, Eric Brown, Robert Holdstock, Steve Baxter, Misha, Barrington Bayley are merely a few of those writers I have not previously mentioned. There are many more, not all working in English, who have continued (often with great difficulty since their work rarely fits commercial categories) to give us an extraordinary variety of outstanding fiction. Literary science fiction is being written all over the industrialised world. Publishing it sometimes proves difficult.

For a while there were very few places where a literary sf story by anyone but an established name would be welcomed. During the mid-eighties semi-professional magazines, not unlike the music fanzines they were frequently combined with, began to proliferate. They steadily improved both in design and content and are nowadays available by mail and through specialist shops. Many of them publish the same writers you will find in *NW* or *Interzone*. They usually publish idiosyncratic talent as a matter of policy. Frequently it is the most daring and curious work around. Some of the titles, more or less at random, are *The Scanner, The Edge, Journal Wired, Nova, Works, Xenos* and *Nova Express*. There are also critical magazines like *SF Eye, The New York Review of SF, Quantum* and *Nexus* which take a frequently uncompromising look at the imaginative fiction available today. Sf is a form which can no longer be considered of minority interest. Its vocabularies and references are familiar to the majority of us who read for pleasure. It therefore urgently needs, I think, some rigorous criticism. Very few of these magazines make much distinction between 'mainstream' and 'fantasy' fiction and quite reasonably, since those distinctions no longer exist in any meaningful sense. At the time of writing, *Nexus* should be available through newsagents. I am looking forward to it. Its editorial policy statement displays a fine impatience with the existing *status quo*.

In other words, *New Worlds* doesn't by any means publish all the good work. By ordering *Back Brain Recluse* and *Interzone* the interested reader should be able to find a great range of other publications providing a wonderful alternative to the cloned ranks of paperbacks you encounter these days whenever you enter a bookshop. Meanwhile, Britton's and Butterworth's crazed ironies continue to erupt from their Savoy imprint, publishing Lord Horror comics or bizarre P. J. Proby records with a quirky, defiant vulgarity which echoes Smollett and Gillray but which thoroughly (some would say terrifyingly) relate to this century's complex realities. Savoy's constant problems with various authorities tend to make their distribution erratic but for those who find contemporary cyberpunk a little bit tame *Lord Horror, Meng & Ecker* and the Hitler Youth Orchestra should restore their faith in excess.

The bulk of commercial sf and fantasy is no more 'imaginative' than the bulk of anything else. Even at their best these books prove that Enlightenment idealism, like magic, works best in a sword and sorcery tale.

The stories published here have about as much to do with those mindless exploitation sf sequels to which the famous add their names, as *Brighton Rock* has to do with *Kane and Abel*. They also have little to do with most 'hard' sf, which generally lacks the excitement and immediacy of any issue of *Nature* and is perhaps sf's least accurate method of examining the future. The stories do deal interestingly with human relationships, eternal dilemmas, new moralities, today's experience. I don't think it matters what label they get as long as people who want to read them can find them. If they share a generic label with a lot of very bad commercial fiction that is scarcely their fault. If *Jane Eyre* is a Gothic, *The Mill on the Floss* a Romance, *Les Misérables* a Mystery, *Chéri* Erotica or *Victory* a Sea Story, then *1984, V, A Clockwork Orange, The Old Men at the Zoo* and *The Handmaid's Tale* are all Science Fiction while George Orwell, Thomas Pynchon, Anthony Burgess, Angus Wilson, Margaret Atwood, Julian Barnes, Salmon Rushdie, Russell Hoban, Peter Ackroyd, Doris Lessing, Robert Nye, Jonathan Carroll, Angela Carter, John Barth, William Burrroughs, Iain Banks, N'guib Mahfouz, William Golding, Fay Weldon, Herman Hesse, Fawzi Mellah and hundreds more are sf writers. Or you could say that, like the authors here, they chose an appropriate visionary medium for a specific literary purpose. Our judgement of their work becomes a question of preference, not of quality. What unites the writers and what you can fairly judge them on is their level of aspiration, not their choice of medium.

An encouraging sign for me is that only three old *NW* hands are represented here — Aldiss, Clute and myself — while there is a preponderance of relatively new writers, including an excellent first story. This confirms my own optimism about restarting *New Worlds*. If this particular collection is predominantly British and predominantly male, future editions should see a wider range of nationalities and genders and I personally hope more non-English-speaking writers will begin submitting translations.

Literary sf has never been more central to common experience, never more valid and very rarely better. I'm sure increasing numbers of readers will find it considerably more satisfying than most of the alternatives. The 'mainstream' is today little more than one exhausted tributary of the literary flood, a *wadi* full of beached arks whose bewildered crews are beginning to ask themselves if the current will ever return. They're a bit like people at a Baghdad bus-stop on 17 January 1991 asking why the Number Seven is so unusually late.

It almost seems a shame to tell them.

Michael Moorcock
London, April 1991

Immaculate

Storm Constantine

For Pat Cadigan

Donna can feel computers dreaming: they reach out and touch her mind, or so she says. In the dark of her room, as the white noise tide of day goes out, and the glowing sky rises, the machines begin to meditate, or so she says. It makes Reeb think of dogs twitching in their sleep, the tongues of slumbering cats licking at invisible bowls of milk; human signs.

'You always have to look for human signs in everything,' says Donna. She's a star, she's a nobody. She sells things.

Reeb is a director, a creative of sufficient reputation to currently work for Say! Play!, a company specialising in leisure software. This is the man who configured the footage that sold the product that juiced the data-suit that excited the customer who paid the cash that went into the accounts of Say! Play! He would not dare to call himself an artist, although his previous campaigns have done much to increase the sales of Say! Play!; his mind is the company's, he can find no other. Donna is their hot package of the moment. In studio, she is a child, innocent and trusting. As a warming light image on your retina, a sound effect between your ears, a grind and stroke of vibro-fabric, she can be your unforbidden lover. Is there such a thing as the girl next door nowadays? Who lives next door, or next floor, another tuned-up commodity? Marketing-wise, Donna is perfection. How young is she: thirteen? Sixteen? Twenty? She also hears voices; there's a market for that, but is she the right product? She can hardly be termed normal. Once, she had a strange pain in her side and when the medics examined her, they found a tiny six-sided die in her liver. Donna was not surprised; she said the People had put it there. The People advise her often, although fortunately for everyone concerned they appear to have a fairly favourable view of her occupation. Neither does Donna punish herself. She has no conscience that Reeb can detect.

Today, she is pouting and blinking at the scanners, sighing softly in a provocative and exciting way. 'Oh! Oh!' Reeb supervises laconically. Later, he will tinker with the footage and, combined with a graphics package, will produce some hard-core delight for the consumer. Donna doesn't have to be too explicit, not like it's the real thing. Reeb can shoot a few limb movements tomorrow, some dildonics the next day; the software overdubs stock effects. Donna puts her tiny hands on either side of her face and grimaces. It is not part of the script.

'What is it?' Reeb asks from the other side of the observation panel.

'Oh, they are speaking to me,' Donna says, putting shaking fingers to her forehead, where the skin is almost translucent and has a damp sheen to it. Today, that suggestion of delicacy repulses Reeb; on other days, it has seemed attractive. She is a child, in mind if not in flesh. Reeb has a desire to tweak her smug piety with a burst of power; he can do that, but he doesn't.

'Who is speaking to you?' He adjusts one of the scan controls, still shooting.

She shrugs, hand flopping into her lap. 'My People. They're gone now.'

'What did they say?'

'Something about an elevator.'

She's making this up; she has to be. 'What?'

'I don't remember.'

She can be convincing when she wants to be. That's why she's here in his studio. Dice and elevators, computers dreaming. Young lips wetted with the tip of a nervous tongue, wide eyes. Donna lives in another world.

If Donna has her aspects of freakishness, Reeb has his own too. Nearly two years ago, he lost half of his body. The accident itself was freakish, like getting hit by lightning. Relaxing in his data-suit at home, living out a hi-res dream, the suit had suddenly turned on him like a swarm of deadly insects, cooking his right side to a frazzle, eating away at his groin and gut. The prostheticians had been delighted by him. (We can redesign this man, they had announced proudly, and proceeded to do so.) Medics could not rebuild his apartment or resurrect the other victim of the accident, his dog.

'You called it to you, that power,' Donna once said. He hated her the day she said that, the very first time he worked with her. For a while, after his therapy had proved so successful, he'd been a reluctant media star himself. Donna had recognised him instantly. 'Electricity is alive too; it's what makes the machines dream,' she told him. His prosthetics are more sensitive than his meat ever was, but there is still a seam, a sense of unreality, a sense that outsiders have moved into his body and might, one day, take over.

'The machines are alive,' Donna says, casting a meaningful glance at Reeb's right side. He puts his hand on his leg; squeezes. It feels like flesh, but slightly rubbery; perhaps like some kind of tough mollusc. This is his first commission since he came out of therapy.

Donna has been one of the company's products for six months – one of Reeb's for three weeks. Her face is burned into a million consumers' dreams. She might have been a little crazy for years and kept it quiet, only now she wants to tell people about her Voices and Visions, her People. She has mentioned them in interviews. People have conjectured whether her peculiarities are the result of how she was conceived. Donna was one of the first of the home-grown 'virgin births'. This fact must be significant, surely? Some people are not only prepared to believe it, but desperate to do so. These people are a cult the media tagged The Immaculates. To Reeb, they are a sad group of crazies that grew up around the virgin birth kick, desperate under-achievers trying to populate the steamed-up, fucked-up world with little messiahs. At the end of the twentieth century the Goddess of Love had tended to stride around with a scythe in her hand, more often than not, and the fear of fatal disease had not only launched the suddenly respectable software porn industry, but had also estranged many people from the desire for human contact. Through artificial insemination, women gave birth who had never known a man's touch, or indeed a woman's. At first, it was just the single women, then the gay women; later, the cult of the Immaculates grew up. Men can be Immaculate too. Reeb thinks the Immaculates should all be locked up, even though he knows the phenomenon is merely a reaction against the fear of death, the de-lustifying of sexuality. There's no need for that any more, but the vein runs deep in human consensus. Too many died back then. The Immaculates were a fringe group wanting to turn it all into a religion. Mercifully, they had never progressed beyond a minority, but they still gushed warmly about Donna in their cult magazines. The company have kept an eye on the media and now wonder whether this is an angle of Donna worth exploiting. After all, if the rumours circulating on the networks are true, Donna is not unique. Many people, whatever their background, are stepping forward to talk about Voices and Visions. Donna, being public property, could very easily be turned into a spearhead for this movement. Her family is totally devoid of fevered religion-mongerers looking for a place to hang their beliefs, but she does have two mothers; hers was a conception of convenience rather than conviction. Alexis, the woman who carried her, is now her agent and manager. Alexis is probably the opposite of any-one's vision of a Madonna. It is doubtful whether her hands have ever met beneath her chin in prayer. She is an eternal teenager, lankily attractive with razor-cut hair and slept-in-look anti-fashion gear. That she could have spawned an angel like Donna is in itself, Reeb supposes, a kind of miracle. And, if your child really does look like an angel, and fulfils everybody's dreams, then you exploit it; in the best possible sense. Especially when your girlfriend is obsessed by graffiti art and the photographic medium; nobody's into anything less than 3D nowadays, so somebody has to see to the family income. Alexis brings Donna over to the studio four days a week, for Reeb to record her. Reeb is also interviewing the girl about her Visions and Voices. Donna is pleased to comply, because she likes to talk. She is one of those pale, tiny people who sometimes become attractive under the right lighting, the right conditions of the mind. Sometimes Reeb likes her very much and is convinced she has a startling clear-sightedness. Sometimes, she irritates him and he thinks she's stupid. He used to feel the same way about his dog, when he had one.

Reeb went back to live with his mother after the accident. It was supposed to be a temporary arrangement – he's still paying rent on his own apartment – but somehow he doesn't have the will to move back home yet. He knows there couldn't be a smell of burning flesh there any more, and the block domestics would have cleaned everything up, but . . . His mother's apartment is spacious, she's never there, she never bothers him. He likes the view, and it's nearer to the studio than his old place. Occasionally, he thinks about ending his lease with the property agency, although it seems a little ungrateful, seeing as they compensated him so heavily for the accident.

Sometimes, he goes over to Alexis and Meriel's for dinner; he has become friendly with them since working with Donna. 'When are you going to let go of Mommy's apron strings?' Alexis says, smiling. They are worried about him. Meriel points a camera at him.

'And when are you going to strip for me?' she says.

He's not sure whether that's an offer or a request.

He goes to the studio early. Alexis and Donna are late today. The trains were down again. 'Someone died, I expect,' Alexis says when she finally arrives, scraping back her artfully ragged black hair. 'Jumpers! I hate 'em. Why do I have to be inconvenienced by their inadequacy? It's so selfish!' Her eyes skitter nervously away from Reeb's body as if she wonders whether she's touched on taboo. 'I can't bear to be held up!' she says.

In the office, after her mother has left, Donna leans demurely against the desktop. Reeb cannot imagine her living with Alexis and Meriel; she is an anachronism, a time-child from years past. She wears a white dress, but that is part of her costume wardrobe. The primness exists in the fabric of the dress, but is it a part of Donna? Reeb doesn't know yet. Is she an example of her mothers' artistic experiments? He would not put it past them. They never talk about Donna to him, and neither is she ever present at the dim-lit, smoky evenings Reeb enjoys in their company. It is as if the women lock her away in a cupboard when she's not working. Once, he tried to talk to Alexis about Donna's problem. 'She's imaginative,' Alexis said. 'That's all. She makes things up.'

'She believes it,' Reeb said.

Alexis rolled her eyes. 'You think so?'

He hadn't meant the voices and visions; the problem, in his opinion, was that Donna had a reality all to herself. Her home, the studio, A to B, and anything in between, like other people, her parents, street bums, commuters, interviewers, even himself, seemed only to touch her awareness on a superficial level. Her only contact with the world outside her own was through performance. And in her room, what did she do in her room? Reeb cannot ask Alexis questions like that; she is clearly not maternal material. The procedure was all the rage back then, of course. New legislation meant women could claim it as a right. Perhaps all Alexis' friends were having children that way. A public statement about her chosen way of life, her chosen lover.

Over the past two weeks, Reeb has been studying the phenomenon that is Donna. There has to be a new angle on her as a product, something the company can use; that's his brief. Has she always heard the voices, had these experiences, and not spoken about them, or are they a more recent phenomenon? Donna cannot remember. She wrinkles her nose, pulls a face. 'One night Merry's laptop dreamed to me,' she says, 'but I don't remember when.'

And what does a computer's dream look like?

She doesn't have the words to describe it; she has grown up that much. 'I could think it to you,' she says, 'but that's all.'

He would dismiss it as fantasy, if it wasn't for the die. The slap-marks which had appeared instantaneously on her arm one day could be explained away as being psychologically self-induced. At the time, when it happened, Donna had told him one of the People had got angry with her.

'So, what are you going to do with this material?' Alexis asks him, through the cloud of smoke she has just exhaled. He is over for dinner again, but only has Alexis' company because Meriel's been called out; a rare offer of work, she can't refuse. Reeb is surprised Alexis wants to discuss it now. Usually, she talks to him about himself.

'Donna is not unique,' he says, 'there are others like her, increasing all the time. They make a market. Understand?'

'A market for what?' Alexis swings her booted feet up on the table, kicking a plate out of the way.

'I'm supposed to be thinking that one up.' He considers the next question before he speaks. 'Aren't you worried about her?'

'She's quite happy,' Alexis says. 'She's always been happy. Completely alien to me, of course, but always happy. I think she gets on better with Merry.' She pulls a face and offers him her joint.

Reeb shakes his head; some things are just too anachronistic.

'I tried to be specific about what kind of donor I wanted when she was conceived. I think they lied to me, don't you?' She grins. 'Sometimes I wonder whether anything of mine went into her at all.' If she feels wistful about that, she hides it.

'Where is Donna?' Reeb asks. 'She's never around when I call.'

'She's in her playroom. All the things she likes are in there.'

Reeb thinks Donna is too old to have a playroom. She should be hanging out with kids her own age, learning to live. Is that discouraged? He can't believe so. Alexis and Merry wouldn't be that enthusiastic about Donna seeing guys, he thinks, but they would never force their lifestyle on someone else, not even if that someone was their daughter.

'What's she get up to in there, anyway?' Reeb asks, jerking his head in the direction of the closed door that is Donna's.

Alexis shrugs. 'Who knows? She doesn't like us going in there, so we don't. We all respect each other's privacy.'

Reeb frowns at the door. Hasn't Donna any friends at all?

'Donna will be okay,' Alexis says. 'Don't you worry about her; she's a survivor. Now, you' – she stabs a finger in his direction – 'you, I worry about.'

She hardly knows him; she hadn't met him before he began working with Donna. He ought to be annoyed at her interference, and would be, if he didn't enjoy it so much. Is that what he wants, motherly concern? Becka, his own mother, doesn't know how to deal with emotional crises; she organised his life and then left him to deal with the burned-out mess of his self-image and feelings. Perhaps that's why he hardly ever sees her. She isn't busy exactly; just busy avoiding him.

'I ought to find myself a place,' he says.

'What's wrong with the one you've got?'

'It's my mother's. I cramp her style.'

'I meant the one you pay for, stupid. Are you never going to go back there?'

He shrugs.

'What reason is there not to?' Alexis demands. 'Your body probably performs now better than it ever did . . .' She drops her eyes, actually blushes. 'Oh, I'm sorry . . .'

More than an arm and leg had been burned away. But they can fix that. They can fix everything. He didn't believe it.

'It's okay,' he says. 'You're right. I just feel . . . I don't know. It's as if someone died in there.'

'You had a dog, didn't you?'

'I didn't mean him. Someone else.'

'Oh.' Alexis shrugs awkwardly. 'I think I understand that. It's terrible.' She brightens and pours him another glass of wine. 'Tell you what. We'll look for a new apartment for you this week, shall we? Somewhere near here, so we can keep an eye on you.'

Reeb is glad he has met these women. He is happy to lean on them.

'Yeah. Fine.'

*

'I heard you talking to Alexis last night,' Donna says, when she arrives at Reeb's studio the following day.

'Oh?' Reeb tries to recall what he said, what Alexis might have said. But Donna isn't interested in what she might have heard about herself.

'You've *never* been back to your apartment?' she says, round-eyed.

Reeb is taken aback. He smiles, laughs unconvincingly. 'Not yet.'

'What are you afraid of?'

'Nothing. Just, well, bad memories.' I lost half my life there, he thinks, half myself, perhaps more than half. A demon hive in the walls had swarmed into his data-suit and sucked away his juice. He feels the place is haunted, perhaps by himself.

'Your dog died there,' Donna says.

'Yeah. Now, tell me what you've been experiencing since I last spoke with you.'

Donna reaches out and puts a delicate hand on his arm, the right arm. 'I want to experience your old apartment,' she says.

'Why? What for?'

She smiles an adult smile. 'The People want me to.'

'And what do they want to do that for?' He smiles back at her, although he feels nervous. He is thinking about the place, his collection of old books, his wall paintings, the way the morning light comes into the main living space, the colour of the floor. He sees himself standing in the kitchenette, mixing an old-style Martini for a shadowy ghost sitting on the couch, out by the hearth. The whole apartment is lit by the flicker of holographic flames. He can hear a body shifting impatiently. The air is full of perfume. The owner of these shadows, these subtle noises, this perfume was, in Reeb's memory, nothing but a human template. Later, he re-created this person as Elna, creature of dreams, modified to his taste. Elna never had to go home, live its own life, but the dream had existed only in the artificial world of recreation and had burned out along with his data-suit.

Donna's small, pale fingers dig into his artificial flesh. He winces a little, brought back to the present. 'When are you going to confront this problem, Reeb?' she asks, in a voice very much like Meriel's. 'Until you confront the dark things inside you, they make you helpless. They are your weaknesses.' She stands up straight, arms folded, and, for a moment, she is a young woman wearing a child's dress. 'Please, take me there.'

He doesn't want to go, even though he's sure the place will be cleaned up. He doesn't want to see that place again and yet, paradoxically, he does. Some of his life is still there.

Donna seems to sense his indecision. She doesn't argue with him as Alexis would. She simply breathes some words at him. 'Please, oh pleeeese, Reeb. I have to go there. I have to see. Let me help you. I can do that. Really I can. Take me there.'

The door is familiar yet strange. He puts his lock-card in the slot and, as if he's never been away, the door opens. Donna steps past, steps inside. He stands on the threshold staring, his right side tingling, his heart beating quickly. He can't go in. He can't. It stinks too much. The smell comes out in a wave of sharp remembrance. Blinking, he watches as Donna goes to the far side of the living room and raises the blind, opens the window. The city comes inside; noise below. The only smell is of disuse, a kind of staleness harbouring memories, but not reeking. The girl turns round, a silhouette against the light.

'I like it,' she says.

The walls have been repainted in a creamy colour. The sofa has been replaced, an inoffensive yet nondescript piece of furniture. Reeb would not have chosen it himself, but he can see Becka hurriedly and distastefully ordering it from the mail-order channel. As he looks at it, a memory resurfaces: frantic barking, teeth closing on the fabric of his suit, pulling desperately, the deadly current passed on. He looks away quickly. Everything else is just the same. His equipment, surprisingly, doesn't even look slightly damaged, although the data-suit has gone. Most of it was burned into him; the medics removed it along with his ruined flesh. Reeb feels sick, yet detached.

Donna crosses the room on light feet and puts her child-like hands on his arms. 'You must come inside,' she says.

'I don't think I . . .'

She pulls him over the threshold. 'You think it's haunted here?' she says, breathlessly.

He doesn't answer. Now he's here, he might as well pack some of his stuff together. The kid can poke around if she wants to. He can see into the small bedroom, the disarray which was caused by his mother throwing things around, looking for the items he asked her to bring him. It isn't too bad for him here. He should have come before. He feels he's been trying to spray plastic skin over a rotten wound. He might as well face reality.

Donna stands in the middle of the room with her eyes closed, humming to herself. One hand is held out towards the far wall, against which the couch rests. Her face is frowning in concentration. Reeb shakes his head and goes into his bedroom. This is where the ghosts would lie, not back in the other room, or splayed out on the floor, but here, healthy and whole. He looks at himself in the smoky mirror behind the bed, pulls down the collar of his shirt, scrapes back his hair. It is impossible to see the join between what is human and what is not human. The two materials have meshed invisibly. He has been told by the medics that his synthetic cells are no less part of him than the cells he had before; if anything, the new ones are more efficient and durable. There is no reason why he shouldn't simply forget half of him is synthetic. He wishes he could. Turning away from the mirror, he opens a wall cupboard, but finds it difficult to summon any interest for his possessions inside. Perhaps he should throw everything away. Begin again.

'Reeb?' Donna is standing in the doorway. 'You're still in the wires.' She looks small, hugging herself. Her words make his spine crawl with unease. Why did he let her talk him into bringing her here? What was the point? There's nothing left for him here.

'Let's go, then.'

She shakes her head. 'No. You need that part of yourself. You need to connect with it again.'

Alexis and Meriel should have done something about her a long time ago. Computers dreaming? She's out of her mind.

'Don't look at me like that,' she says. 'I know what you're thinking, but it's true. Part of you is in the wires here.'

'We're going, Donna,' he says. 'Come on. Don't scare yourself.'

'I'm not scared.' She submits passively as he tries to lead her out of the apartment. Before they reach the door, she says, 'You were in a dark red room, like a womb. The light was red. Someone was with you. They were very dark. Their hair felt like feathers under your hands. They were like a shell-fish, like a cat, like a bird. The name was Elna.'

Reeb drops the girl's arm as if it has burned him. A hi-res dream, a ghost's dream. How can she know the last thing that was playing in his mind before the swarm came down the line? Donna looks troubled. 'I don't want to invade you,' she says, 'but I have to make you see I know what I'm talking about. I'm not mad.'

'How do you know that?'

She shrugs. 'It's in the walls, your leisure-station, the heating ducts. It's all there, and the People thought it all to me.'

'What *are* the people, Donna?' He wonders whether they could actually be real. Has she been telling the truth?

Donna turns away from him. 'Oh, the People are only parts of me, that's all. I call them People because I want it to be like a movie, or like having friends. I'm friends with all the parts of myself, and they speak to me. Some are smarter than others.' She holds out her hands to him, as if she wants to touch him. 'Your data-suit's been replaced, Reeb. It's in the drawer under the monitor. You can take back what you lost, if you want to.'

'I can't take back the flesh,' he says sharply.

'That is replaceable, it doesn't matter about that,' Donna replies. 'You've left stuff behind, though, that does matter. Feedback.'

*

He feels awkward putting the suit on in front of Donna, he feels vulnerable. She is quite familiar with the equipment, which surprises him. 'I have stuff like this in my room at home,' she says.

Is that all? Reeb hadn't imagined her secret playthings would be anything as mundane as data-suits.

'There are two suits here,' she says.

'There shouldn't be.'

Donna pulls a face and shakes out the wired fabric. 'But here it is. For me. I need it, so here it is.' She smiles. 'You see?'

It's only further compensation, Reeb thinks. Two suits left in the apartment to replace the one that fried him. Most people would never think of putting one of the damn things on again. If the suits are a gift from the property agency, it's in the worst taste.

'Ready?' says Donna. For a moment, Reeb wonders whether he is afraid. Not of being hurt again, but of Donna herself. There's something too eager about her. The hood goes over his eyes.

'Relax,' Donna murmurs. 'You're on your way.'

He feels claustrophobic for a few seconds until Donna connects him. At first, it is all fuzzy; black and white static, noise-sight. He is hooked into nothing but the main power system. The program they are running is the daytime purr of appliances ticking over, the nowhere hiss of mindless, directionless, formless energy. This is crazy. The girl is crazy. There's nothing here. Nothing.

Then, out of nowhen, he is aware but dreaming, jacking into a tactile visualisation. The light is red around him. His body throbs in anticipation and there are feathers beneath his hand. For the first time since the accident, he senses a feeling of desire, his body is waking up, but this is only a dream, isn't it? He is in a dark place, surrounded by a sense of breathing, perhaps his own. There is also a feeling of confinement. Reeb flexes his arms, his fingers, breathes in through his nose. He does not know where he is. 'In the wires,' says Donna, close by, yet far away. This is not real, Reeb thinks and attempts to extend his awareness. He feels the presence of Elna, his animal-human companion, but cannot see it. Part of him can sense the touch, but it is incomplete. There is no sound, no chirrup of welcome, no sensuous brush of fur. Red light pulses swiftly round him, and for an instant he is back fully in the old dream: that of feathers and sex, warmth and envelopment. He sees Elna's slanted slitted eyes, open mouth, small pointed teeth. The eyes blink in greeting, the velvety throat purrs. Then it has flashed past him, just a fragment, like an echo of a cry.

'Come to *me*,' Donna says.

'Where are you?' Reeb gropes blindly, fighting vertigo, nausea. He has never experienced anything like this before. He is nowhere. What if he can't return? That is ridiculous. All he has to do is disconnect, press the stud in his arm, which in reality will end the program run. But there is no program. He's hooked into nothing.

'Here!' He blinks and Donna is standing beside him.

'How did you get in here?' he asks. A stupid question. Donna knows what she is doing. He is aware of that.

She holds out her hand. 'Come to my room,' she says. 'My playroom. All my things are there, the things that I like.'

Ahead of them is a plain white door. It could be any door, but Reeb knows it is the one that leads to Donna's playroom. As they approach it, it swings open and a strong light pours out.

'Here we are,' Donna says, gripping Reeb's hand. 'Home again.'

The room is full of things. Things and people. Creatures like automatons, beautiful dolls. Puppets hang from the ceiling, which is a blue sky, the impossible blue of childhood memories. The puppets swing on invisible strings. They are objects of human desire: cars, gleaming household goods, jewellery, expensive consumables, silk and real leather, but at the same time they are effigies of people. There are no walls to this room, only a ceaseless rush of colour and visual noise; scenes flashing by. Reeb sees dark forests, beaches, city-scapes, alien lands, the interiors of immense houses.

'Look,' Donna says, pulling on his hand, pulling him out of a stunned stasis. 'I have something of yours here too.'

They push their way through the dangling feet of the puppets and Reeb sees two yellow eyes glowing from the darkness of a forest. There is a throaty purr and a sinuous shape slinks towards him, dragging its landscape with it.

'Elna,' he says. 'You reconstructed her.'

Donna shakes her head. 'Oh no,' she says. 'No need to. I have the dreams of all the machines here, the computer dreams. I collect them. I bring them through.'

Elna drops to its belly in front of them.

'Part of you,' Donna says. 'Take it back now.'

Reeb has to fight to escape Donna's tight-fingered grip. His hand is damp. So real. It feels so real in here. He could almost believe she's somehow flipped them out of his apartment into her own surreal world. He never doubted it wasn't real for her. Is it possible to share a dream?

'Open the door.' Donna's voice has become hard. She is holding the hand that Reeb wrenched himself away from to her breast, as if he has hurt her. 'Open the door, and you'll find Merry and Alex getting stoned, as usual. You doubt me, don't you?' She smiles at him and walks towards the door, which is closed.

'Don't open it,' he says. 'Donna, get me out of here. It's too crazy. Take me back.'

'You are back,' she says. 'Stupid. I let you into my world and you're too stupid to believe it.'

He knows, if she opens the door, and he steps out into reality as she described it, he will go mad. If he walks out into Merry and Alex's apartment, the shock could kill him, because it wouldn't be possible. It isn't possible. Why even be afraid that might happen? Even if it did, it couldn't be true reality, but only further evidence of Donna's virtuosity in programming leisure software. She's always been on the wrong side of the camera, he realises, but perhaps this is all too weird for public consumption, too detailed to be comfortable. Elna has curled a fingered paw around his ankle. Instinctively, he extends a hand to caress the feathered head. Elna has never felt so real to him before.

'Do I open the door or not?' Donna asks.

He shakes his head. 'No, I believe you.'

She relaxes, folds her arms. 'Good. Now, fuck your animal-person. Do you mind if I watch?'

'Donna!'

'Oh, you're not shy are you? It's easy. I can do it, so can you. I only want to help you, Reeb. Take back what you lost. Be a man again.'

'I'm not into this, Donna.' He feels for the disconnect stud, the bump on his non-real arm that corresponds to the button on the data-suit, back in the apartment. He tries to concentrate on the fact that he never left there: this is just an illusion. No need to be worried.

'Don't bother doing that,' Donna says. 'It won't work. I brought you here, down the wires. To my playroom. I collect the dreams of machines here. I collected the dreams of your machines. Aren't you pleased? You thought Elna was dead, didn't you?'

Reeb puts his hands against his eyes, shakes his head. Donna makes a sound of distress and hurries towards him on her tiny feet. 'Oh, I've scared you. I'm sorry. I was showing off. Silly. Like a kid. I'm not that, I don't want you to think I'm that. Look, the animal has gone. I made it go. But there's me. There's me!' She leans against him, a Reeb that is not real, that cannot be flesh and blood, a dream icon. He closes his eyes and she puts her arms around him. She feels warm and solid against his body.

'Whatever is given to you here can be taken back,' she says, and kisses him. 'I promise.'

Child-woman, dream lover of a multitude of leisure sleepers, at home in her true medium; the non-real, the fantastic. There are no feathers beneath his hands.

Donna can feel computers dreaming, or so she says. She collects the dreams of machines, or so she thinks. The dreams of people are in the machines, a planet network of active imaginations hooked into their made-up, make-believe worlds. Artificial reality is taking over; it has its own children.

Donna feels the dreams of people. There are others like her.
She is not unique.

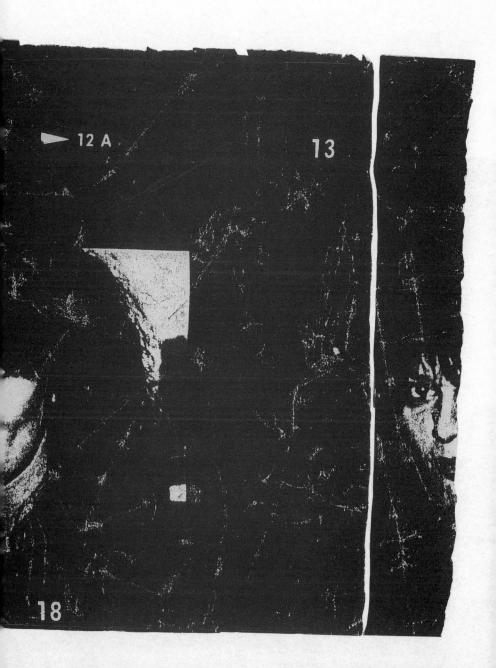

ANY MAJOR DUDE

Paul Di Filippo

Taylor's room was costing him twenty thousand *pesetas* a day. A few years ago, the civil authorities had closed down the building as unfit for human habitation. Only minimal repairs had been made since.

The room boasted a single window that opened onto a sooty brick airshaft, a tall dark box full of smells and sounds, capped with a square of blue Spanish sky. Into Taylor's room from this central well, dotted with other windows, drifted odours of oily foreign cooking.

Hotplates were prohibited in theory by the management, and, yes, the fat hotel-owner had agreed, there was a possibility of starting a fire, but really, *Señor*, what can we do? We agree it is dangerous, but most of these people are too poor to eat in restaurants, having spent all of their money on a promised passage across the Strait. Ah, *Señor*, everyone wishes to cross to Africa, and we are just helping. Were we younger ourselves . . .

Helping yourself get rich, you old hypocrite, thought Taylor, but said nothing at the time.

Filtering in through Taylor's window along with the Mediterranean scents were snatches of music and conversation, and tepid, torpid breezes that idly ruffled the dirty white gauze curtains, like an old woman sorting remnants of fabric at a sale.

Taylor lay half in shadow on the narrow bed with bad springs. He rested on his side, facing the peeling, papered wall, wearing the rumpled linen suit he had been too abstracted to shed. At some point in the past the plaster had cracked, splitting the mottled wallpaper and erupting in a line of chalky lava. It reminded Taylor of the white calcareous strata beneath the Channel, so perfect for tunnelling. How was the work going now? he wondered. Did anyone miss him? Did anyone puzzle over why he had left so precipitously, with the job so near completion? Did anyone care . . ?

It was very hot in Algeciras that July. So hot, so enervating, that it affected Taylor's thinking. He found that unless he continually reminded himself of his goals, his mind would wander, he would forget what he had to do next. Not that there was much he could do, of course, except to wait.

He hadn't been like that a week ago, when he had arrived fresh in the swarming port town, on the trail of his runaway wife. Then, he had been all fire and determination. Everything had been clear and uncomplicated as vacuum, his course laid out simply before him.

He would cross the border, cross the sea, to Maxwell's Land. He would find Aubrey. He would ask her if she intended to come home. If she agreed, well and good. (Although how they would travel home, return through the global interdict, he had no idea.) If she said no, he would kill her. Then he would kill Holt. It was as simple as that.

Now, however, after seven days of delay, seven days of brain-broiling heat which even the advent of night could not annul, things no longer seemed so simple. There seemed to be a lag between every action he took and its consequences. Hysteresis was the technical term, he dimly remembered. (Always the engineer, Taylor, even when you were numb or hurt or raving mad. How fucking pitiful.) Or else the proper order of his actions seemed muzzy and doubtful. (For this latter effect, there was unfortunately no convenient scientific term.)

Perhaps he would kill Holt first. The entire affair was, after all, his fault. He was responsible for the whole mess, both in Taylor's personal life, and on an international scale. Surely his death would be a good thing, and might perhaps send Aubrey back into Taylor's arms without even the necessity of asking.

On the other hand, was he even sure any longer that he wanted Aubrey back? Perhaps she and Holt deserved each other, the damn traitors. Perhaps he would kill Aubrey and Holt together, without a word . . .

No, that wasn't right. He was not a man who sought idle

revenge. He would not have abandoned a job he deemed important, travelled all this hot and dusty way, along with hundreds of thousands of other pilgrims and emigrants, just to achieve that entropic end. It was Aubrey he wanted, alive and sweetly tangible and his once more, not the nebulous and twisted satisfaction of seeing her dead. And Holt. Even he could live. Yes, Taylor would let him live. True, he had done wrong. But Taylor could understand what had driven him: a love of elegant solutions, a lifelong affair with the muse of physical precision and grace. After all, he and Taylor were *simpatico*, both engineers, albeit at different ends of the spectrum.

Up from the airshaft, preternaturally clear in an unusual moment when competitive noises were missing, floated a string of Spanish vocal and musical *non sequiturs*, as someone tuned across the radio band. Unctuous ads, flamenco guitars, the unmistakable transcultural inanities of a soap opera . . . Finally the unknown dial-twiddler settled on a station playing some ubiquitous old American rock. In utter disbelief, Taylor listened as half-forgotten lyrics tumbled over his windowsill.

Taylor laughed without pleasure. '"Demon at your door . . .,"' he repeated into the blankets. Oh, yeah, the demons were at the door now, sure enough.

That song was over twenty-five years old. Steely Dan's 'Any Major Dude'. It had been old when that campus DJ had used it as his closing theme, when Taylor and Holt had both been in grad school together a decade ago.

MIT, on the banks of the Charles. Studying and sailing, fireworks on frosty First Night, a fire in their guts, to be someone, to do something important. Taylor in macro-engineering, Holt in the barely nascent field of nano-technology. Two divergent personalities, yet somehow fast friends. Given to endless bullshitting sessions, each man half-seriously defending his specialty as more vital than the other's.

'All the really important work left is in the big projects, Des,' Taylor would tell his friend. 'Orbital stations, a bridge across the Bering Strait, harvesting icebergs, mid-Atlantic islands—'

'Show-off stuff,' Desmond Holt would contend. 'Megalomania, pure and simple. Old ideas writ large. The same impulse that leads flower-breeders to produce bigger and bigger blossoms with less and less scent. Distinct lack of imagination there, boy. No, Nick, the age of materials is over. You've got to face it some day. The real action in the future will be on the atomic and molecular levels, and in information theory.'

'You've been listening to Drexler and Fredkin again. Those guys're crazy. Can you heat your house with information, or drive your car on it? You're building castles in the clouds, buddy.'

'We'll see. Time will tell. But I know one thing. Your kind of engineering promotes heavy social control.'

'And yours promotes chaos.'

'Fascist.'

'Anarchist.'

And, thought Taylor, recalling that archetypical conversation, a composite memory distilled out of so many, the cliché Holt had employed had, as clichés disconcertingly will, embodied truth.

Time had indeed told. With the passage of the last few years, there could be no doubt now as to who had been right about the relative importance of their work.

Taylor's own projects had not been without results. But not on the scale of Holt's.

Aubrey had been someone utterly foreign to their scene, a communications major from Emerson. Doing the unusual, drawn solely by the subject matter, they had seen her in a play – a stage-adaptation of Capek's *Absolute at Large*; Aubrey had the role of Ellen – and been instantly smitten. Both had dated her, one had wed her.

Since then, Taylor had, off and on, harboured doubts about whether Aubrey hadn't chosen arbitrarily between them, seeing little differences between their cognate manias, entranced merely by their common hard-edged vision. Now he feared he knew the bitter truth: that she had cast her lot with the one she thought stood the greatest chance of worldly success, and, upon a shift in fortunes, abandoned the downward-bound man for the one on the rise.

He didn't really want to believe it about her, but it was the only explanation he could accept. Surely that other drivel contained in her goodbye letter was just a façade for her real motives . . .

Nick, she had written, *I can't accept feeling useless any more. Too many things are happening in the world right now. I need to take part. You think I should just kick back and enjoy the London theatre, the Paris stores, but I can't. I need to feel useful, like I'm doing something to help humanity. It sounds corny, but I know you'll understand. You share the same sentiments – or used to, until the projects became their own reason for existence. But since I'm no use under the Channel with you I'm going where I can make a difference.*

The old song continued to filter in: 'Any minor world that comes apart falls together again . . .'

Was that true? He doubted it. Two months now, and the shattering pain he had experienced upon returning from the worksite to their London flat to find that letter hadn't diminished. It had taken him that long to pick up Aubrey's trail. At first he believed she had gone back to America, perhaps to help in some relief effort or other, such as the rebuilding of Mexico City after the quake. When he couldn't find any trace of her there, he turned in desperation to the list of self-exiled emigrants to Maxwell's Land, printed by international edict in all major newspapers.

Searching backwards through the online London *Times*, not really expecting to encounter her name, he had been stunned to see it starkly confronting him in the pages for May 15.

Their anniversary. What a fine joke. *Dear John, I'm going far away, where you'll never find me* . . .

Don't count on it, honey.

The music had ceased. The radio, powered off, was replaced by a baby's cries. Taylor felt himself falling asleep. His brow was stippled with sweat. It trickled down through a week's worth of stubble. The bisecting line of light moved slowly over him, pulling back through the window, as the sun sank.

After he had lain wholly in shadow for some time, he awoke, hungry.

* * *

Narciso was waiting for him down in the shabby lobby of the crowded hotel.

Taylor smiled ruefully when he saw the boy. Narciso appeared to be the last beggar left in Algeciras, all the others having emigrated by one means or another. For some reason, out of all the gullible marks thronging the town, he had picked Taylor to fasten himself to. The man vacillated between suspecting that Narciso was either the stupidest or the smartest beggar out of all those 'Hey Joes' who had once inhabited the community.

'You want some *comida* now, huh, *Señor* Nick? I bet you sick of my brother's food, huh? He not such a good cook. But today, for special, I take you to a new place. Run by my own Tia Luisa.'

Taylor knew from a week's experience that it was impossible to shake Narciso, so he mutely let the boy lead him out the door, to his relative's restaurant.

The transient population of Algeciras had more than quadrupled from its Pre-Max heights, and the streets were thronged. Even in the old days, when the port at the southern tip of Spain had filled with Euro-Africans each summer as they headed home on vacation, it had not resembled the current combination of Bedlam and Mardi Gras.

The town was filled with an atmosphere of impatience, of throttled anticipation. Everyone seemed ready and eager to shed old ways and inhibitions, to get where they were going, their common destination, and begin their lives anew. There was no sense of menace, but Taylor still felt scared somehow at the prospect of so much change.

He had paused in the doorway, leery of mingling with the crowd. They didn't share his purity of motive, he didn't belong with them, he wasn't really hungry . . .

But Narciso, waiting patiently a few feet away, beckoned, and Taylor began to shoulder his way after his guide, who wove lithely in between larger figures.

The hot twilit air carried scents of the Mediterranean, not all of them pleasant, from that biggest and most utilised of the world's open sewers. But there were fewer odours than last year, and even fewer than the year before that.

Holt and his loyal team-mates, the technocratic saviours of Maxwell's Land, were responsible. They had seeded the sea with toxin-disassemblers, claiming that they needed untainted water for their small but high-throughput desalinisation plants. It was one of the few unilateral actions they had taken outside their own borders. Official communiqués and press releases had explained, quite patiently, that they did not wish to give offence, had no plans for expansion where not invited, but on the other hand maintained the right to ensure their own prosperity, to claim their share of the world's common resources – especially if they improved them in the process.

The people in the narrow, dusty, cobbled streets of the old town were of all nationalities, of every class and type, here for the same reason Taylor ostensibly was. As one-way emigrants, they all sought passage to Maxwell's Land, and this was one of the busiest points of entry, along with Marseilles, Naples and Athens. Those favouring an overland route usually chose Israel, rather than attempt travel through the unsettled African nations to the south of Maxwell's Land. (So far, the Israelis had resisted assimilation, forming a stubborn eastern bulwark against the new country. But Taylor had read just yesterday, in the *International Herald Tribune*, that the Knesset was preparing to vote on a merger with the globe's youngest nation – if such an anarchistic system could even be called such.)

As Taylor followed Narciso down to the waterfront, he noticed that there seemed to be even more demonsign graffiti than yesterday. These emblems were in a variety of media and styles: stencilled, drawn freehand, pasted as preprinted posters and stickers, spraypainted, chalked in colours. But they all took the same form, the inward-pointing circle of arrows representing anti-entropy.

Taylor wondered how soon the symbolic invasion would become a literal one. Surely two such incompatible realms could not coexist on one globe forever.

Walking behind the small, raggedly dressed figure of Narciso, Taylor had been following the boy without much thought given to his reality as an individual. Suddenly, however, he was struck by the desire to communicate, to learn what at least one inhabitant of this land so close to the alien continent thought of that strange shore. He caught up with the boy and laid a hand on his shoulder, halting him.

Indicating one of the demonsigns with a curt gesture, Taylor said, 'Who draws these, Narciso? The pilgrims? The emigrants? Your own people?'

Narciso looked up, brown eyes lively beneath a fall of black hair. There was a smudge of grease over one eyebrow, like misapplied makeup. 'Mostly those first two you name, *Señor* Nick. The people who still live here have no time for such things.'

'Don't you fear the day when Maxwell's Land will reach out and take Spain?'

Narciso shrugged with a fatalism beyond his age. 'What good is worrying? If America can do nothing about the demons, then certainly I cannot.'

'You expect life to be good when they come?'

'*¿Quien sabe?* Things do not seem so bad there, from what I hear. Let them come. I will make out. But now, you are hungry, *Señor* Nick, and my aunt's place is not far.'

The boy turned and set off down the crepuscular alleys they had been traversing, and Taylor was forced to follow.

Tia Luisa's restaurant was situated right on the waterfront. Before going inside, Taylor stood on a rust-stained concrete jetty and strained his eyes, trying to make out significant details of the land only a few miles south across the Strait of Gibraltar.

Lit extravagantly, the African coastline was a far cry from its old self. Just five years ago, it had been possible, by squinting, to pretend nothing had changed there since Roman times. But now the lavish display of power was like an alluring billboard advertising the new world order with all the subtlety of a campaign for the latest blockbuster film.

Taylor, his brain still stunned from the heat and the drastic changes in his own life, hazily tried to envision what inexhaustible energy might mean. The concept seemed hard to credit, flying in the face of all the precepts of physics he had always cherished. Something for nothing. Hadn't Szilard dealt the final blow to that possibility?

The lights reflected in the black waters of the Strait spelled out, plain as any textbook, that Szilard had been wrong.

Inside, Taylor ordered sangria and squid sandwiches. The latter arrived with the deep-fried meat still hot, a nest of tentacles covered with crisp golden batter, the flesh inside white as a lily and succulent as a kiss. Only the bread was unsatisfying, being made of that peculiar yellow Spanish meal and baked till absolutely dry. Taylor discarded the stuff after a few bites and ate the squid with a fork, washing it down with long draughts of the fruity, brandy-spiked wine.

Suddenly, with laden fork poised halfway to his lips, Taylor looked nervously at Narciso, who was waiting nearby like a vest-pocket *maître d'* to make sure everything was all right.

'Was this fish caught locally?' Taylor asked.

'Oh, *si, Señor* Nick. Very fresh.'

Taylor regarded the squid. How many of Holt's toxin-disassemblers had these creatures ingested? Taylor knew the nanomechanisms were supposed to be biologically inert, with a limited lifetime, but still –

Hell, he'd been eating local catch all week without thinking about it. Too late now . . .

Taylor continued his meal in silence, without company, Narciso having vanished into the kitchen. He meditated on tomorrow's departure. Spain is a land to flee across. That sentence was from a book Aubrey had once tried to get him to read. The author's name was Gauss – no, Gaddis. He had never gotten into it, too convoluted, not precise enough. The equations of fiction eluded him. Aubrey was always unsuccessfully pressing new books on him – at least, during the first few years of their marriage. Now Taylor wished he had read some.

Was she with Holt? He was convinced of it. Holt had always read what Aubrey suggested, the bastard. Why else would she have entered Maxwell's Land, if not to yoke her wagon to his rising star . . .?

Narciso, uncannily sensing when Taylor was ready to leave, emerged from the kitchen. 'You want some fun now, *Señor* Nick?'

'No,' said Taylor wearily. 'Just take me back to the hotel.' He stood clumsily, the empty pitcher on the table silent witness to his condition.

Narciso led him back to his hotel and tumbled him into bed. Taylor sensed his eyes closing, his breath settling into a stertorous rhythm.

His last thought was, *You are what you eat.*

Or what eats you.

Taylor awoke with a hangover, sharp as the nail driven through Holofernes' head by his lover Judith. His suit was spotted with sangria stains, the mirror told him, his eyes were pouched in shadow, and he looked like a bum. He didn't care, though, because soon, one way or another, this whole abominable business would be over with.

Prior to leaving, patting down his jacket pockets for his passport, which he was gratified to find, Taylor soon learned that Narciso had relieved him of fifty thousand *pesetas*, all his remaining money.

Taylor swore mildly, unable really to bear any grudge against Narciso. He imagined how the boy had rationalised it: the crazy American would be gone tomorrow morning to the land of demons – where, so everyone said, money was of no use whatsoever, and all the streets were paved with gold. Under law, he would never return.

And the boy was probably right.

He only hoped there would be no further palms to grease prior to his departure.

Taylor found his duffel bag beneath the bed, opened it, saw the gun, and zipped it shut. Luckily, his missing wallet had not held the all-important ferry ticket; that was still safe in his shoe.

Out on the streets, Taylor joined the flow toward the docks. Nothing like this atmosphere had existed since the Iron

Curtain crumbled. He assumed some of these people would be his fellow passengers, but that most of them were merely going to gaze wistfully south, or try once more to bargain for an earlier departure date. Had Taylor not come to Algeciras liberally supplied with cash, he, too, might have been among the idlers. Even as it was, the earliest passage he had been able to secure had involved waiting a miserable week. Not wishing to entrust his fate to the privateers in their small craft – stories abounded of passengers taken only halfway across the Strait and then chucked overboard – Taylor had chosen to wait for one of the more reliable conveyances.

There was a chain-link fence topped with concertina wire around the dock where the ferry was berthed. The gate was manned by UN Peacekeeping Troops, part of *Operacion Transito*. Ticket in hand, Taylor joined the line leading up to the guards. There seemed to be no customs check of baggage, so Taylor made no attempt to slip his gun into the lining of his duffel bag, as he had intended.

Under the strengthening sun, time passed. Eventually Taylor came to the head of the line.

A Scandanavian guard, big and blond, demanded, 'Passport, please.'

Taylor handed it over.

In a bored voice the guard recited his speech: 'You understand that according to UN Security Council Resolution Number 1050, approved by a majority of member nations, you are hereby permanently renouncing your citizenship in the land wherein you are currently enfranchised. Do you understand this?'

'Yes.'

'Do you still wish to board?'

'Yes.'

The guard waved Taylor through, keeping his passport. His name would appear in newspapers around the world tomorrow, separated from his wife's by months, though to any future historians the time differential would disappear and the separated lovers would merge into the statistics of the mass exodus, united at last, if only cliometrically.

As he passed beneath the coiled wire, a miasma seemed to

lift off his shoulders. For the first time in a week, he felt he was truly moving under his own volition.

The craft moored at the dock was one of the old hulking multi-tiered ferries which had once plied a more sedate trade across the Strait. Its suddenly wealthy owners, operating under government franchise, had made minor alterations – filling the cargo space with cheap seats – thereby converting it into a shuttle for the one-way emigrants. Now the craft was showing signs of wear. Kept so busy it had forgone drydock for over a year, the vessel was rusting and untrustworthy-looking.

Its crew, already wearing surplus CBW gear and breathing bottled air, was forbidden to set foot on Maxwell's Land, or traffic in African goods, under penalty of the same permanent expulsion the guard had outlined to Taylor.

Small boats and their owners who opted not to seek a government licence for passage to Maxwell's Land were deemed by the authorities to be in instant violation of the UN interdict, and were sunk when sighted. Twenty had gone down in the week Taylor had been waiting.

Taylor boarded by means of a shaky wooden ramp and took his place at the already crowded rail. He wished he had someone to wave goodbye to, and he idly looked at the people on the shore for any familiar face, even that of the mercenary Narciso.

Gulls wheeled overhead. Next to Taylor stood two black youths, mountaineering backpacks dwarfing them, by speech and dress obviously American. They seemed almost giddy with the adventure they were embarked on.

'Back to Africa, huh, man!'

'Yeah, but nobody cogged it'd ever be like this!'

'Hey, how many demons does it take to change a lightbulb?'

'None, 'cuz they don't never wear out!'

Soon the ship was full. A horn blared. With a noisy blast and a belch of black smoke, the ship's diesels roared into life, the lines were cast off, the ferry pirouetted and headed out to sea. Taylor felt the breeze of passage begin to dry the sweat from his brow. Today the sun felt different somehow. Still as hot, it seemed less dulling than stimulating. Taylor supposed it was all in his mind, the result of being at last in motion.

Midway through the passage, the ship's engines abruptly ceased to stink and bellow, the thrumming they imparted to the hull disappearing, more as if they had suddenly winked out of existence than as if someone had throttled back on them. None the less, the ship continued to surge forward, perhaps even more swiftly, under some unknown impulse.

Taylor puzzled over the curious phenomenon briefly, then discarded it. He was certain he would encounter many mysteries in Maxwell's Land, none of which had any real bearing on his strictly personal mission.

The trip to Tangier was over sooner than Taylor could have wished. In transit, he had been both active and passive, moving toward his destiny, yet helpless for the moment to do more than he was doing. With landfall came an end to such suspension, and a necessity for further decisions.

The trouble was, Taylor had no idea what he was going to do next. Disembarking with the excited immigrants, he realised that he had thought ahead no further than this point. Where Holt and Aubrey were, and how he was to get there without money, were points he had neglected.

As on the other side, no port officials bothered to rummage through personal possessions. It was as if they were saying, *Nothing you bring in can matter as much as what's already here*. And they certainly did not enquire as to the intended duration of anyone's stay.

There was, however, one formality to undergo.

A European woman wearing a Red Crescent pin on her shirt held a modified injection pistol connected by a hose to a stainless-steel tank. Each traveller came under her ministrations.

When it was Taylor's turn, he knew what was expected. Dreading it, he took off his jacket and exposed his bare skin.

The woman pressed the wide muzzle against his flesh and squeezed the trigger.

When she withdrew it, the demonsign was tattooed brightly in red on the underside of his forearm. A single drop of blood appeared, but no more.

'Self-organising and ineradicable,' she said, responding to Taylor's look. 'Even if you were to cut it away, it would reform. Think of it as your passport as a citizen of Maxwell's Land. Oh, and you've just gotten the standard viral disassemblers too. Anti-trypansomiasis, anti-AIDS, and all that. Good luck.'

Clutching his duffel bag in one hand, rubbing his sore new trademark with the other, still without immediate goals, Taylor decided to wander around the city and learn what he could of the changes that had come to North Africa in Holt's wake.

* * *

Five years ago, the government of President Zine al-Abidine Ben Ali of Tunisia – one of the more liberal, secular Arab nations – had extended an invitation. Hearing of a certain Desmond Holt, whose field trials of his potentially revolutionary nanodevices had been forbidden in America, the Tunisian government offered to help finance his work and to give him *carte blanche* in terms of implementing any of his discoveries.

One year after Holt had relocated with his small staff to the impoverished but eager Arab country, there was no more Tunisia.

It still existed in the physical sense. The land – its earth, its people, its buildings – had not vanished off the map. But in a metaphysical and legalistic way Tunisia was no more. As a separate political entity, the country had disappeared. President Ben Ali had, all unknowingly, engineered a coup against himself.

Details of what was quickly dubbed the 'Gadget Revolution', how it had been accomplished so easily, were scant. Other nations, recognising a peril to their own integrity even if they could not define it, had exhibited great alacrity in slapping quarantine on the infected nation. But the fact of great changes was soon plain.

After dismantling the government of his host, Holt and the technology he embodied had absorbed Libya to the southeast and Algeria to the west. Both had immediately stopped pumping oil. The rest of OPEC, picking up the slack, prevented more than a slight hiccup in the world economy. The closing of these markets to Western goods and the repudiation of foreign debts was actually more troublesome, and corporations agitated for a quick return to normalisation of relations – assuming, of course, that the offending nations could be forced to give up their dangerous new technology.

Morocco, where Taylor now found himself, entered into the union a year later. Mauritania, Mali, Niger, Chad and the Sudan followed in short order. Egypt proved more stubborn, but had acquiesced just six months ago. And now, as Taylor had recently read, Israel looked likely to follow.

These countries, then, made up the strange and unlikely amalgam known, to the Western press at least, as Maxwell's Land.

Home to demons.

Taylor didn't know what he expected to see as he walked idly through the noisy city. Perhaps alien scenes of unhuman construction, swarms of semi-sentient mechanisms, perhaps upheaval and confusion . . . Instead, everything appeared utterly mundane. Tangier was in fact flourishing, despite the seemingly airtight trade embargo imposed by the rest of the world.

He had never visited North Africa before, but a thousand travelogues had prepared him for the innocuous, albeit colourful reality. In the *medina*, the old town, the *soukhs* were all busy, heaps of produce and piles of carpets, booths full of brass and basketware, jewellery and clothing, all proudly on display.

The only traditional element missing from the city, in fact, was misery. Taylor saw no beggars, no faces ravaged by untended controllable illnesses. He passed many clinics, staffed by Westerners: immigrants in their new jobs. Also, he realised that there were no draught animals or conventional vehicles. Instead, small carts and scooters, impelled noiselessly by odd engines – Taylor's trained eye recognised them as Stirling cycle devices, powered by demon heatpumps – were everywhere.

The whole city seemed slightly inebriated, in fact. There

was an almost physical euphoria, something in the air like ozone on a mountaintop. Taylor found his attention drifting again, and forced himself to recall his mission.

He stopped, attracted by a tea-stand. Having stood in the sun since before noon, he was parched. He watched the proprietor prepare numerous cups of hot dark tea for his customers. Each cup of water was heated to boiling individually over a small black cube emblazoned with a demonsign. The cube had a single control.

Taylor stared at this device with almost as much interest as he held for the drinks. Here was one of Holt's products – the most revolutionary – in its simplest form: inside the cube was nothing but a number of self-replicating Maxwell's demons – sophisticated nanomechanisms, silicrobes – and a quantity of plain air at ambient temperatures. The demons, intelligent gates, were layered in a screen that divided the interior of the cube in half. By segregating molecules of common air with non-uniform velocities, the silicrobes produced heat in one half of the cube, while the other half grew frigid. (Some of this energy they used for themselves.) The control regulated how many gates were switched on.

Endless free power. A local reversal of entropy.

This was what had toppled governments and transmogrified societies. Inside this small featureless cube was a power that was well on its way to remaking the globe.

Taylor watched as customers exchanged *dinars* for drinks. A few seemed to partake without paying, failing to arouse any protest from the man running the booth. Taylor was just on the point of daring to do so himself when a voice spoke from his side.

'You are just off the boat, I wager.'

Taylor turned. A young Arab man with five-o'clock shadow, wearing jeans, a T-shirt emblazoned with the demonsign, and cowboy boots, stood beside him.

'Yes,' admitted Taylor.

'Understandably, you are perplexed. It is a common reaction. Money, you see, is on the way out here. In a society of growing abundance, it is losing its value. Many cling to it still, out of habit, but are willing to give freely of their products and labour if asked, knowing they may take freely in return. But enough of theoretical economics. It was my field of study, and I think sometimes I was on my way to becoming quite a pedant. You are thirsty.' The man spoke in Arabic to the proprietor, who quickly fixed Taylor some tea.

Tea in the Sahara, he thought, sipping. That was both an old song and a chapter in one of Aubrey's books. Things seemed suddenly to converge in a rush upon Taylor, and he felt dizzy.

'Please,' said the Arab, taking Taylor's arm, 'my name is Azzedine, Azzedine Aidud. Allow me to find you some shade.'

Taylor finished his tea quickly, nearly scalding his mouth, returned the cup, and allowed the man to lead him off.

Walls old as life, alleys narrow as death, shadowy doorways – Taylor lost all sense of where the port was. His attention wandered, and he followed Azzedine as he had followed Narciso. Used to giving orders and leading, he now found himself reduced to a child's role.

They ended up in a walled garden, water purling gently in a fountain. Taylor vaguely remembered the Arab saying something about his family. Azzedine was speaking.

' – and when I heard what was happening in my homeland, I left my studies in America – I was at Stanford, do you know it? – and returned. It was the only thing to do, obviously.'

Taylor was seized by a sudden feverish energy. He grabbed Azzedine's wrist.

'Listen – do you know where Holt is now?'

Azzedine's face filled with near-religious awe, then disappointment. 'The great man. How I wish I could meet him! It would be an honour to thank him personally, something I could tell my children about some day. But, sad to relate, I do not know.'

'Is there some way we could find out?'

'There is a branch of Holt's tribe in town. They might know.'

'His tribe?'

'That is what the ones who work with Holt call themselves.'

'Please, would you take me there?'

'Certainly.'

The office of the tribe was a former Army building denoted by a special demonsign that featured a capital H in its centre. The place was bustling with activity. The chain of command was hard to distinguish: no receptionists, no private offices, no obvious executives. After some time, Taylor found himself talking to a dark-haired Canadian named Walt Becker, Azzedine listening attentively.

Taylor tried to lie convincingly. 'Listen, you've got to tell me where Holt is. It's imperative that I see him. I have crucial information for him.'

'About what?'

'It's – it's information about an attempt on his life.'

'It wouldn't be the first. Holt can handle it.'

'No, this is different. He's not prepared. Please, he's an old friend. I couldn't stand it if anything happened to him.'

'You know Holt personally?'

'We went to school together . . .'

Becker seemed unconvinced, on the point of turning away. Taylor rummaged desperately through his small bag of tricks.

'The woman with him, Aubrey. She's my wife.'

Becker perked up. 'What's your name again?' Taylor told him. 'And what project were you just working on?'

'Chunnel Two.'

Becker nodded. 'She said you might show up.'

Taylor's heart skipped. What kind of tripwires had she set?

It looked, however, as if no alarms had gone off. Becker picked up a phone. 'We'll get you transportation right away.'

Azzedine interrupted. 'No. I claim the right to take him. My family were always *marabouts*, guides. I brought him here. It is only fair.'

Becker shrugged. 'Why not? Holt's in the desert, the Tanzerouft, not far from Taodani. He got a project going with the Tuareg. Exactly what, I'm not sure.'

Taylor laughed bitterly. 'Out in the field himself. Holt always did have a weakness for micromanaging things.'

Becker chuckled. 'Call it nanomanaging now.'

Outside, Taylor said to Azzedine, 'Do you know the way?'

'The new Tangier to Tombouctou highway passes near to Taodani.'

'How far is it?'

'Not far. A thousand miles, more or less.'

'You call that "not far"?'

'In the past, yes, it would be a long distance. But not on the new road. You'll see. Let's get your bag, and we'll be off.'

Azzedine's transportation was a two-seater, a teardrop-shaped, three-wheeled vehicle with a canopy laminated in gold to reflect the desert heat. Powered by demons, it needed no refuelling. The man was immensely proud of it, and seemed able to discourse endlessly on it, much to Taylor's annoyance.

'Classical physics, you know, Mister Taylor, claims that our power source is impossible. Information theory was supposed to have put a final nail in the coffin of Mister Maxwell's demon, you see. In sorting molecules, the demon was supposed to discard information, which was thermodynamically costly, thereby negating all the work it had done. Holt's insight was to see that a mechanism with a large enough memory could increase the entropy of its memory in order to decrease the entropy of its environment. When saturated, it would replicate a fresh heir, then self-destruct. Thus the problem of thermodynamic irreversibility is sidestepped.'

As they moved slowly through the streets of Tangier, Taylor, eyes closed, reclined alongside the driver in his comfortable seat. The amber light filtering in through the one-way transparency coloured his face like a marigold.

'It's all bullshit, Azzedine. There's some hidden payback down the road. There has to be.'

Azzedine seemed hurt. 'Then, Mister Taylor, I must affirm that this car is powered on bullshit. Seriously, do you believe Mister Holt would set something loose like this if it were not perfected? He is a unique soul. Why, to aid the Tuaregs qualifies him as a holy man.'

'Why's that?'

'The Tuaregs are not even really Arabs. They claim to be an ancient noble race, but I do not trust them. Do the men not veil their faces, so you cannot read them?'

'If you say so.'

'I do. Holt is brave to work with them. As you might say,

he's one "major dude". I know many in other lands vilify him, claiming he is irresponsible and crazy to unleash such forces so rapidly. But he knows just what he is doing. Some day the whole world will acknowledge him as its saviour, as we here do now.'

'We'll never live to see if it happens as you predict.'

'Only God knows. And as there is no God but Allah, Holt is his prophet.'

On the outskirts of Tangier began a golden road of almost supernatural smoothness, heading south-east straight as a surveyor's wetdream. The road was lined with young palms fed with a continuous length of trickle-irrigation tubing, studded with demon-powered pumps.

'Look,' said Azzedine with admiration, 'fused from sand by more of Holt's creatures of genius.'

'Wonderful,' said Taylor. He was simultaneously keyed-up and weary. There definitely seemed to be something in the air that sharpened the senses and quickened the pulse. Conversely, his mind was burdened with its weight of fatality, the self-imposed geas to regain Aubrey and put an end to Holt's madness.

Azzedine cranked the little car up to one hundred and twenty kilometres an hour. Twelve or fifteen hours, and they should be there.

Taylor managed to doze off during one of Azzedine's impassioned monologues about the miracle of North Africa. He awoke as they passed through Fez and began to ascend into the Grand Atlas Mountains. They crossed the nonexistent border near Chaouf, and entered the true desert. Even here, the road flew out ahead of them, indomitable, lined with hopeful trees.

Azzedine drove like one possessed by the Holy Spirit. Taylor, waking at intervals in the night, tried vainly to imagine what was going on in the Arab's mind. Did he view himself as divinely appointed by Kismet to find the stranger in the marketplace and convey him to his meeting with Saint Holt?

Around midnight, after eight hours of driving, they stopped for a brief rest at an oasis.

Hive-shaped buildings with thick walls, constructed by

nanomachines from sand, sat beneath date-palms and *talha* trees. Camels were hobbled by the well. A man in a flowing *gandourah* appeared, and bowed them welcome. He brought them inside and roused his whole family: two wives and six children. The women, their hair modestly concealed from the strange males by cloth wraps, served Taylor and Azzedine *couscous* with chunks of lamb and a milk drink called *zrig*, followed by dates and honey.

Taylor was curious. 'Ask them why they live out here, so far from anywhere.'

Azzedine enquired. The husband launched into a long impassioned speech. Azzedine's eyes grew large.

'He claims that wherever Holt has rested becomes a *haram*, a holy place, and he hopes to gain heavenly merit by staying here and helping travellers.'

'Oh, Jesus, this is really too much – '

After Azzedine had a short nap, the travellers were off.

Fifteen hours after their departure, as dawn was breaking in shades of apricot and cream, they reached Taodani, a small town in the north of a Mali that was no more.

They parked. Outside the car, the heat smote them like a velvet-covered hammer, dazing Taylor.

'Now what?' asked Taylor.

'We will find a local who knows where the Tuaregs are camped and can serve as guide. Then, I'm afraid, it will be camels for us. There are no roads in the Tanzerouft.'

A shopkeeper, instantly cooperative at the mention of Holt's cursed name, directed them to a man called Mahfoud.

Mahfoud, apparently in his fifties, was desert-thin, desert-dark. 'Of course I can bring you to Holt. Did I not guide the *azalai*, the salt caravans, for years?'

'How far is he?'

'Twenty-five miles. With luck, eight hours' travel.'

Taylor groaned. 'When can we start?'

'Tonight. Travelling by dark, we will avoid the heat.'

Taylor and Azzedine spent an hour or two buying, under Mahfoud's direction, a few supplies. They napped in the house of the town's prefect. By moonrise, they had all assembled on the edge of town.

The camels wore wooden butterfly-shaped saddles. Mahfoud tied the waterskins, the *girbas*, to the saddles. Each camel was controlled by a bridle to which was attached a rope.

Mahfoud couched the camels. 'Mount now.'

Taylor and Azzedine ascended. The camels rose, making half-hearted protests at the weight.

'Your beasts will follow mine. But do not drop the head-rope, whatever you do, or they will bolt.'

Mahfoud moved to the fore of the caravan. Holding his camel pole across his shoulders, he started the train in motion.

Mounted on his camel, Taylor, still wearing his filthy linen suit, found the riding deceptively easy.

Two hours later, his whole body felt like a single giant bruise. The night, while cooler, was still in the nineties. The monotony of the trek, the slowness after the speed of the drive, made him want to scream. Would he never reach Holt?

Rocking atop the smelly beast, Taylor was suddenly taken by the ironic notion that his whole journey was more comedy than tragedy. A plane to Spain, a boat to Africa, a car to the desert, a camel to some filthy nomad encampment. It was all too much like one of those movies where the characters experience successive degradations in their quest, until they end up pedalling on a child's bicycle . . .

Seeking reassurance, Taylor reached beneath his jacket. Tucked into the waist of his trousers was his gun. It felt hot against his skin.

Constellations spun; the desert drifted past them.

The Tuaregs had not moved, and were easily found. They were camped in a depression which even Taylor could recognize as a dry wadi. From a distance, their flattened oval tents of *dom* fibre looked like some abandoned circus, dropped impossibly into the waste of sand. In the middle of the encampment was a modern tent, obviously the ringmaster's, Holt's.

Taylor tried urging his camel to greater speeds, but found it as unresponsive as stone. After a seeming eternity, they arrived in the midst of the camp.

It was so early, pre-dawn, that no one was yet up.

Taylor painfully dismounted.

He stumbled at an awkward trot towards Holt's tent. Azzedine hung back out of respect, while Mahfoud was busy with the camels.

Taylor pulled back the tent flap and an unexpected blast of air-conditioning smacked him in the face, utterly disconcerting him for a moment. Recovering, he saw in the dim light two sleeping figures on separate cots: Aubrey and Holt, both in T-shirts.

If they had been together in bed, he knew he would have shot them.

But as they were, looking like children, his wife and his best friend, they drained everything from him except self-disgust.

With a roaring in his ears, Taylor raised the gun to his own temple.

He pulled the trigger –

Once, twice, a number of times.

No flare, no aroma of gunpowder, nothing but dull clicks.

Taylor dropped his hand and looked down in befuddlement at the traitorous weapon. He ejected the full clip, studied it as if expecting it to voice an explanation, then tossed it aside. He began to cry.

Holt and Aubrey were awake now. A light came on. Holt manoeuvred a campstool behind Taylor, and pressed his shoulders. He sat.

'Aubrey, I could use some tea. And I'm sure Nick could too. Would you mind?'

Aubrey's single nod was like a wordless recrimination that drove straight through Taylor's heart. His sobs deepened.

Holt, damn him, was acting all apologetic, as if it were he who had attempted the suicide, and not Taylor.

'It's a shock at first, Nick. I know. Hell, I remember when I discovered it. And you should have seen the faces on the UN troops when they tried firing at us. But certain entropic reactions from the old paradigm are just impossible now, within a large radius of the demons. You can't get an internal combustion engine to function within miles of Maxwell's Land. It's a local accumulation of anti-entropy, put out as a byproduct of the demons' sorting. God knows why our metabolisms still work. Sheldrake thinks it's got to do with the morphogenetic field. But shit, it's all beyond me – I admit it. One thing I do know. The field should reach Europe pretty soon. After that, they'll have no choice but to use my demons. I figure America has about another ten years, tops, if she stays stubborn. Although I'd go back to help any time sooner, if they asked.'

Taylor's sobs diminished. 'What . . . what are you going to do with me?'

Holt looked at Aubrey, his face – as youthful as it had been in their school days – honestly ingenuous. 'Gee, I don't know. There's so much to be done, whole continents to convert, a hundred countries, thousands of societies. Take what we're doing out here. We're going to restore the wadi. There's plenty of water, it's just three hundred feet down. These new silicrobes we've engineered form micro-capillaries and bring the water up one molecule at a time. We could sure use you to help restore the biosphere – but maybe you have some ideas.'

Taylor was silent. Holt turned as Aubrey approached with tea.

'Aubrey, what do you say we should do with Nick?'

His wife looked at Taylor, and he managed to meet her eyes. He thought he had never seen her so radiant or self-possessed. That drivel in her farewell letter – had all been true. He waited with trepidation for her to speak.

'Put him to work,' she said forcefully. 'What else? Even now,' she said, 'nobody gets something entirely for nothing.'

For Paul Bowles

Heat

J. D. Gresham

The clink of ice cubes gave a momentary illusion
of coolness. Mara smiled her thanks as she took the drink,
sipped, and glanced sympathetically at the man mopping his
brow with a large white handkerchief.

'Madness to be in town really.' His tone implied that he could
be on a yacht off the Needles, or holed up in his second home in
Wales, instead of in a stuffy terrace in Finchley on a stifling
August evening.

'Yes.' Mara thought wistfully of the Pennines. 'But think how
unbearable it would be trying to travel anywhere on a Friday,
stuck in a tailback on the motorway, probably.'

'True.'

They smiled at each other again, already certain that they had
nothing to share, the man's eyes searching beyond Mara for
someone else to talk to. Taking pity on him, Mara began to
move past him.

'Bathroom,' she murmured, threading cautiously through the
people grouped in Eva's sitting-room.

'Awful,' a woman in a backless dress was saying to the
nodding faces nearest to her. 'You have a shower, and two
minutes later you're as hot as you were before.'

Mara edged into the hall and decided she probably did need
the bathroom. She wanted to splash cold water on the back of
her neck, and perhaps on her feet, too.

'Mara.'

She peered over the banister and Sandy was in the hall,
looking hot and damp.

'Haven't seen you in ages. Come and say hello.'

'In a minute. Just . . .' She gestured upwards.

'Right. We're in the kitchen. Find us when you come down.'

She made it sound, thought Mara, as if it would require the
skills of a detective. In fact, she knew so few people at the party
that familiar faces shone out like beacons. Especially Sandy's
scarlet one, she thought, splashing her own burning cheeks. It
would be nice to talk to Sandy again – and Phil, who was so
decent, though somewhat monosyllabic. She wished she had
not accepted Eva's invitation, but Eva was so anxious for the
party to be a success that she had felt obliged to promise to be

there. If it had only been cooler, it would have been less of a duty and perhaps more of a pleasure. As she combed back her hair, grimacing when her fingers touched the dampness at the roots, she felt a faint sensation of unease. She looked at her reflection, which stared unsmilingly back. Drank those two glasses too fast, she told herself. Better ease up now.

Not that Eva would care if she got drunk. As long as everyone had a noisy good time, Eva would be happy; she was looking a little tipsy herself, though it was hard to tell with Eva. Mara could hear her rather loud voice as she went down to the kitchen, where Sandy was standing by the fridge.

'I see you've found the coolest spot.' She accepted a glass from Sandy.

'If only I could stick my head inside it!' Sandy flapped her hand ineffectually in front of her face. 'I must look like I've been boiled. Well, what have you been doing for the last three months? Phil said he'd seen you the other week, by the way.'

Mara nodded, smiling, at Phil, who had turned his head on hearing his name. 'Yes, we bumped into each other at the Van Gogh do. I was really glad to see him. Pretty dreadful crowd.'

'Rather like this lot.' Sandy's voice dropped. 'Why do we come, for God's sake? Do you know any of these people? Do you want to?'

They giggled; Mara was aware that her third glass was nearly empty as Sandy reached for the bottle and refilled it.

'Get some ice, Mara. There must be some in the fridge.'

She bent to open the fridge door. As the cold air streamed out, she felt the unease again, stronger this time. Her head was suddenly startlingly clear, then fuddled with heat. She straightened up with the ice tray. Dropping cubes into Sandy's drink, she felt the muscles tighten across her shoulders and she frowned.

'What is it?'

'Nothing. The ice was cold.'

'Isn't it wonderful?' Sandy held her glass out. 'Shove another one in. Brilliant.' She looked at Mara again. 'Are you all right?'

'Yes, fine.' Mara swallowed, felt for a tissue. 'It's just so hot in here.' The sharp clarity filled her head again; her stomach contracted in response. Oh no, she thought. It can't be. Not now.

Sandy was talking, her red face animated. Mara nodded, tried to focus on what she was saying. She was aware of phrases floating past, but there seemed to be gaps that were filled with the all-too-familiar sharpened reality that segued in and out.

Sandy came back into focus. '. . . so we could be moving in a couple of months, if we don't get gazumped or something dreadful. You can never be sure until you're actually in, though.'

Mara heard herself recounting the details of her flat purchase with Karen. Sandy had heard it before, of course, but Mara could talk while part of her stood back and examined the state she was in.

Clammy hands that she could not blame on the weather; rapid changes from heightened awareness to a drowsy dullness; pressure on the back of the neck and the shoulders; prickly skin and a gradual tightening of the muscles; a growing sense of unease and, suddenly, damningly, a finger-trail of desire across her belly, slow and insidious, a snake uncoiling.

She set her glass down sharply. It rapped on the worktop, making heads turn.

She said, urgently, 'Sandy!'

'What is it?' Sandy put out a hand. 'Do you feel ill?'

She couldn't say it. She ran her tongue across her dry lips, swallowed, tried again.

'Phone a taxi.'

'What's wrong?' Sandy was pulling at Phil's arm. 'Phil . . . sorry to interrupt. Mara's not very well.'

He turned to them at once, his expression concerned. 'Isn't she? What's up, Mara?'

Mara was trying to steady her breathing. Slowly, she told herself. Hold it, slow it down, and you can control it until you get home. Just get out of here as fast as possible, before they all realise.

She said through her teeth, 'Something I ate, I expect. Could you call me a cab, Phil? I need to go home.' She could not look at him, fought to master her breath.

'I wish we'd driven here.' Sandy was apologetic. 'But there's always an argument about who's going to drink, so we came on the Tube. But I'm sure someone would give you a lift.' She looked vaguely round the kitchen.

'No!' Mara dropped her voice hastily, seeing the surprise on Sandy's face at her vehemence. 'No, don't ask anyone. I don't know any of them. I'd much prefer to take a taxi. Could you phone for me, Phil?'

'Of course.' He went to the door and she heard him call to Eva. She kept her face averted from Sandy, filled her lungs, waited, let the air out slowly. It shuddered out of her and Sandy put an arm across her shoulder.

'Oh, Mara, you poor thing. Do you feel sick?'

She shook her head, shrugged off Sandy's arm. 'I'm okay. Just . . . I had some fish for lunch, maybe that . . .' Even as she spoke, she felt the horrifying clarity that seemed to open her to everyone's attention, and made her catch her breath as the full awareness of the men in the room struck like a punch.

She felt, rather than saw, that there were three of them, one considerably older than the other guests, the other two about her age. They were glancing her way, probably unaware as yet as to what was drawing them. They seemed to be very large, menacing.

She said quickly to Sandy, 'It's too hot in here. Eva's room.'

Sandy nodded and took her elbow, guiding her upstairs into Eva's tiny bedroom, and on to the bed.

'Do you want to lie down until the taxi comes?' Sandy was beside her, face anxious.

'No.' Mara was rigid with concentration, counting the seconds as she breathed. Her mind clouded suddenly and she relaxed. 'I'm okay, really.' She leaned back against the headboard and curled her legs up.

A hand tapped; Phil's head came around the door. 'About half an hour, I'm afraid.'

'Half an hour!' Mara sat up, trembling.

'It's Friday night. You know what it's like.' Phil was apologetic, helpless.

Sandy was brisk. 'That's all right. I'll sit with Mara till it comes. You go back down and enjoy the party.'

'Well . . .' Phil was uneasy now. Mara guessed that he was affected.

Sandy got up and went over to the door. Mara could hear her whispering and then Phil's footsteps receded. Sandy's face was hard as she came back to the bed.

'You're on, aren't you?'

'I . . . think so.'

'Why the hell did you come here tonight?'

'I didn't know . . . It's three weeks early. Sandy, I'm never early.'

Sandy grunted. 'I'd better tell Eva.'

'No!' Mara caught her arm. 'You don't need to. I'll be gone in half an hour. It's only just coming on.'

'Phil's realised.'

'You mean you told him.'

'No. I mean he's noticed.'

'Already?'

They looked at each other, Mara seeking a little sympathy, Sandy some contrition.

'Damn it, Mara, what's the first thing you learnt, the first time you came on? You don't go out!'

'Sandy, I swear I didn't know. I told you, it's early. I'm usually on the nail.'

Sandy let her breath out in a sigh. 'I have to tell Eva. You know what it'll be like in a few minutes.'

Mara knew only too well. The social groupings downstairs would be ruined, the men unsettled by lust, the women trying to pretend it wasn't happening. She knew, too, how it would be when she went down to the taxi, how the faces would stare, the men's frankly appraising, the women's tight with anger. She would not be a guest of Eva's again, or Sandy's probably. She heard a moan come from her dry lips.

'Maybe Eva's got some SuPress.' Sandy began to rummage through the dressing-table drawer.

'No. Can't stand the side-effects.' Mara remembered the blinding headache, the dried-up mouth, the eyeballs which felt as if a pair of thumbs were pushing them relentlessly from behind. 'Doesn't really suppress it – just makes you feel like death. Stay with me, Sandy,' she added miserably.

Sandy patted her hand. Mara felt the insincerity of the gesture, bit her lip.

'I have to tell Eva. I'll come straight back. You'll be all right here.' She went out, closing the door firmly.

Mara lay back, feeling the tears start. Even they were false, she thought bitterly, invoked by the hormonal surge in her body rather than by emotion. She wondered why she always felt so self-pitying – and so vulnerable. If it were not so hot, she would slide under Eva's duvet, bury her head under the pillow.

A tap on the door.

'Sandy?' she said nervously.

A man's head came round the door. 'Mara?' it said, smiling.

'Who are you?' Mara could barely get the words out.

The man edged around the door. 'Richard's the name. Haven't met, I don't think.'

She could see the glisten of perspiration on his brow. 'Please don't,' she said faintly.

'Got my car outside,' the man said, staring openly now. 'If you didn't want to wait for the taxi . . . Get you home in a jiffy.'

'Get out.'

'Better than staying here and letting them all know.'

'Get out of here!'

He stood unmoving by the door. He passed a hand quickly across his face; his lips gleamed.

'You'd feel better in your own bed.'

The leer in his voice brought her upright. She looked him full in the face. 'How did you know?' she said. It was not what she had meant to say at all.

'Knew when you came upstairs.' The man took a step towards her. 'Mara . . . The car's just outside.'

'No.' She heard, with relief, footsteps, and then the door was opening and Sandy was there. She gave the man a contemptuous glance.

'Well, if you change your mind.' He ignored Sandy completely, watched Mara's face.

'I won't.'

He smiled again, his tongue darting between his lips for an instant, and then he was gone.

'You see?' Sandy banged the door shut. 'I had to tell Eva.'

'What did she say?'

'She's pretty bloody angry. But she says she believes you didn't know. It's ruining her party, of course. Horrid little staggy groups forming, the women whispering in the kitchen, you know the sort of thing. Oh, don't start crying,' she added crossly. 'That won't do any bloody good.'

'Can't help it.' Mara blew her nose fiercely.

Sandy's face softened momentarily. 'Yeah, it's a bitch, isn't it?' She moved over to the dressing-table. 'Christ, look at this lot. Eva must spend a fortune.'

Mara watched her toy with Eva's bottles and jars, saw her unstopper the perfume, sniff it and pull a face. The heavy odour flooded the room as Mara's intensified awareness returned, taking hold of her and gripping her, making her conscious of the sweat that started on her brow, the crawling of her skin, the aura that Richard had left behind him. She could hear the rising murmur of male voices downstairs; her insides twisted. There was a ragged chorus of a rude song that degenerated into a roar of laughter. She rolled over on to her stomach, clenched her fists.

'Getting strong?'

She nodded, unable to answer.

'You come on quickly.' Sandy's voice was neutral; she put down the perfume bottle, wandered over to the wardrobe.

'Look at this.' She pulled out a blue dress, held it in front of her. 'Not me, is it? Not really Eva, either, I wouldn't have thought.'

Mara tried to concentrate on the dress, on Sandy. The image of Richard standing at the door was in her head. She could see the moistness of his mouth, the hair on the back of his hand, could smell his skin.

'Oh God.' She pushed her face into the pillow, tried to block out the picture.

The door opened and Eva came in. She crossed the room and sat down beside Mara.

'How is it?'

'Strong.'

The two women looked at each other, Eva struggling to hide her feelings beneath the mask of the concerned hostess. She exchanged glances with Sandy, who was closing the wardrobe door.

'What's it like downstairs?' Sandy's tone was casual. She might have been asking about the weather.

Eva dabbed at her neck with a tissue. 'Difficult. The single women are starting to leave, of course. I'm afraid no one will give you a lift, Mara. You can imagine the hostility. The men are behaving well on the whole. One or two are getting impossible – all suggestive comments and bottom-pinching.'

'Sorry, Eva.' Mara despised the tears in her voice, hated her body for doing this to her. 'I really didn't know. I'm not due for weeks.'

'Sandy said.' Eva got up. 'I'd better go back down. You *will* leave as soon as the taxi comes?'

'Yes, of course.'

'Are you staying here, Sandy?' Eva paused at the door. Mara suspected she was half-enjoying the drama. The raised voices of the men floated up, raucous with suggestiveness.

'Yes.' Sandy sat down in front of the dressing-table. 'I'll stand guard, Eva. Don't worry.'

'It's not funny.' Eva glared at them both and banged the door behind her. Sandy raised one eyebrow at Mara, stuck her legs out in front of her and began to whistle under her breath. They did not look at or speak to each other. Mara concentrated on breathing, holding each intake of air, letting it go slowly.

Sandy got up, came around to the bedside table to look at the clock. 'Any minute now, kid. How're you doing?'

'Getting there.' They smiled, Sandy magnanimous now that her job was nearly over.

'Karen'll look after you when you get in.'

'She's away for the weekend. I'll have the place to myself. Better really.'

'Yes. You can roll around and groan and no one'll care.' Sandy picked up a china pot and toyed with it. Her voice was deliberately casual again. 'Anyone you might call up?'

'No.' Mara thought of the men she knew. There was not one she would consider when she was not on and she knew that, although her perceptions of them would be altered during the next few days, to invite any of them would be to hate herself – and them – afterwards.

'Oh well. A few days in the flat then.'

'Yes. Catch up on my letter writing.' They laughed.

Footsteps came quickly up the stairs and a hand knocked. Phil's voice: 'Taxi.'

'Right, here we go.' Sandy was on her feet, glancing around. 'Got everything?'

'Yes. Only had this bag.'

'Money for the taxi?'

'Yes. It's all right, Sandy.' She came over to the other woman for a moment, knowing that to get too close would be to invoke an aggressive reaction that Sandy could no more control than the men downstairs could master their arousal. 'Thanks for everything. I know it's hard.'

'Forget it. Let's get you out of here.' Sandy was listening to the men, frowning at the words they were chanting. 'Go straight to the front door and don't look at them. Keep your head down and it won't be so bad.'

Mara took a deep breath, followed Sandy downstairs. She saw before she reached the bottom that Phil had stationed himself at the front door, which he was holding open. The taxi's motor was running and she made for the sound gratefully, trying not to hear the bellow of lewd singing that came from the kitchen.

At the foot of the stairs, Sandy stopped and stood aside to let her go by. She was, Mara realised, blocking the entrance to the sitting-room, ensuring that no one came out and touched her. The man called Richard was lounging against the wall by the kitchen. She recognised his odour, though she only looked at his legs and feet as she hurried past. He whispered her name, but she was at the front door now, turning to thank Phil. The words dried in her mouth as she saw his expression. For a moment, she was back in Eva's bedroom and Richard's leer was in front of her. She took in the glazed look, the parted lips and perspiring brow, and then she was running out, down the steps and into the lighted rear of the cab. The front door slammed and they were moving. She did not look back at the house. Eyes closed, she allowed herself the luxury of a few tears of relief.

'Where to?' The driver's voice through the intercom brought her to abruptly. Male. Middle-aged.

She opened her eyes, met his in the driving-mirror. I know you know, her look told him, but you won't do anything. Probably a family man, she thought as she leaned forward to give the street name. Protected by the glass barrier that, by law, separated all taxi drivers from their fares, she could relax. He would not risk his job, a prison sentence.

She sat back, thinking about the next few days. She had enough food to last until Karen came back, although she would have to drink her tea milkless on Sunday. She would need to ring work on Monday, of course, but, apart from the Milsom project, nothing would suffer during the two-week compulsory absence. Actually, it was better to be on now from the work point of view. Next month was a busy one, and they would be glad when she went in and removed her 'biannual leave' sticker from the wallplanner.

'Comfortable in the back?' The driver's voice, as intrusive as the gaze that watched every move. She ignored him, turned her head to the window. Just drive, she thought. Just get me home.

'A little music maybe?' He didn't wait for an answer, but the cab filled with the sound of Nina Marron, heavy, sexual, pleading, the rhythm insistent, the saxophone wailing. She swallowed, crossing her legs. She would not meet the driver's eyes again, although she knew they were fixed on the mirror, staring at her. The snake coiled and uncoiled across her belly, making her pant. She clenched her knees together, almost crying out as the burning took her, shook her.

'Baby,' the voice crooned over and over. 'You know what I want. You know what I want.'

In her mind a man's hands were touching her, stroking her, curling around her breasts, running down to where the heat filled her. She pushed into the corner of the seat, reaching into her bag for a tissue to dab at her neck and forehead.

If only it were not such a hot night. That made it worse. And she had two days and nights of this to bear, forty-eight hours in which she would be gripped and shaken by a need that made her ashamed of her body one minute, and desperate to satisfy it the next. If she took sleeping pills, there would be appalling dreams in which every enactment of lust that she could imagine would possess her, leaving her wrecked when she woke up, full of self-disgust. Experience had taught her that the only way, when there was no man that she could consider, was to sweat it out, for at least when she was awake she could control the fantasies to some extent, could re-direct them to involve men she did not find repulsive and who did not want to degrade her. There might even be some pleasure there.

And her thoughts strayed to Colin. Oblivious of the cab driver, her body uncurled, stretched. Their mouths met; his body was against hers. The memory was bitter. She had realised that this was what it was all for, for the pleasure, the satisfaction, the promise of renewal. She had even thought that they might pair, have children, that she would fulfil what they had taught her at school was her biological destiny.

But maybe that was the fantasy, she thought grimly, opening her eyes and seeing the glint of the driver's gaze as he watched. She was aware of her hand, drew it hastily away. This was the reality, and Colin could certainly be no more than a fantasy now. He had found another woman, and then others, for it was Colin's tragedy, as well as hers, that he could not resist, any more than the pathetic Richard at Eva's party, the pull exerted by a woman's heat. And since Colin there had been no one that she wanted, except in the nightmares and the terrible daydreams that her present condition invoked. Even you, she thought, catching the eye of the fascinated taxi driver again. Even you, God help me.

The voice of the singer filled the cab, making her squirm in its insistence. She leaned forward, spoke into the intercom. 'Turn it off, please.' She pretended not to see the curl of the driver's lip, tried to think of something neutral. To concentrate, she began a climb she had done last summer in Derbyshire. She closed her eyes, seeing the handholds above her, thinking about where she would place her right foot, sliding her knee up, testing the ridge. She looked up and Colin's face was laughing down at her.

She shook her head and turned back to the window. Nearly home. There was the church. Another five minutes. She looked at the streets that she would be unable to walk for the next few days, thinking about the men who would follow her home when she did go out again, calling, pleading. She remembered the little ginger-haired man who had hung around their building for nearly a week last time. She and Karen had joked about him, while preserving a stony-faced indifference every time they went past him. It had been good to have someone to go with her when she went out. She did not regret having bought the flat with Karen, even though it was an acknowledgement that she would not, after all, have a future that involved Colin.

They were turning into her street. She tapped on the intercom. 'Just here, thanks. How much is that?' She tipped the money into the connecting drawer, waited while he slid it through and checked it, avoiding his stare. The automatic lock clicked open and she was outside. She crossed the road, looked around. Empty. She began to walk slowly towards the flat, controlling the impulse to break into a run. The taxi remained at the kerb. She slowed down even further, willing him to drive on. She would not enter until he had driven past, did not want him to know which building was hers. Please, she screamed silently, go. Her heart was pounding. Finally, she heard the gears engage and the cab moved forward. It drew level and she saw the man lean out of the window. His head turned towards her and he called, low but penetrating, an obscenity that made her blush. Then he was accelerating away from her. She waited until the cab turned out of the street and then she was running to the front door, fumbling with the key, hurrying up to the second floor.

She let herself into the flat, slamming the door in her relief, and stood still for a moment to get her breath. Then she put down her bag and went towards the bathroom to run cold water into the bath. Humming deliberately, she made for the kitchen to get juice.

And stopped. Her body prickled. The sitting-room. It was in darkness, but there was someone there; she could sense it. Breathless again, she opened the door. She smelt, rather than saw, that a man was lying on the sofa.

'Karen?' His voice was heavy with sleep.

She switched on the light. 'No, it's Mara. What are you doing here?'

He was trying to struggle out of his sleeping bag. 'Karen gave me her key, said I could . . .' His voice trailed away.

They stared at each other, Mara seeing her dismay mirrored. Awareness stretched taut between them. The man pushed his hair back off his forehead.

'This heat. Isn't it terrible?'

Mara could feel her legs trembling. She sat down heavily in the armchair. 'What's your name?'

An uncertain smile began to form on the man's mouth. Mara looked away hastily.

'I'm Peter. An old college friend of Karen's. I expect she's mentioned me.'

Mara fixed her gaze on her knees. The silence seemed to press against her ears. 'Are you here for the weekend?' she managed at last.

'That was the idea. But I can go if it's . . . not convenient.'

'It's okay.' Mara raised her face, met his eyes. 'What are your plans? Sightseeing?'

He did not answer, dropped his gaze. She watched his face, saw the play of feelings there. She thought of her own emotions, twisted out of her control by her body chemistry, the unwilling lust of men like Phil, the instinctive hostility of Sandy and Eva. Anger and self-pity filled her. Peter glanced up at her. The expression in his eyes was familiar; she had seen it in Colin's, in a dozen others. His confusion was palpable as he struggled against her attraction. She felt her pity transfer from herself to him, and in that moment she was free. She stood up, stretched her arms above her head, luxuriating in the feeling, knowing he could not look away any longer.

'Feels like it's getting a little cooler.'

She put a hand on his arm, felt him shiver. The half-smile was back on his lips as he stood up, but this time she did not turn away.

FLOATING DOGS

Ian McDonald

And there in a wood, a Piggy-wig stood . . .
Edward Lear: *The Owl and the Pussy-cat*

On the third day beyond the womb we come to the cool cool river. Peeg and Porcospino and Ceefer and papavator and I. We stand among the trees that come down to the edge and watch the river flow. The sun is high above us; light shines and gleams from the moving water. Peeg is fascinated. He has never seen true water. Only the dream water when he was a seed high in heaven. He goes down over the stones to touch his trunk to the flowing river.

'Alive!' he says. 'Alive.'

It is only water, I tell him but Peeg cannot accept this. There cannot be enough water in the world for all this flowing: no, it must be some great coiling creature, flowing across the earth, up into heaven and back to earth again. A circle of never-ending movement. For a creature of no hands and very little words, Peeg has much opinion about the hardworld. Opinions should be left to beings like me who have much words, and clever hands. Why, he does not even know his own true name. He calls himself *Peeg* because that is the name he found on his tongue when he woke in the womb of mamavator. I tell him, *You are not a pig, a boar, you are a tapir. A tapir, that is what you are. See, you have a trunk, a snout, pigs do not have trunks or snouts.* He will not be told. *Peeg* is his name, peeg is what he is. Creatures with few words should not toy with powerful things like names.

Ceefer flexes her claws, cleans between her toes.

'What it is is not important,' she says. 'How we get across it is.' She is a law to herself, Ceefer. She has as many words

as I; this I know because she has the smart look in the back of her eyes. You cannot hide that look. But she keeps her words much to herself. If she has a name, one she found on her tongue in mamavator, she keeps that also to herself. So I have my own name for her. Ceefer. Ceefer Cat.

We follow the river to a place where the smooth shining water breaks over rocks and stones into white spray.

'Here we will cross,' I say. 'Ceefer will go first to make sure there are no traps or snares.' She grimaces at the white water; she loves to fish but hates to get her fur wet. In a few bounds she is across, sitting on the far side shaking water from her feet. We follow; Porcospino, then Peeg, then papavator, then me. The Team Leader must be last so he can watch over his team. I can see that Peeg's small feet are far from safe on the slippery rocks.

'Peeg!' I say. 'Be careful careful careful.' But the glitter and shimmer of the running water have dazzled him. His small feet lose their balance. In he goes. Screaming. Splashing. Feet clawing, kicking, but there is nowhere for them to catch hold. And the current has hold of him, is sweeping him towards a gap in the rocks to wedge him, drag him down, drown him.

Flash blue silver: papavator steps over me, straddles his long, thin metal legs to form a good steady base, unfolds an arm. *Down* goes the arm, *in* go the fingers locking in the mass of hair and circuitry at the back of Peeg's neck, *up* comes Peeg thrashing and squealing. In three strides papavator is on the far bank. Peeg is a dismal, dripping huddle on the shore.

'Up, up,' I say. 'Move move. We must go on. We have far to go this day to get to our Destination.' But Peeg will not move. He stands shivering, saying over and over and over again these words: *Bit me bit me bad being bad being bit me bit me bad being bad being.* The river being that seemed so wonderful, so friendly to him has turned evil and hostile. I go to talk to him, I stroke the coils of circuitry around his head, stroke the bulge on his side that covers the lance. He will not be consoled by my words and my touching. He is beginning to upset the others. I cannot allow that. We shall have to wait until Peeg is ready before we go on. I signal for papavator to unfold the arm with the needleful of dreams on it. Great dreams there are in the needle. Perhaps the flying dream: that is the one Peeg loves best: that he is back in heaven, flying, laughing and crying and pissing himself with happiness as the angels look down upon him and smile at their Peeg. He lifts his trunk to touch the needle. Dream good, Peeg.

Papavator settles on his metal legs, opens his belly. Time to feed. Porcospino and I suck greedily from the titties. Ceefer flares her nostrils in displeasure. She prefers the taste of gut and bone and blood. Tonight, she will hunt by the light of the moon and the shine of her eyes. She will kill. She will swallow down blood and bones and guts and all. Disgusting creature. Not a being at all.

Ceefer. Peeg. Porcospino. Papavator. Me, Coon-ass. One more in our team to make it the full one-hand's-worth-and-one. Here she comes now, down the beams of light that slant into the shadows among the trees of the river's edge: she does not need dreams to fly in. Only Peeg and I have the gift of colour-seeing, and Peeg is rolling and grunting in his needle-dream. The others cannot see as I do how the colours flow from blue to green across her wings and back, the cap of brilliant red, the beak and feet of brightest yellow. This, I think, is the word called *beautiful*. She settles on papavator's outstretched arm. No pulp, no pap for her. She feeds on pellets from the hand of papavator himself. But for all her colours, she has only one word; that is the trade the angels made: one word, two syllables that she sings over and over and over. Bir-dee. Bir-dee. Bir-dee.

Ceefer Cat looks up from her eternal cleaning, cleaning, cleaning, sudden, sniffing. In the backs of her eyes are the red moving shapes that are her gift from the angels. She stiffens, bares her teeth, just a little. That is enough. One of the things that goes with having hands and colours, and much, much words, is more fear than others: the fear that looks at what might be and shivers. *Anxiety*, that is the name for it.

Danger. Bir-dee leaps up into the air again, darting and many-coloured, brilliant, dashing through the air, and then I can see her no longer through the canopy of tree-tops. But I do not fear that she will fly away out of all seeing and never come back, she is keyed to my scent, she will always come back to me, however far she flies.

Ceefer is waiting in the shadows beneath the trees, Porcospino is ruffling and rattling his quills, papavator has closed himself up and is lurching on to his silly thin legs. But Peeg sleeps on. He grumbles and mumbles and drools in his dream. It must be a very good dream that papavator has in his needle. Peeg, Peeg, danger coming, danger coming! Awake! Awake! The others have reached the dark of the deep forest, they are looking back; why do we not come?

I do not have the senses of Ceefer, but I can feel the thing she feels; huge and heavy, moving through the forest on the other side of the river.

There are secrets that mamavator gave only to me, to be shared with none other; secrets whispered to me in the warmth of the womb, in the dream-forest that is so like, and so unlike, this hard-forest. The middle finger of my left hand is one of the secrets told to none but I. It is made from the same almost-living stuff as the emplants that trail almost to the ground from the sockets behind my ears, from the skulls of all my team.

Quick. Quick. Out comes the emplant in the back of Peeg's head.

Quick. Quick. In goes the middle finger of my left hand.

Up, I think. *Up*. Peeg twitches in his sleep, a great heaving twitch. *Up*. He staggers to his feet. *Forward*, I think and the thought pours out of my finger into his head and as he moves forward, still dreaming his needle-dream, I hop up on his back, ride him with my finger. *Move. Move. Run. Run. Fear.* He wails in his dreams, breaks into a trot, a canter. I lash him into a gallop. We fly over the dark, dark earth. Porcospino and Ceefer run at my side, papavator covers the ground with his long, clicking strides. The trees rise up all around us, taller and darker and huger than any dreaming of them. *Run Peeg run.* The dream of the needle is beginning to wear thin, the hardworld is pouring in through the tears and cracks in the dream, but I do not release him from my mind. From far behind comes a tremendous crashing, as if the dark, huge trees are being torn up and thrown into heaven; and the sound of mighty explosions. We run until all running is run out of us. Full of fear, we stop, listening, waiting. Presently, there is the smell of burning. The red shapes in the backs of Ceefer's eyes flicker and shift: she is scanning. She sits to clean herself.

'Whatever it is, is gone now,' is all she will say. She licks her crotch.

We sit, we pant, we wait. The rain begins, dripping in fat drops from the forest canopy. Soon the smell of burning is gone. As I sit with the rain running down my fur, Bir-dee comes to me, perches on my hand, singing her glad two-note song. I stroke her neck, ruffle her feathers, smooth down her glossy blue wings. Only when the others are asleep with the rain from high high above falling heavily upon them, do I extract the reconnaissance chip from her head and plug it into the socket beside my right eye.

Flight. Soaring. Trees and clouds and sun, the bright shine and coil of a river, the curved edge of the world: all crazy, all turned on end. Then, something huge as the moon: huger even than mamavator when we saw her for the first time, steaming in the forest clearing where we were born: something earthbound and stamping, stamping out of the forest, into the river, standing with the water flowing around its feet while it fires and fires and fires, explosion after explosion after explosion tearing apart the trees and rocks of the river bank where we rested. Before it stamps away down the river it sets the smashed trees alight with flames from its chest.

I blank the chip with a thought, extrude it, give it back to Bir-dee. To have hands, and colour, and much, much words, to *know;* this is the worst punishment of the angels.

> The bravest animals in the land
> Are Captain Beaky and his band.
> *Captain Beaky*

Who made you?
The angels made me from a seed.
The angels planted a seed in the womb of mamavator and

*nurtured it, and grew it. Flesh of the flesh of mamavator. She
suckled and fed us.*

The servants of the angels, the agents of their work upon
this world.

*Two natures of service, two natures of servant have the
angels; the soft and the hard; those of the inorganic and those
of the organic. The service of the inorganic is not greater
than the service of the organic, the service of the soft is not
greater than the service of the hard; both were created in the
likeness of the angels to complement each other in their
weakness.*

Recite the weaknesses of the organic.

Pain. Hunger. Tiredness. Sleep. Emotion. Defecation.
Death.

Recite the weaknesses of the inorganic.

Noise. Expense. Energy. Breakdown. Vulnerability.
Stupidity.

*Why have the angels, themselves perfect, created such
imperfection?*

Because the angels alone are perfect.

*Because no created thing, no thing of the hands, may
assume to the perfection of the angels, that is the great sin.
What is the name of the greatest sin?*

Pride.

How may we purge ourselves of the sin of pride?

By the faithful service of the angels. By the humble obedi-
ence of their will. By the execution of their assignments.

To the letter.

To the letter.

I have always wondered what that final part of the Litany
means. *To the letter.* I think that it has something to do with
the dark marks on papavator's skin; those regular, orderly
marks; and they have something to do with *words*, but the
understanding of it is not a gift the angels have chosen to give
this Coon-ass. Perhaps they are the prayers of the inorganic:
papavator himself takes no part in our nightly recitations; his
own hard, inorganic devotions he makes well apart from us;
long, thin legs folded up under him, arms and antennae

drawn in. It is not sleep, the inorganic do not sleep, not as we sleep. Strange, the lives of the inorganics. How marvellous, the will of the angels, that has made us so different, so weak in ourselves, yet so strong together to their service.

Every night, when Ceefer has sniffed out a place free from traps and poisons for us, we gather in a circle in the forest for the Litany. I lead, they respond as best they can. Bir-dee has only two words, yet no matter how far she is flying, however high, she always returns to sit with the others, shifting from foot to foot because she is not made to stand on the ground, cocking her head from side to side as if the wonder of the words is being communicated to her by some spiritual channel I do not understand. And Peeg loves the Litany, would have me say the words over and over and over because though I know that he does not understand what he is saying – they are just sounds he was born with in his skull – inside the words he can see the angels reaching down to lift him up into heaven and set him flying among the stars.

I have said that papavator does not take part in our worship. There is another, sad to say. Ceefer says that she does not believe. There are no angels, there is no heaven, she says. They are comfortable words we have invented because we know that we all must die and the knowing frightens us. She thinks that is brave. I think it foolish. It is certain that we must die, and that is frightening, but would she say it is wrong to comfort ourselves with dreams, like the dreams papavator keeps in his needle? I have tried to steer her right but she will not believe. She is a stubborn animal. Our arguing upsets Peeg; he has a great faith but the light shines through it, like sun through the leaf canopy, easily stirred by the wind. I would order Ceefer to believe, but she would laugh that dreadful cat-laugh at me; so every night when we recite she sits and cleans herself, licking licking licking. That licking, it is as bad as any laughter.

At the end, after Porcospino has scraped a hole in the leaf-litter and one after the other we shit into it, Peeg asks for a bible story.

'What story would you like to hear?' I ask.

'Angels. War,' says Peeg. 'Lights. Flying.'

Ceefer growls. She stalks away. She thinks it is a stupid story. She thinks all the bible stories she was taught by mamavator are stupid. I must admit there is much in them that does not make sense to me, but Peeg would have them told over and over and over again, every night if he could. He rolls on to his side, his safe side, closes his eyes. The tip of the lance slides out of the fold of skin on his side, like a metal penis. He seems to have forgotten all about the river. He does not have the circuits for long memory. Fortunate Peeg.

'In the days of days,' I say, 'there were only angels and animals. The animals looked like us, and smelled like us, but they were only animals, not *beings*. They were called animals by the angels because all they possessed was an *anima*, a living-ness, but no words or spirit. The angels and the animals had existed together in the world for always so that no one could remember which had made the other, or whether they had both been made by something different altogether.

'In those days of days, as in these days of days, animals served angels, but the angels, being as they were mighty creatures, with moods and feelings that are not to be judged by *beings*, grew tired of the animals and their limitations and created new servants to be better than the animals. They created servants stronger than you, Peeg' – he hears my voice in his near-sleep, the high-pressure lance slides out to almost its full length – 'that could see better and farther than you, Ceefer' – though she is out, patrolling in the darkness, it is part of the story – 'that could fly higher and carry more than you, Bir-dee, that were smarter and could remember better and think faster than me, an old raccoon; and that could kill better and more than you, Porcospino.

'So excellent were the new servants that the angels were able to fly up into heaven itself, where they have been flying ever since with their hands held out at their sides.

'Now I have said that the wisdom of the angels is greater than the wisdom of beings, and if the angels turn to war among themselves, as they did, not once, but many times in the days of days, what are we to question them? But there was war, a great and terrible war, fought by the terrible servants they had made for themselves; servants that could knock flat whole forests, that could set fire to the sky and turn the sea to piss. A war so terrible that it was fought not just upon the hard world, but in heaven also. So mighty a war that the angels in the end called upon their old servants, the animals, to aid them, and from those wordless, spiritless creatures created, by the shaping of their hands, *beings* like us.

'Though lowly and lesser and stained by the sin of our failure to serve the angels as they wished to be served, we were permitted to redeem ourselves by aiding the angels in their war. Thus we were given wonderful weapons, mighty enough to destroy the works of angels, both organic and inorganic; mighty enough' – and here I always draw my words into a hushed whisper – '*to destroy the angels themselves.*'

As they gaze into my words and in them see the angels smiling and holding out their hands to them, I go to them in turn, as I have every night since we came into the hardworld, and touch the third finger of my left hand to the sockets between their eyes, the finger that sends them down down into holy sleep.

Unseen, unheard, black as the night herself, Ceefer returns from her patrol as I end my story.

'Stupid,' she says. 'What kind of a god is it that can be killed by beings?'

'I do not know,' I say. 'That is what faith is for. So we can believe what we cannot know.'

'I hope it is a big faith you have,' says Ceefer, extending her hard inorganic claws to lick off the forest dirt, carefully, carefully. 'Big enough for another to sit on the back of it. I will have need of your faith tomorrow.'

'What do you mean?' I ask.

She blinks her round round eyes at heaven, flares her nostrils. Sensing.

'It will be a hard day, tomorrow,' she says, and, refusing any further words with me, stalks away to find a comfortable nest among the root buttresses of the great great trees.

> 'Bonedigger, bonedigger, dogs in the
> moonlight . . .'
> Paul Simon: *Call Me Al.*

I have these pictures in my head. I suppose they must be the vision of angels, for I can see the forest spread out below me, from sea to shining sea, all its hills and valleys and rivers and lakes laid out before me. But it is more than just as if seeing from on high; it is as if I can see through the canopy of the trees, see through the trees themselves. I can see with a detail surely not possible from so great a height: I can see the place where mamavator left us before returning to the sky in lights and fire; that is a ball of blueness. I can see us, the Team, five yellow dots with a sixth moving some way ahead of us. And I can see the place where we are to go. Our Destination. The shape of that is a black, pulsing star.

The six yellow points are now closer to the black pulsing star than they are to the blue ball.

Every time Bir-dee returns with her pictures for me, my heavenly sight becomes clearer. I see now the war machine that destroyed the river bank where Peeg dreamed as a red triangle moving off to our left, along the river we crossed. It has lost interest in us. Between us and the black star is an area of open ground. When I look at it in my head, the words 'lumpy ground' come to me. It is little more than a morning's walk for us to the lumpy ground.

On the lumpy ground we will decide what we are to do when we reach the Destination. So our orders go.

Between the lumpy ground and the black star the picture looks as if ten, twenty, many many red stars have fallen out of heaven on to the earth.

The outer defences.

Ceefer leads us through the dark beneath the great trees towards the Destination, sensing for any traps and nets and snares that might await us. Now it is we who must ride on her back. We must have faith that she can see and hear and smell what we cannot, we must trust her to see what cannot be known, for to know, to see, to taste and touch, would be to die. I have learned a new word today. Ceefer's words of the night before have made it come bubbling up out of my head like deep deep water. *Foreboding*. Such a duty, the angels have laid upon us. But would they have given us a task they knew we could not perform?

Ceefer's screech sends my angel-pictures whirling away in many many torn pieces. The wail dies slowly into a growl: Ceefer crouches, eyes wide, whiskers and ears folded flat, staring at the thing she has found in the dark under-forest.

It has been dead a long long time. The smell of it has been dissolved away into the smell of forest: guts and eyes pecked out by pecking pecking birds and insects, skin pulled away from teeth bared in the final snap at death. Pelt a dried tatter of fur and leather. The metal spike of the spring trap is driven out through the back of its neck. Some kind of possum, or small, biting marsupial: I cannot tell, it is so old and dead.

There are bright metal sockets beneath its ears, and torn strands of circuitry. Nestled among its bare ribs are long, thin, steel somethings.

Cat-cool recovered, Ceefer brushes past, moves on. Porcospino pauses to sniff at the dried corpse, papavator steps past on his metal legs. He is a machine, he does not have the weakness of feeling. But Peeg is terrified. Peeg will not go past it. Peeg cowers away from it; it is a bad sign, he says, *bad sign, bad sign, bad sign.*

'It cannot harm you,' I say. 'Its duty is done. Its soul flies in heaven with the angels. You too have a duty, given you by the angels, that you must do.'

I do not want to have to use the circuits in my finger again. Wide-eyed with terror, Peeg approaches. Any moment he will break and run, I think. I have circuits in my hand for that possibility, too. Keeping as far as he can from the dead impaled thing, Peeg edges past. Ceefer waits, head turned, eyes shining red, tail lashing impatiently.

But Peeg is right. It is a bad sign.

We enter a clearing. Ceefer is suspicious, looking to the sky, sniffing all around her. Nothing registers on her sensors but she is not happy. If Ceefer is not happy, I am not happy. Porcospino, too, is uncomfortable; blinking his tiny eyes in the light. He is a creature of the forests, of the darkness of the forests; he is naked in open terrain. Naked sky frightens him. Peeg looks across the clearing to the great great trees.

'Look at the trees, Coon-ass,' he says, pointing with his trunk. 'Dead dead trees, with leaves on them.'

I look where he is pointing. And I am afraid. For the great trees are dead, bare, blasted wood, killed by black air and war, but the branches are hung with black leaves.

'Quick, quick!' I cry. 'This is a trap!'

And the leaves rise from the branches of the dead trees and we understand. They are not leaves at all. They are bats, rising up in a cloud of beating, roaring wings so dark they shut out the sun.

Those red dots in my inner vision, as many as the stars in heaven . . .

'Quick! Quick!' I try to watch the sky as we run across the clearing beneath the wheeling, chittering mass of bats. They swoop down upon us: I can see the shine of circuitry in their fur. I can see the shine of weapons clutched between their feet.

'Quick! Quick!'

The ground rises up in front of me in a burst of noise and earth: the explosion sends me reeling backwards. I plunge onward, blindly, guided by older, baser, truer instincts. The bats release their bombs and flap away. Explosions to the right of me, explosions to the left of me, explosions before me, explosions behind me. We run on; the sky is gone. There are only bats, wheeling, croaking, screaming. The edge of the forest is close, the cover of the trees. So many bats could not safely fly there. Not day-bats, as these are. I look back, see papavator lurching unsteadily across the clearing. Then the bright bombs fall, there is an explosion, flying metal and machine juices. Arms and legs wave, flail, fall dead.

When I am sure I can no longer hear the beating of wings or the sound of bat-voices, I call a halt. We have lost more with papavator than needle-dreams, I say. Without his picking and purging and preparing digested pap for us to suck from his titties, we must take the time to forage and find our own food. This is a dangerous thing for us to do: we cannot be certain that food we find is not enemy food, or tainted with the black air poisons that papavator's stomach removed, and there are always the traps and snares and nets.

'Hungry now,' says Peeg. 'Hungry *now*.'

'We all must feed ourselves,' I say. 'There is no more papavator.'

For me to grub and dig for food is a fearful, animal thing; the fat maggots and wild honey I dig with my hands, my fine, clever hands, from the hollow of a dead tree and share with Peeg and Porcospino are crude and disgusting compared to the milk of papavator. For Ceefer to hunt, to bring some small forest thing back dripping in her jaws, is a joy. Her sensor eyes glow red as she tears the small thing she has killed with her steel claws. She offers me a piece of hairy flesh gently grasped in her teeth.

'You are a raccoon,' she says, setting it down before me in the way of a wicked joke. 'You are an omnivore. You can eat anything.' I would sooner eat my own shit. Clever clever Ceefer with your smart, clever words, and your smart eyes that can see things no one else can, and your sharp little claws, and your confident belief in disbelief.

We come to the lumpy ground as the day is growing old. It is a strange terrain indeed; full of hummocks and mounds and hollows and dark pits. As if something huge and unshapely had died long ago and let the forest grow over it. Scattered across the open space are strange spires and pillars of heaped earth. There is a smell to this place I cannot identify but which stirs the hairs along my spine; a smell, and a sound, a deep, deep humming, everywhere and nowhere.

There is a dark shape moving among the shadows and hollows: a creature. A peccary, rooting. I order Porcospino forward. He raises his quills, growls in his throat.

'Tell him to put his spines down,' says Ceefer. 'It is not a being. It is just an animal. Come, Peeg, with your lance. That is our evening meal, out there.' Off she goes, a black shadow flowing across the lumpy ground. Poor, silly Peeg trots after her. The peccary looks up, bolts for the forest edge. The vague troubling noise has become a definite sound, a buzzing, a droning.

Streams of black vapour pour from the strange earth pillars.

'Ceefer! Peeg! Come back at once!' I say. They need no warning from me, they are already flying back across the lumpy ground. The dark vapour forms a cloud around the

peccary. The frantic animal tries to flee but the swarm follows
it. The peccary twists, turns, plunges; and falls. And I understand. It is not black air, as I had feared. It is much worse. It
is insects. Flying, stinging insects. Millions upon millions of
insects. They swarm up from the dead peccary, a dark,
droning tower looming above the lumpy ground, leaning over
us.

What is this Coon-ass to do if he is to obey the will of the
angels? I stare, mesmerised, at the whirlwind of insects,
moving slowly across the open ground towards me. We
cannot fight. We cannot run. We cannot escape. Then I hear
Porcospino's voice.

'In. Now.'

Has the fear overloaded his circuitry? What is he talking
about? He is scratching at a dark hole at the foot of an oddly
shaped green mound.

'Others already in. You. Now.'

'Bir-dee,' I say. 'What about Bir-dee?'

'If she is out there, already too late,' says Porcospino. 'In.
In.'

I scuttle into the hole as the storm of insects breaks.
Porcospino works with his strong feet, kicking at the dirt to
seal up the tunnel. A few insects have crawled inside, I strike
at them with my hands and feet, crush them into the earth.

'Come. Come. Fast. Fast,' says Porcospino as he leads me
down, down, downward. To me, a being of the light, with
hands and much much words, this is a foreboding of death;
dark, pressing close all around, fear, down down downward
into the gnawing earth. To Porcospino this is his place of
places, underground, grubbing, sniffing.

When I was a seed in the womb of mamavator, adrift in
highest heaven, I had a dream in which I was shown the
shape of the world. In this dream the world was a bubble of
light and air and life surrounded by earth and soil and stone
that went on and on and on beyond all counting, for always.
In the dream, a voice told me that somewhere lost in this
never-endingness of earth and soil were other worlds like our
own, of light and air and life.

Of course, it is the foolish imagining of a raccoon, but

when I find myself in light and air and space after so long in the dark I think that we have dug our way through the bottom of the world and emerged in some other earth.

It is a very small world, this bubble of air and light, barely big enough for Ceefer and Peeg and Porcospino and Coon-ass. The air is stale, dead, and tastes of old, used-up poison. The light is strange, dim, blue, coming not from one sun, but from flat squares above us. It is a square world altogether, this world, square-sided, everything sharp-edged. It has the smell of a work of angels.

Peeg is looking as if he is going to cry with confusion.

'I think this must be an old defensive position,' I say. I hope that he will trust my words and knowledge. 'It must come from the very very early time of the war, so long ago the forest grew over it and forgot it. Look: see?' I point at more flat, square things fixed to the sides of the world. They are covered in tiny red and yellow lights, like the shapes in the pictures in my head. 'Machine servants. This is a place made by angels.'

'More than machine servants,' says Ceefer. 'Come. See.'

She leads us through an opening, along a tunnel into another blue-lit square-cut chamber. There are more inorganics on the walls with their red and yellow stars. On the floor are the bodies of organics.

The dead possum-thing we encountered on the forest path was frightening because it still retained a memory of life. These things are so long dead that they are not even memories. Beyond fearing, they are merely curious.

'What beings these?' asks Porcospino. I cannot answer, I have never seen creatures like these before. Very tall they are, very thin. Long long legs, very big and fine hands at the ends of their forelegs. Fur only on the tops of their heads. Double-skinned: that is the only way I can describe them. Over the middle of their bodies and their legs they wear a second skin, very soft and fine, though ill-fitting. When I touch it, it falls into dust.

'I will tell you what manner of beings are these,' says Ceefer. 'They are angels. That is what they are. Dead angels.'

Peeg whimpers.

'No,' I say. 'That cannot be. The angels are all in heaven.'

'The stories say that the angels fought upon earth and heaven,' says Ceefer. 'And this is a very old place. And the stories say that the angels can die. Can be destroyed by beings.'

'No,' I say, though fears and doubts rise up around me like stinging insects. 'No. No. They are monkeys. That is what they are. See the skull, the jaw? Monkeys, created and shaped to the will of the angels, but no more than monkeys.'

Ceefer sniffs at the body, delicately bares her teeth and picks up a bone. She coughs, spits it out.

'Piss and dust, that is how angel-meat tastes,' she says.

> *Sit Ubu, sit. Good dog.*
> American TV sit-com production company sound-byte.

Peeg will destroy.

How?

Peeg will know.

How will Peeg know?

You will give Peeg the knowledge.

Knowledge that I do not myself know?

Strange indeed, and wonderful, are the ways of the angels.

Peeg slept a black sleep last night, down in the square chamber among the strange bodies. There was no papavator with his needleful of dreams to send him flying through the night. I listened to him crying and whimpering, under the blue square lights. The world is too much for him.

Ceefer's eyes, which see in any darkness, lead us through many chambers under the earth full of the strange dead beings before finding a scratchway up into the the real world again. It is little more than a scrape; bulging with weapons, Peeg can barely fit through. For one moment we think he has jammed good. He screams and screams and screams in terror as Porcospino digs around him to widen the tunnel. I can understand the fear of the earth closing in all around, I have been learning much about fear.

We emerge into the morning. The sun is high above us.

The ground is covered in dead insects, like black dust. They are too dangerous for their angels to allow them to live long. From the lumpy ground we pass into forest again. We scavenge. We scratch. We shit.

From the forest we pass into the smouldering land.

The line between the two is as sharp as the edge of a claw. From the cover of the root buttresses, we survey a land burned clean of life: trees, creepers, ferns, fungi, every living thing, every creature, swept away, stripped down to the sick, shit-coloured earth. A dusting of white ash covers the earth, the smell of burning is strong; here, there the charred stump of a tree has resisted the burning.

There is a shadow on the land. A giant shadow. Before us, above us, on the edge of the burnt land that smoulders further than my eyes can see, stands the hulk of a huge war machine. Some terrible weapon has blown away the upper half of its body, the ground is littered with its torn metal flesh. The wind from across the ashlands moans over the jagged, ripped shell.

'The outer defences,' I say, quietly. Porcospino rattles his quills. Peeg whimpers in dread. Ceefer hisses. No one need ask *What could have done this?* There are forces here that can shatter even mamavator: that is why we were set down on earth so far from the Destination, to trek through dread and danger and death. Yet we beings, in all our sinful imperfection, may slip through to work the will of the angels where the mighty machines fail.

We pass between the feet of the destroyed war machine. The wind-blown ash stings my eyes. In the picture in my head, the Destination has grown huge, throbbing like a black heart, filling all my inner vision with its beating, throbbing. The ground is warm beneath my hands and feet. Ceefer quests ahead of us, sniffing a path through the soft white ash.

One scream. One warning. That is all we get. That is all Ceefer is allowed before the dogs, bursting up from under the ground, are upon her. Black hurtling dogs, many many many of them; in an instant she is snatched up, tossed into the air. I see her little steel claws flex, her teeth bare in rage, then the waiting jaws catch her, shake her, tear her in two, shake out her guts and blood and bones and scatter her across the burning earth.

Peeg squeals, lowers his stupid head. The tip of the metal lance slides from its housing on his side.

'No Peeg, no. Let Porcospino!' I say.

The dogs hurl themselves upon us. Porcospino hisses, raises his spines. He flicks loose a flight of quills. The lead dogs go down, kicking their paws and writhing and twisting until their backs snap from the pain of the poisons the angels have put on Porcospino's quills. The second wave of dogs comes bounding on, over the bodies of their brothers. They have red eyes and silver metal jaws. Emplants stud the backs of their necks. Again Porcospino throws his neurotoxic spines and they go down on the right and on the left. A black dog leaps: I see his metal jaws open in my face, smell the stinking steam of his breath. Porcospino raises his tail but Peeg catches the dog in the belly with his high-pressure lance. Intestines bursting from its open mouth, blood spraying from its eyes, it goes spinning away to fall among the bodies of its littermates.

And the third wave is on us. They have ferocity, but no conception of strategy. All they know is to run, and to leap, and to savage. Squealing with excitement, Peeg thrusts with his lance, again, and again, and again: the black evil dogs go down, shattered, smashed, impaled and spasming, stuck full of Porcospino's needles.

Then there are no more for they all lie dead on the soft white ash beneath the war machine. All the dead dogs. And the sun is low on the edge of the world, red and huge behind the thin smoke that rises from the smouldering land.

'Come,' I order.

'Ceefer . . .' says Peeg. Soon it will hit him, and I have no dreams to stop him crying.

'She is gone. The angels hold her in their hands. Believe me.'

But I am no longer sure I believe what I am telling them they must believe. Where do the faithless go? Is there a lonely place, dark and sad, for those who deny the angels? Or is death death? Nothing? *Nothing?* As we pick our slow and careful way through the ashlands under the rising moon, I find myself drawn to this thought, over and over and over. *Nothing.* It is a terrible thought. I cannot imagine it. Yet over and over and over, I am drawn to it.

Peeg snuffles out a hollow between the burned roots of a tree stump, digs a small scrape where we lie together.

'Hungry,' says Peeg.

'We are all hungry,' I say. 'There is nothing here for us. We will have to be hungry a little longer.'

I lie in the scrape. The moon stands over me. A little lower than the moon, strange lights cross the sky, moving fast, fast, from horizon to horizon in a breath. I cannot sleep. I dare not sleep. If I sleep, I will see Ceefer broken apart and all her words and knowledge and strange unbelief that, in truth, was a kind of belief, spilled out and lost.

In the night, Peeg wakes.

'Coon-ass.'

'Yes.'

'Give me.'

'Give you what?'

'Give me knowledge.'

'I do not know how. I do not know what this knowledge is.'

'Peeg know. Mamavator give Peeg words. Mamavator say: "Say Coon-ass: *Load File B13 echelon 7.*"'

And it is as if those words, which Peeg could not possibly know unless he had, indeed, been given them by mamavator, gather all my *beingness* and roll it up like clay in a hand, push it away away to the very back of my head so that I may watch but am helpless to act as I feel my hands reach round to the back of my neck and pull out an emplant. And I see those hands that look like my hands reach out and slide the emplant into an empty socket beneath Peeg's ear. And the ears that hear like my ears hear Peeg sigh, and gasp, and say, in a voice I have never heard Peeg speak in before:

'Reset normal sentience simulation parameters.'

I shake my head, try to shake my *Coon-ass* back into every corner of my being. I am frightened: clever, proud, wise Coon-ass, mastered and ridden like a . . . like an *animal.* I lie and watch the lights crossing the sky, feeling small, small, smaller than the smallest thing I can imagine. *Nothing.*

The black, beating star beat-beats all night, so huge and close it has spilled out of the place in my head where the pictures are to fill everything with its beating.

> *All together now, all together now, all together now.*
> *In No Man's Land.*
> The Farm.

In the morning my eyes and hands are raw sore with the white ash that covers the burned lands. We are all very hungry but we know among ourselves it is better not to speak about such things. Peeg offers to let me ride on his back. I am glad to accept. With Porcospino trotting beside us, we enter the inner defences. The borderline is clearly marked. A metal arm jutting from the ash bars our path. Clenched in its steel grip is a rodent-like being, furious even in death. The steel fingers crush the rodent's neck, the rodent's teeth are sunk into the arm's brightly coloured wiring. Both are long, long dead.

It is both warning and welcome.

Much occupied with our own thoughts, whatever kind of thoughts the angels have given us to think, we pass into a landscape of terrible, terrible destruction. As far as we can see, the ash is littered with bodies of beings organic and inorganic, locked together in embraces that seem to this Coon-ass almost tender. Paws clawing for the light; mouths open to snap bright teeth one last time at the sun. Torn and twisted metal; gnawbones, jawbones. Hanks of hair and wind-dried hide. Dead birds, pulled out of the sky, sky-wise wings splayed out, feathers rustling in the wind, beaks and eyeless eyesockets silted up with drifting ash. Standing guard over them, half-clogged to the waist in ash and mud, the machines: shattered, crushed, twisted apart by ancient explosions, smashed metal limbs swinging, creaking, red sensor eyes dull dead dark.

A cat hanging from a wire noose.

A bird shot through with a metal spike.

Three bloated dogs floating in a crater full of rainwater.

Porcospino lets out a cry. It is the first sound to break the silence of the ashlands. He has seen the body of a brother porcupine, lying close by in a hollow in the ash, surrounded by the skin-draped skeletons of dogs.

'Leave it, leave it,' I say. 'You can do nothing here. It is dead, it has been dead for time beyond counting.'

But Porcospino will not listen; it is as if this rattle of dead, dry quills and spines is a comrade to him, a comfort in the dreadfulness all around him. A lost littermate he never had. He nuzzles the dead thing, pushs it with his nose, as if he might push life back into it, push it into movement and joy. He pulls at its pelt with his teeth; clumps of emplants come away in his teeth.

'Leave it leave it leave it!' I say. 'There is too much danger here!'

The ash hears me. The ash stirs. The ash moves. The ash opens. Like a flower blooming, the machine unfolds from beneath the earth. Its head quests; back, forth, back, forth. Red machine eyes open, staring.

'Run run run!' I say, but the weaving head on the long flexing neck has fascinated Porcospino, like the snake I once saw in my mamavator dreams, which could dazzle you with its dancing, weaving, flexing. The huge red sensor eyes fasten on Porcospino. He gazes up into the huge red eyes.

The machine spews out a sheet of fire. Porcospino goes up in a shriek of burning. He tries to beat at the flames with his tiny useless hands, rolls on to his back to roll them out. The fire roars up and eats him.

The head on its long neck wavers, collapses into the ash. Its red sensor eyes go black. Its work is done. I curl my fingers into the circuitry on Peeg's neck, urge him onward.

'To the Destination,' I say. 'The Destination.'

A thin trail of smoke goes up behind us; the wind changes direction and bends it low over us as we pick our way across the battlefield. As Peeg carries me along, he tells me about what the chip has told him about the Destination he is to destroy. It is a *strategic manufacturing installation*, he says.

His words are large and strange, not Peeg words. It builds machines and grows beings, this *strategic manufacturing installation*.

Like mamavator? I ask.

Like mamavator, says Peeg, but this one does not fly in heaven. This one is buried deep under the ground. Deep deep, way down deep. It is very old. Very very old. The angels have been trying to destroy it' for long long years. Attack after attack after attack they have sent, from heaven first, and then by machine, and then by beings. Attack after attack after attack. After so many attacks, it must be tired now, old. It cannot have much energy left. That is how we will be able to reach the Destination.

How will we know when reach the Destination? I ask.

We will know, says Peeg. That is what the chip tells me.

And then you will destroy it?

And then Peeg will destroy it.

How?

Peeg does not know. But Peeg trusts that the angels, in their great wisdom, having told him much already, will tell him that also when he needs to know.

Angels, in their great wisdom. Peeg would have cried, once. Peeg would have cried for Porcospino. Peeg would have cried for each one of those many many beings, more than many many hands can count, that died so that Peeg and Coon-ass can reach their Destination. What did the angels take away to make room for their great wisdom?

We will know, the angel voices in the chip said. Why must they be so very very true in everything they say? We will know, I will know, I have known, since I stumbled, blinking from the warm wet womb into the forest morning. The Destination is the great black star in the picture in my head taken out and pressed into the earth; real, actual. Huge. The black star is bigger than I can cover with both hands spread out in front of my eyes. Many many hours walk across. Heat shimmers and dances over the star: I cannot see its further edge. Now that the shock is passing. I see that it is not the same as that other star, my inner star. It is not as sharp-edged, as definite; it has many many rays, the shiny black of it is streaked and stained with colours, its surface is crazed and cracked, like something that has fallen from heaven to earth.

Fallen, or cast down? We stand at the edge of the great black star, a raccoon riding on the back of a tapir.

'You must get down now,' says Peeg. 'I am to go on on my own.'

'Where?' I touch the blackness with my hand, it is smooth, slippery, warm to the touch.

Peeg points with his trunk out across the black.

'I hear voices,' he says in that voice, with those words, which are not his own. 'Voices, coming from big bright lights. Wonderful wonderful lights.'

'Peeg, you cannot go, I must go too, you need me.'

'On my own,' Peeg says, looking far into the heat haze. 'I will destroy it on my own. Then I will come back to you.'

'You will come back to me?'

'Yes.'

'Do you promise?'

'I do not understand what that means.'

'It means that when you say that you will come back, you will come back, that nothing will stop you coming back.'

'Yes.'

'Then I will do as you say.'

'It is the will of the angels,' says Peeg, and walks out on his little, neat feet, out across the black glass star, until the heathaze swallows him and I can see him no more. I sit. I wait. The sun moves across the sky, I watch it reflected in the blackness before me. In the reflection I can see where the wars of the angels have left their marks even there. The face of the sun is scarred with dark pock-marks. Craters. Black starbursts. The heathaze runs over the black, melted land like water. In the shiver and the shimmer I am no longer certain what is true, what is false. For in the silver shining I see a distant dark figure standing. Then the heathaze flows and runs and I see clearly: it is Peeg out there in the black lands.

'Peeg!' I shout, 'Peeg!' but he cannot hear me. He is looking into the sky, questing up with his trunk, like one who has been given a vision of angels.

'Peeg!' I call again, and start to run to him, across the black glass star. 'You have come back!' I run and run and run; the soles of my feet and hands blister on the burning black glass, but however hard I run, however much I call, I never seem to come any closer. Peeg remains a tiny, wavering dark figure in the huge silver shimmer of the heathaze.

'Peeg!' I call one final time.

And Peeg looks round.

And the sky turns white with a light so bright that it burns through my closed eyelids as if they were not there, burns through my hands that I clamp over my eyes, a burning burning light as if the sun has burst and died. Belly, hands, face are seared by the light, the fur shrivels and crisps away in an instant.

And after the light, is darkness.

And after the darkness is a thunder like the sound of heaven falling, so loud that it becomes more than sound, it becomes a voice, a cry of angels.

And after the thunder is a rushing mighty wind; a screaming, scorching wind that does not seem like a thing of air, but a thing of earth, a solid, material thing that strikes like a fist, strikes the breath from me, sends me hurling, tumbling backward in the tearing whirl of ash and dust and roaring air, away away away from Peeg's Destination, into the ashlands.

And after the rushing mighty wind is darkness again, beautiful darkness, and in the beautiful darkness; silence.

> *. . . and dance by the light of the moon.*
> 'Thirtysomething': Production company sound-byte.

Am forgetting. Am losing. Words. Rememberings. Knowings. Feel with fingers, for darkness still in eyes; feel the chips, feel the emplants; they feel not right, they feel melted, burned. The blast must have damaged my circuitry. Words come, words go, sentences, memories. Words from deep deep in the chips. Words that I once knew. Words that I have forgotten. Words I was meant to forget. Words I now remember, stirred up like silt in a river by the explosion. Words like *implanted nanotok warhead*. Words like *containment field generator*. Words like *mass/energy conversion*. I take the words in these clever hands of mine and understand. Everything. I understand what has been done to me, to Porcospino and Ceefer and Bir-dee, and every other creature trapped and impaled and dismembered and burned to nothing out there in the ashlands. Most of all, I understand what has been done to Peeg.

Enough intelligence to carry out the mission, but not to understand. Never to understand, merely to obey.

Blind, burning, I crossed the ashlands. Nothing harmed me, nothing knew of my existence. Dead. All dead now. In my blindness I pushed down down down into my memories, down into the deep deep river of remembering, down beyond our birth from the womb of mamavator into this hardworld, down past the dreamforest in which we ran and played and swam while we were yet seeds in the metal womb. And there I found words. Words like *programmed neural simulation*, and *pre-natal environmental conditioning*, like shadows in a heathaze.

I came to the forest. The trees were tumbled and fallen, brought down by the blast. I felt my way over the trees, picked out fat grubs and beetles with my fingers, crunched them down with my small teeth. *Anima*. The spirit of livingness. When I felt coolness and shade on my pelt, and smelled dampness, and growing, I knew I had passed under the canopy of the living forest.

Grubbing. Sniffing. Feeling. When will seeing be again? When will hearing be again? When this hissing, ringing no more?

There. Do I hear? Look up in darkness, turning turning, under cool cool trees, *again*, do I hear, a whisper, a whistle, a call? Two notes. Two tones. Hi-lo. Hi-lo. Hi-lo. *Hush*, you whistling, chirping, rustling things, in my head or in the world, Coon-ass must listen. Hi-lo. Hi-lo. Hi-lo. Two words.

Blind, I hold up my hand into the warmth of a beam of sunlight. And, light as light, she comes to rest on my fingers, singing her two-word name. Bir-dee. Bir-dee. Bir-dee.

Colours gone. Sweet flashing darting movement, up through leaves, branches, into heaven: gone.

'Bir-dee.' Name remains. 'Bir-dee.' She sings her two-note

song. I feel her bobbing, impatient, on my finger. *Chip. Chip. Pull chip. See pictures. See pictures.*

No, Bir-dee, no. Gently gently, I bring her in front of my face, gently gently move close until my lips touch the back of her head. No fear. Trust. I press my lips to her blue blue feathers, then, one by one, pull the chips and emplants from their sockets and drop them, one by one, to the ground. When they are all gone, I lift Bir-dee high, high as my arm will reach, into the warmth of the sun.

'Go, Bir-dee, go. Be animal again. Be full of joy. Fly!' I cast her up into the light. Wings beat, I imagine bright darting colours rising up, rising up, above the forest, into light. I look up into the light: do I see shapes, movings, loomings, like motion of angels? I touch long, trailing coils of circuits and chips, trace them back to the metal sockets in my skull.

Then one by one, I pull them out and let them fall.

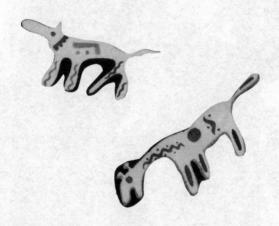

Übermensch!

Kim Newman

On the way from the aeroport, the cab driver asked him if he had ever been to Metropolis before.

'I was born here,' Avram said, German unfamiliar in his mouth. So many years of English in America, then Hebrew in Israel. In the last forty years, he'd used Portuguese more than his native tongue. He had never been a German in his heart, no more than he was now an Israeli. That was one thing Hitler, and his grandparents, had been right about.

He had been – he *was* – a Jew.

This was not the Metropolis he remembered. Gleaming skyscrapers still rose to the clouds, aircars flitting awkwardly between them, but on this grey, early spring day their façades were shabby, uncleaned. The robotrix on traffic duty outside the aeroport had been limping, dysfunctional, sparks pouring from her burnished copper thigh. Standing on the tarmac, Avram had realised that the pounding in the ground was stilled. The subterranean factories and power plants had been destroyed or shut down during the war.

'That's where the wall was,' the driver said, as they passed a hundred yards of wasteland which ran through the city of the future as if one of Mr Reagan's orbital lasers had accidentally cut a swath across Germany. The satellite weapons were just so much more junk now, Avram supposed. The world that needed the orbital laser was gone.

Just like the world which needed his crusade.

Perhaps, after today, he could spend his remaining years playing chess with a death-diminished circle of old friends, then die from the strain of playing competitive video games with his quick-fingered grandchildren.

'That used to be East Metropolis,' the driver said.

Avram tried to superimpose the city of his memory on these faceless streets. So much of Metropolis was post-war construction, now dilapidated. The cafés and gymnasia of his youth were twice forgotten. There wasn't a McDonald's on every corner yet, but that would come. A boarded-up shack near the wall, once a security checkpoint, was covered in graffiti. Amid the anti-Russian, pro-democracy slogans, Avram saw a tiny red swastika. He had been seeing posters for the forthcoming elections, and could not help but remember who had taken office the last time a united Germany held a democratic election.

He thanked the driver, explaining, 'I just wanted to see where it was.'

'Where now, sir?'

Avram got the words out, 'Spandau Prison.'

The man clammed up, and Avram felt guilty. The driver was a child, born and raised with the now never-to-be-germinated seeds of World War Three. Avram's crusade was just an embarassing old reminder. When these people talked about the bad old days, they meant when the city was divided by concrete. Not when it was the shining flame of fascism.

The prison was ahead, a black mediaeval castle among plain concrete block buildings. The force field shone faintly emerald. Apparently the effect was more noticeable from outer space. John Glenn had mentioned it, a fog lantern in the cloud cover over Europe.

The cab could go no further than the perimeter, but he was expected. From the main gate, he was escorted by a young officer – an American – from the Allied detachment that had guarded the man in the fortress for forty-five years.

Avram thought of the Allies, FDR embracing Uncle Joe at Yalta. Old allies, and now – thanks to the baldpate with the blotch – allies anew. If old alliances were being resumed, old evils – old enmities – could stir too.

Captain Siegel called himself Jewish, and babbled sincere admiration. 'As a child, you were my hero, sir. That's why I'm here. When you caught Eichmann, Mengele, the Red Skull . . .'

'Don't trust heroes, young man,' he said, hating the pomposity in his voice, 'that's the lesson of this green lantern.'

Siegel was shut up, like the cab driver had been. Avram was instantly sorry, but could not apologise. He wondered when he had turned into his old professor, too scholarly to care for his pupils' feelings, too unbending to see the value of ignorant enthusiasm.

Probably, it had started with the tattoo on his arm. The bland clerk with the bodkin was the face that, more than any other, stayed with him as the image of National Socialism. These days, almost all young men looked like the tattooist to Avram. The cab driver had, and now so did Captain Siegel. So did most of the guards who patrolled the corridors and grounds of this prison.

Not since Napoleon had a single prisoner warranted such careful attention.

'Jerome,' Siegel said, summoning a sergeant. 'Show Mr Blumenthal your rifle.'

The soldier held out his weapon for inspection. Avram knew little about guns, but saw this was out of the ordinary, with its bulky breech and surprisingly slender barrel. A green LED in the stock showed it was fully charged.

'The beam-gun is just for *him*,' Siegel said.

'Ahh, the green stuff.'

Siegel smiled. 'Yes, the green stuff. I'm not a scientist . . .'

'Neither am I, any more.'

'It has something to do with the element's instability. The weapon directs particles. Even a glancing hit would kill him in a flash.'

Avram remembered Rotwang – one of 'our' Germans in the '50s – toiling over the cyclotron, trying to wrestle free the secrets of the extra-terrestrial element. Rotwang, with his metal hand and shock of hair, was dead of leukaemia, another man of tomorrow raging against his imprisonment in yesterday.

Jerome took the rifle back, and resumed his post.

'There've been no escape attempts,' Avram commented.

'There couldn't be.'

Avram nearly laughed. 'He surrendered, Captain. Green stuff or not, this place couldn't hold him if he wanted to leave.'

Siegel – born when the prisoner had already been in his cell twenty years – was shocked. 'Mr Blumenthal, careful . . .'

Avram realised what it was that frightened the boy in uniform, what made every soldier in this place nervous twenty-four hours a day.

'He can hear us, can't he? Even through the lead shields?'

Siegel nodded minutely, as if he were the prisoner, trying to pass an unseen signal to a comrade in the exercise yard.

'You live with the knowledge all your life,' Avram said, tapping his temple, 'but you never think what it means. That's science, Captain. Taking knowledge you've always had, and *thinking what it means . . .*'

After the War, he had been at Oak Ridge, working with the green stuff. Then the crusade called him away. Others had fathered the K-Bomb. Teller and Rotwang built bigger and better Doomsday Devices – while Oppie went into internal exile and the Rosenbergs to the electric chair – thrusting into a future so bright you could only look at it through protective goggles. Meanwhile, Avram Blumenthal had been cleaning up the last garbage of the past. So many names, so many Nazis. He had spent more time in Paraguay and Brazil than in New York and Tel Aviv.

But it had been worth it. His tattoo would not stop hurting until the last of the monsters was gone. If monsters they were.

'Through here, sir,' Siegel said, ushering him into a bare office. There was a desk, with chairs either side of it.

'You have one hour.'

'That should be enough. Thank you.'

Siegel left the room. Even after so short a time on his legs, Avram felt better sitting down. Nobody lives for ever.

Almost nobody.

When they brought him in, he filled the room. His chest was a solid slab under his prison fatigues, and the jaw was an iron horseshoe. Not the faintest trace of grey in his blue-black hair, the kiss-curl still a jaunty comma. The horn-rimmed glasses couldn't disguise him.

Avram did not get up.

'Curt Kessler?' he asked, redundantly.

Grinning, the prisoner sat down. 'You thought perhaps they had the wrong man all these years?'

'No,' he admitted, fussing with the cigarette case, taking out one of his strong roll-ups. 'Do you mind if I smoke?'

'Can't hurt me. I used to warn the children against tobacco, though.'

Avram lit up, and sucked bitter smoke into his lungs. The habit couldn't hurt him, either, not any more.

'Avram the Avenger,' Kessler said, not without admiration. 'I was wondering when they'd let you get to see me.'

'My request has been in for many years, but with the changes . . .'

The changes did not need to be explained.

'I confess,' Kessler said, 'I've no idea why you wanted this interview.'

Avram had no easy answer. 'You consented to it.'

'Of course. I talk to so few people these days. The guards are superstitious about me.'

Avram could understand that. Across the table, he could feel Kessler's strength. He remembered the old uniform, so familiar in the thirties. The light brown body-stocking, with black trunks, boots and cloak. A black swastika in the red circle on the chest. He'd grinned down from a hundred propaganda posters like an Aryan demi-god, strode through the walkways of Metropolis as Siegfried reborn with X-ray eyes.

He felt he owed Kessler an explanation. 'You're the last.'

Kessler's mouth flashed amusement. 'Am I? What about Ivan the Terrible?'

'A guard. Just a geriatric thug. Barely worth the bullet it'd take to finish him.'

'"Barely worth the bullet." I heard things like that so many times, Avram. And what of the *Führer*? I understand he could be regrown from tissue samples. In '45, Mengele – '

Avram laughed. 'There's no tissue left, Kessler. I burned Mengele's jungle paradise. The skin-scraps he had were of dubious provenance.'

'I understand genetic patterns can be reproduced exactly. I try to follow science, you know. If you keep an ear out, you pick things up. In Japan, they're doing fascinating work.'

'Not my field.'

'Of course. You're an atom man. You should have stayed with Rotwang. The Master Engineer needed your input. He could have overcome his distaste with your racial origins if you'd given him a few good suggestions. Without you, the K-Bomb was ultimately a dead end.'

'So?'

Kessler laughed. 'You are right. So what? It's hard to remember how excited you all were in the fifties about the remains of my home planet. Anything radioactive was highly stimulating to the Americans. To the Russians, too.'

Avram couldn't believe this man was older than him. But, as a child, he had seen the brown streak in the skies, had watched the newsreels, had read the breathless reports in the *Tages Welt*.

'If things had been otherwise, I might have been a Russian,' Kessler said. 'The Soviet Union is the largest country on the planet. If you threw a dart at a map of the world, you'd most likely hit Russia. Strange to think what it'd have been like if my little dart had missed Bavaria. Of course, I'd have been superfluous. The USSR already had its "man of steel". Maybe my dart should have struck the wheatfields of Kansas, or the jungles of Africa. I could have done worse than be raised by apes.'

'You admit, then, that you are him?'

Kessler took off his glasses, showing clear blue eyes. 'Has there ever really been any doubt?'

'Not when you didn't grow old.'

'Do you want me to prove myself? You have a lump of coal for me to squeeze?'

It hit Avram that this young-seeming man, conversing in un-accented German, was hardly even human. If Hitler hadn't got in the way, humanity might have found a champion in him. Or learned more of the stars than Willy Ley imagined.

'Why weren't you in the army? In some SS élite division?'

'Curt Kessler was – what is the American expression? – 4F. A weakling who wouldn't be accepted, even in the last days when dotards and children were being slapped in uniform and tossed against the juggernaut. I believe I did my best for my *Führer*.'

'You were curiously inactive during the war.'

Kessler shrugged. 'I admit my great days were behind me. The thirties were my time. Then, there seemed to be struggles worth fighting, enemies worth besting.'

'Only "seemed to be"?'

'It was long ago. Do you remember my enemies? Dr Mabuse? His criminal empire was like a spider's web. The *Führer* himself asked me to root it out and destroy it. He poisoned young Germans with drugs and spiritualism. Was I wrong to persecute him? And the others? Graf von Orlok, the *nosferatu*? Dr Caligari, and his somnambulist killers? The child-slayer they called "M"? Stephen Orlac, the pianist with the murderer's hands?'

Avram remembered, the names bringing back *Tages Welt* headlines. Most of the stories had borne the Curt Kessler byline. Everyone had wondered how the reporter knew so many details. Germany's criminals had been symptomatic creatures then, twisted and stunted in soul and body, almost an embodiment of the national sickness. And Kessler, no less than the straight-limbed blonds trotted out as exemplars of National Socialism, made the pop-eyed, needle-fingered, crook-backed fiends seem like walking piles of filth. As a child, Avram's nightmares had been of the whistling "M" and taloned *nosferatu*, not handsome tattooists and smart-uniformed bureaucrats. It was possible for a whole country to be wrong.

'They're all gone,' Kessler said, 'but they'll never go away really. I understand Mabuse's nightclub is due to re-open. The Westerners who've been flooding in since the wall came down like to remember the decadent days. They have the order of history wrong, and associate the cabarets with us, forgetting that we were pure in mind and body, that we closed down the pornographic spectacles. They'll have their doomrock rather than jazz, but the rot will creep back. Mabuse was like the hydra. I'd think he was dead or hopelessly mad, but he'd always come back, always with new deviltry. Perhaps he'll return again. They never found the body.'

'And if he returns, will others come back?'

Kessler shrugged again, huge shoulders straining his fatigues.

'You were right. Adolf Hitler is dead, National Socialism with him. You don't need X-ray vision to see that.'

Avram knew Kessler could never get tired as he had got tired, but he wondered whether this man of steel was truly world-weary. Forty-five years of knowing everything and doing nothing could be as brutally ache-making as the infirmities visited upon any other old man.

'Tell me about your childhood.'

Kessler was amused by the new tack. 'Caligari always used to harp on about that, too. He was a strange kind of medieval Freudian, I suppose, digging into men's minds in search of power. He wanted to get me into his asylum, and pick me apart. We *are* shaped by our early lives, of course. But there's more to it than that. Believe me, I should know. I have a unique perspective.'

'There are no new questions for us, Kessler. We must always turn back to the old ones.'

'Very well, it's your hour. You have so few left, and I have so many. If you want old stories, I shall give you them. You know about my real parents. Everybody does. I wish I could say I remember my birthplace but I can't, any more than anyone remembers the first days of their life. The dart was my father's semen, the Earth my mother's womb. I was conceived when the dart ejaculated me into the forest. That is my first memory, the overwhelming of my senses. I could hear, see, smell and taste everything. Birds miles away, blades of grass close to, icy streams running, a wolf's dung attracting flies. I screamed. That was my first reaction to this Earth. My screams brought people to me.'

'Your parents?'

'Johann and Marte. They lived in the woods just outside Kleinberg. Berchtesgaden was barely an arrow's-reach away.'

'How were you raised?'

'There was a war. Johann and Marte had lost four true sons. So they kept the baby they found.'

'When did you realise you were different?'

'When my father beat me and I felt nothing. I knew then I was privileged. Later, when I joined the Party, I felt much the same. Sometimes, I would ask to be beaten, to show I could withstand it. There were those among us too glad to oblige me. I wore out whips with my back.'

'You left Kleinberg as a young man?'

'Everyone wanted to go to the big city. Metropolis was the world of the future. We would put a woman on the moon one day soon, and robots would do all our work. There would be floating platforms in the seas for refuelling aeroplanes, a trans-atlantic tunnel linking continents. It was a glorious vision. We were obsessed not with where we were going, but with how fast we would get there.'

'You – I mean, Curt – you became a reporter?'

'Poor, fumbling Curt. What a big oaf he was. I miss him very much. Reporters could be heroes in the thirties. I was on the *Tages Welt* when Per Weiss made it a Party paper. It's hard to remember when it was a struggle, when the Mabuses and the Orloks were in control and we were the revolutionaries. That was when it became exciting, when we knew we could make a difference.'

'When did you start . . .?'

'My other career? An accident. Johann always tried to make me ashamed of what I was, insisted I keep myself hidden. That was the reason for the eyeglasses, for the fumbling idiocy. But "M" was at large, and I knew – knew with my eyes and ears – who he was. I could not catch him as Curt Kessler and the police would not listen to me, so the man inside came out.'

The man named 'M' had been turned over to the police, eventually. There had been little left of him. He had spent the rest of his life in Caligari's asylum, in the cell next to the often-vacant room they reserved for Dr Mabuse. He never killed again, and he would have been unable to rape even if the opportunity arose.

'Why the uniform?'

Kessler smiled again, teeth gleaming ivory. 'We all loved uniforms then. All Germans did. The cloak might have been excessive, but those were excessive times. Theatre commission-aires looked like Field Marshals. I was at the rallies, flying in with my torch, standing behind the *Führer*, making the speeches Luise wrote for me. All men want to be heroes.'

'You were a Party member? A Nazi?'

'Yes. Even before I came to Metropolis. We prided ourselves in Bavaria on seeing the future well before the decadents of the cities.'

'They say it was the woman who brought you into the Party?'

'Luise? No, if anything, she followed me. The real me, that is. Not Curt. She always despised Curt Kessler.'

'Was that difficult for you?'

'It was impossible,' Kessler smiled. 'Poor Luise. She was born to be a heroine, Avram. She might not have been blonde, but she had everything else. The eyes, the face, the limbs, the hips.

She was born to make babies for the *Führer*. Goebbels was fond of her. She wrote many of his scripts before she began broadcasting herself. She was our Valkyrie then, an inspiration to the nation. She committed suicide in 1945. When the Russians were coming. Like many German women.'

'Luise Lang would have faced a War Crimes tribunal.'

'True. Her other Aryan quality was that she wasn't very bright. She was too silly to refuse the corruptions that came with privilege. She didn't mean any of the things she did, because she never thought them through.'

'Unlike you?'

'By then I was thinking too much. We stopped speaking during the war. I could foresee thousands of differing futures, and was not inclined to do anything to make any of them come to pass. Goering asked me to forestall the Allies in Normandy, you know.'

'Your failure to comply was extensively documented at your own trial.'

'I could have done it. I could have changed the course of history. But I didn't.'

Avram applauded, slowly.

'You are right to be cynical, Avram. It's easier to do nothing than to change history. You could have given Truman the K-Bomb, but you went ghost-hunting in Paraguay.'

'I'm not like you,' he said, surprised by his own vehemence.

'No one is.'

'Don't be so sure.'

Kessler looked surprised. 'There've been other visitors? No, of course not. I'd have known. I scan the skies. Sometimes things move, but galaxies away. There were no other darts, no tests with dogs or little girls. Since Professor Ten Brincken passed away, no one has even tried to duplicate me as a *homunculus*. That, I admit, was a battle. The distorted, bottle-grown image of me wore me out more than any of the others. More than Mackie Messer's green knives, more than Nosferatu's rat hordes, more even than Ten Brincken's artificial whore Alraune.'

Ten Brincken had been second only to Rotwang as the premier scientific genius of Metropolis. Either could have been the equal of Einstein if they had had the heart to go with their minds.

'I am reminded more and more of the twenties and thirties,' Kessler said. 'I understand they want to get the underground factories working again. Microchip technology could revive Rotwang's robots. *Vorsprung durch technik*, as they say. The future is finally arriving. Fifty years too late.'

'You could be released to see it.'

The suggestion gave the prisoner pause. 'These glowing walls don't keep me in, Avram, they keep you out. I need my shell. I couldn't soar into the air any more. A missile would stop me as an arrow downs a hawk. The little men who rule the world wouldn't like me as competition.'

Avram had no doubt this man could make the world his own. If he chose to lead instead of follow.

'I've seen swastikas in this city,' Avram said. 'I've heard Germans say Hitler was right about the Jewish problem. I've seen Israelis invoke Hitler's holocaust to excuse their own exterminations. The world could be ready for you again.'

'Strength, Purity and the Aryan Way?'

'It could happen again.'

Kessler shook his head. 'No one eats worms twice, Avram. I was at the torchlight processions, and the pogroms. I wrestled the *nosferatu* beyond the sunrise, and I saw shopkeepers machine-gunned by Stormtroopers. I was at Berchtesgaden, and Auschwitz. I lost my taste for National Socialism when the stench of ovens was all I could smell. Even if I went to China or Saturn, I could still taste the human smoke. I surrendered, remember? To Eisenhower personally. And I've shut myself up here. Buried myself. Even the human race has learned its lesson.'

Avram understood how out of date the man of tomorrow's understanding was. 'You're an old man, Kessler. Like me. Only old men remember. In America, seventy-five per cent of high school children don't know Russia and the United States fought on the same side in the Second World War. The lesson has faded. Germany is whole again, and Germans are grumbling about the Jews, the gypsies, the Japanese even. It's not just Germany. In Hungary, in Russia, in the Moslem countries, in America and Britain, in *Israel*, I see the same things happening. There's a terrible glamour to it. And *you're* that glamour. The children who chalk swastikas don't know what the symbol means. They don't remember the swastika from the flag, but from your chest. They make television mini-series about you.'

Kessler sat back, still as a steel statue. He could not read minds, but he could understand.

'When I was a boy, a little Jewish boy in Metropolis, I, too, looked up at the skies. I didn't know you hated me because of my religion, because of the religion my parents practised no more than I did. I wore a black blanket as a cloak, and wished I could fly, wished I could outrace a streamlined train, wished I could catch Mackie Messer. Do you remember the *golem*?'

Kessler did. 'Your rabbi Judah ben Bezalel raised the creature from clay in Prague, then brought it to Metropolis to kill the *Führer*. I smashed it.'

The echo of that blow still sounded in Avram's head.

'I saw you do it. I cheered you, and my playmates beat me. The *golem* was the monster, and you were the hero. Later, I learned different.'

He rolled up his shirtsleeve, to show the tattoo.

'I had already seen that,' Kessler said, tapping his eyes. 'I can see through clothing. It was always an amusing pastime. It was useful at the cabarets. I saw the singer, Lola. . .'

'After you killed the *golem*,' Avram continued, 'all the children took fragments of the clay. They became our totems. And the brownshirts came into the Jewish quarter and burned us out. They were looking for monsters, and found only us. My parents, my sisters, my friends. They're all dead. You had gone on to Nuremberg, to present Hitler with the scroll you snatched from the monster's chest.'

'I won't insult you by apologising.'

Avram's heart was beating twice its normal race. Kessler looked concerned for him. He could look into another's chest, of course.

'There's nothing I could do to make reparation. Your family is dead, but so is *my whole planet*. I have to live with the guilt. That's why I'm here.'

'But you are here, and as long as you remain you're a living swastika. The fools out there who don't remember raise your image high, venerate you. I know you've been offered freedom by the Allies on six separate occasions. You could have flown out of here if you'd consented to topple Chairman Mao or Saddam Hussein, or become a living weather satellite, flitting here and there to avert floods and hurricanes. Some say the world needs its heroes. I say they're wrong.'

Kessler sat still for a long time, then finally admitted, 'As do I.'

Avram took the heavy metal slug from his cigarette case, and set it on the table between them.

'I've had this since I was at Oak Ridge. You wouldn't believe how much of the stuff Rotwang collected, even before they found a way to synthesise it. The shell is lead.'

The prisoner played with his glasses. His face was too open, too honest. His thoughts were never guarded. Sometimes, for all his intelligence, he could seem simple-minded.

'You can bite through lead,' Avram said.

'Bullets can't hurt me,' Kessler replied, a little of the old spark in his eyes.

'So you have a way out.'

Kessler picked up the slug, and rolled it in his hand.

'Without you in the world, maybe the fire won't start again.'

'But maybe it will. It started without me last time.'

'I admit that. That's why it's your decision, Curt.'

Kessler nodded, and popped the slug into his mouth. It distended his cheek like a boiled sweet.

'Was I really your hero?'

Avram nodded. 'You were.'

'I'm sorry,' Kessler said, biting through the lead, swallowing.

He did not fade away to mist like the *nosferatu*, nor fragment into shards like the *golem*. He did not even grow old and wither to a skeleton. He just died.

Guards rushed in, confused and concerned. There must have been a monitor in the room. They pointed guns at Avram, even though their beams couldn't hurt him. Doctors were summoned, with enough bizarre machinery to revive a broken doll or resurrect a *homunculus* from the chemical stew. They could do nothing.

Avram remembered the destruction of the *golem*. Afterwards, the brown streak had paused to wave at the children before leaping up, up and away into the skies of Metropolis. They had all been young then, and expected to live forever.

Captain Siegel was upset, and couldn't understand. Doubtless, his career would be wrecked because this had happened during his watch. The Russians would insist an American take the blame. Siegel kept asking questions.

'How did he die?'

'He died like a man,' Avram said. 'Which, all considered, was quite an achievement.'

Indeterminacy

Jay Summers

*H*is face, as society would desire to derive it – configured – is unknown. As a person with no face, he is known only through the performances, the work, and the name: Baptiste Rand. He sees his face on videoscreens: few other people watching would know its name. He hears his name cited, and a stranger's face appears, apparently attached to it. An intrinsic aspect of his life; a life within life.

The Gallery is nearly empty of visitors at this time of day – early – when people stay separate, travelling alone to arrive and gather at destinations, or leaving somewhere and selecting something from a choice of purposes. The name has just arrived. Now: standing facing the exhibit of huge print panels; the exhibit of enlarged handwritten notes; the exhibit he has come to see. Hand-penned text in blow-up print hanging hard behind plexiglass: some of the words have lines through them. Many diagrams, like characters in Arabic and Chinese, have been overlaid; the white space between them makes a distinct pattern.

Rand opens the chitin-paper catalogue and glances at the photograph of the artist; a familiar face, showing resented beauty and the narrow eyes of improvised drama. As he reads, nootropic substances massage his mind. He dosed himself earlier, now the effect is kicking in, opening out and up. The Gallery sinks through his mind, releasing scents like an identification parade of materials; pliable, translucent, solid, cubic, white, colourless, dry and smooth. Tracer bullets of perfume, flares of verbal exclamation from the other viewers in the space, and the slow shift of clothing against flesh. Salient music of blurs, quiver-quakes, undulations and zooms fill the space of white walls and body cavities with lounging sub-sonics. Quiet light breathes into him, from holograms that fall inside the walls, where mirrors hang in faded spaces; mirrors glowing, reflections which are reflections without source, without reality, as a skin breaks sweat, lipstick prints on the glass hazily erasing, all in minute melting movements.

He reads from the catalogue:

Ex-Semination:
The third exhibition of the Noteworks of Remy Yassah.

Star City, an abandoned complex of diseased concrete near Moscow. Once the heart of Soviet space exploration, now a Remy Yassah Site. The Soviets were always the realists of space exploration; to the Americans space was made for television. Yassah has installed an **Isolated Image Laboratory** of video screens hidden amongst the remains of the complex. It takes several days to find all the screens, with a **compass** (a small lcd vid-screen that tells you where you aren't). The screens are your maps; apparently the images change every 30 seconds. Vid-cams mounted on bizarrely constructed animal-like robots follow you around, putting your image into unknown scenes on the screens.

Found Ghosts is a memorial, quite separate in concept from the rest of the installation. It centres on living things sent out into space. Astronauts, cosmonauts, animals. They are brought together here as the dead, although the imagery concerns parallels with life on Earth and in Space, using audio as well as visual effects; again video screens are used. This use of the medium is yet more of Yassah's obsession with the twentieth century, something which seems to have come from her work with Baptiste Rand. His only statement, concerning his work, on record is:

> 'Anonymity of the artist allows society a sensory
> deprivation of image in this, the virtual age,
> enabling it to project desires around the artist.
> Here and now, nothing is true, experience is everything.
> The New Age Reality State war is over.
> Emerge from the cubicles.
> Free access to the Fourth Dimension.'

There is no visual record of Rand; these words were the soundtrack to a viddisc, his only press release from some years ago. There were no visuals on the disc, though it did release an image virus.*

The manifesto is dust, yet it is still his skin. He is still aware of its impact.

Before Yassah and Rand collaborated together on **The Globe**, at the **Silent Container Site** (Dublin Free Trade Plaza), Rand used a virtual package, which had been developed by Yassah, as part of his **Persisting Perform-**

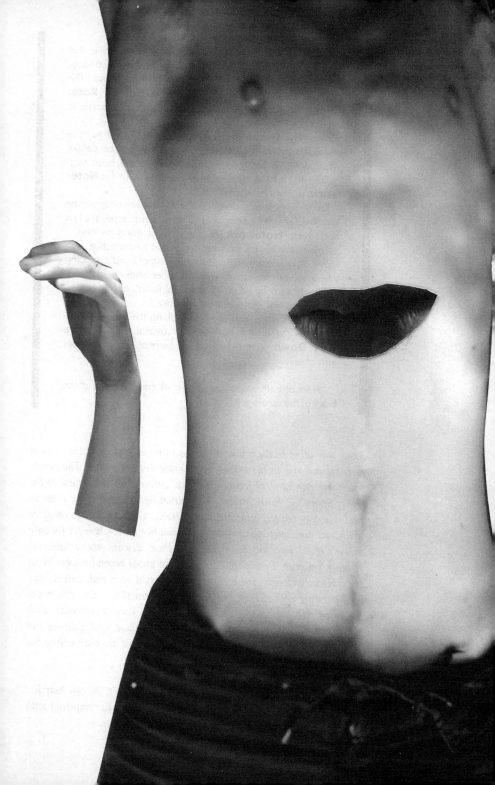

ance. This was a travelling interactive theatre Site that opened nearly half a decade ago in Vancouver, Canada, and travelled around the globe to New Zealand. The package he made use of was **For a Human Race: Changing Room**. Its intention was to enable people to experience different cultural identities first hand.

Since **The Globe** installation, Rand is not known to have released any work. However, it is impossible to be certain whether this is so, given his anonymity. Some have suggested that his hand was actually responsible for this **Notework**, rather than Yassah's.

Remy Yassah has been prolific since her collaboration with Rand. As well as designing Sites across Europe, she has had several **Notework** exhibits, of which this is the third.

This exhibit is also the most linear and introspective, with many critics describing it as too revealing of Rand's ongoing influence, an obsession with the phenomenon of Rand. Others have called it an 'antithesis of Rand', or a 'performance of the anti-real within the hyper-real'.

The book Rand published, containing the incident mentioned by Yassah in the exhibit, is still available. Titled **Write Way Down**, it is published by Serpents Tail, in paper format only.

*A list of both artists' previous work can be found at the back of the catalogue.

Rand goes blind to the catalogue, keeps in mind to stare at the rows of text. He can take in individual words made distinct by ink. The panels cover over one hundred feet of wallspace, curving out of his view to the right. Scanning words, finding the section he has specifically come to read. He does not feel completely comfortable. Galleries always conspire to distract him; other viewers, thinking him like them – here for the sake of being here – force him to interact with them, discuss other exhibitions at other galleries. People wouldn't have vocalised beyond a whisper in the original galleries. These places, when they'd been real, would have been bursting with silence, but now nervous reaction insists otherwise; the alien idea of silence and static display doesn't compute with contemporary observer intelligence. Many of these new galleries are converted from old shopping malls; perhaps people are channelling the ghosts of dead consumers.

Now, he starts to read, to engage meditation.

As he thought he would, as he hoped he wouldn't, he can hear her voice speaking to him immediately. Designer American competing with Arabic roots and a dreamy Japanese childhood: her voice.

*

I don't know how you live the way you do. I don't know if you
are living. Life is a question: 'Who is?'

*He disengages his attention. This experience can be reached slowly. He
responds to her silently, because she is there, in her written words, on
the wall. I live – I do – uncertainly. I needed you to make it this way.*

I have thought, though never written or talked, about you
before. People will be reading this, they take it as sign language,
an invitation to experience. It's the way things have gone since
we worked together, in another time. An alienation of ego; the
voyeuristic environment of my Notes is as popular as my real
works and, for me, as necessary. My installations have been
displaced by expositions of the artist.

*Personal. Is it some idea she has of 'how to be an artist?' Really for me?
Or only to be seen to be for me?*
    *He reads on; each phrase is separated by diagrams that are made of
other, smaller diagrams. Each pattern is a description of the elements
that become words on the paper; a design of objects within a design of
space, each representation is an effect of itself.*

I've snuck these pages in, because they define the origin of my
practice of writing Notes. As you can see, my Notes go on
display synchronous to the release of my works. These Notes
are the inner and outer, the precepts and the post-conceptual, a
post-meditation. My works have become secondary, taking on
the role that notes would serve if I were another. I think I *am*
another. Now.

*He doesn't empathise with what she is doing. Introspection should
remain as something for critics to fantasise about. Critics must own her
now. This is what's happened: she's entered into a symbiotic pact with
the lost, and she needs me as reference, as witness. But who is he to be
critical, to be lost?*

Some guy came and interviewed me about you. He wasn't a
journalist. He wasn't working for any of the Big Authorities

either. He only wanted to know if I had any idea where you were and, more strangely, by insinuation, if you had ever existed at all. Same old thing.

I couldn't answer that, seriously.

He'd found out I was doing a live discussion for TV. I was waiting in the green room, which was white, and this guy came along. I thought he was another guest; young, dressed in a suit, with a shaven head and grey contacts. Then, he started chatting at me, asking all these questions. It was only for a few minutes, just before I was ushered out to the studio. I never saw him again. This was recent; I didn't think anyone remembered you.

Rand's attention slips away from the wall. He senses approach, breathing, and a cautious shuffle.

There is a vocal crack from a larynx.

'What does it mean?'

Rand meets a gaze that falls short of his eyes by several inches. Art becomes life: grey suit, shaven head, grey eyes: too grey.

'What?' He tries to sound like someone who doesn't want to be interrupted by talk.

'Is it art?' The man gestures at the panels, flapping a rigid hand on a rigid arm, like a tool he doesn't know how to use, at waist height.

Rand gives a pointed answer to deflect further conversation. 'Up to you, your perception, how you are affected by the work, and how you apply the result of that affect.'

The small, grey-suited man turns his body toward the display, his neck tightening as his head remains fixed in space, his vision glued to an imaginary dust mote between Rand and himself.

'Yah! Are you affected?' He speaks like an actor, uneasy with the line, as though the question is a risk.

'This dialogue we're having now could be termed an effect of the work. Perhaps.'

The grey-suited man shakes his head, getting into an argument, causing Rand to wish he hadn't responded to the initial question.

'Nah!' Now grinning. 'Our dialogue is me affecting you, not the work affecting us.'

Rand hasn't the desire to continue the conversation but, as though it is a social obligation, he cannot resist another attack. 'I disagree. The work is affecting me through you, and therefore I am affecting your perception of the work.'

The man is noise posing as message. An empty body, waiting to be transplanted. He obviously wasn't satisfied simply to have met Remy and talked with her; now he has to perform in the exhibition room as though he is a feature of her work. Perhaps he believes that she and the Notes have become a feature of his work. Rand wonders what the man would say, what he would want, should he discover who he's speaking to. The body has moved down the row of panels a little, perhaps seeking for more evidence of his presence in the artist's life.

Rand is still reading.

Thinking about it, that guy might even have been you, I suppose; anything's possible with you, although he shared no quality I identify as you. Considering all the wild rumours he was coming over with, though, it's feasible.

So, Baptiste Rand: *Are* you *you? Have* you had some radical surgery, personality re-imprinting? Because, you know, it's impossible for me to really remember you. The way you were: always camouflaging your existence realtime with the drugs. I can't stop the past from changing, from absorbing discharges from the present. Remembering you, and the states we made together, it's like part of me is fighting to sleep and part of me is fighting to wake, and all of me is resisting both surges. So I can't distinguish . . .

'This is art, this conversation?' The grey bug is back.

What conversation? 'The result, maybe.'

'This conversation gives the work meaning, is that what you are saying?'

'Yeah.'

'Is this work art, or is only the result of our conversation about the work art?'

'It's literature, I think, so: is literature art?'

'Your answer?'

'I don't have one.'

. . . between body and mind, memory and experience.

Rand is aware that some are always looking for evidence to disprove his existence, almost as if they could control his work if there were a face to the name – or many faces, with which they could defame the work. As someone said, 'The trouble with artists these days is they live longer and you can't collect their works.'

He is slightly provoked by Remy's questions about his possible existences. Does she really think he would do any of those things? Does she really think he'd ever choose to be like that grey-suited object? He would never gamble his abstract conditioning simply for the chance to re-live himself; that indulgence is for the already muddled and over-moneyed.

You were the one who was changing, Remy. Too much realism. Too much.

In some way, we encountered at a virtual gig – EventElation – and if it wasn't for that gig these Noteworks wouldn't exist.

You cracked the sequences the band and I were running and fed in one you were carrying.

He remembers that night. He'd wormed the band's system long before, another time and place; it had just been waiting for a signal from his dataform, his virtual skin. A success, that night, it seems, to Rand.

'Well, I think I do!'

The grey object has come back with an answer to Rand's last remark, which had been designed to terminate their interaction.

'What?'

The object is defiant to negative response. 'Literature! Art! This isn't art at all!' He wags a finger near Rand's face, grinning. 'But it isn't literature either, because it pretends to be both these things! See? I agree with you that only our conversation can give it any meaning, which means, inherently, that the piece has no meaning, except exactly what it says, and that meaning is a message from one person to another, which is private yet public. So its meaning, intended meaning, belongs only to two people. Therefore, to us, it is meaningless, and that is the art. . .'

Rand notices even a blank response is response enough.

'Are you an artist?' The object, perhaps at last perceiving the boredom of its audience, now sounds plaintive.

'No.'

'Ha.' Disappointment. 'You understood what I was trying to say? I find it easier to communicate with artists.'

'I took the message.'

'Ahh, fine! Most people don't.' He hesitates a moment, and then points to the panel section where Remy describes her meeting with him in the TV studio. 'She's writing about me there. I've met her.'

'Realised that.'

The grey-suit man pauses in his tightly animated body, perhaps picking up on the tone in Rand's voice. The remark could be interpreted as mocking or complimentary. Accepting someone's view of themselves is a tactic Rand uses regularly, especially when they haven't prepared themselves for it.

Rand looks back at the panels, but there are no more questions, no remarks, no noise. The grey zombie has gone, perhaps to lurk in the background until the next person comes along to read 'his' section. Up ahead, a cluster of bodies that move each other with words: for this phrase or that, a face changes, hands handle gestures and the whole shuffles and pulsates.

Interrupted, Rand goes back to the virtual gig, with Remy, on the wall.

I was there as a kind of special guest/instrument; the group made the music while I co-created the experience realtime. The audience would experience whatever I laid down as visuals and tactiles, in compliment to the sound.

Everyone was standing around in the arena, wired up in reality-skin. The music was a kind of random reception of ethno-funk and old metal-guitar-thrash, like Stockhausen was the program template for their AI mixer. I thought I was doing fine work, bringing in colours with different surfaces and impact-pressures, configuring from clouds and deep-sea life-forms. People were 'bodying' the creations, and having a time of a time. So was I.

It all started imploding; at first, a gentle decay, the music was still coming through. Everything went dark and senseless, followed by a white brightening of punctures, like stars filling the sky at sundown, and a skate-board sensation of movement. I'd never experienced anything like that in a virtual; moving from the abstract to the inter-real, from the synaesthetic to the subjective. Then, it really began.

My own hand was scribbling, with myself as the hand. I was reminded of those cortical map diagrams, feeling ink trickle onto a tectonic-like surface, seeing the words being written by my own hand. It lasted an eternity, a second. I realised my hand had finished writing. I felt a distant no-sense, and saw pages flutter into place, between a cover, as if real leather was growing around them, split around its depth. My hands returned to my control, and I picked up the book, but my hands were everybody's hands, and my eyes were everybody's eyes, and we read it all, page by page.

No one could escape it.

Mektoub; it is written.

It was.

'Do you believe it?'

Another voice, another interruption. The images in Rand's head, so clear, so vivid, splinter and dissipate. Should he respond this time? The voice is female.

'What you think? You believe it's for real?'

She wants an answer. She dances slightly on the spot, her thin clothes fluttering as though attached to her ragged hair; an automatic marionette, part of the word-dancing group.

'Well, that depends on which aspect you're referring to,' *he replies, trying to discern skin tone from make-up. Skin wins.*

The woman screws up her face, and waves a hand at the panels. 'What I mean is, all this seems so raw – too sensitive! Suppose that I was Remy Yassah, and you were this Rand guy. Suppose I published our intimate details like this: how would you feel?'

He can almost believe she's aware of who he is. 'You think this piece has some specific intention? I'm wondering if it's dissimulation, for publicity.'

The young woman shakes her head, shakes her hair. 'It has intention.' *She gestures wildly at the wall.* 'Take a look at the rest of Yassah's Notes; they're nothing like this, no real narrative, no autobiography. If she'd left Rand's name out, I might understand it better. It's like she wants everyone to know about their relationship. It didn't end too good, did it?'

She shakes her head again, and speaks in a lowered voice: the deference of woman for woman, he thinks.

'Doesn't it disturb you?' *she asks.*

'No, why, you?'

The woman nods. Her hands are clasping each other loosely at waist level; she looks very young. 'Yeah,' *she says.* 'It makes me feel used.'

'Because you sympathise?' *he asks.* 'Or it's antagonistic because it exposes too much about the people involved? Careful. It might catch on, then you'll all have to do it! Yassah might be setting a social standard!'

She frowns. 'That's not how it makes me feel used,' *she says. Rand thinks through, how people affect, infect themselves with acquired sensations, structures of identity.*

The EventElation group would have sued you, if you'd been anyone else, but your guerrilla attack shocked-up their rating, so they accepted the publicity and the kudos as damages.

It was strange to read myself, strange to write, because I hadn't written words for so many years. I expect that most of the people there had never written anything by hand in their lives. How can I describe what we wrote? There was nonsense, there were pictures, there were rips and blotches. At the time, it was terrifying in what it revealed. In retrospect, it was theatre.

I finally did write something, with my own hand, months later; it seemed so similar to the handwriting I'd automatically traced back there; perhaps I'd learned, or remembered, a skill.

Though he reads anything, even if it is about himself, Rand had always avoided Remy's written work. Now is the change. He flicks through the catalogue again, remembering there is an extract from the book in there.

> Existent velocity, as an archaeologist, I dig for nutrients of the past. To re-uncover. Here, I preceding. Current is exposure. Arouse the world throughout an intensification of sapphire sound. I sketch my heart and my feet on ground. The interspace of unfolding online. My muscles are here, and now is skin. My body echoes; I am the silence between mirrors. I motion my form and I am soundless in a contrasting space.

He feels she is grasping blindly for shreds of that virtual experience, pulling words out of the signal at random, trusting they have the essential power.

The woman at his side has approached the panels, one hand outstretched as if to touch them. She looks back at him. 'You know how this makes me feel? It's like I'm nothing but a fiction, like everyone is nothing but fiction, if you analyse them enough. It's as if, to Yassah, people – including herself – are just projections from an environment, like we only exist as words or these sketches, and those lines come from external sources, not from within.'

'Yah, you've rilly hit on exactly what the artist's trying to say with this.'

She is complimented and touches her neck. 'Have you been to The Globe?' *she asks.*

'No, but I was at that gig she describes.' *One lie, one truth.*

The woman looks impressed. 'Rilly? Did you know her, are you in the book?'

He shakes his head. 'No, I was a blotch.' *He was the book.*

She smiles. 'Ah!' *A pause.* 'You go Siting at all?'

'Sometimes.'

She takes a disc from the pack strapped to her upper arm. 'Great! Well, here's my card. Give me vision, maybe . . .'

'I'll do that.' *He takes the disc.*

'Soontime, yah.'
'Soontime.'

Of course, <u>you</u> were the book, and you published it, didn't you? I've never read the copy your publishers sent me. I put it on the floor of my studio, and went and bought a boxful of other books, just to keep it company, just so I could lose it. I've never read any of those other books either, although I glance at the titles sometimes: *Simulations, War and Peace in the Global Village, The Telephone Book.* They're classics, I'm told.

I used to think of words as something over which I had no control. Reading old books, or writing on paper, could result in a kind of drug abuse; my creative muscle would atrophy, a fixed solid state like the ink, but destructible by any number of other elements or actions. I have no control over what my words do.

She is right; she does have an addiction. She has imprisoned herself by thinking in language and tries desperately to release herself through the act of writing. She has become a critic, too conscious to be creative. She has lost the language she once developed. Now, there is nothing of uncertainty; she is secured, restrained.

I met you for <u>real</u> a week or so after that gig, at a virtual exhibition; some old videography team retrospective, digital collage, kind of primitive dynamic feel. You were there with that Europolitic from the Free Dream party. She didn't even know who you were, though she said later, in an interview, that she'd known you very well from years ago.

I remember I was looking at a still. I was fascinated by the deconstruction that somehow failed to really change the image at all. It simply imitated and exaggerated what the eye of an observer could already do. No challenge. But perhaps people had <u>needed</u> the effect to be demonstrated to them back when the image had been created. The image was manipulated against its context, like no-mind of zen, like thinking 'thinking' when you're thinking. The mind and image became one psycho-form, with skin, and a flatline of consciousness.

You came across to me, without the MEP. She was otherwise occupied, telling someone, 'When laws are outlawed, only out-laws will obey the law', repeating it to penetrate an argument.

Only a politician would find that a conundrum, and worth repeating.

Of course, I didn't recognise you, and didn't know you were the one who'd wormed the virtual-gig.

You said, 'You're Remy Yassah, aren't you? Used some of your work recently.'

I didn't know about that, but didn't want to appear ignorant of my own business. So I was real offhand and asked if I'd received payment for it. You didn't answer. Downloaded a vid and said, 'My card.' I was still watching an exhibit as you disappeared; images of the Earth, using different methods of observation, so that continents of heat lay over other continents of mineral deposits: cities as patterns of constructions fell on mountain ranges and oceans. It was absorbing.

Rand wonders: perhaps everything he's thinking of Remy now is actually what he knows of himself. He dislikes self-consciousness – too much like lying. He wouldn't have behaved like that. Perhaps he'd been up on some neural cocktail when he'd approached her; that or possibly he'd missed a hit of something.

I remember accessing the vid later. Nothing on it, but hours of miles of cinéma vérité. Street sounds of places, voices of faces and your reflection or shadow slipping off surfaces like a ghost, your virtual image. I never asked you about it, but I was sure a lot of it was artificially generated. The whole damn thing was just you re-creating the world, slightly changing things. All the people came from you. All the places were sketched by you.

I watched it a hundred times though, and then followed the visual clues. Through the labyrinth of moving history from Vigo and Jarman, from the First world to the Fourth. Images of post-industrial Europe from a train, deserts with modern Western cities and Islamic genes. The surreal exposure of the ruins of Euro-Disneyland. Rooftops that hovered in an antique strata below the modern world. From old JouJouka villages to new Dublin. I followed the clues.

The last time I'd visited the city, it had still been recovering from the twentieth century, when it had suffered the repression of a short sharp recognition of past. Since then, Europe had invaded with technology and social ideas, like sex toys for adolescents. I didn't just go there to look for you, but because I wanted an excuse to return anyway. I was interested in going to a Site like the Silent Container, because I hadn't been to a non-virtual since I was a kid, and then I'd been using all the usual drugs. So I thought, go there. Of course, I was really curious to meet you, because I still didn't know who you were. There was no name on the vid you'd given me, and no address, just the clues: of the Silent Container; a pyramid in black. I saw your silhouette entering the lobby, there were no more screen options.

I went to Dublin.

Rand feels uneasy; how much is she going to reveal? Memories open and shut in his mind, settling, focusing, like a fragment of conversation, when someone says something and leaves before you can reply, and you didn't hear what they said but, like some subliminal, the garbled message eventually gains meaning, perhaps in minutes or even years later. So Rand remembers the hotel room. Remy naked, barely standing and shuddering against a soft wall. His tongue, his jaw and lips, feel as if he is swimming and eating, a mixture of endorphin high smoothing out fatigue ache, and a compulsion to reach for a taste and take breaths that draw in deep fragrance, incense trance. She collapses. They meet with mouths. His penis: the tip alive, the only sense of gravity, transmitting through the spine, urging shocks to the tension of skin that surrounds his muscles. They slide through each other. The ceiling is at his feet. A slow rain spins drops like tears onto his face. He balances on arms that feel like body, but act as roots of wood. His legs want to stretch away, tear him across the wall. Remy's hands dance gentle impressions across his skin of sweat, like sunlight falling on a breeze. She fixes his legs straight and vertical, tight against the wall. Her mouth slow-action-paints him inside out.

I spent a few days in a hotel, an old Stark design. It was like a bio-mechanical womb that fed from those inhabiting it. I was profoundly sedated by the whole building, like flying in an airliner that had the dimensions of a cathedral, reminding me of a fantasy I'd once had as a kid, when I'd seen a picture of an airship.

I looked out over the city, through windows of liquid that altered refraction with the weather, changing the focus of the skyline. I saw winter-scraped old-town Dublin through half-closed eyes; it looked like black and white electron micro-photography of different surfaces. I was waiting for you to hear I was in town.

I made sure I was visible, had plenty of guests. A gang of kids wanted to broadcast a live party from my suite. The director of <u>Finnegans Wake</u> wanted me for a cameo part. I couldn't act, and didn't want to spend days in a vision lab, either. I've seen the movie since; it incorporates the footage that was on the vid you gave me. A dream sequence, only a lot shorter than your version. It's a dream of Beckett's <u>Film</u>, with you playing <u>O</u>; it's not really the same as the original, you don't seem to be running from anything, you're running towards something.

He hadn't known he was the reason she'd been in Dublin. It wasn't important why other people did things, only why you do things. She'd never revealed that. She'd wanted him to take her to a Site, wanted him and a Site.

The owner of the Silent Container, a woman who manifested on-screen only, had suggested a commission from her. It was something she couldn't refuse, and Rand had decided he had the time, playing her assistant.

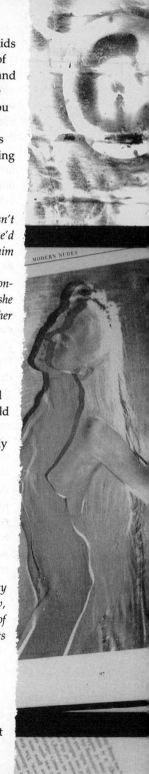

MODERN NUDES

Eventually, you arrived and called me, grinning on the vid screen. I think you were pleased but surprised. We met up and talked. We met up and fucked. I told you about myself. You told me about your work. You told me your name.

Next day, you took me to the Silent Container. It was the only place we really happened. I've made a habit of this in my life now: I don't have any working or social relationships that exist outside a Site. Moving through Site culture, as a traveller (but not a tourist), making attachments, trading. That's how I eat, fuck, sleep and work – although I never go to the Silent Container.

Rand no longer goes to Sites at all. He realises now how badly Remy had wanted success. It isn't unreasonable. Many do, some don't. Now, she has achieved it and, unlike others, she has resisted the cliché of becoming reclusive. He doesn't feel this realisation; although he wants to, it remains a concept.

Since our work at the Silent Container, non-virtual Sites are the thing in Europe. The Zombie Birdhouse; my latest Site design. It's past-time; concrete, iron struts, pool tables and stage. I like it there. It's probably the last one I'll do, because I think the concept is as bankrupt now as the early virtual stuff was when it was first performed. There's nothing like playing billiards while some performance is going down on the stage. It's alive, that sensation; so basic. Had to commission someone to find the billiards stuff. If the revolution was virtualised, I found life through the Birdhouse that I had forgotten.

Entering the Container was nothing like that; it was like stepping out of an air-lock into a place that affected obscurity. I felt the same as when I'm in the intimacy of some drug-transfigured people, and I'm as straight as a nervous system can be, sensing the way I appear to them; my senses tuning in and analoguing the surreality they're perceiving. Conversion to rhythms; an interplay atomic.

The main chamber used figure-ground altering patterns, animated on chameleon reactive walls; fast-mo ambient light moving through twenty-four hours in twenty minutes. No colour, just black, white and a million shades in between. It had the most complex lighting system available, although I recall there were flashbacks of colourisation. People were hanging and dropping through a set of stretch ropes and nets, spindling through the webs. The whole thing squirmed with flex and tension. If you didn't wear rubber or sim-leather, you went total nude with a layer of paint slick for décor and friction protection. Hovering or falling, you had to use your eyes like a frog; watching for movement, then focusing on it, and surfing the shock through. Trickle of static charge on the breath. Silent. Almost. You could hear your body, your body only: deep bass, like an ocean pounding, seeming to phase its duration into a reverse loop. Siren diva-chant-howl of the nervous system. Ringing tone over remote images, like talking on the phone, without screen or camera, in a room with no light. I did a radio interview like that. Disembodied conversation. It seemed contextually accurate for stimulating words for radio broadcast.

Rand considers this information, and thoughts of starting his own radio station, phoning random numbers and asking people to describe themselves and their environment, tangle his mind.

The mind can be still, but not silent. When you can't feed words to images, the word erupts. A constant dream of syllables

become the only abstraction. Not heard and not seen. The
source is the body, with no final destination. Flesh becomes the
word. The pattern drifts through space of consciousness. Without time, it floats; a quiet roar that has no sequence. The silent
scream of sex; pleasure that is not, is more, with no pain.
Talking eyes, deep body searching. Touch was like a first
contact with life. Silence and movement were instrumental to
variances of communication, and the results of this sign
language created a social vernacular of dreams.

I was commissioned to design a new concept chamber, you
posing as my assistant. We spent most of our space without
time at the Soul Bay, dreaming it out, in a simple ultra-violet
luminated pool. So obvious; no artist needed to create this place,
although I imagine nature could, with a little bio-hazard.

I could only love you there, under the mirror skin surface.
Processions of echoes tumbling through: this was the feedback
from the rest of the Site, all the lost vocals, piped like muzak
into the pool. Generating heat, with sonic friction. It felt like a
mountaintop wind; molecules breaking and making like strobe
light, sensory fission. Breaking water skin of noise for silent
breaths.

Our installation: The Globe. We slowly designed it on the
premises in a silent suite and managed to construct it in half the
allocated time. It had a surface of projection skin for holograph-
ics; images moved from the surface into space. We made the
animated images appear three-dimensional, though we configured them to moving on two-dimensional planes that revealed
other planes, if you moved. True to life: a deception. That is the
life we have derived from the video screen, which has become
installed in human perception. I've heard a theory that humans
were unconscious until a few millennia ago, and find it strange
that this has resulted in such misdirected consciousness. History
is a video-disc and the present is artificial sentience.

We demonstrated this aspect of perception: stand anywhere
in The Globe and see a different silent story. Roll up, roll up,
youngsters need it special! We took 3D design graphics of
buildings, objects and machines, we took old street graffiti,
abstract-impressionist and old movie clips of erotica and images
of brains functioning; molecules and fashion models, war and
space footage, I could list forever. I remember seeing a helicop-
ter gunship attacking Picasso's 'Guernica'; a urinal; AIDS activ-

ists rioting against an Astronaut on the moon; the Earth, its continents a mass of winking eyes.

And what did they make? A story. A possibility. He can dream it now The story comes to him complete.

This is what he and Remy had made: a demonstration of how th twentieth century had become the sum of reality multiplied by th infinite realities it contained. This was the inheritance, as if every tex every audio and visual recording, had been spliced up and consigned t vessels, which had then been dropped as bombs, delivered by guide missiles as people huddled in shelters. Pieces left after the blasts had bee gathered up and delivered to those people thought to be wisest. The wi pieced it all together, using machines that reduced everything to i origin. Then, the machines produced strange stories of words an pictures which, said the wise, were the definition of the world. No on said the wise, must question our sensory apparatus or that of th machines that we, in our wisdom, have given to you, the people.

Nobody noticed the people who asked questions, because even th wisest existed by definition alone.

And so the people of the definition slept without dreaming, becau the definition itself was their dream.

Then, the questioners took some of the machines. If they wanted t they could have changed the definition then, simply by using th machines as they'd always been used: gathering missing pieces an adding them to the definition. But instead, the questioners changed th machines. They instructed the machines to examine every piece information they stored, and every piece of a piece, and then to compa each piece with all the others, finally making an interpretation of eac comparison.

*Thus the definition of the world, the **origin of the pieces**, becam just one definition, among more interpretations than pieces.*

People told the wise: we have found the machines to be wiser than ye are, and that is because we have found ourselves to be wiser the machines. We didn't ask for answers, we asked for new questions.

Rand daydreamed; it was enhanced by the nootropics. His imaginin were augmented by the Gallery music, shunting and blipping. It plac cartoon images in his head, comic strips from a childhood – not his, b remembered all the same. 'Wake up,' he tells himself.

The images became hieroglyphs that told tales of the word and the image. A word is moments on a calendar; the calendar measure of its meaning, its dynamics, its constantly unpredictable message. Meaning is culture, experience, a virus of objectivity that we create. We are genetic electromagnetic compasses, directing word particles into a sight scape.

We were synaesthetic guerrillas.

The technedelic history of every semiotic fragment reveals itself through the body; moving through nerves, the anatomy, to the mind and minds within. And your image is in there, mixing with that of everyone and everything. Mutating with the heuristics that evolve. We lose subjectivity, we become a living architecture, a narrative that is the territory and not the iconographical representation we thought we were.

Working in The Globe, its huge volume drowning us with each new configuration playback, was like trying to escape from the increasing intrusion of mundanity, only to be overwhelmed by the topography of the new landscape, so that mundane action served as a transformation in itself.

In the Container, we combined. Outside, we shattered. We spent sixteen days there. I spent another two weeks, with you, outside.

Remember we didn't give interviews, we didn't attend the opening. We, because on completion I said who you were, that it had been a collaboration. The critics said it was revolutionary. I've never been there since.

I stayed at your studio. Its only window was the skylight roof. The walls were light-emitting holograms, on which you had sprayed patterns of paint. The rest was gantries of concrete, shaped as though by natural elements, glazed in shades of blue. The floor, almost a forest of white, tree-trunk-like gantry supports, was thick glass, stained colours that lived according to the lighting, over heated concrete, solid and warm. You had one workstation, for communications and projects, a simple shower stall and latrine, a kitchen, and something you called the organic shelf, where you grew things with hydroponics. No pets. Everywhere there were things, objects of every possible type: bones, shells, circuit boards, books, musical instruments, old things. You slept anywhere you cared to, and at any time.

Whenever you said my name, you alienated me. I heard you mutate my name into more forms than a person can recall. Yet I can't remember recognising my name; you always made it sound unfamiliar, like a word from another language read with no clues to pronunciation. It played with my body, or maybe my body played with it. Through you, my name became identified with ambient configurations; place, time, emotions, my thoughts prior to hearing my name. And the environment would absorb my being, the experience that my name had become. Sometimes, I would feel a slight tremble, as though my nerves were sensing shudders in the continuum that previously I had never perceived.

Why was she relating her experience to him? Can't she allow herself to respond to herself? Perhaps she is afraid of something within, something that she has to project on to others, so that her own sense of being is preserved. Living through others, she makes them all that she resists.

There, I came to understand something, although at the time I was a conflict of definitions, and I could only sense it: many different types of drugs, sex, sound from hidden sources, and objects to lose myself in, while you came and went from your workstation.

Now, I am able to express it. I could be trapped as an artist without this ability, to write words about experience. My notes are so popular, because they reveal a human process before and after each work. The interface between, the work itself, is an act of artificial intelligence. The concept form is an experience. Those that observe my work think they share this experience. But all they can perceive is information, evidence of <u>their</u> action, not mine, an artefact of this, our indeterminacy.

And that was our relationship outside, beyond The Globe, the Bay, The Container. This, because I cannot experience the act of <u>observing</u> my work either. It's like being a movie director, except only the actors know the script.

And she is a writer now. Perhaps she's seen beyond the mind, the body as interface. She has given him evidence of his existence that otherwise he would never have known. She's proved that his experiments reverberate through people like unconscious imprints. The written word was lost to him, but now he knows what he is to another person, and can become real. Could anything or anyone else have given him that? Words are not the experiences, but they can induce responses that no other sensory stimuli can achieve.

In the Site, we were complete in our combined consciousness.

Outside, as this state gradually dissolved, as we passed our convergence, we altered. Our impact split us apart. We lost the system form, separated by light in a spectrum of sound that together we had charted. As if the algorithmic bond was erased on return to external conditions. The gravitational climate altered the space between us, or rather our sense of space, the secret life of sound and time.

Maybe. You became a stranger to me, I became a stranger to myself. Because we knew each other. When strangers meet, knowing absolutely nothing about one another, to an observer the event is simply that – strangers meeting – but in reality this is a semiotic mirage, because the mutual awareness of strangers unites them; they have their essential unfamiliarity in common.

I remember leaving you, by night, as I'd arrived. Never having left your studio all the time I'd been there, I'd not seen the outside by day. It was a large building, with its guts spilled over the walls. An elevator and a lobby and a drive, where the taxi was waiting. You just said 'okay', and handed me a record deck and a collection of records to play on it. I hadn't seen one before, never mind heard one. People saying words as though they mean something, or maybe to show they meant nothing. Who knows? I can't tell. The noise of needle on vinyl was a distance that held the recordings, making the medium tangible, like the shaft of light from a cinema projector. I remember that from childhood, seeing it on television, watching dust shiver as the images winged towards the screen.

Everything's a hidden laser now, the eroticism of the flicker is gone. Maybe I'll design a cinema, maybe not.

He has read as much as he can, as much as he needs to. He wants to leave. He glances around and watches the writing as if it is receding, erasing itself as it passes a curve in the wall, leading to a section hidden from view.

He sits down on a chair made of vat-grown bone – white, dry and smooth – and reads some more of the catalogue. Its chitin-paper pages click apart with static.

It is worth considering that since completion of The Globe, her first post-virtual work, Remy Yassah has only worked with past media such as video and real environments. Zombie Birdhouse sites are notable for the lack of even a vid screen. In a recent interview she answered a question about her recent work:

'I was originally renowned (laughter) – **reverbed** would be better – for being ahead of my time. A critical cliché. But I was, in a sense, ahead of myself. So now I'm going way back with my work, and I hope to find, or at least engage, a search for **my time**. We all live in different time streams, and life is full of chronographical locations where we change our time flow. I'm trying to chart these places in my life.'

He closes the pages, stands up and begins to walk towards the doo There is a figure in his path, but other than that the gallery is no empty. The figure is female; white-blonde dreadlocks partly obscure h Asian features.

He is sure it is Remy, and accelerates his pace, very slightly, planni words. The woman gestures to him with both hands as he draws nea as if she is a friend. She has a vid-cam; eye-antenna a bulge around h thumb, a black-hole leading reality to microcosmic isolation. The ma pack is strapped to her shoulder; two cables lead from there to her hea one clings to her cheekbone, tracing a thin line into her eye socket.

'Excuse me a second,' she says.

It isn't Remy; it couldn't be. She's somewhere else, working. S wouldn't visit her exhibits. This woman has the same manner as Ren though, even if the voice is different. Her melatonin-treated skin a wide eyes are simulacra of Remy's features.

'I've been recording you,' she says. 'I know who you are.' She lets t words reach him like smoke exhaled.

'Could say I'm whoever you think I am,' he says, aware that his voi though low in tone, sounds agitated.

'I think you are Baptiste Rand,' she says.

'Rilly . . . You're free to do whatever you like with that recording He walks away, but she follows him, reaching out to touch his arr 'What you want? My agent will give any permission you require.'

'Like I said, I've been watching and listening. When other people re that stuff, it's like they're reading their own experience. They seem react that way. You, though, you're different. You just read it straigl didn't you?'

'You trying to ask something?'

'No, yeah, I'd like an interview.'

'An interview with a man who you think is Rand?'

The woman scrapes dreadlocks from her eyes. 'I've made a compos of your face from all the glimpses of it you've sprinkled through yo work over the years. I think it's time you went public. You've se yourself up there: respond!'

'Who the hell are you to tell me that?'

She shrugs. 'The virtual age is over, Rand. Give me an interview!'

He hesitates. 'Another time. Maybe.'

'You might not have another time. She's captured some of it herself, and if you don't fill the space someone else will. You'll keep losing time as other people strip you down. You've got to drop the myth, or you'll burn up with it.'

* * * * *

'Baptiste Rand, what do you think about Yassah's Ex-Semination exhibit?'

You look strange, Baptiste, they've found a good camera angle for your face. Did you choose the backdrop? Suppose they had to show it on TV, bring it all round full circle.

'It's well written.'

Like I said, if it wasn't for that gig . . .

'This is your first real media appearance. What prompted it?'

I did, you did. I repayed you, anyway.

'I'd become so virtual only others could perceive me, which was my intention, except I was no longer experiencing myself. I was addicted to information about myself from the real world. Now, I'm coming into reality, because it's become, to me, that which I thought I would become.'

'And what exactly is that?'

'I don't know, I never did, I could say an impression of a dream. It's like a joke, vu ja de? This has never happened to me before.'

'So this is a passive statement, it's not an activation, not symbolic?'

No, this is television.

'It's a beginning. This "me" has never existed before. It is an act, a process.'

'A reaction, a response. Is this studio your current Site?'

'My current Site is the mind of anyone watching this, whenever it is being watched or remembered. This is a simulation of previous appearances.'

'You mean this is a version of a you that never existed, because the previous appearances, like in Yassah's text, are not the real you either?'

'This is a version of me constructed from previous versions, this is a re-appropriation, and that's about as real as I can be at this moment.'

Remy watches as the image processor pulls his image into the back-drop graphics of Globe footage mixed with panning shots of her Notes. The camera tunnels through visual storms to a single eye, injecting itself into the shiny deep, pupil night of his soul: a black screen on which the viewer can only see itself reflected.

Remy is laughing as a group of critics appear, projected by studio lights, with ironic faces. Their eyes casually acknowledge the viewer, their compressed lips say 'Yes, we know, we'll advise on what this all means', their chatter fades in as they tune up for a performance. She knows that somewhere Rand is laughing too: he has recognised himself, realised his image. He is real again, for Remy.

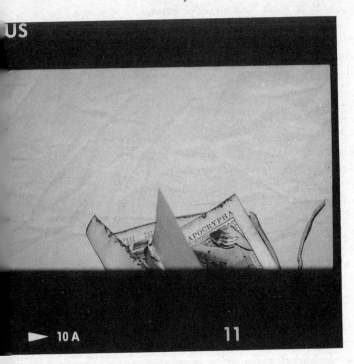

COLOUR A SHORT STORY

Michael Moorcock

The very nature of our dreams is changing. We have deconstructed the universe and are refusing to rebuild it. This is our madness and our glory. Now we can again begin the true course of our explorations, without preconceptions or agendas.

Lobkowitz
For John Fogerty.

1. A VICTIM OF THE GAME

The heat of the New Orleans night pressed against the window like an urgent lover. Jack Karaquazian stood sleepless, naked, staring out into the sweating darkness as if he might see at last some tangible horror which he could confront and even hope to conquer.

'Tomorrow,' he told his friend Sam Oakenhurst, 'I shall take the *Star* up to Natchez and from there make my way to McClellan by way of the Trace. Will you come?'

(The vision of a sunlit bayou; recollection of an extraordinarily rich perfume, the wealth of the earth. He remembered the yellow-billed herons standing in the shallows moving their heads to regard him with thoughtful eyes before returning their respect to the water; the grey ibises, seeming to sit in judgement of the others, the delicate egrets congregating on the old logs and branches; a cloud of monarch butterflies, black and orange, diaphanous, settling over the pale reeds and, in the dark green waters, a movement might have been copperhead or alligator, or even a pike. In that moment of silence before the invisible insects began a fresh song, her eyes were humorous, enquiring. She had worked for a while, she said, as a chanteuse at *The Fallen Angel* on Bourbon Street.)

Sam Oakenhurst understood the invitation to be a courtesy. 'I think not, Jack. My luck has been running pretty badly lately and travelling ain't likely to improve it much.' Wiping his fingers against his undershirt he delicately picked an ace from the baize of his folding table.

For a moment the overhead fan, fuelled by some mysterious power, stirred the cards. Pausing, Oakenhurst regarded this phenomenon with considerable satisfaction, as if his deepest faith had been confirmed. 'Besides, I got me all the mung I need right now.' And he patted his belt, full of hard dollars, better than muscle.

'It looked for a moment as if our energy had come back.'

Karaquazian got on to his bed and sat there undecided whether to try sleeping or to talk. 'I'm also planning to give the game a rest. I swear it will be a while before I play at the Terminal.' They both smiled.

'You still looking to California, Jack?' The black man stroked down a card. 'And the Free States?'

'Well, maybe eventually.' Karaquazian offered his attention back to the darkness while a small, dry, controlled cough shook his body. He cursed softly and vigorously and went to pour himself a careful drink from the whiskey on the table.

'You should do it,' said Oakenhurst. 'Nobody knows who you are any more.'

'I left some unfinished business between Starkville and McClellan.' Quietly satisfied by this temporary victory over his disease, the Egyptian drew in a heavy breath. 'Anywhere's better than this, Sam. I'll go in the morning. As soon as they sound the up-boat siren.'

Putting down the remaining cards, his partner rose to cross, through sluggish shadows, the unpolished floor and, beneath the fluttering swampcone on the wall, pry up one of the boards. He removed a packet of money and divided it in two without counting it. 'There's your share of Texas. Brother Ignatius and I agreed, if only one of us got back, you'd have half.'

Jack Karaquazian accepted the bills and slipped them into a pocket of the black silk jacket which hung over the other chair on top of his pants, his linen and brocaded vest. 'It's rightfully all yours, Sam, and I'll remember that. Who knows how our luck will run? But a sad year down here, I think, win or lose.' The Egyptian found it difficult to express most emotions; for too long his trade had depended on hiding them. Yet he was able to lay a pale, fraternal hand on his friend's shoulder, a gesture which meant a great deal more to both than any amount of conversation. His eyes, half-hidden behind long lashes, became gentle for a moment.

Both men blinked when, suddenly, the darkness outside was ripped by a burst of fire, of flickering arsenical greens and yellows, of vivid scarlet sparks. In the narrow streets the *mechanish* squealed and wailed as if in torment, while other metallic lungs uttered loud, depressed groans occasionally interrupted by an aggressive bellow, a shriek of despair from xylonite vocal chords, or a deeper, more threatening klaxon as the steel militia, their bodies identified by bubbling globules of burning, dirty orange plastic, gouting black smoke, roamed the Quarter in search of flesh — human or otherwise — which had defied the city's intolerable curfew. Karaquazian never slept well in New Orleans. The fundamental character of the authority appalled him.

2. TWO OF A KIND

At dawn, as the last of the garishly decorated, popishly baroque *mechanish* blundered over the cobbles of the rue Dauphiné, spreading their unwholesome ichor behind them, Jack Karaquazian carried his carpet-bag to the quayside, where other men and women were making haste to board *L'Étoile d'Memphes*, anxious to leave the oppressive terrors of a Quarter where the colour-greedy *machinoix*, that brutal aristocracy, allowed only their engines the freedom of the streets.

Compared to the conscious barbarism of the machines, the riverboat's cream filigree gothic was in spare good taste, and Mr Karaquazian ascended the gangplank with his first-class ticket in his hand, briefly wishing he were going all the way to the capital where at least some attempt was made to maintain old standards. But duty — according to Jack Karaquazian's idiosyncratic morality and the way in which he identified an abiding obsession — had to be served. He had sworn to himself that he must perform a certain task and obtain certain information before he could permit himself any relief, any company other than Colinda Dovero's.

He followed an obsequious steward along a familiar colonnaded deck to the handsomely carved door of the stateroom he favoured when in funds. By way of thanks for a generous tip, he was offered a knowing leer and the murmured intelligence that a high-class snowfrail was travelling in the adjoining suite. Mr Karaquazian rewarded this with a scowl and a sharp oath so that the steward left before, as he clearly feared, the tip was snatched back from his fingers. Shaking his head at the irredeemable vulgarity of the white race, Karaquazian unpacked his own luggage. The boat shuddered suddenly as she began to taste her steam, her paddle-wheel stirring the dark waters of the Mississippi. Compared to the big ocean-going schooner on which, long ago, the gambler had crossed from Alexandria, the *Étoile* was comfortingly reliable and responsive. For him she belonged to an era when time had been measured by chronometers rather than degrees of deliquescence. He was reminded, against his guard, of the first day he had met the Creole adventuress, Colinda Dovero, who had been occupying those same adjoining quarters and following the same calling as himself.

(Dancing defiantly with her on deck in the summer night amongst the mosquito lamps to the tune of an accordion, a fiddle, a dobro and a bass guitar while the Second Officer, Mr Pitre, sang 'Poor Hobo' in a sweet baritone ... *O, pauvre hobo, mon petit pierrot, ah, foolish hope, my grief, mon coeur ... Ai-ee, no longer, no longer Houston, but our passion she never resolves. Allons dansez! Allons dansez!* The old traditional elegies; the pain of inconstancy. *La musique, ma tristesse* ... They were dancing, they were told in turn, with a sort of death. But the oracles whom the fashion favoured in those days, and who swarmed the same boats as Karaquazian and his kind, were of proven inaccuracy. Even had they not been, Karaquazian and Dovero could have done nothing else than what they did, for theirs was at that time an ungovernable chemistry ...)

As it happened, the white woman kept entirely to her stateroom and all Karaquazian knew of her existence was an occasional overheard word to her stewardess. Seemingly, her need for solitude matched his own. He spent the better part of the first forty-eight hours sleeping, his nightmares as troubled as his memories. When he woke up he could never be sure whether he had been dreaming or remembering, but he was almost certain he had shouted out at least once. Horrified by the thought of what he might reveal, he dosed himself with laudanum until only his snores disturbed the darkness. Yet he continued to dream.

Her name, she had said, was West African or Irish in origin, she was not sure. They had met for the second time in the Terminal Café on the stablest edge of the Biloxi Fault. The café's sharply defined walls constantly jumped and mirrored, expanding space, contracting it, slowing time, frantically dancing in and out of a thousand minor matrixes, its neon sign (LAST HEAT ON THE BEACH), usually lavender and cerise, drawing power directly from the howling chaos a few feet away, between the white sand and the blue ocean, where all the unlikely geometries of the multiverse, all the terrible wild colours, that maelstrom of uninterpretable choices, were displayed in a smooth, perfect circle which the engineers had sliced through the core of all-time and all-space, its rim edged by a rainbow ribbon of vanilla-scented crystal. Usually the Terminal Café occupied roughly the area of space filled by the old pier, which itself had been absorbed by the vortex during the early moments of an experiment intended to bore into the very marrow of ultra-reality and extract all the energy the planet needed.

The operation had been aborted twenty-two seconds after it began. Since when, many adventurers of many persuasions and motives had made the sidestep through the oddly coloured flames of the Fault into that inferno of a billion perishing space–time continua, drawn down into a maw which sucked to nothingness the substance of whole races and civilisations, whole planetary systems, whole histories, while Earth and Sun bobbed in some awkward and perhaps temporary semi-parisitical relationship between the feeding and the food: their position in this indecipherable matrix being generally considered a fluke. (Or perhaps the planet was the actual medium of destruction, as untouched by it as the knife which cuts the throat of the Easter lamb.) Even the least fanciful of theorists agreed that the engineers might have accelerated, or at least were witnesses to, a universal destruction. They believed the engineers had drilled through unguessable dimensions, damaging something which had until now regulated the rate of entropy to which human senses had, over millions of years, evolved. With that control damaged and the rate accelerating to infinity, their perceptions were no longer adequate to the psychic environment. The multiverse raced perhaps towards the creation of a new sequence of realities, perhaps towards some cold and singular conformity; perhaps towards unbridled Chaos, the end of all consciousness. This last was what drew certain people to the edge of the Fault, their fascination taking them step by relentless step to the brink, there to be consumed.

On a dance-floor swept by peculiar silhouettes and shifts of light, Boudreaux Ramsadeen, who had brought his café here by rail from Meridian, encouraged the zee-band to play on while he guided his tiny partners in their Cajun steps. These professional dancers travelled from all over Arcadia to join him. Their hands on their swaying hips, their delicate feet performing figures as subtly intricate as the Terminal's own dimensions, they danced to some other tune than the band's. Boudreaux's Neanderthal brows were drawn together in an expression of seraphic concentration as, keeping all his great bulk on his poised left foot, describing the steps with his right, he moved his partners with remarkable tenderness and delicacy.

(Jack Karaquazian deals seven hands of poker, fingering the sensors of his *kayplay* with deliberate slowness. Only here, on the whole planet, is there a reservoir of energy deep enough to run every machine, synthetic reasoner or cybe in the world, but it is energy not transmittable beyond the Terminal's peculiar boundaries. Only those with an incurable addiction to the past's electronic distractions come here and they are all gamblers of some description. Weird light saturates the table; the light of Hell. He is waiting for his passion, his muse.)

Colinda Dovero and Jack Karaquazian had met again across the blue, flat sheen of a *mentasense* and linked into the wildest, riskiest game of Slick Image anyone had ever witnessed, let alone joined. When they came out of it, Mrs Dovero was eight guineas up out of a betting range which had allowed psychic bids most seasoned players never cared to imagine. It had caused Boudreaux Ramsadeen to rouse himself from his mood of ugly tolerance and insist thereafter on a stakes ceiling that would protect the metaphysical integrity of his establishment. Some of the spectators had developed peculiar psychopathic obsessions, while others had merely become subject to chronic vomiting. Dovero and Karaquazian had, however, gone into spaceless together and did not properly emerge for nine variations, while the walls expanded and turned at odd angles and the colours saturated and amplified all subtleties of sensation. There is no keener experience, they say, than the act of love during a matrix shift at the Terminal Café. 'That buzz? It's self-knowledge,' she told the Egyptian, holding him tight as they floated in the calm between one bizarre reality and another.

'No disrespect, Jack,' she had added.

3. IL FAIT CHAUD

Karaquazian found her again a year later on the *Princesse du Natchez*. He recognised, through her veil, her honey-coloured almond eyes. She was, she said, now ready for him. They turned their stateroom into marvellous joint quarters. Her reason for parting had been a matter of private business. That business, she warned him, was not entirely resolved but he was grateful for even a hint of a future. The old Confederate autonomies were lucky if their matrixes were only threadbare. They were collapsing. There were constant minor reality melt-downs now and yet there was nothing to be done but continue as if continuation were possible. Soon the Mississippi might become one of the few geographical constants. 'When we start to go,' he said. 'I want to be on the river.'

'Maybe chaos is already our natural condition,' she had teased. She was always terrifyingly playful in the face of annihilation, whereas he found it difficult even to confront the idea. She still had a considerable amount of hope in reserve.

They began to travel as brother and sister. A month after they had established this relationship, there was some question of her arrest for fraud when two well-uniformed cool boys had stepped aboard at New Auschwitz on the Arkansas side as the boat was casting off and, suddenly in mid-river, they had no authority. Yet they made their threats. They insisted on entering the ballroom where she and the Egyptian were occupied. And then Karaquazian had suffered watching her raise promising eyes to the captain who saluted, asked if she had everything she needed, ordered the boys to disembark at Greenville and said that he might stop by later to make sure she was properly comfortable. She had told him she would greatly appreci-ate the attention and returned to the floor, where a lanky zee-band bounced out the old favourites. With an unsisterly flirt of her hands she had offered herself back to her pseudo-brother.

Jack Karaquazian had felt almost sour, though gentleman enough to hide it, while he took charge of the unpleasant feelings experienced by her cynical use of a sensuality he had thought, for the present at least, his preserve. Yet that sensuality was in no way diminished by its knowing employment and his loyalty to her remained based upon the profound respect he had for her — a type of love he would cheerfully have described as feminine, and through which he believed he experienced some slight understanding of the extraordinary individual she was. He relished her lust for freedom, her optimism, her insistence on her own right to exist beyond the destruction of their universe, her willingness to achieve some form of immortality in any terms and at any cost. She thrilled him precisely because she disturbed him. He had not known such deep excitement since his last two and a half weeks before leaving Egypt and his first three weeks in America; and never because of a woman. Until then, Karaquazian had experienced profound emotion only for the arts of gaming and his Faith. His many liaisons, while frequently affectionate, had never been allowed to interfere with his abiding passion. At first he had been shocked by this realisation, that he was more fascinated by Colinda Dovero than he had ever been by the intellectual strategies of the Terminal's ranks of Grand Turks.

The mind which had concentrated on gambling and its attendant skills, upon self-defence and physical fitness, upon self-control, now devoted itself almost wholly to her. He was obsessed with her thoughts, her motives, her background, her story, the effect which her reality had upon his own. He was no longer the self-possessed individual he had been before he met her; and, when they had made love again that first night, he had been ready to fall in with any scheme which kept them together. Eventually, after the New Auschwitz incident, he had made some attempt to rescue his old notion of himself, but after she revealed her business had to do with a potential colour-strike valuable beyond any modern hopes, he had immediately agreed to go with her to help establish the claim. In return, she promised him a percentage of the proceeds. He committed himself to her in spite of his not quite believing anything she told him. She had been working the boats for some while now, raising money to fund the expedition, ready to call it quits as soon as her luck turned bad. Since Memphis, her luck had run steadily down. This could also be why she had been so happy to seek an ally in him. The appearance of the cool boys had alarmed her: as if that evening had been the first time she had as much as been accused by anyone. Besides, she told him, with the money he had they could now easily meet the top price for the land, which was only swamp anyway. She would pay the fees and expenses. There would be no trouble raising funds once the strike was claimed.

At Chickasaw they had left the boat and set off up the Trace

together. She had laughed as she looked back at the levee and the
Princesse outlined against the cold sky. 'I have made an enemy, I
think, of that captain.' He was touched by what he perceived as her
wish to reassure him of her constancy. But in Carthage they had
been drawn into a flat game which had developed around a
random hotspot no bigger than a penny, and played until the spot
faded. When the debts were paid they were down to a couple of
guineas between them and had gambled their emergency batteries.
At this point superstition overwhelmed them and each had seen
sudden bad luck in the other.

Jack Karaquazian regretted their parting almost immediately and
would have returned to her, but by the time he heard of her again
she was already lost to Peabody, the planter. It had been Peabody
that time who had sent his cool boys after her. She wrote once to
Karaquazian, in care of the Terminal. She said she was taking a rest
but would be in touch.

Meanwhile Karaquazian had a run of luck at the Terminal which,
had he not cheated against himself and put the winnings back into
circulation, would have brought a halt to all serious gambling for a
while. Karaquazian now played with his back to the Fault. The sight
of that mighty appetite, that insatiable mystery, distracted him these
days. He was impatient for her signal.

4. LA POINTE A PAIN

Sometimes Jack Karaquazian missed the ancient,
exquisite colours of the Egyptian evening where shades of yellow,
red and purple touched the warm stone of magnificent ruins, flooded
the desert and brought deep shadows, as black and sharp as flint
upon that richly faded landscape, one subtle tint blending into the
other, one stone with the next, supernaturally married and near to
their final gentle merging, in the last, sweet centuries of their material
state. Here, on the old *Étoile*, he remembered the glories of his
youth, before they drilled the Fault, and he found some consolation,
if not satisfaction, in bringing back a time when he had not known
much in the way of self-discipline, had gloried in his talents. When
he had seemed free.

Once again he strove to patch together some sort of consistent
memory; of when they had followed the map into the cypress
swamp; of times when he had failed to reach the swamp. He had a
sense of making progress up the Trace after he had disembarked,
but he had probably never reached McClellan and had never seen
the Stains again. How much of this repetition was actual experience?
How much was dream?

Recently, the semi-mutable nature of the matrix meant that such questions had become increasingly common. Jack Karaquazian had countless memories of beginning this journey to join Colinda Dovero and progressing so far (usually no closer than Vicksburg) before his recollections became uncertain and the images isolated, giving no clue to any particular context. Now, however, he felt as if he were being carried by some wise momentum which allowed his unconscious to steer a path through the million psychic turnings and cul-de-sacs this environment provided. His obsession with the woman, it seemed to him, his insane association of her with his Luck, his Muse was actually supplying the force needed to propel him back to the reality he longed to find. She was his goal, but she was also his reason.

5. LES VEUVES DES LA COULEE

They had met for the third time while she was still with Peabody, the brute said to own half Tennessee and to possess the mortgages on the other half. Peabody's red stone fortress lay outside Memphis. He was notorious for the cruel way in which his plantation whities were treated, but his influence amongst the eight members of the Confederacy meant he would inevitably be next Governor-General, with the power of life and death over all but the best-protected *machinoix* or guild neutrals like Mr Karaquazian and Mrs Dovero. 'I am working for him,' she admitted. 'As a kind of ambassador. You know how squeamish people are about dealing with the North. They lose face even by looking directly at a whitey. But I find them no different, in the main. A little feckless. Social conditioning.' She did not hold with genetic theories of race. She had chatted in this manner at a public occasion where, by coincidence, they were both guests.

'You are his property, I think,' Karaquazian had murmured without rancour. But she had shaken her head.

Whether she had become addicted to Peabody's power or was merely deeply fascinated by it, Karaquazian never knew. For his own part he had taken less and less pleasure in the liaison that followed while still holding profound feelings for her. Then she had come to his room, one evening when he was in Memphis and she in town with Peabody who attended some bond auction at the big hotel, and told him that she deeply desired to stay with him, but they must be so rich they would never lose their whole roll again. Karaquazian thought she was ending their affair on a graceful note. Then she produced a creased read-out which showed colour-

sightings in the depths of Mississippi near the Tombigbee not far from Starkville. This was the first evidence she had ever offered him and he believed now that she was trying to demonstrate that she trusted him, that she was telling the truth. She had intercepted the report before it reached Peabody. The airship pilot who sent it had crashed in flames a day later. 'This time we go straight to it.' She had pushed him back against his cot, sniffing at his neck, licking him. Then, with sudden honesty, she told him that, through her Tarot racing, she was in to Peabody for almost a million guineas and he was going to make her go North permanently to pay him back by setting up deals with the white bosses of the so-called Insurgent Republics. 'Peabody's insults are getting bad enough. Imagine suffering worse from a white man. No disrespect, Jack. But that's what it means.'

Within two weeks they had repeated their journey up the Trace, got as far as McClellan and taken a pirogue into the Streams, following, as best they could, the grey contours of the aerial map, heading towards a cypress swamp. It had been Fall then, too, with the leaves turning; the tree-filled landscape of browns, golds, reds and greens reflected in the cooling sheen of the water. The swamp still kept its heat during the day.

'We are the same,' he had suggested to her, to explain their love. 'We have the same sense of boredom.'

'No, Jack, we have the same habits. But I arrived at mine through fear. I had to learn a courage that for you was no more than an inheritance.' She had described her anxieties. 'It occasionally feels like the victory of some ancient winter.'

The waterways were full of birds which always betrayed their approach, but they were certain no humans came here at this time of year, though any hunters would assume them to be hunting, too. Beautiful as it was, the country was forbidding and they saw no evidence of Indians, a sure sign that the area was considered dangerous, doubtless because of the snakes.

She foresaw a world rapidly passing from contention to warfare and from warfare to brute struggle, from that to insensate matter and from that to nothingness. 'This is the reality offered as our future,' she said. They determined they would, if only through their mutual love, resist such a future.

They had grown comfortable with one another and when they camped at night they would remind themselves of their story, piecing it back into some sort of whole, restoring to themselves the extraordinary intensity of their long relationship. By this means, and the warmth of their sexuality, they raised a rough barrier against encroaching chaos.

It had been twilight, with the cedars turning black and silver, a cool mist forming on the water, when they reached the lagoon marked on the map, poling the dugout through the shallows, breaking dark gashes in the weedy surface, the mud sucking and sighing at the pole, and each movement tiring Karaquazian too much, threatening to leave him with no energy in reserve, so they chose a fairly open spot, where snakes might not find them, and, placing a variety of sonic and visual beacons, settled down to sleep. They would have slept longer had not the novelty and potential danger of their situation excited their lusts.

In the morning, sitting with the canvas folded back and the tree-studded water roseate from the stately emerging sun, the mist becoming golden, the white ibises and herons flapping softly amongst the glowing autumn foliage, Karaquazian and Colinda Dovero breakfasted on their well-planned supplies, then studied their map before continuing deeper into the beauty of that unwelcoming swamp. Then, at about noon, with a cold blue-grey sky reflected in the still surface of a broad, shallow pond, they found colour — one large Stain spread over an area almost five feet in circumference, and two smaller Stains, about a foot across, almost identical to those noted by the pilot.

From a distance, the Stains appeared to rest upon the surface of the water, but as Karaquazian poled the boat closer they saw that they had in fact penetrated deep into the muddy bottom of the pond. The gold Stains formed a kind of membrane over the openings, effectively sealing them, and yet it was impossible to tell if the colour were solid or a dense, utterly stable gas.

'Somebody drilled here years ago and then, I don't know why, thought better of it.' Colinda looked curiously at the Stains, mistaking them for capped bores. 'Yet it must be of first quality. Near-pure.'

Karaquazian was disappointed by what he understood to be a note of greed in her voice, but he smiled. 'There was a time colour had to come out perfect,' he said. 'This must have been drilled before Biloxi — or around the same time.'

'Now they're too scared, most of them, to drill at all!' Shivering, she peered over the side of the boat, expecting to see her own image in the big Stain and instead was surprised, almost shocked.

Watching her simply for the pleasure it gave him, Jack Karaquazian was curious and moved his own body to look down. The Stain had a strangely solid, unreflective depth, like a gigantic ingot of gold hammered by some alien blow deep into the reality of the planet.

Both were now aware of a striking abnormality, yet neither

wanted to believe anything but some simpler truth and they entered into an unspoken bond of silence on the matter. 'We must go to Jackson and make the purchase,' Karaquazian said. 'Then we must look for some expert engineering help. Another partner, even.'

'This will get me clear of Peabody,' Mrs Dovero murmured, her eyes still upon the Stain, 'and that's all I care about.'

'He'll know you double-crossed him as soon as you begin to work this.'

She had shrugged.

She had remained, at her own insistence, with the claim while he went back to Jackson to buy the land and, when this was finalised, buy a prospecting licence, without which they would not be able to file their claim, such were Mississippi's bureaucratic subtleties; but when he returned to the cypress swamp she and the pirogue were gone. Only the Stains remained as evidence of their experience. Enquiring frantically in McClellan he heard of a woman being caught wild and naked in the swamp and becoming the common possession of the brothers Berger and their father, Ox, until they tired of her. It was said she could no longer speak any human language, but communicated in barks and grunts like a hog. It was possible that the Bergers had drowned her in the swamp before continuing on up towards Tupelo where they had property.

7. VALSE DE COEUR CASSER

Convinced of their kidnapping and assault upon Colinda Dovero, of their responsibility for her insanity and possibly her death, Jack Karaquazian was only an hour behind the Bergers on the Trace when they stopped to rest at *The Breed Papoose*. The *mendala* tavern just outside Belgrade in Chickasaw Territory was the last before Mississippi jurisdiction started again. It served refreshment as rough and new as its own timbers.

A ramshackle, unpainted shed set off the road in a clearing of slender firs and birches, its only colour was its sign, the crude representation of a baby, black on its right side, white on its left and wearing Indian feathers. Usually Jack Karaquazian avoided such places, for the stakes were either too low or too high and a game usually ended in some predictable brutality. Dismounting in the misty woods, Karaquazian took firm control of his fury and slept for a little while before rising and leading his horse to the hitching post. A cold instrument of justice, the Egyptian entered the tavern. It was a mean, unclean room; even the sawdust on the floor was filthy beyond recognition. His weapon displayed in an obvious threat, he walked slowly up to the *mendala*-sodden bar and ordered a Fröm.

The two Bergers and their huge sire were drinking at the bar wit
every sign of relaxed amiability, like creatures content in th
knowledge that they had no natural enemies. They were honest
surprised as Karaquazian spoke coolly to them, his voice hard
raised, yet cutting through the other conversations like a Masc
knife.

'Ladies are not so damned plentiful in this territory we can affor
to give offence to one of them,' Karaquazian had said, his eye
narrowing slightly, his body still as a hawk. 'And as for hitting one o
cursing one or having occasion to offer harm to one, or eve
murdering one, well, gentlemen that looks pretty crazy to me. Or
it isn't craziness, then it's dumb cowardice. There's nobody in th
here tavern thinks a whole lot of a coward, I believe. And even les
I'd guess, of three damned cowards.'

At this scarcely disguised challenge, the majority of *The Bree
Papoose*'s customers turned into discrete shadows until only M
Karaquazian, in his dusty silks and linen, and the Bergers, still in the
travelling kaftans, their round Ugandan faces bright with swec
were left confronting one another along the line of the plank ba
Mr Karaquazian made no movement until the Bergers fixed upon
variety of impulsive decisions.

The Egyptian did not draw as Japh Berger ran for the darkness o
the backdoor convenience, neither did his hand begin to move o
Ach Berger flung himself towards the cover of an overturned benc
It was only as Pa Ox, still mildly puzzled, pulled up the huge Vicke
9 on its swivel holster that Mr Karaquazian's right hand moved wit
extraordinary speed to draw and level the delicate silver stem of
pre-rip Sony, cauterizing the older Berger's gun-hand and causin
his terrible weapon to crash upon warped boards – to slice awa
the bench around the shivering Ach, who pulled back witherin
fingers with a yelp, and to send a slender beam of lilac ca
cinogens to ensure that Japh would never again take quite the sam
pleasure in his private pursuits. Then the gambler had replaced th
Sony in its holster and signalled, with a certain embarrassment, for
drink.

From the darkness, Ach Berger said: 'Can I go now, mister?'

Without turning, Karaquazian raised his voice a fraction. 'I hop
in future you'll pay attention to better advice than your pa's, boy
He looked directly into the face of the wounded Ox as the olde
man turned, holding the already healing stump of his wrist, to mak
for the door, leaving the Vickers and the four parts of his hand in th
sawdust.

'I never would have thought that Sony was anything but
woman's weapon,' said the barkeep admiringly.

'Oh, you can be sure of that.' Jack Karaquazian had lifted a glass in cryptic salute.

8. LES FLEMMES D'ENFER

It had been perhaps a month later, still in the Territory, that Karaquazian met a man who had seen the Bergers with the mad woman in Aberdeen a week before Karaquazian had caught up with them.

The man told Karaquazian that Ox Berger had paid for the woman's board at a hotel in Aberdeen and made sure a doctor was found and a woman hired to look after her 'until her folks came looking for her'. The man had spoken in quiet wonder at her utter madness, the exquisite beauty of her face, the peculiar cast of her eyes. 'Ox told me she had looked the same since they'd found her, wading waist-deep in the swamp.' From Aberdeen, he heard she had been taken back to New Auschwitz by Peabody's people. In Memphis Karaquazian heard she had gone North. He settled in Memphis for a while, perhaps hoping she would return and seek him out. He was in a state of profound shock.

Jack Karaquazian refused to discuss or affirm publicly any religion; his faith in God did not permit it. He believed that the moment Faith turned to Religion it inevitably became Politics. He was firmly determined to have as little to do with Politics as possible. In general conversation he was prepared to admit that both provided excellent distraction and consolation to those that needed them, but he believed they were often bought at too high a price. Privately he held a quiet certainty in the manifest power of Good and Evil. The former he identified simply as the Deity; the latter he personified as The Old Hunter, and imagined this creature stalking the world in search of souls. Until now he had always congratulated himself on the skill with which he avoided the Old Hunter's traps and entice-ments, but now he had been thoroughly deceived. He had been made to betray himself through what he valued most: his honour. He was disgusted and astonished at the way his most treasured virtues had destroyed his self-esteem, and robbed him of everything but his uncommon luck at cards.

She did not write. Eventually, he took the *Étoile* down to Baton Rouge and from there rode the omnus towards the coast, by way of McComb and Wiggins. It was easy to find Biloxi. The sky was a fury of purple and black for thirty miles around, but above the Fault was a patch of perfect pale blue. It had been there since the destruction began. Even as continua collided and became merely elemental you could always find the Terminal Café, flickering in and out of a thousand subtly altering realities, pulsing, expanding, contracting, pushing unlikely angles through the after-images of its own shadows, making unique each outline of each ordinary piece of furniture and equipment, and yet never fully affected by that furious vortex above which the solar system bobbed, as it were, like a cork at the centre of the maelstrom. They were not entirely invulnerable to the effects of Chaos, that pit of non-consciousness. There were the hot-spots, the time-shifts, the perceptual problems, the energy drains, the odd geographies. There had been heavy snow over the Delta one winter, a general cooling, a coruscation, but the following summer, most agreed, was perfectly normal. And yet there remained always the sense of borrowed time. She had seen that winter as an omen for the future. 'We have no right to survive this catastrophe,' she had said. 'Yet we must try, surely.' He had recognised a faith as strong as his own.

Boudreaux Ramsadeen brought in a new band, electrok addicts from somewhere in Tennessee where they had found a hot-spot and brained in until it went dry. They had been famous in those half-remembered years before the Fault and they played with extraordinary vigour and pleasure, so that Boudreaux's strange, limping dance took on still more complex figures and his partners, thrilled at the brute's exquisite grace and gentleness, threw their bodies into rapturous invention, stepping in and out of the zig-zagging after-images, sometimes dancing with themselves, it seemed, their heads flung back and the colours of hell reflected in their eyes. And Boudreaux cried with the joy of it all while Jack Karaquazian, on the raised floor of the main game section where the window looked directly out into the Fault, took no notice. Here, at his favourite flat game, his fingers playing a ten-dimensional pseudo-universe like an old familiar deck, the Egyptian still presented his back to that voracious Fault, its colours swirling in a kind of glee as it swallowed galaxies, and gave himself up to old habits. Now, however, he was never unconscious.

And so Jack Karaquazian remained in the limbo of the Terminal Café, while up in Memphis, he heard, bloody rivalries and broken treaties must inevitably end in the Confederacy's absolute collapse, unless they made some sort of alliance with the reluctant Free States. Either way, wars must begin. It seemed that Colinda Dovero's vision of the future had been more accurate than most of the oracles.

Karaquazian had left Egypt because of the civil war but now he refused to move on or even discuss the situation. He always kept his back to the Fault, which he had come to believe was the antithesis of God, nothing less than the personification of the Old Hunter. Yet, unlike most of his fellow gamblers, Jack Karaquazian still hoped for

some chance at Heaven, a reconciliation with his Deity. His faith was
made more painful but not diminished by his constant outrage at the
obscene arrogance which had led him to ruin innocent men. Yet
something of that arrogance remained in him and he believed he
could not find reconciliation until he had rid himself of it. He knew of
no way to confront and redeem his action. To seek out the Bergers,
to offer them his remorse, had seemed to him a way of compounding
his action, of attempting to shift the moral burden and, what was
more, of further insulting them. He remembered the mild astonishment in Ox's eyes and he at last understood the man's expression as
he sought to defend himself against Karaquazian who, to Ox, could
only be a psychopath blood looking for a coup.

Sam Oakenhurst wondered, in the words of a new song he had
heard, if they were not 'killing time for eternity'. Maybe, one by one,
they would get bored enough with the game and stroll casually
down into the mouth of Hell, to suffer whatever punishment, pleasure
or annihilation was their fate. But Karaquazian became impatient
with this and Sam apologised. 'I'm growing sentimental, I guess.'

Oakenhurst and Brother Ignatius had borrowed two of Karaquazian's systems for the big Texas game. They had acted out of good
will, attempting to re-involve him in the things which had once
pleased him. Oakenhurst had told of an illegal poker school in New
Orleans where they were playing acoustic cards. Only a few people
still had those old skills. 'Why don't you meet me down there, Jack,
when I get back from Texas?'

'But they're treacherous dudes, those *machinoix* — outlaws or
otherwise.'

'What's the difference, Jack? It'll make a change for you.'

So, after a few more hands and a little more time on the edge of
eternity, he had joined Oakenhurst in New Orleans. Ignatius was
gone, taken out in some freak pi-jump on the way home, his horse
with him. Karaquazian discovered the *machinoix* to be players more
interested in the nostalgia and the pain than the game itself. It had
been ugly money, but easy, and their fellow players, far from
resenting their losses, grew steadily more friendly, courting their
company between games, offering to display their most intimate
scarifications.

Jack Karaquazian had wondered, chiefly because of the terror he
sensed resonating between them, if the *machinoix* might provide
him with a means of salvation, if only through some petty martyrdom.
He had nothing but a dim notion of conventional theologies but the
machinoix spoke often of journeying into the shadowlands, by which
he eventually realised they meant an afterlife. It was one of their
fundamental beliefs. Sam Oakenhurst was able, amiably, to accept

their strangeness and continue to win their guineas, but Karaquazian became nervous, not finding the sense of danger in any way stimulating.

When Sam's luck had turned Karaquazian had been secretly relieved. He had remained in the city only to honour his commitment to his partner. He felt it might be time to try the Trace again. He felt she might be calling him.

9. LOUISIANA TWO-STEP

'The world was always a mysterious dream to me,' Mrs Dovero had told him. 'But now it is an incomprehensible nightmare. Was it like this for those Jews, do you think?'

'Which Jews?' He had never had much interest in history.

She had continued, probably to herself, as she stood on the balcony of the hotel in Gatlinburg and watched the after-shocks of some passing skirmish billow over the horizon: 'Those folk, those Anglo-Saxons took no special comfort in dying. Not for them the zealotry of the Viking or the Moor. They paraded their iron and their horses and they made compacts with those they conquered or those who threatened them. They offered bargains, a notion of universal justice. And this gradually prevailed until Chaos was driven into darkness and ancient memory. Even the Normans could not reverse what the Anglo-Saxons achieved. Their ideas gradually prevailed, but with them, Jack, also vanished a certain wild vivacity. What the Christians came to call "pagan".' She had sighed and kissed his hands, looking away at the flickering ginger moon. 'Do you long for those times, Jack? of pagan semi-consciousness?'

Karaquazian thought it astonishing that some people at least had managed to create a kind of order out of ungovernable Chaos. And that, though he would never say so, was his reason for believing in God and, because logic would have it, the Old Hunter. 'Total consciousness must, I suppose, suggest total Anti-Consciousness — and all that lies between.'

She told him then of her own belief that if the Fault were manifest Evil, then somewhere there must be an equivalent manifestation of Good. She loved life with a positive relish which he enjoyed vicariously and which in turn restored to him sensibilities long since atrophied.

When he left the steamboat at Greenville, Karaquazian bought himself a sturdy riding horse and made his way steadily up the Trace, determined to admire and relish the beauty of it, as if for the first time. Once again, many of the trees had already dropped their leaves. Through their skeletons a faint pink-gold wash in the pearly sky showed the position of the sun. Against this cold, soft light, the details of the trees were emphasised, giving each twig a character of its own. Jack Karaquazian kept his mind on these wonders and pleasures, moving day by day towards McClellan and the silver cypress swamp, the gold Stains. In the sharp, new air he felt a strength that he had not known, even before his act of infamy. Perhaps it was a hint of redemption. Of his several previous attempts to return, he had no clear recollections; but this time, though he anticipated, as it were, forgetfulness, he was more confident of his momentum. In his proud heart, his sinner's heart, he saw Colinda Dovero as the means of his salvation. She alone would give him a choice which might redeem him in his own eyes, if not in God's. She was still his Luck. She would be back at her Stains, he thought, maybe working her claim, a rich machine-baron herself by now and unsettled by his arrival; but once united he knew they could be parted only by an act of uncalled-for courage, perhaps something like a martyrdom. He felt she was offering him, at last, a destiny.

Karaquazian rode on up the red-gold Trace, between the tall, dense trees of the Mississippi woods, crossing the Broken and New Rivers, following the joyfully foaming Pearl for a while until he was in Chocktaw country where he paid his toll in *piles noires* to an unsmiling Indian who had not seen, he said, a good horse in a long time. He spoke of an outrage, an automobile which had come by a few days ago, driven by a woman with auburn hair. He pointed. The deep tyre tracks were still visible. Karaquazian began to follow them, guessing that Colinda Dovero had left them for him. At what enormous cost? It seemed she must already be tapping the Stains. Such power would be worth almost anything when War eventually came. He could feel the disintegration in the air. Soon these people would be mirroring the metaphysical destruction by falling upon and devouring their fellows. Yet, through their self-betrayal, he thought, Colinda Dovero might survive and even prosper, at least for a while.

He arrived in McClellan expecting to find change, enrichment from the colour strike. But the town remained the pleasant, unaltered place he had known, her maze of old railroad tracks crossing and recrossing at dozens of intersections, from the pre-Biloxi days when the meat-plants had made her rich, her people friendly and easy, her whites respectful yet dignified.

Karaquazian spent the night at the Henry Clay Hotel and was disappointed to find no one in the tidy little main street (now a far cry from its glory) who had heard of any activity out around the streams. Only a fool, he was told, would go into that cypress swamp at any time of year, least of all during a true season. Consoling himself with the faint hope that she might have kept her workings a

secret, Karaquazian rented himself a pirogue, gave an eage
kiddikin a guinea to take care of his horse, and set off into th
streams, needing no map, no memory — merely his will and th
unreasoning certainty that she was drawing him to her.

10. SUGAR BEE

'I had been dying all my life, Jack,' she had sai
'I decided I wanted to live. I'm giving it my best shot.'

The swamp fog obscured all detail. There was the sharp sound c
the water as he paddled the pirogue; the rustle of a wing, a muffle
rush, a faint shadow moving amongst the trunks, so Jack Karaquc
zian began to wonder if he were not in limbo, moving out of on
matrix to another. Would those outlines remain the outlines of tree
and vines? Would they crystallise, perhaps, or become massive cliff
basalt and obsidian? There was sometimes a clue in the nature c
the echoes. He whistled a snatch of 'Grand Mamou'. The old danc
tune helped his spirits. He believed he was still in the same reality.

'Human love, Jack, is our only weapon against Chaos. And ye
consistently, we reject its responsibilities in favour of some mor
abstract and therefore less effective notion.'

Suddenly, through the agitated grey, as if in confirmation of h
instinct, a dozen ibis flapped low beneath the branches of th
cypresses and cedars, as silvery as bass, so that Mr Karaquazian i
his scarlet travelling cloak felt as if he somehow intruded on all th
exquisite paleness.

When eventually the sun began to wash the sky in the West an
the mist was touched with the subtle colours of the tea-rose, warmin
and dissipating to reveal the tawny browns and dark greens it ha
been hiding, he grew more comfortable with his growing certain
that this time, inevitably, he and Colinda Dovero must soon reunit
He was half-prepared to see the baroque brass and diamonds c
the legendary Prosers, milking the Stains for his sweetheart's securit
but only herons disturbed the covering of leaves upon the wate
only ducks and perpetua geese shouted and bickered into the co
air, the rapid flutter of their wings having every resemblance to
mechanish engine. The cypress swamp was avoided perha
because it was genuinely timeless, the only place on Earth complete
unaffected by the Biloxi error.

But why would such changelessness be feared?

Or had fundamental change already occurred? Something tc
complex and delicate for the human brain to comprehend, just as
could not really accept the experience of more than one matri
Jack Karaquazian, contented by the swamp's familiarity, did not wi

to challenge its character. Instead, he drew further strength from it so that when, close to twilight, he saw the apparently ramshackle cabin, its blackened logs and planks two storeys high, riveted together by old salt and grit cans, still advertising the virtues of their ancient brands, and perched low in the fork of two great silvery cypress branches overhanging the water and the smallest of the Stains, he knew at once that she had never truly left her claim; that in some way she had always been here, always waiting for him.

For a few seconds Jack Karaquazian allowed himself the anguish of regret and self-accusation, then he threw back his cloak, cupped his hands around his mouth and, with his white breath pouring into the air, called out:

'Colinda!'

And from within her fortress, her nest, she replied:

'Jack.'

Then she was leaning out over the veranda of woven branches, her almond eyes, the colour of honey, bright with tears and hope, an understanding that this time, perhaps for the first time, he had actually made it back to her. That he was no longer a ghost. When she spoke to him, however, her language was incomprehensible; seemingly a cacophony, without melody or sense. Terrible yelps and groans came out of her perfect lips. He could scarcely bear to listen. *Is this*, he wondered, *how we first perceive the language of angels?*

The creosoted timbers lay in odd marriage to the pale branches which cradled them. Flitting with urgent joy, from veranda to branch and from branch to makeshift ladder, she was a tawny spirit.

Naked, yet unaffected by the evening chill, she reached the landing she had made. The planks, firmly moored by four oddly plaited ropes tied into the branches, rolled and bounced under her tiny bare feet.

'Jack, my *pauvre hobo!*' It was as if she could only remember the language through snatches of song, as a child does. '*Ma pauvre pierrot.*' And she smiled in delight, seeming to recognise him at the same time as she brought back the words to her tongue.

Then he stepped from the pirogue to the landing and they embraced, scarlet engulfing dark gold, and it was the resolution he had so often prayed for; but without redemption. For now it was even clearer to him that the mistake he had made at *The Breed Papoose* had never been an honest one. He also knew that she need never discover this; and what was left of the hypocrite in him called on him to forget the past as irredeemable. And when she sensed his tension, a hesitation, she asked in halting speech if he had brought bad news, if he no longer loved her, if he faltered. She had waited for him a long time, she said, relinquishing all she had gained so that she might be united with him, to take him with her, to show him what she had discovered in the Stain.

She drew him up to her cabin. It looked as if it had been here for centuries. It seemed in places to have grown into or from the living tree. Inside it was full of naïve luxury — plush and brass and gold-plated candelabra, mirrors and crystals and flowing *muralos*. There was a little power from the Stains, she said, but not much. She had brought everything in the car long ago. She took him on to the veranda and, through the semi-darkness, pointed out the burgundy carcass of an antique Oldsmobile.

'I thought . . .' But he was unable either to express the emotion he felt or to comprehend the sickening temporal shifts which had almost separated them forever. It was as if dream and reality had at last resolved, but at the wrong moment. 'Some men took you to Aberdeen.'

'They were kind.' Her speech was still thick.

'So I understand.'

'But mistaken. I had returned to find you. I went into the Stain while you were gone. When I tried to seek you out I had forgotten how to speak or wear clothes. I got back *here* easily. It's never hard for me.'

'Very hard for me.' He embraced her again, kissed her.

'This is what I longed for.' She studied his dark green eyes, his smooth brown skin, the contours of his face, his muscular body. 'Waiting in this place has not been easy, with the world so close. But I came back for you, Jack. I believe the Stain is not a sign of colour but a kind of counter-effect to the Fault. It leads into a cosmos of wonderful stability. Not stasis, they say, but with a slower rate of entropy. What they once called a lower chaos factor, when I studied physics. I met a woman whom I think we would call "the Rose" in our language. She is half-human, half-flower, like all her race. She was my mentor as she could be yours. And we could have children, Jack. It's an extraordinary adventure. So many ways of learning to see and so much time for it. Time for consideration, time to create justice. Here, Jack, all the time is going. You know that.' She sensed some unexpected resistance in him. She touched his cheek. 'Jack, we are on the edge of chaos here. We must eventually be consumed by what we created. But we also created a way out. What you always talked about. What you yearned for. You know.'

'Yes, I know.' Perhaps she was really describing Heaven. He made a gesture, awkwardly for him. 'Through there?' He indicated, in the gathering darkness, the pale wash of the nearest Stain.

'The big one only.' She became enthusiastic, her uncertainties fading before the vividness of her remembered experience. 'We have responsibilities. We have duties there. But they are performed naturally, clearly from self-interest. There's understanding and charity there, Jack. The logic is what you used to talk about. What you thought you had dreamed. Where chance no longer rules unchecked. It's a heavenly place, Jack. The Rose will accept us both. She'll guide us. We can go there now, if you like. You must want to go, *mon chéri, mon chéri.*' But now, as she looked at him, at the way he stood, at the way he stared, unblinking, down into the swamp, she hesitated. She took his hand and gripped it. 'You want to go. It isn't boring, Jack. It's as real as here. But they have a future, a precedent. We have neither.'

'I would like to go to such a place.' He checked the spasm in his chest and was apologetic. 'But I might not be ready, *ma fancy.*'

She held tight to his gambler's hand, wondering if she had misjudged its strength. 'You would rather spend your last days at a table in the Terminal Café, waiting for the inevitable moment of oblivion?'

'I would rather journey with you,' he said, 'to Paradise or any-where you wished, Colinda. But Paradise will accept you, *mon honey.* Perhaps I have not yet earned my place there.'

She preferred to believe he joked with her. 'We will leave it until the morning.' She stroked his blue-black hair, believing him too tired to think. 'There is no such thing as earning. It's always luck, Jack. It was luck we found the Stains. It's luck brought us together. Brought us our love. Our love brought us back together. It is a long, valuable life they offer us, *bon papillon.* Full of hope and peace. Take your chance, Jack. As you always did.'

He shook his head. 'But some of us, my love, have earning natures. I made a foolish play. I am ashamed.'

'No regrets, Jack. You can leave it all behind. This is luck. Our luck. What is it in you, Jack, this new misery?' She imagined another woman.

He could not tell her. He wanted the night with her. He wanted a memory. And her own passion for him conquered her curiosity, her trepidation, yet there was a desperate quality to her love-making which neither she nor he had ever wished to sense again. Addressing this, she was optimistic: 'This will all go once we enter the Stain. Doesn't it seem like heaven, Jack?'

'Near enough,' he admitted. A part of him, a bitter part of him, wished that he had never made this journey, that he had never left the game behind; for the game, even at its most dangerous, was better than this scarcely bearable pain. 'Oh, my heart!'

For the rest of the night he savoured every second of his torment, and yet in the morning he knew that he was not by this means to gain release from his pride. It seemed that his self-esteem, his stern wall against the truth, crumbled in unison with the world's collapse; he saw for himself nothing but an eternity of anguished regret.

'Come.' She moved towards sadness as she led him down through the branches and the timbers to his own pirogue. She still refused to believe she had waited only for this.

He let her row them out into the pastel brightness of the lagoon until they floated above the big gold Stain, peering through that purity of colour as if they might actually glimpse the paradise she had described.

'Your clothes will go away.' She was gentle as a Louisiana April. 'You needn't worry about that.'

She slipped over the side and, with a peculiar lifting motion, moved under the membrane to hang against the density of the gold, smiling up at him to demonstrate that there was nothing to fear, as beautiful as she could ever be, as perfect as the colour. And then she had re-emerged in the shallow water, amongst the lilies and the weeds and the sodden leaves. 'Come, Jack. You must not hurt me further, sweetheart. We will go now. But if you stay, I shall not return.' Horrified by what she understood as his cowardice, she fell back against the Stain, staring up at the grey-silver branches of the big trees, watching the morning sun touch the rising mist, refusing to look at Jack Karaquazian while he wept for his failures, for his inability to seize this moment, for all his shame, his unforgotten dreams; at his unguessable loss.

She spoke from the water. 'It wasn't anything that happened to me there that turned me crazy. It was the journey here did that. It's sane down there, Jack.'

'No place for a gambler, then,' he said, and laughed. 'What is this compensatory heaven? What proof is there that it is real? The only reason for its existence appears to be a moral one!'

'It's a balance,' she said. 'Nature offers balances.'

'That was always a human illusion. Look at Biloxi. There's the reality. I'm not ready.'

'This isn't worthy of you, Jack.' She was frightened now, perhaps doubting everything.

'I'm not your Jack,' he told her. 'Not any longer. I can't come yet. You go on, *ma chérie*. I'll join you if I can. I'll follow you. But not yet.'

She put her fingers on the edge of the boat. She spoke with soft urgency. 'It's hard for me, Jack. I love you. You're growing old here.' She reached up one of her arms, the silver water falling upon his clothes, as if to drag him with her. She gripped his long fingers. It was his hands, she had said, that had first attracted her. 'You're growing old here, Jack.'

'Not old enough.' He pulled away. He began to cough. He lost control of the spasm. Suddenly drops of his blood mingled with the water, fell upon the Stain. She cupped some in her hand and then, as if carrying a treasure, she slipped back into the Stain, folding herself down until she had merged entirely with the colour.

By the time he had recovered himself she was completely vanished. There was a voice, an unintelligible shriek, a rapidly fading bellow, as if she had made one last plea for him to follow.

'And not man enough either, I guess.' He had watched the rest of his blood until it had mingled entirely with the water.

11. POURQUOI M'AIMES-TU PAS?

He remained in her tree-cabin above the Stain for as long as the food she had stored lasted. She had prepared the place so that he might wait for her if she had to be absent. He forced himself to live there, praying that through this particular agony he might confront and perhaps even find a means of lifting his burden. But pain was not enough. He began to suspect that pain was not even worth pursuing.

More than once he returned to the big Stain and sat in the pirogue, looking down, trying to find some excuse, some rationale which would allow him this chance of paradise. But he could not. What he had left to him was a partial truth. He felt that if he lost that, he lost all hope of grace. Eventually he abandoned the cabin and the colour and made his way up the Trace to Nashville, where he played an endless succession of reckless games until at last, as fighting broke out in the streets between rival guilds of musician-assassins, he managed to get on a military train to Memphis before the worst of the devastation. At the Peabody Hotel in Memphis he bathed and smoked a cigar and, through familiar luxuries, sought to evade the memories of the colour swamp. He took the *Étoile* down to Natchez, well ahead of the holocaust, and then there was nowhere to go but the Terminal Café where he could sit and watch Boudreaux Ramsadeen perform his idiosyncratic measures on the dance floor, his woman partners flocking like delicate birds about a graceful bull. As their little feet stepped in and around the uncertain outlines of an infinite number of walls, floors, ceilings and roofs, expertly holding their metaphysical balance even as they grinned and whooped to the remorseless melodies of the fiddles, accordion and tambourines, Jack Karaquazian would come to sense that only when he lost interest in his own damaged self-esteem would he begin to know hope of release.

Then, unexpectedly, like a visitation, Ox Berger, a prosthenic better than the original on his arm, sought him out at the main table and stood looking at him across the flat board, its dimensions roiling, shimmering and cross-flashing within the depths of its singular machinery, and said, with calm respect, 'I believe you owe me a game, sir.'

Jack Karaquazian looked as if a coughing fit would take control of him, but he straightened up, his eyes and muscles sharply delineated against a paling skin, and said with courtesy, almost with warmth, 'I believe I do, sir.'

And they played the long forms, sign for sign, commitment to commitment, formula for formula; the great classic flat-game schemes, the logic and counter-logic of a ten-dimensional matrix, a quasi-infinity held in a metre-long box in which they dabbled minds and fingers and ordered the fate of millions, claimed responsibility for the creation, the maintenance and the sacrifice of whole semi-real races and civilisations, not to mention individuals, some of whom formed cryptic dependencies on an actuality they would never directly enjoy. And Ox Berger played with grace, with irony and skill which, lacking the experience and recklessness of Jack Karaquazian's style, could not in the end win, but showed the mettle of the player.

As he wove his famous 'Faust' web, which only Colinda Dovero had ever been able to identify and counter, Jack Karaquazian developed a dawning respect for the big farmer who had chosen never to use a talent as great as the gambler's own. And in sharing this with his opponent Ox Berger achieved a profound act of forgiveness, for he released Karaquazian from his burden of self-disgust and let him imagine, instead, the actual character of the man he had wronged and so understand the true nature of his sin. Jack Karaquazian was able to confront and repent, in dignified humility, his lie for what it truly had been.

When the game was over (by mutual concession) the two men stood together on the edge of the Fault, watching the riotous death of universes, and Karaquazian wondered now if all he lacked was courage, if perhaps the only way back to her was by way of the chaos which seduced him with its mighty and elaborate violence. But then, as he stared into that university of dissolution, he knew that in losing his pride he had not, after all, lost his soul, and just as he knew that pride would never earn him the right to paradise, so, he judged, there was no road to heaven by way of hell. And he thanked Ox Berger for his game and his charity. Now he planned, when he was ready, to make a final try at the Trace, though he could not be sure that his will alone, without hers, would be sufficient to get him through a second time. Even should he succeed he would have to find a way through the Stain without her guidance. The Egyptian shook hands with his opponent. By providing this peculiar intimacy, Ox Berger had done Karaquazian the favour not only of forgiving him, but of helping him to forgive himself.

The gambler wished the map of the Stain were his to pass on, but he knew that it had to be sought for and that only then would the lucky ones find it. As for Ox Berger, he had satisfied his conscience and required nothing else of Jack Karaquazian. 'When you take your journey, sir, I hope you find the strength to sustain yourself.'

'Thanks to you, sir,' says Jack Karaquazian.

The olive intensity of his features framed by the threatening madness of the Biloxi Fault, its vast walls of seething colour rising and falling, the Egyptian plays with anyone, black, white, red or yellow, who wants his kind of game. And the wilder he plays, the more he wins. Clever as a jackal, he lets his slender hands, his woman's hands, weave and flow within the ten dimensions of his favourite flat game and he is always happy to raise the psychic stakes. Yet there is no despair in him.

Only his familiar agony remains, the old pain of frustrated love, sharper than ever, for now he understands how he failed Colinda Dovero and how he wounded her. And he knows that she will never again seek him out at the Terminal Café.

'You're looking better, Jack.' Sam Oakenhurst has recovered from the *machinoix*'s torments. 'Your old self.'

Jack Karaquazian deals seven hands of poker. In his skin is the reflection of a million dying cultures given up to the pit long before their time; in his green eyes is a kind of courtesy never there before. Coolly amiable in his silk and linen, his raven-black hair straight to his shoulders, his back firmly set against the howling triumph of Satan, he is content in the speculation that, for a few of his fellow souls at least, there may be some chance of paradise.

'I'm feeling it, Sam,' he says.

THE END

Thanks to Garth Brooks, Doug Kershaw, all the artists on Swallow Records, Ville Platte, La., and friends in Atlanta, New Orleans, Houston, West Point MS, Hattiesburg MS, Oxford MS and Oxford UK, where this was written. Special thanks to Ed Kramer, Mustafa al-Bayoumi and Brother Willie Love . . .

The Descent of Man

Matthew Dickens

When I first met Olaf, I was tumbling out of control in the midst of a Downdraught. The cold air was too heavy to rise, and carried everything caught up in its chilly downward spiral to a speedy destruction. My teeth were chattering, and I was cursing my ill-fortune in hitting the icy 'draught. I was wondering how I could stop my spin when I plummeted into a cloudbank.

The shock of the cold clammy moisture, even chillier than the surrounding 'draught, made me gasp. I could see nothing but drifting grey water-droplets. Icy water beaded on my clothes, and soon I was drenched and shivering.

This was serious. Getting wet could be fatal. I remembered a luckless uncle of mine, whose leg had frozen while he was asleep, developed gangrene and had to be cut off. It was essential that I get out of this cloudbank, and out of the Downdraught. I could feel my extremities beginning to go numb, and tried to flex them, to keep the blood circulating.

The next moment I was out of the cloudbank. The 'draught was still there, but it was weaker. I fought the spin, and managed to steady myself, so that I was falling in a more or less upright position.

I breathed a sigh of relief – a tiny Thermal which vanished into the hurtling wind. But I was still shivering, and although the wind generated by my fall dried my clothes, it also chilled me to the bone. I needed to warm up again – and that meant locating a Thermal.

That was when I spotted Olaf.

*

'Hey! My friend! Over here!'

He was leaning back, legs crossed, one arm folded on his belly, the other holding a book, lounging on the wind of his fall. He ignored me. I shouted again, more desperately. I was above him, but falling faster, my damp clothes doing nothing to slow my fall. If I missed this opportunity . . .

The man looked around, then up, in surprise.

'May I share your Thermal, friend? I've just been chilled to the marrow in a Downdraught.'

'Oh . . . I see . . . Very well.'

Rather reluctantly, it seemed to me, he moved towards my trajectory of fall, and I did my best to swim towards him. I calculated my speed, compared it with his, and readied myself.

He held his arms out, and I grabbed them gratefully. We pushed back to his Thermal. The rising column of warm air was bliss on my numbed body.

'Many thanks,' I said to my benefactor.

'Think nothing of it,' he replied, and moved away. He took out his notebook again, and returned to studying it, a deep frown twisting his wind-beaten, sun-tanned features.

I felt a little offended at his indifference. After all, I *had* been severely chilled, and people *did* get gangrene that way; when that happened, there was nothing for it but to amputate, and if there were no saws, axes, glass-cutters or similar makeshift surgical instruments to hand, then the infection would spread . . . Not a pleasant fate. My relief had made me garrulous, and I felt the need to talk to someone.

'My name's Georg, by the way,' I called across to him.

'Olaf,' he mumbled.

I felt a jolt of excitement. The name Olaf was familiar. What was more, it was firmly connected in my memory to Thermals. Here was an Olaf and here a Thermal. Could it be that *this* was that same Olaf?

'Pardon me,' I said doggedly, 'but are you by any chance the Olaf who . . .?'

He looked up and fixed me with an expression that was two parts exasperation, three parts weariness. 'Yes, I am *the Olaf who invented a means of calculating the whereabouts of Thermals*. Now if you don't mind, I'm busy. I came here to escape all the autograph hunters.'

This shut me up, but not because I felt abashed by the rebuff; I'm made of sterner stuff. I was silent out of wonder at the coincidence of meeting the esteemed Olaf, inventor of the Thermal Detection method. By a highly ingenious though complex series of calculations, it was possible to work out where to find a Thermal. One had to include in the equation one's approximate rate of fall, wind speed (whether resistance or Downdraught), cloud distribution and concentration of freefalling objects such as bottles, corpses, and lengths of timber. One could then draw up a distribution graph showing the probable location of a given number of Thermals. There was no doubt that it was one of the greatest steps backwards humanity had ever made. It was a subtle mathematic, and few had mastered it. But I for one had benefited from the method, and would have used it again had I not had the extraordinary good fortune to fall into the very Thermal occupied by the inventor of the technique!

I marvelled some time at this remarkable turn of events. I had heard of Olaf as a child, had painfully taught myself his miraculous calculus, dreamt vertiginous dreams of meeting him, of us falling together, not down but up, up to the top of the sky. I had even dreamt of him the night before; and now, here he was. It was another of those extraordinary coincidences which made life so baffling, and so strange.

I looked again at Olaf. A host of compliments thronged into my head, but I felt he would not have appreciated them. I determined, there and then, that if he would permit me, I would stay with him.

We fell in silence for some time. Eventually, I said, 'May I enquire as to what you are working on now, sir?'

He looked up from his notebook. Then, sighing, he put it back in his pouch, along with his pen, and sealed it.

'Just a little notion of mine. A system of rotating blades, affixed to the ankles, which would turn very rapidly, powered by the wind. They would generate wind resistance, and could arrest the rate of fall by an appreciable margin . . .'

I felt a thrill of excitement. 'Why, that's a brilliant idea, if I may say so! Is the design sound? Do you have any of the materials necessary to construct the device? May I see the sketches you've made?'

He seemed surprised at my last request, but passed me the notebook. I studied the finely drawn lines of the machine eagerly. I had always been fascinated by mechanical things, and always made great efforts to understand the principles involved in the occasional machines which I had encountered falling: sometimes small, light contraptions which I gained on, as I had gained on Olaf today, sometimes heavy, bulky affairs which plummeted from the sky I'd left behind me.

The brittle pages fluttered furiously in the wind. I smoothed them, holding the book flat with both hands. The device was simple, a series of wooden blades radiating from a central spindle. An arrow showed the direction of wind, and a simple equation demonstrated the exponentially multiplying power generated by the blades as the accumulating wind was channelled into the tiny system. I admired the simplicity of the conception . . . but was there not a flaw?

'Pardon me, sir,' I said, 'but isn't it a mistake having the central shaft positioned in such a way? Surely lateral interference would put the whole contraption at risk – the force of the wind captured by the blades might be deflected away from the circle you've drawn here' – I pointed to the diagram – 'and mistakenly directed at the spindle. Could it withstand such pressures? Perhaps a modified design for the blades is called for? I was thinking perhaps of a flap which could contain the air generated by the blades within a kind of tunnel. Do you see the idea?'

I turned to a blank page. 'May I?'

He nodded, once. I scrawled a design on the page. Olaf studied it, frowning deeply. Then he looked at me in amazement.

'My dear sir,' he faltered. 'I had no idea that you were an engineer . . .'

I bowed. 'Merely an enthusiastic amateur. I'm honoured if you see merit in my suggestion.'

'Indeed I do.' He frowned, and studied his design, flipping over the page to examine my own contribution.

He looked up, clearing his throat.

'Pardon me . . . What did you say your name was?'

It had been only relatively recently that I had been able to get rid of my mother. Like many mothers, mine was of the kind that couldn't bear to let their progeny go. I had been a part of her life for so long that she couldn't face the prospect of losing me. In fact, she never let me out of her sight. So it was a considerable relief when I finally managed to sever our connection.

When I speak of severing our connection, I mean it quite literally. My mother, in common with many others, believed that by neglecting to cut the umbilical cord after birth she would actually arrest her rate of fall, reasoning that because I weighed so much less than her, I would counteract her descent. This of course was sheer nonsense; it was perfectly obvious that the more any object weighed, the faster it would fall, and since my mother and I, while connected by the umbilicus, counted as one heavy object not one heavy one and one light one, it was an inevitable fact that we would fall faster. But Mumma refused to acknowledge this simple truism, insisting that my relative lightness would help to retard our fall – a view to which she adhered with such perversity that I gradually became convinced that in reality she only maintained our link out of sheer cussedness.

At any rate, after some sixteen years of this unhappy union, the opportunity of escape at last presented itself. We had found a Thermal, by luck rather than judgement. Mother was snoozing some thirty feet away from me. Over the years the umbilicus had stretched – though it refused to snap. I was dangling a little above her, disconsolately surveying the surrounding air for useful flotsam. Then something caught my eye; a tiny black object, coming up on the starboard side.

I stared at it closely. Then my heart leapt. I couldn't believe my good fortune. This was precisely the find I had sought for so many years: a pair of scissors.

The scissors were rising steadily towards me. I stole a glance at Mumma. She was still snoring. Our paltry stock of food floated a few feet above her, attached to her by a rope, while fluttering absurdly above that was a kind of blanket of pigeon and sparrow-feathers, woven into a length of fabric – another of Mumma's hare-brained ideas intended to slow our fall.

There she sprawled, ropes and umbilici stretching away from her broad leather belt like the tentacles of some grotesque octopus. I had to escape from her clutches, and I knew that if I missed this chance I was finished; opportunities like this only came once in a lifetime, if that. I couldn't afford to fluff it.

I pushed away, cleaving through the air with a powerful stroke. I readied myself to snatch.

Then Mother woke up.

'Georg? Where've you got to? Georg?'

I cursed silently. She spotted me. 'What are you doing? Come here; fetch me an apple from the stock.'

Then she saw what I was after, and gave a shriek of terror. Wasting no more time, she began to haul me in, looping the slack over her flabby forearm. Another moment and I would be out of range. Desperately, I lunged.

She uttered a cry of despair, I one of triumph. But there was no time to savour it. She had returned to hauling, feverishly slinging loops of umbilical cord over her shoulders. Another few feet and she'd be close enough to seize my prize, hurl it away forever, and give me a sound box on the ears into the bargain. Without more ado, I cut the cord.

The feeling of relief at seeing the hated umbilicus part and float away from me was indescribable. Mother bellowed with rage, and tried to flail through the air towards me. But she was already beginning to fall away beneath me.

'Sorry, Mumma,' I shouted. 'But it's for the best; I keep on telling you, we're only dragging each other down by staying together. It's time we went our separate ways.'

'Ungrateful pup,' she wailed. 'After all I've done for you – I don't know how many years I lost when I was pregnant with you; you were such a fat little baby. And now you cut me off as if I was a stranger. Your father would never forgive you.'

A ridiculous statement. I had never known my father, and neither had she, beyond a brief casual dalliance.

'You wait,' yelled mother, faintly. 'I'll find you again one day. I'll get a Remission. And when I do I'll . . .'

Her voice faded on the wind. I watched her fall, a plump, vainly struggling form, gradually dwindling to a speck, and vanishing into the blue.

I felt a twinge of poignant regret. We'd had some good times together – when she wasn't attending to one of her fly-by-night lovers, the loins of one of whom must have engendered me.

'Goodbye, Muvva,' I murmured.

I flung the scissors away. Another adolescent would find them, and would cut away the dead weight of his mother.

That was how Regress was made.

Abruptly, the Thermal vanished, and we were once more falling swiftly through air that suddenly felt very chill. Olaf immediately began the calculations necessary to locate another. A task that normally took me fifteen minutes he accomplished in three. Soon I was following him, swimming through the air towards it.

Olaf did not object to my company, so I suggested that we tie ourselves together, to prevent drifting apart. He agreed, and when were ensconced in the new Updraught, I voiced a point which had been troubling me.

'Pardon me, but you must be at least twice my age, Olaf. Have you been riding the Thermals for so long?'

He glanced across at me, and nodded briefly. 'I've devised many other ways of arresting fall – as I just showed you – but it's very hard to get the materials necessary for their manufacture. You just have to pick up what you can get – a hammer, a box of nails, tools for shaping metal. There's always plenty of driftwood about, of course, but most of it is unworkable.' He sighed. 'I had ideas of constructing a kind of platform with huge canvas wings, like a bird – wings which would catch the wind, and which could be controlled by a system of pulleys, so you could steer – not fall, but *fly*, like a pigeon or an albatross. But it's just a dream. I could never assemble the materials. It's maddening to think that right now, as I speak, all those materials are falling past us somewhere out there' – he swept his arm, taking in the vast emptiness of the sky – 'falling past, out of reach, unusable. The probability of them ever falling close enough for me to retrieve them is – well, quite ludicrous.'

'It could happen, though,' I said encouragingly. 'Think of the odds against my falling into your Thermal back there. Things like that are mathematically infinitely improbable – yet they happen all the time.'

This curious phenomenon had struck me in the past, and I was looking forward to finding out if Olaf had any ideas which might explain it. But he merely nodded gloomily.

'It drives me mad to think that all the best tools and materials are probably falling into the hands of the most incompetent fools imaginable, instead of into those of people with even the smallest ability to make use of them. No wonder Regress is so slow. All I get is junk – bottles of perfume, false teeth, inflatable castles, ironing boards. I don't know, sometimes I wish . . .'

He trailed off into a sullen silence. I could sympathise with him. It was so rare that anything useful appeared; most of the flotsam which fell around us was useless – or, if it had a utility, it was either impractical without certain other accessories, or incomprehensible. The popular theory was that the gods flung us the artefacts to make use of as we could, amusing themselves at our expense by the hopeless improbability of our (a) having the good fortune to get hold of the things and (b) having the intelligence to know what to do with them. Our food likewise came predominantly from above; pigeons, though numerous, were notoriously difficult to catch, as well as being unpalatable. Flying fish were less elusive, but tended to congregate inside clouds, where it was hard to see them. We ate what we could when we could.

Not far away, to our left, a group of Colinites plummeted past, their orange robes fluttering like flames in the wind. They were a heretical sect who believed that the sooner man reached Hell, which they believed awaited us all at the end of the fall, the better. They formed into circular groups of up to thirty believers. Arms locked, they hurtled Hell-wards, praying and singing hymns, eager to plunge into the everlasting fire. One of those in this particular congregation spotted Olaf and me.

'Join us,' he shouted, and beckoned, nearly causing the whole group to break up.

They were quickly out of sight. Olaf watched them moodily.

'You know, I sometimes think they may be right . . .'

I stared at him in amazement. Here was one of the greatest scientists and inventors of all time – one of the few true innovators to appear in history – expressing tentative approval of the most pathologically progressive set of lunatics in society. 'You can't be serious,' I said.

Olaf only grunted, eyes still following the dwindling speck of the Colinites.

We fell to talking of our past lives. I told Olaf of my recent escape from Mother. Olaf spoke of his childhood – he had been brought up in a scattered community by parents who had encouraged his interest in things mechanical, letting him play with any small gadgets or bits of machinery which came along.

Eventually, the little community had fallen apart, its members gradually drifting away from each other, as always happens sooner or later. Olaf was left alone, and in his solitude spent more and more time with his notebooks, doodling ever more recondite mathematical abstractions, trying to grasp the dynamics of his world as an equation. He had had some truly fundamental insights, only a few of which, it turned out, were known of by others; the communications which existed between individuals were deplorable. Although lateral movement was possible, it was physically extremely tiring. Besides this, it seemed pointless: one part of the sky was very like another, after all. So most people remained in more or less the same position all their lives.

As for written communication, that was little better. Paper could be written on, and then flung to the sixteen winds, placed inside bottles or other receptacles, or occasionally tied to the legs of pigeons, all of which methods had a negligible chance of successfully delivering a message. Olaf had produced many copies of his Thermal Detection method, and one or two of these had been found. Such was the fame of the discovery that news of it had travelled up and down the sky – incidentally, one of the most concerted attempts at mass communication on record – and the name of Olaf was revered.

'I always had an affinity for mechanical things,' said Olaf, rather dreamily. 'I'll never forget the time when – '

He was rudely interrupted. A flying fish landed smack in his eye.

Startled, Olaf made a grab for it with both hands. The shiny silver-blue fish flailed desperately in his grasp, landing a couple more dabs in the face before Olaf clouted it against his foot, silencing it.

Then the fish were all around us, a flock of them, their scales seeming to sparkle.

'Catch them, catch them!' roared Olaf, and made a dive at the nearest fish.

Bewildered, I tried to capture one of these elusive fishy denizens of the air. I had never been keen on fish-hunting, and my efforts now were inept. Olaf, however, had caught five fish, and had stuffed them into the various pockets of his tunic.

Then the flock was gone, winging away on some mysterious migration of its own.

'I'm very partial to flying fish,' explained Olaf, revealing an unexpected side to himself. 'Come on, let's eat.'

'That's better,' sighed Olaf, tossing a fishtail over his shoulder. 'Sometimes I just forget to eat – it's easily done.'

I nodded, wishing that flying fish did not leave such a rancid after-taste. Olaf seemed quite disposed to adjourn his scientific researches for the while, so I reminisced about the brief period I had spent in a community as a child. I recalled the floating rafts of food and drink, tethered together, their weight carefully gauged so as to match the falling-velocity of the people. Such communities were rare; apart from the practical difficulties presented by maintaining the rafts, most people found the semi-permanence of relationships which went with them too demanding; casual *amours* were far less trouble for both parties, and it was brief encounters such as these, rather than ongoing affairs, which maintained the population even at its present low density.

There had even been roving gangs of bandits in those

days – rogues who travelled the skies by slinging crude harnesses to the giant albatross, pillaging the food-stocks of communities such as ours. A few of the more flamboyant had even adopted names for themselves – 'Pettigrew's Pilfering Pigeon-men', 'ffrench's fflying ffilibusters'. Where were they now, I wondered, those swaggering pirates of the skies?

Olaf listened absently, but it wasn't long before he took out his crumpled notebook again, and began once more to pore over his spidery diagrams.

'Can I help?' I offered. But he shook his head briefly, a gesture so abstracted that it could just as well have been a rejection of some hypothesis in his train of thought as of my tentative question. Either way, I decided, I had better leave him in peace. I moved away, and let the wind lull me to sleep.

Time passed, immeasurable and elusive. We fell through space and time, growing slightly older as we fell, falling towards whatever awaited us.

And what was that? More and more, I found myself preoccupied by this question. Was there really a Hell down there? Or was there something else – something less metaphysical, perhaps?

Olaf and I discussed it, though curiously he found the issue less intriguing than I.

'I remember hearing legends, as a child,' I said. 'Did you ever hear tell of the *Myth of the Ground*?'

He shrugged. 'I have vague memories of it.'

'I always found that a fascinating idea,' I said. 'The notion of there being something *solid* below us, a kind of anti-sky which one would traverse *horizontally* – I made a cutting motion with my hand – 'rather than fall through vertically.'

Olaf sniffed. 'Materialism,' he said dismissively.

I was about to point out that science itself was a form of materialism, when a voice hailed us.

'Ahoy there! Friends, may I share with you God's Remission?'

A plump figure was falling slowly past on our left. His blue gown identified him as a member of the Order of Saint Hudibras. Olaf curtly signalled his permission for the cleric to join us, and he came flapping awkwardly towards our trajectory.

'Thanks, friends,' he puffed. He had positioned himself a little above us; evidently he intended to talk for some time, for his rate of fall was slightly faster than ours, and he had clearly arranged the gap between us deliberately, so that he would not fall away from us too soon.

The priest introduced himself as Brother Peter, then remarked, 'You have much grace of God that you have found this Remission, friends. Are you believers?'

The Order called Thermals 'Remissions'; because since an Updraught slowed the rate of fall somewhat, it gave more time to remember and repent of one's sins; hence its place in the sect's theology. Remissions could be bought from the sect for tradable items, but whether the buyer would actually *find* his Thermal Dispensation was another matter; the sect claimed that it was a matter of faith – 'Have faith, and thou shalt rise.' The rival sect of Brother Colin despised Remissions, calling them 'Devils' Farts'.

Both Olaf and I shook our heads in answer to the priest's question. He tutted, and said, 'Perhaps, friends, you are ignorant of the *Tenets*? Wait; I possess a copy . . .'

Brother Peter rummaged inside his robe, and produced a book, its pages crackling, doubtless from the many occasions on which it had been soaked in clouds and then held out to dry in the wind. So these were the legendary *Tenets*, one of the very few printed books that were known to exist, exhaustively copied by diligent Brothers who had little else to occupy them on their long descent. Interested in spite of ourselves, Olaf and I attended to the priest.

Brother Peter opened the book and began to read.

'Long, long ago, Man lived high up, at the Top of the Firmament, at the Zenith of Creation, in that place known as Heaven. By any Standards, Heaven was an ideal place to live, for it had everything that a Man might need: Food, Water, Tools, Wax, Clothes, Pigeons, Paper, and a host of others.

'Man was happy here, and longed to stay there Always.

'But Man was not Alone in Heaven; another Race lived there. This Race was the *Gods*, or God. God resembled Man in many ways, but they were stronger than Man. God was happy in Heaven, but he was not very happy, because he envied Man. He envied, and it liked him not to see Man so happy. Also, he envied Man his women (which in those Days were far different from now, and were in fact more like young Boys).

'Therefore God ordered Man to worship them. A few obeyed, but most argued, and demanded Wherefore. God became exceeding Wroth, and one of them proposed that Man be ejected from Heaven.

'It was done immediately. God picked up Man (for he was the Stronger) and *Cast him from Heaven*.

'And God said, "You shall Fall many cubits and will Learn to Adore us."

'They also Cursed women, and made them change into their present Form, so that they would have to bear Children, the weight of which would, like lumps of Rock in their bellies, drag them quickly to Hell.

'But, in their Mercy, God granted Man Remission: "When you have Learned the Error of your Ways you may Regress and live once more in Heaven. Those who repent, and pay homage in piety and true Devotion, them will I, reaching down from Heaven, Pluck up and Return to their Original Place. But those who remain Unregenerate shall be passed over, and will continue their Fall until they plunge into the very Fires of Hell."

'All this was and is So. Therefore must we Adore and worship God; only then will we Regress unto Heaven, our Original home, and make our peace with God.

'Here Endeth the First *Tenet*.'

Brother Peter closed the book. Weighing more than Olaf and I, he had fallen faster, and was now almost level with us. He beamed at us beatifically: were we converted?

'When were the *Tenets* written?' inquired Olaf.

'No one knows, friend. Brother Hudibras, their author, is in all probability back in Heaven now, even as we speak; he would have been Plucked by the Hand of God some time ago now. There is a constant traffic of the Regressing Ones, brothers; as we Fall, so they Rise. But we can't see them.'

'Why not?' I asked.

'Best not to ask "Wherefore", lad. Remember, that was the word that undid our ancestors. "Seek not after vain Wisdom, that your Bones be not filled with Lead that you may Fall the Faster into Hell." So says Brother Hudibras, brother, and – '

'And he was utterly wrong,' snarled Olaf, taking us both by surprise. '*Lead in our Bones is precisely what we want!*'

With which cryptic remark he seized Brother Peter, and cast him out of our Thermal.

'Heretic!' screamed the priest, evidently aware of the symbolic quality attaching to Olaf's action. 'When the Fires of Hell make the Lead in your Bones run molten, then you'll recant your Colinite heresy!'

Taken aback, I watched him fall away. His threats and curses dwindled to nothing and, a little later, so did he.

'What was all that about?' I demanded. 'Why did you throw him out like that?'

'Don't you see, I was doing him a favour? It suddenly struck me, while I was listening to all that nonsense about Divine Regression, and the Hand of God plucking us up again – *it's precisely the opposite of what we ought to be seeking.* No, I'm not talking about the Colinites – they're just as fatuous as that flabby imbecile who was preaching at us. What I'm talking about is the notion of *Regress* – the belief that *falling more slowly*, or of actually *going up* and falling back the way we've come – is utterly misguided. *Progress* is what we should be seeking if we wish to enter Heaven.'

I was baffled, and asked him to expand.

'What's the fastest speed at which anything can travel, Georg? The Speed of Light. Our own rate of descent varies, but it is always considerably *less* than the Speed of Light, correct? Now, what would happen if an object travelled faster than light? Obviously it would disappear, since light would travel too slowly to illuminate it and enable us to see it. But more than that – not only would it disappear, but it would actually pass out of a universe in which a physical constant, the Speed of Light, had been broken. In short, having violated the structure of that universe, *it would no longer be able to exist in that universe; it would have passed into a realm in which an entirely different set of physical laws would operate.* Do you see? The point at which an object reached this velocity and slipped into another universe would be utterly beyond the energy of light – a, um, *Dark Fissure*, you might call it, or perhaps a *Black Hole*. That's what we have to do: attain a faster-than-light velocity, punch our own Black Holes in this universe, and thereby pass into another!'

The idea was extraordinary; only someone of Olaf's genius could have made this breathtaking intuitive leap.

'But how are we to attain such a speed?' I asked. 'Our velocity should be constantly multiplying – yet it fluctuates, always stays below the Speed of Light.'

'That's because of air resistance,' stated Olaf. 'For centuries, scientists – myself included – have been seeking ways of increasing that resistance; but I now believe that that is a fundamentally unscientific notion. Science is about moving *forwards*, not back. Backwards is for religion.'

Sensing a diatribe on the priests, I hurriedly said, 'That's all very well, but how do you propose to achieve this unprecedented acceleration?'

The great inventor frowned deeply. 'I don't know. But I'll think of something. I'll find a way – you watch!'

*

At first Olaf had been reluctant to let me help him with his invention, but at last I convinced him that I had every right to share in the work. However, while he agreed to let me help construct his machine, he refused to divulge its principle, and though I studied it at length, I could not fathom its secret.

We collected driftwood, fashioned it into long tubes with funnels at one end. No elaborate machine, with whirling spindles or adjustable flaps; I could have puzzled that out. But *tubes*? Even tubes with funnels at one end seemed unlikely devices by which to achieve faster-than-light velocities.

When we had four of these contraptions, Olaf decided that the time had come to reveal all.

'This,' he announced, waving one of the tubes at me, 'is it. By means of these tubes – *propulsors*, as I have chosen to call them – we will attain a speed faster than that of light.

'I had the idea for these not long after the initial concept of FTL travel. The devices are strapped the length of the back – so – the funnels directed down-wards. They fit comfortably on either shoulder; their purpose is to gather the wind – to scoop up the air resistance that slows our falls – and to funnel it along these tubes. They thus turn resistance into *propulsion* – a driving force which, concentrated in the tubes, whistles out of the narrow rear orifices, driving the wearer down at an astounding rate. And the effect is cumulative; the faster one falls, the greater the air resist-ance encountered – so the more air is sent hurtling through the system. The more air passes through here, the greater the speed. With these, we can go shooting out of this universe and into the next!'

I had known that simplicity was the essence of great inventions; but this surpassed all my expectations.

I had resented Olaf's secrecy over the propulsors; but his exposition captured my imagination; his genius had triumphed once more! All my old admiration returned, and I wanted nothing more than to put this, his latest masterpiece, to the test. Incredible as it seemed, we were going to try to enter a new universe.

Olaf was never one for pompous speeches. We helped each other strap on the propulsors.

With an encouraging grin he said, 'Now or never. The next time we speak together, Georg, it will be in another reality!'

Then we were shooting downwards at a rate so rapid as to make our previous falling seem like the drift of a pigeon-feather. Cold, invisible fire roared from our pro-pulsors, an artificial Thermal that could have lifted a man a thousand feet back into the air. My mouth opened in a scream which I could not hear above the roar of the wind. My ears were singing, my eyes streaming. Could the puny human frame endure such velocities?

It was too late to worry about such things now; I was hurtling down like an arrow from Heaven – an arrow sent by God to dispatch these blasphemers who denounced the *Tenets* of Divine Regress. With this thought, a sudden rush of pious dread gripped me, and with it my revived respect for Olaf evaporated; was I really hastening my descent only to plunge into Hell like a damned wretch with the sins of all humanity on his head? I cursed myself for a fool: I had thrown away my life on the whim of a mad inventor, a crank who had had the monstrous audacity to reverse the direction of twenty generations of science!

I burst through a cloudbank, and would have gasped in amazement, had I had any breath with which to gasp.

Below was that thing which was the stuff of legend, of myth: not the leaping fires of Hell, but something more substantial – a vast flat surface, mottled with green and brown, an endless panorama of substance, a rushing enormity, a frantically expanding volume of solidity, of not-air.

The Ground.

The myth was a reality!

But I didn't have long to contemplate it. In a single

microsecond, it rose up to engulf me, and everything went black.

No, not everything; that was an exaggeration.

I found myself drifting through a void at a leisurely pace. It was very cold. I could see odd points of bright light, punctuating the blackness.

Was this the Ground? Had I *landed*? Or was this Hell?

Then a familiar voice hailed me.

'Georg! Over here! We made it! We broke the Light-barrier! We made our own black holes and shot through them! This is it – *our new universe*!'

It was Olaf, drifting a short distance away from me. The cord by which we had been attached to each other had snapped – presumably we must have attained faster-than-light speed at different moments, and the umbilicus had been neatly cut in two by the respective universes.

I looked around me in consternation, bewildered by the darkness; our surroundings were gloomier than the interior of even the thickest cloudbank. I wondered briefly if Olaf was wrong, and that *this* was a black hole – that we were still falling through it towards an unknown destination.

But if so, why were there lights here? Reluctantly, I acknowledged that this void was indeed the new universe we had hankered after. Clearly I had crossed the Light-barrier in the nick of time, slipping through my black hole a mere instant before impacting with the Ground. A miraculous escape; so why did it feel like an anticlimax?

'What do we do now?' I asked.

Olaf, who was drifting a little ahead of me, looked nonplussed. 'Well . . . Could we think about that later? After all, we've only just arrived. Let's just appreciate the . . . er . . . view a little first, shall we?'

We both stared at our surroundings.

'What are those lights?' I demanded.

'Oh . . . clearly those are black holes – they appear *white* here, of course, because this universe is the converse or negative of the one we knew; there we couldn't see them because they transcended light, here we can because the light shining through them from our old universe is still visible. Interesting that there are so many . . . er . . . *white holes*. We're evidently not the first people to have had the idea of FTL travel. At least we won't be lonely.'

I gazed about me, but could see no sign of anyone else sharing the void with us; we had our new universe to ourselves, it seemed.

We drifted on in silence for a while. I began to feel hungry, and hoped that perhaps a cooked pigeon or some other delicacy would float past.

'We're undoubtedly in the *anti-universe* of our old one,' commented Olaf. 'As you will have observed, we're not falling, but *drifting* – a significant difference.'

Fascinating, I reflected sourly. I don't know what I had expected our new universe to be like, but I hadn't envisaged such a place as this. I began to wonder if Olaf's *Progress* had really been such a wonderful idea after all; it had sounded so ingenious back there in the old universe. But I remembered the tantalising glimpse of the *Ground* which I had been vouchsafed just before blinking out of that reality. I couldn't help thinking, perhaps it would have been better to stick to the old ideas – Regress rather than Progress; that way, perhaps we would have invented a means of slowing our descent so much that we could have actually *landed on the Ground*, and begun a new life there.

Could *that* be Heaven? A fruitful expanse of solidity, where everything stayed still and you could be sure of finding food, rather than relying on dumb luck to put a morsel your way? That was it, I felt sure; Creation was the wrong way around – instead of shooting back up the way we'd come, the Ground was our destination all along; Olaf had been partly correct in saying that science had got its priorities mixed up. But it was really our *theological* notions that were back-to-front: Heaven was actually *below us*.

And we hadn't worked out a way of getting there yet. No sooner had we beheld this wondrous promise than we slammed into it at an inconceivable velocity and that was that.

There must be a way out of this impasse, I thought furiously. Turning over hypotheses in my mind, I suddenly recalled that fact which had several times struck me as singular, and which, thanks to the perfecting of the FTL drive, I had never got around to discussing with Olaf: the occasional correspondence between the mind and reality.

Consider. The scissors with which I had cut my umbilicus. A monumental coincidence, their appearing just when I needed them. I had been thinking seriously about escape prior to finding them; had those thoughts crystallised, so to speak – actually *given rise to* the desired object of my cogitations?

And the further 'coincidence' of my meeting with Olaf; I had dreamed of him shortly before meeting him. Had this dream-reality become translated into the external one? A strange, hitherto unexamined process of causation linking the ideal with the real?

The possibilities this opened up were immense. If my speculations were true, what could be achieved by consciously manipulating the process! Could we *think* ourselves to the Ground? Was it, finally, a question of Mind over Matter?

Olaf was starting to drift away. He was saying something to me; I couldn't hear.

'Olaf!' I shouted. 'Come back! I've realised how we can get out of here!'

Too late. He was dwindling in the darkness, caught in some anti-Downdraught. I tried to follow him, but my movements were clumsy, and soon he had vanished into the darkness.

Silently, I saluted him, this genius with whom I had travelled so far.

But this was no time for sentiment; I was eager to test my theory.

I summoned a picture of the old universe to mind. I tried to imagine myself there. Nothing happened. Had I been wrong? Or did ideal causation simply not operate in this reality?

Surely not; I was simply being too impatient. I would sleep; and when I awoke I would find myself back there. Then I could set about landing on the Ground. And when I got there I would help others to land, too.

I closed my eyes. I would dream myself into reality. And when I arrived – why, there would be so much to do!

Something Sweet

Simon Ings & Charles Stross

One

Above them the sky is neon wash-out pierced by airship running lights.

'It's cold out here,' says the Man in her soft, hoarse voice. 'Won't you come in?'

The car is long and low and shiny. Jimmy gets in.

He perches on the jump-seat opposite the Man. She wears a long gabardine coat. He looks in her eyes and thinks of video cameras. Next to her sits Hired Muscle, staring at him like Jimmy has a target pasted between his eyes.

The Man can be crude in some ways.

'Two days, Jimmy.'

He glances out of the window. The sky is mirrored in the gutters.

'How much longer?' Her manner is exquisitely polite – utterly threatening.

He shrugs. 'It didn't come with a spec. sheet.'

The Man gives him a long look. 'What needs the work?' she asks.

The car swings into Peckham High Street. The buildings here are a century old; chopped up and accreted to, they're no more substantial now than a series of abandoned theatre flats. Skips piled high with cartons conceal the pavement every fifty yards. Jimmy watches out the back window: an old man wrestles a shopping trolley over a length of abandoned cable; a woman in overalls and a works helmet is leant up against a building site hoarding, fussing over her throatmike.

Jimmy explains, 'I've got as far as the core's final input. Breaking it is a semi-random process: two seconds or two weeks. Plus, I've got to find a suitable cover each time I do it.' Out the rear window he sees shadows drift beneath a sign for bathroom fittings.

'Remember who owns you,' says the Man.

One of the shadows throws something. Jimmy blinks.

It is a smart grenade. It detonates two metres above the

Mercedes; a charge-sequence compresses a slug of uranium into a white-hot dart the size of an ice-pick and spits it out.

The Man and her companion lose their heads. Blood and fluid borne on a wave of expanding air drench Jimmy's face and clothes; his skin prickles as bone shards nick and scratch him. Bits of flesh and windscreen spray the street.

The car swerves, picks up speed, grates its nearside across a row of parked cabs and shudders to a halt, at right angles to the road.

Jimmy opens the door and pools the tarmac with vomit. He falls out, gets to his feet and totters to a rank of skips. He crawls between them, sits down in the garbage and drips blood over crumpled sushi cartons; his nose is gushing.

He watches the street.

People are running about; their mouths open and close, but he can't hear them.

Steam curls from the glassless windows of the car. The interior is all red, like someone took a spray-can to it. The Man's driver climbs out of the car, unhurt, and crouches by the nearside headlight; the back of his head is covered with someone else's blood. He's looking back the way the car has come, wondering whether to run.

Jimmy wants to yell to him but he's winded, nearly deaf, he can't find his voice.

The driver turns round, sees Jimmy. There is something black and heavy held in the ball of his fist; he points it.

Behind Jimmy, someone shouts something incoherent, guttural – a cry of warning or dismay. Jimmy closes his eyes. A sound like a thousand Velcro fasteners being pulled apart—

The driver is blown in two. His legs have been knocked under the car. The rest of him slides smoothly back down the slick plastic bonnet and lands upright on the tarmac; his head bobs.

Jimmy turns on to his front, ready to heave again. There's someone standing right behind him. The hem of a black plastic raincoat swishes past his face, and the figure is gone.

The air stinks of kebabs and gunshot and urine. Before him, a pavement's breadth away, there is an amusement arcade. There is a neon sign over the door, telling him to BOMB THE BASTARDS.

His ears ache.

Doctor Gordon Dexter, a research director at Protein Technologies PLC, enters an exclusive Japanese restaurant just north of Covent Garden.

He has been invited here by Josephine Barr; she is the manager of Protein's UK Patents Department.

They take their seats. Dexter orders ginger and water chestnut vermicelli. Josephine picks the biggest lobster in the tank.

Dexter has a bad feeling about this.

He says: 'I am pleased you will be taking personal charge of this case. I do not want a repetition of yesterday's action.'

Josephine Barr picks up her chopsticks and clacks them together moodily like they were a claw she's just grown. 'The initial choice of subject for your experiment has provided some, shall we say, unique challenges.'

Dexter makes a placatory gesture with the hand that's not pouring them tea. His back aches. Not enough squash this month, he thinks to himself and he shuffles uncomfortably on his cushion. 'I was unfairly rushed, and now your department takes the brunt – it's in the nature of things. You don't know how much pressure I was under. We're in a race with Achebe, not to mention Hoffmann la Roche; but the real threat is Achebe. If they win, the consequences will be serious. If we don't get our biologic systems interfaced with the human central nervous system successfully – and on the market first – they'll wipe the floor with us using self-annealing optical implants. I'd like to remind you of the projections for turnover of integrated bionic control systems within the next ten years. And, what's more, you must understand the unique opportunity the lad represented.'

'Which is?'

'He has an inaccessible tumour in his amygdala. Surgical excision is impossible because of the probability of brain damage, and death due to subarachnoid haemorrhage is likely in one or two years.' Dexter smiles to himself. He likes people who ask questions. He thinks back with some regret to his promising teaching career, since blighted by Protein's multi-million-ECU research grant.

'Unfortunately,' Josephine points out, not without venom, 'your subject worked for the biggest data pirate in the country.'

'That was no excuse to indulge in one of the most absurd and bloody – ' Dexter raises his voice as he speaks. He does not like being put on the defensive. His voice carries to a party of senior execs squatting three tables away towards the window.

A woman glances round at him. Light glints off her monocle. The glass is tinted red – a print surface for her e-mail link.

From Bowmaker, he thinks, reading in her appearance her company's aesthetic: all pinstripe and old-style cyberware.

A waiter crosses the room between their tables, bearing Josephine's lobster. Dexter blanches. The lobster is raw. He looks at Josephine and catches the ghost of a smile on her lips. She does not move. He swallows, hard. 'Please, don't wait for me,' he murmurs.

'Oh, it's not hot, I'll wait.' She drains her cup.

Dexter fills it for her again and says, 'Hydrostatic shock alone could have brain-damaged him.'

Josephine Barr sighs. 'The action was my responsibility, I grant you, but the purpose of this meeting as I understand it is to *prevent* similar incidents.'

Dexter nods enthusiastically. 'Of course.' His vermicelli arrives and before he can lift the bowl to his mouth Josephine Barr has made her first attack upon the lobster. Dexter sees that its claws and skull have been crushed by something serrated. It's probably not even dead yet.

'I've told you before,' Dexter says, 'we need keep only the most cursory tabs on the poor lad; in the fullness of time *he* will make his whereabouts known to *us*.'

'Ah, but when will that be, Doctor?'

'Does it matter?'

'I think so,' says Josephine Barr; she allows herself another, barely perceptible smile. 'You see, at this very moment he is breaking open the cores on Something Sweet.'

Dexter chokes on his seaweed.

Sergeant Tina Gullam Hussein of the Westminster Constabulary Mobile Response Unit enters Tower Bridge Control and makes straight for Booth 110.

She palms open the door. Foster sits with his back to her, watching seven traffic monitors at once. She creeps up behind him and swipes the back of his head, lightly, with her glove.

He twists round. 'Oh. Hi.'

'You forgot your watch,' she says to him and takes a worn men's Swatch out of her jacket pocket and dangles it in front of him.

'Oh. Thanks.' He thinks a second. 'Look, could we meet after work? I know – I know we've really got to talk but I'm kind of . . .' He laughs, uncertain, and gestures at the monitors.

'Jo on the desk told me it's your coffee break in five. Why d'you think she let me in here?'

'Oh. Right. It's just I figured maybe we should take longer . . .'

'I don't want to be around you any longer than I have to,' she says, and in spite of herself she lets a little of the anger out.

He bridles. 'Well, if that's the way you've taken things, I guess . . .'

'Things?'

He doesn't know how to respond to that, which is good because she doesn't want him to respond. She just wants him to sit there looking stupid and that is precisely what he does. 'Well,' she says, 'are you just going to sit there looking stupid or do I get a coffee?'

Foster curses under his breath. 'Yes, of course, I'm sorry.' He glances at his naked wrist, clicks his tongue in annoyance, and takes his watch from Tina's outstretched hand.

He stands up and heads for the door. 'I know somewhere quiet.'

She likes the tone of self-deprecation in his voice, likes the trust it implies, but she hopes he won't be like that to her now, because now, with him gone from her bed with only stupidity and platitudes for explanations – right now, she wants to hate him. Just a little. It helps. She's been here before and she knows.

'You hear the Man is dead?' she says, when they're on the street. Foster doesn't answer, just leads her down an alley to the door of a café she's never seen before. The tables are marked out for chess. Two women with headscarves tied tightly under their chins are playing against each other in the back of the room, otherwise it's empty. The coffee tastes like piss. 'You and your buddies really screwed up the lights,' she says. 'Took us four minutes to get there through cross-traffic. Lost a witness.'

Foster nods. 'Messy. Whose was the hit?'

'Corporate.'

'How come?'

'Intelligence hasn't thrown up any urban grouping with that kind of firepower since the Stockwell raids.'

Foster nods. 'It figures. We've been working over the Man's apartment, breaking open her cores. When we bust them, seems the Man was reading up on bio-logic.'

Tina smiles, polite. 'It seems you've hit the big time.'

Foster shrugs. 'Just picked the right straw.'

She stares into his eyes. 'What is it?'

He sighs. 'Please, not again.'

'Why leave? Why cancel your diary?'

'Huh?'

'I've been doing some detective work, that being what we do best, right? It's not just me, is it? It's Caroline and Thursday nights at the alley and – '

He drains his cup and says, 'Look, I just need some time on my own, and I *know* it sounds like the words came off the back of a cereal packet but it's true.'

She smiles at him. He is so naïve. 'Has anyone else bought this line?'

He, in his turn, can't help but laugh. 'No.'

All right, she thinks, enough of this. She says, 'I don't know what you've got into, but if you need me I'll be there, right?'

He looks like he'll plead honesty again, then gives it up and says, 'Right. Thanks.'

Before the platitudes get any worse she's out the door and in the daylight again, breathing fast. She heads towards the station parking lot.

Her bike, leant up against the kerb, spots her. It powers up.

Two

Foam effluents drift down the Thames like melting ice sculptures. Automatics on Tower Bridge scan the traffic. The shadow of an airship falls across him. Jimmy thrusts his hands deeper into the pockets of his jacket and turns from the view across the river. He leans into the breeze as he walks.

He's got the scanalyser on a strap at his belt. It looks like a ThinkMan. It burbles to itself, testing a new combination every eight-tenths of a millisecond. Worth a lot of cash on the fence – two K maybe, because the big companies are trying to stamp them out. But how can he fence it? Incriminating. He feels exposed, naked. Jimmy wants rid of it but he can't afford to trash it.

He's near the City, now – the old financial heartland of the capital. He's not as conspicuous as he thinks he is; there are as many builders as execs on the streets, on a break from the dozen construction projects sited in the area. Jimmy looks like one of them – young, dirty, covered in dust, cut about some on his face and hands. He crosses Bank by the underpass and when he surfaces there's a bright window; a bar. Jimmy rummages in his pocket and feels cash – enough for a drink. He goes in.

There is more to life than shooting Ants, but nobody told the games designers. On his way in, Jimmy is assaulted by reverberations from Tank Battle Antarctica. Global graphics and incoming missiles in green, Ants in white, Aussies in traditional communist red. Two kids are playing it like it's for real; Jimmy slides through the gap between them and the door. The barman has nobody else to serve.

'Something Sweet,' Jimmy says, then double-takes. There's a throbbing at his temples – the usual sign. Cluster headaches that make him want to vomit. He knows there is something wrong up there, but the clinic found nothing. He remembers with a pang that the Man paid his MedicAid. He had owed her, liked her even – it isn't something he wants to think about. He wobbles a bit and leans on the bar, watches incuriously as the barman makes up something turquoise. 'What's that?' he says.

'Something sweet. IBM Special – cocktail, one ECU fifty.'

Floating in the foam on his drink are flakes of sugar shaped like microprocessors. Jimmy sips, then pushes the glass away and puts the scanalyser on the bar top. He looks at the display and sees a red light, burning steady. His head pounds in time with the Tank Battle riff.

He is in.

Dexter doesn't know how he got here but he's in a car next to Josephine Barr and they are on the way to her flat in the West End. He doesn't understand this; Barr doesn't get paid enough to afford an apartment around here. He wonders precisely where it is.

Josephine Barr is giving him hell. 'You knew Jimmy worked for the Man; she paid you to dice his brain.'

'He came into my surgery complaining of headaches. The Man paid his MedicAid bill; maybe she liked him.'

'To the tune of thirty thousand ECUs?'

Doctor Dexter shrugs uncomfortably. 'So maybe I strung her along a little.'

'With what?'

Dexter folds his arms – a self-protective gesture. 'I gave nothing important away.'

'The Man got wind of the project. Not necessarily by name – but she knew something was going down. Right now there's a scanalyser eating at Protein Technologies' cores. We can't keep it out indefinitely so I bought a discreet police wringer on the would-be core breaker. Turns out he's an ex-employee of the man. You have three guesses.'

Dexter rubs his face with his hands. 'Fuck.'

'Now tell me – *precisely* – what you told her.'

Dexter sighs. 'I spoke only in the most general terms – that we've designed a retrovirus which attacks tumours. I told her the virus contains genes that modify the cancer cells – they create conditions similar to those in the brain tissue of a foetus, where brain cells form synapses when they divide.'

'And?'

'That's all.'

'Dexter, the Man would not have splashed five figures on a

nothing like Jimmy if you hadn't told her of the system's capabilities – its *commercial* capabilities.'

Dexter squirms. 'I told her the tumour is shaped into a logic-processing system – a physical embodiment of a mathematical idea known as a Turing machine; by doing that we narrow the man–machine gap to the thickness of a gene. The only prerequisite is cancer.'

Josephine Barr stares at him. 'You *sold* it to her,' she says, amazed.

'Listen,' Dexter insists, angrily, 'I'm getting just a little sick of the way Protein dumps all its shit on my doorstep. This may surprise you but, much as the Board wanted a full field test, their experimental protocols did *not* include human experimentation. If anything goes wrong with this, I and I alone go to jail. The Board refused even to help me look for a suitable subject. The only patients I could draw on were those attending my clinic. Three presented with the right symptoms: a mother of four, the PR chief of BZW – and Jimmy.'

'An employee of London's biggest hood.'

'A street kid with no family. I knew nothing of his . . . connections. The Man approached me only after I'd diagnosed him.'

'Why? Why should she?'

Dexter laughs weakly. 'It's not something that figures on balance sheets, Ms Barr – she *liked* him. I wrote "at death's door" on my Employer's Diagnostic Report, figuring he'd be kicked off whatever payroll he was on as a bad insurance risk. I figured the fewer the connections he had with people, the more secure the experiment would be. Instead the Man rings me up and asks how much I need to keep Jimmy alive.'

'And you said thirty thousand ECU.'

'In return for a cut of the business.'

'Somewhat mercenary, no?'

Dexter purses his lips. 'Think of it as an insurance policy. If news of the project ever leaked out I could trace my funding to the Man, not to Protein.'

'Your loyalty to Protein seems out of character.'

'Pure self-interest. If I could frame the Man, then Protein would be free to buy my sentence and I'd be back at work in a matter of a year.'

Josephine Barr stares at him in surprise, then says, 'That makes a great deal of sense.'

'Thank you.'

'Nevertheless, Jimmy *is* about to crack Protein's cores.'

Dexter brushes away her remark. 'Even if he succeeds, he'll only read what he'll come to know about in a few days anyway. Something Sweet may on-line any day now.'

Josephine Barr frowns. 'Any day now? And should we find Jimmy sitting atop the Telecom Tower reciting the Dow Jones index, how will you explain the phenomenon to the world's press?'

'No problem,' Dexter replies easily. 'Something Sweet is primarily a cure for a kind of cancer. Without this programme, a thousand people a year will continue to die of subarachnoid haemorrhage.'

'And what of his other abilities?'

Dexter pats Josephine Barr on the knee, quite tenderly. 'My dear,' he says warmly, 'if Something Sweet works as well and as publicly as you suggest, we are sitting on top of a market turnover estimated at twenty billion a year. Let the press suck on *that*.'

Josephine Barr smiles sweetly and brushes Dexter's hand off her knee. 'I'm bringing him in, Doctor. I'm calling in the wringer.'

'What?' Dexter cannot conceal his incredulity. 'This is supposed to be a *field test*. Why risk an arrest? The boy's running scared. Think, woman, he nearly had his head blown off! And what if it went wrong? He knows this city well enough to hide places we may never find him. I don't deny taking Jimmy into Protein's custody would save white hairs, but can we really risk it?'

'I'm not taking him into Protein's custody,' says Josephine.

Dexter shakes his head. 'I don't understand.'

'Jimmy is about to open the cores on Something Sweet. I want to see what comes out of them. I want Jimmy there with me. And I want you.'

Dexter would have politely declined Josephine's invitation, but right now he's noticed something curious.

The doors in this car have no handles.

Tina is on a routine patrol. She stares through the head-up pasted to the front of her visor. She sees the road through an overlay of ghostly images and smeared rain drops. Beneath her, the fuel cells of her bike convert methane into power – enzyme systems looted from electric eels. Fat tyres rumble across pot-holed tarmac and the world swings by. Stretch out and you can touch it, leave your foot behind.

Of a sudden, data haemorrhage across the head-up like blood

from a severed artery: a mole's been sighted, caught supping copyrighted data from a scanalyser. It only takes a moment for the police computers to confirm the target.

SatNav overlays lead her to him.

Jimmy is in an all-night café, reading:

It is possible to tap a computer terminal at a distance with a directional aerial and the right decoder. The ear of a cat is sensitive to noises so faint that the limit on its hearing is imposed by quantum uncertainty. No one has conclusively proven that the transmission of messages between nerve cells is a purely chemical process by excluding electromagnetic effects. The system is designed to be more than just a passive supercomputer, a child prodigy. It has to talk . . .

He looks up and sees himself reflected in a mirrored visor.

'Shut it down,' says the policewoman.

Jimmy's guts twist.

'Shut it down and put your hands on the table.'

He reads her name badge. 'What kind of bit-player are you, Hussein?' he says. It's a line from a cop show he used to watch; it's not convincing.

The tiny camera built into Tina's helmet assimilates his portrait, then transmits it and waits. He can't do anything – she has him pinned like a butterfly on a cardboard mount.

A cursor blinks inside her helmet, muddy under a film of condensation. The demisters come on automatically. Writing scrolls across the visor.

Tina reads it and says, 'I hereby inform you that as of 09:08:14 today you have been found guilty of violation of Article IV of the Data Control Act, and I warn you that – ' She pauses to read.

DETAIN PENDING CIVIL EXTRADITION ORDER

' – anything you say will be recorded and offered for sale to the registered purchaser of your sentencing licence. You have the right to request a loan from public funds for purposes of your appeal procedure before their courts.'

She turns the helmet speaker off and talks to her helmet. It confirms: SECURITY VIOLATION CLEARED * PROTEIN TECHNOLOGIES PLC SOLE BIDDERS * EXTRADITION GRANTED [NOV 9] 09:12:02 * SQUAD MOBILE AS OF [NOV 9] 09:12:43.

Tina stares at her head-up.

Squad? she thinks.

Squad?

She turns the speaker back on and the speech stress analysis package and says, 'What's your name?'

'Jimmy,' says Jimmy.

'What were you aiming?'

'Don't know,' he says. He rubs his forehead. 'The Man put it on me.'

Bells go off inside Tina's head. The Man – and now this kid with his face all scratched up. She leans towards him. 'Were you in the hit?'

'Yeah,' says Jimmy. He closes his eyes. 'It was *real* sick.'

'I heard. Any guesses what this is for?' She taps the scanalyser.

'Payroll, design specs, how the hell should I know? The Man just told me, get it.' He looks up at her and his eyes are haunted. 'You think it was – *this*? You think *this* killed her?'

Tina shrugs. 'Curiosity killed her. Bio-logic. That link in?'

Jimmy looks down at the scanalyser screen and frowns. 'Maybe. Yeah.' He rubs his forehead. 'Can I have one of my pills?'

'Show me.'

Hesitantly he reaches into his jeans pocket and gets the pack out.

'What for?'

'Migraine.'

She's not listening. She's watching data spool from the speech stress programme.

Level. All of it – level. Jimmy's not stringing a line; he's not even that tensed up, or maybe fear's such a habit with him it doesn't change his speech pattern any more. Why, Tina wonders, does Protein want to *buy* this zero?

She thinks hard. The Man died while her employee was cracking Protein's cores.

The Man died in a corporate hit.

Protein –

There is very little time.

'Stand up,' she says. 'You can come with me and sort this out or wait for the big boys to get here – it's up to you.'

They go outside. Tina puts a control cuff on him: explosives and a radio receiver slaved to her command-key. The traffic is terrible. Tina thumbs her siren, rolls through a U-turn and rumbles away with her compliant passenger. While they ride, Tina calls Control and files a holding order on the extradition.

Tina leaves Jimmy in the holding area and goes upstairs to the Intelligence suite. She sits at her terminal and runs a wringer on

Jimmy – a fifth-generation descendant of the old HOLMES and INTERPOL systems. For the first half-hour she's alone and glad of the silence.

Jimmy is a spear-carrier for the Man. No convictions. No history.

Tina sucks her teeth.

The door swings open.

Gloria settles into a seat beside her, snaps on a monitor and scans his 'In' tray. 'Well, smack my butt.' Gloria left the US aged three but he makes up by watching Swanson and Dietrich on cable. He rummages in his jacket pocket and takes out a bottle of nail varnish. 'Looks like I'm in for the afternoon.'

Tina leans back in her chair and rubs her eyes. 'How many wringers you got to do?' she asks him.

She first met Gloria during a SWAT operation on an exotics factory in New Cross. She got in the van and all the while she was field stripping her Seiko-Tally .45 she was trying to work out who this freak was opposite her, straightening a bullet-proof vest over his gold lamé trouser suit. 'Live hard, die young, and leave a beautiful corpse,' he explained to her, removing his *diamanté* earrings, and then he took the pieces of her gun from her and put them back together without ever taking his eyes off her.

'Twenty,' he replies, with a sigh. 'You?'

'I'm on a chase.'

'Lucky bitch.'

'I'm fighting a civil. Not so lucky.'

If Tina fails to find anything substantive about Jimmy's case that warrants her holding action, then every hour he's in her custody is an hour she doesn't get paid. On top of that, the law gives her only four days before the restraining order expires. She accesses the standard suite – DSS, Health, Neighbourhood Watch.

'You still balling Frost-face?' says Gloria.

'Fuck off,' says Tina, but gently.

'Never trust a straight boy,' says Gloria. He blows on his fingers. 'What you reckon?'

Tina looks at his nails. 'Like a paracetamol OD upchucked on 'em.'

'So young and so embittered.'

Tina laughs, sardonic, and turns back to the screen.

Jimmy's health records make strange reading. Migraines. MedicAid. Lots of MedicAid. Now, where did *that* come from? It doesn't take her long to trace the connection. A familiar alias. The above-board tax-and-benefits face of the Man. Not so surprising. MedicAid is a standard employee perk, and Jimmy ostensibly had a bona fide job with her. But so much money . . .

'What's eating Frosty these days, anyway?'

'Fuck knows,' says Tina, not really listening. She reads the file more closely. PSR scan, four days in hospital—

Four days?

'He say anything to you?'

'Just yelled a lot.'

'How come?'

'He found I got *teeth* inside.'

'Fancy.'

'Now stuff it, Gloria, I'm busy.'

For the most part, it reads like a standard exploratory routine for persistent head pain. They tested his sight (20/20) and intra-ocular pressure (normal), his balance (excellent) and his co-ordination (better), they gave him diet and allergy advice, offered him a psychiatric consultation (he refused), and scanned him with a PSR spectroscope (clear). Four days in hospital.

Four days.

Migraines.

'Hey, you hear the one about – ?'

Tina waves Gloria into silence and thumbs on the speaker to the holding area, grille seventeen. 'Hey Jimmy, you ever had an operation?'

Jimmy looks up at her, his face grey and distorted and grainy in the monitor above her head. 'Sure,' he says, unnerved by her voice coming out the ceiling. 'Uh . . . last year.'

'Mind telling me what? I guess I should tell you you needn't answer that. It doesn't show on your health records, so if there's a reason I shouldn't – '

'Must be a mistake,' Jimmy says. 'Sure, I don't mind. They opened my skull. Exploratory. Nothing there. Migraines, remember? Used to be real bad. Worse than now.' He winces – he's still got the attack he was getting in the bar. 'I guess.'

Tina stares at the screen, and she is very glad Jimmy cannot see her face. Oh you stupid kid, she thinks. Exploratory surgery? After a clear scan? Her mind is awhirl with pity and horror and plain greed as it slowly clicks home that Jimmy is her meal-ticket.

She snaps off the monitor. She thinks: the Man reads up on biologics, then pays for an operation; Jimmy's migraines . . .

'Hey, chile,' Gloria drawls. 'You hear the one about the dog called Porky?'

'Save it for my promotion party.'

'Happy session?'

Tina breathes deep. 'Happy-scary.'

Gloria sighs. 'Like I say. Lucky. Me, look what I get. Grid eighteen – real big-time.'

'Is?'

'Someone calling himself the Flyer.'

'He got wings?'

Gloria shrugs. 'No ID snap. Still, there's this vicar, see – '

Tina leans over to examine Gloria's monitor. There's a big black hole where the mug-shot should be. 'Glitch on your system?'

'That or they couldn't find his right side. Let's have a look at him anyway.' He patches the surveillance cameras in the holding bay and turns a couple onto bay eighteen. 'Come hither, my angel – '

And all the screens go dead.

Three

The holding area is gridded with sockets at three-metre intervals, some of them occupied by two-metre-high aluminium Christmas trees with periscopes – a taser fence. Anyone crossing between the branches walks into a painful electric shock. By using tasers they can regularly reconfigure the holding space: it foils escape plans. Jimmy isn't alone; in the adjacent cell is a person who calls himself the Flyer. He wears an old sheepskin jacket and does break-and-enter, searching apartments for their telebank numbers. Everyone keeps them on a slip of paper somewhere, in case their diary malfunctions. The Flyer flies by night, usually on dexamphetamine, which is how PowerGen caught him doing over an employee's flat; he kept typing his name over and over again on a kitchen terminal until the local Tesco got suspicious. Or so he maintains.

Jimmy stands as far away from him as possible, uncomfortably aware of the taser fence behind him and the cameras slung from the ventilation fans. The Flyer is a bearish shape, and his jacket stinks of dead skin.

Jimmy's palms are damp and his migraine pulses like a badly programmed drum kit.

The Flyer talks incessantly.

' – then Greta moved into the Isle. Bye-bye salad days. Took to the commuter lifestyle, you get me. No, I never gave Greta much line 'cos she had it in her to carve me if I fucked up. Mind, we weren't the worst of friends; I got this jacket, see, off her for a run of one of her pieces. She wanted to talk to this uppity shopkeeper's central heating. Bang!'

Jimmy blocks his ears against the Flyer's laughter and wonders what happens if you throw up on a taser?

The Flyer gesticulates wildly, hands lurid in the blood-orange light. 'I got a contact will see I get out of here in a couple of weeks, which is better than Greta. A registered bidder, like. Buying herself my sentence!' He sniggers drunkenly.

Jimmy figures that the Flyer is either on the payroll or mad. He is manic, a demented devil lost in a hell of coldly burning lights and electrified silver trees. A sudden wave of nausea grips Jimmy's stomach. He gasps for breath as his sense of balance dissolves in a crazy whirl, but his migraine refuses to let him throw up.

The Flyer won't stop talking. 'Like I says, it was them Tottenham girls zeroed Mac Morcambe. You hear about that? One of those smart bullets with a dum-dum head. Must've been quite a sight. They figured he was gunning for their wirehead operation down in Kennington.'

Jimmy shivers.

The Flyer smiles at Jimmy and whispers: 'I can give you a new identity and get you out of this shithole for free. Or my friends can finish what the grenade began. They're all around you.'

Jimmy looks about him.

Every taser in the room is aimed at him.

The cameras turn their backs and examine the far corner of the holding area for cobwebs.

Jimmy's neck prickles.

The Flyer grins and he walks through what should be fifty kilovolts. Nothing happens. 'Come on, son,' he says, and takes Jimmy by the shoulder, leading him towards a service door.

There is a corridor, lined in blue acrylic. Jimmy and the Flyer run along a catwalk which is slung two feet above ground. The handrails shake. Beneath them, fat pipes squiggle along the floor. Jimmy follows the Flyer, his viewpoint shifting and swirling in crazy migrainous patterns. There are lights in the pipes below him, pulsing. They frighten him. As they run, the fluorescents set into ceiling alcoves dazzle then go past, dazzle then go past, like they were moving too, the other way, like they were growing bright then dim as they rush past, then things get worse and they snap on off on off, thundering in his head and when the Flyer glances back his face is all collapsed, fallen in, like there was a singularity in his left eye, blinking, on off on off, and when Jimmy glances away to the near wall the light from the fluorescents is threaded and latticed upon the rough white surface and it spells words behind his eyes and the words say *Something Sweet*.

Ideograms etch their way across Jimmy's eyes.

Fragments of speech rumble like trucks through the paths of his mind.

The tunnel seems to compress and expand in all directions at once. Suddenly he is aware of the network of service ducts behind the wall, the fistulae and abcesses in the city's iron intestinal tract.

The Flyer leads Jimmy to the end of the tunnel. A spiral staircase as stark as the skeleton of some vast sea creature drills its way down to the basement.

They go down, reach doors painted red for Fire Exit, and past the doors, down, where the air gets stale, past more doors, painted blue for Car Park, and down, through other doors that should be locked (they glimmer and spark behind Jimmy's eyes and when he looks back he sees wires coming out of them, amber running lights and loops of bell wire and black tape and all the paraphernalia of the Flyer's trade) and down.

Jimmy's veins churn in the rumble of traffic – a road, above them and to the right. He stumbles on the steps and the Flyer tells him to look where he's going but all he can see are brake servos, stereos, fuel counters, cabin spies, lights and cigarette lighters and heaters and coolant pumps and fans and radio presets and CB slang.

'I think I'm blind,' Jimmy says and in his voice there's the upswell of raging panic.

The Flyer manhandles him down the steps; little by little, the further down they go, the better things get, till at last Jimmy gets his eyes back.

The spiral steps burrow into the corpse of a metro system; the London Underground has been disused for a decade, ever since the Front hit it with nerve gas. On Black Monday the bodies of a thousand civilians were laid out on the platforms at King's Cross.

'Come on now,' says the Flyer. 'We've got a train to catch.'

Jimmy follows him onto the platform.

Instantly, he becomes aware of something itchy; a feeling he's had every time he passed a power cable since leaving the holding area.

There is electricity about, an active power supply.

A hiss emanates from the tracks. Seconds later the far end of the tunnel is lit by the eerie lights of a thirty-year-old train. There is only one coach. In the driver's compartment, a grinning skeleton made out of old coat-hangers. The doors drift open and Jimmy and the Flyer get in.

'Who are we meeting?' Jimmy asks, then regrets it. It's as if, when he opened his mouth, a hot pin stabbed Morse code into his eyes.

'The Flyer just shakes his head. 'She scares the shits out of me.'

Tina hits the alarm plate. Gloria thumbprints a pad protruding from a white cabinet. It recognises him, clicks and opens: inside it are three Weizenbaum A100-E 'ware-guided rifles and a rack of Zeiss protocol cartridges. Tina comes over, picks out two and hands one to Gloria. She plugs the other into the ROM-port behind the chamber of her rifle.

Gloria thumbs open another cabinet, hands Tina her helmet and jacket, then puts on his own. Print surfaces come to life inside their visors. Tina eyeballs the operations suite on her rifle.

The rifle obediently chambers a round.

Gloria opens the door and they sprint down the stairs. There are others at their backs; security personnel from the floor above. Others will follow – they are still suiting up. Ahead of them, the service door opens; Control has Tina's commslink and is helping them. Tina darts into the tunnel, rifle ready, guessing that Jimmy and the Flyer won't have hung around for her.

Her helmet video prints up a message; the wringer on the Flyer is all fucked up – a mish-mash of crossed files and corrupt data.

Gloria comes up beside her. 'A plant,' he says, unnecessarily.

They come to the staircase. Now Tina knows where they've gone.

She radios Control and negotiates the operation. She tells the police around her and her superiors what she's found out about Jimmy. Her mind is racing. Between calls she dials the surveillance library for a picture – any picture – of the Flyer. Archive time for the holding bays is sixteen hours but she can't patch anything; something must be already scrubbing them. The Flyer has sewn up Control's surveillance systems.

Then Gloria, his helmeted head tilted at an odd angle and his gloved fingers jittering as he dials systems and reads from the print surface on the inside of his visor, lets out a curse. 'Lobby footage,' he says to Tina. 'He didn't get to the lobby footage.' Then – an uncharacteristic gesture – he reaches out and touches Tina's arm, gently, with his datagloved hand. 'You won't like it.'

The fingers of his left hand writhe, and he ports the picture to the inside of Tina's visor.

It's Foster's face inside her helmet.
Then it comes together.
The cancelled diary.
Four minutes' delay and a lost witness.
Foster?
Foster.

The train rattles through a couple more stations, then Jimmy feels a shift in his balance on the seat as the train slows down. A needle beneath a dusty dial cover in the seat opposite him stirs itself as the brake pressure climbs.

The sign on the platform reads E M B A N K M E N T.

The train stops and the doors open. The Flyer gets out and waits impatiently for Jimmy.

'Come here,' says the Flyer. Jimmy obeys and follows him to the end of the platform, and an exit blocked by a massive armoured door. Looking up, he sees the eye of a camera gleaming at him.

With a grating of rusty metal, the flood barrier rolls up until it is poised like a giant guillotine above the doorway. They go through.

Bonsai oak trees, a waist-high avenue of foliage between walls rich in Picasso, Seurat and Tanguy. Jimmy doesn't recognize most of them but he knows they are originals. They stink of time and money.

'Jimmy, say hello to Josephine.'

Jimmy stares at the Flyer's employer, whose name is Josephine, and sees the realisation of his fears. The Man could be her twin sister. Her retarded twin sister.

'Hello,' he says tentatively. The Flyer steps back and removes his jacket.

'Hello, Jimmy.' She moves towards him and takes his hand. 'Come on in.' Her hand is small and cool in his. 'Do you like this place?'

Jimmy nods, taking the path of least resistance.

'It's not mine. I borrowed it, from a friend of yours. You know who I mean, don't you, Jimmy?'

Jimmy can guess.

'Listen,' says Josephine, 'I need something of yours, something very special. Do you remember Doctor Dexter?'

Jimmy lifts a hand to his forehead without thinking. A blur of red lines has smeared across the centre of his vision. His mind is becoming more sensitive to electrical fields.

'My headache,' Jimmy mumbles. He cradles his forehead in

his hands. 'Dexter looked after me in the clinic.' The red lines are firming up. They twist and turn like angry snakes. They menace his sanity.

Josephine glances at the Flyer. 'Get the doctor. We're leaving in five. You sure you want to stay here?'

The Flyer nods. 'I'll have to join you later. I've got to pull the suckers on Protein's cores.'

'I don't imagine you have more than fifteen minutes.'

The Flyer grins. 'Don't worry about it.'

'Don't get shot,' says Josephine, carelessly, like she was a mother telling her child to mind the roads.

Behind Jimmy's eyes, the red lines shimmer into place – alphanumerics. Abstracts from research papers. Foetal cerebellar tissue left over from abortions used to cure Parkinsonism. Embryonic nerves reproduced, grown to replace the burnt-out tissue of the *substantia nigra*. Immature brain tissue used to patch up the living. Jimmy sees another document.

A self-referential one.

Something Sweet.

He shouts, and lashes out, and spins, and spins, and spins.

Pixel by pixel, the world is going out.

Four

WAKE UP.

Jimmy is slumped against someone. His head is tilted on one side – his cheek is pressed against something scratchy. Overstarched fabric stretched tight over a padded shoulder.

Josephine, he thinks.

He groans.

SHUT UP. KEEP STILL.

It is very dark. He cannot see anything. He does not recognise the voice.

YOU ARE IN DANGER.

He feels his arms and legs moving of their own accord, stretching and twisting with an idiot's intensity, simulating the movements of sleep. There is a blanket thrown over him, up to his chest; it prickles his hands.

Below the padded shoulder, he feels hardness, an arm from shoulder to elbow – Josephine's. It presses against him and draws back and then it hits him hard, to hurt, in the ribs.

EASY.

Jimmy whimpers and leans away from her. He is barely conscious; his head is too heavy and it falls to the other side; it collides softly with another shoulder, a different, more abrasive fabric. A sports coat. Jimmy sniffs, smells bad, expensive aftershave – a brand he recognises.

DOCTOR DEXTER.

The voice could easily be mistaken for the promptings of memory, or for the monologue of conscience -- but it is not a voice at all.

Control seconds Tina to the day's SWAT team. Gloria's on the list today, so they ride together in the van.

There is someone new in booth 110 – someone reliable. The armoured carrier rises three feet into the air and sweeps towards Embankment, the Man's old fortress, riding green lights all the way.

Automatics divert traffic away from Embankment then seal the road.

Southern & Eastern PLC clears Hungerford rail bridge and terminates all EMR services from Charing Cross until further notice.

Control assigns local patrols to Villiers Street. They clear the area around the old Tube station seconds before the SWAT van swings side-on to its northern entrance.

Tina runs across the street, takes cover behind the concrete hulk of a WundaLoo and calls Control.

There has been no contact with the core-breaking team assigned to the Man's old home in Embankment for at least five hours. Jo on the desk hadn't thought anything of it, figuring they'd got sick of the sight of the Man's terminals and were maintaining e-comms silence in a pub somewhere.

Tina scrolls the manifest; instantly, Jo is forgiven.

Rowley, James, Lydgate, Topor: Piss-heads, all. And Foster.

Tina routes Hendon Archives' groundplans of Embankment through her helmet into the rifle's Zeiss interface, then watches for when the team can cover her as far as the station entrance.

Her rifle wishes her luck.

Jimmy is in the back seat of a car, slumped between Josephine and Doctor Dexter. The seat beneath him surges uneasily.

MS JOSEPHINE BARR WANTS SOMETHING SWEET. SHE KILLED THE MAN FOR IT. SHE BROKE PROTEIN TECHNOLOGIES' CORES FOR IT. SHE WILL KILL YOU.

Dexter? Dr Dexter? Dr Dexter works for Josephine – Josephine

Barr? Jimmy senses betrayal, wakes up a fraction, opens his eyes. There is no light anywhere. Jimmy has never known a night as black as this.

THE TIME IS 14:14 GMT. And before Jimmy can utter his dismay: DEXTER HAS ANAESTHETISED YOUR OPTIC NERVE.

Jimmy makes to cry out but his voice gets cut off, strangled, as if the owner of the voice which is not a voice has somehow put a hand round his throat.

THEY HAVE BLINDED YOU TO CONTROL YOU MORE EASILY. THEY DO NOT CARE ABOUT YOU. THEY CARE ABOUT ME.

Jimmy at last recognises the voice – it is himself; it is the ceaseless, organic tirade of his own conciousness. Something Sweet is coming on-line, heading for synergy; picking up emissions with its neural antennae, adding Jimmy's optic and speech centres to its own calculation spaces. Lay every cell in Jimmy's tumour end to end, they would stretch to the moon and back.

'There's this country vicar, right?'

'For fuck's sake, Gloria,' Tina mutters through her throat-mike, as she shimmies along the wall towards the dead escalators. Someone – she can guess who – has turned off all the lights. The rifle looks through its IR targeting eye and ports a super-real monochrome simulation of the station onto the print-surface of her visor: better than night goggles.

'He says goodbye to his congregation, swings shut the mossy oak door, locks up the porch gate and walks through the churchyard; he sniffs the pollen-scented air and smiles. It's a bright June day, a light breeze, a few cotton-wool clouds – '

'*This* is a joke?'

'He lets himself out through the lych-gate and wends his way home through an avenue of lime trees.'

'Levy, run a bike on remote down the Up escalator.'

'*Check.*'

One of the team's five Yamahas rumbles forward on automatic, fat tyres squeaking on the slip-proof tiles, and begins its descent.

'Cover me, I'm watching the bike,' says Tina, and she eyeballs a new commslink. The monochrome station dissolves; now she is looking through the bike's IR eye as it rolls down to the tunnels below.

Something twists its way into Tina's head-up. Something red. Her helmet peeps.

'Fuck,' Tina says, and the bike explodes.

'*No playing on the escalators,*' says Levy, once they've had a chance to shake the concussion out their ears.

'*Hand-enamelled, too,*' says Finn, with a sigh.

Gloria snakes towards the escalator mouth. '*And as he walks he spies in the distance a little girl, five, six years old, dressed all in pink, with a pink ribbon in her hair, and she is walking a little dog on a leash . . .*'

My eyes. Jimmy thinks, desperately, *my eyes . . .*

YOUR EYES HAVE BEEN PERMANENTLY DAMAGED.

Doctor Dexter –

Suddenly the blackness is punctuated by bursts of white light. They shimmer and resolve themselves into letters from an alien alphabet, then shift in a way Jimmy cannot follow into readable English.

Jimmy wants to cry out with relief, but his throat is cramped once again.

YOU DO NOT NEED TO SPEAK.

Jimmy reads, feverishly, more for the relief of seeing than to understand what has been written:

CHAIR BY SNOWDON

SOFTWOOD TABLE WITH METAL TRESTLE SUPPORT AND SEPIA PLASTIC LAMINATE WORK SURFACE WITH DESIGN DERIVED FROM 23 ENVELOPE ALBUM COVER

A PAIR OF POLISH IMPORT WORKING TROUSERS TORN AT LEFT KNEE

'SHITTED' BY GILBERT AND GEORGE (ORIGINAL)

The words dissolve, to be replaced by others, and the process repeats, faster and faster, until Jimmy in his confusion forgets to panic – and he wonders almost idly whether the list unfolding before him is simply a clever ruse by which to calm him, or whether there is more to it.

ANTIQUE KENWOOD MUSIC SYSTEM, STEREO FOAM-BACKED INDUSTRIAL-WEAR GREY CARPET, WALL-TO-WALL, HAND-FITTED, CRUDE WORKMANSHIP

The words in his eyes swim and coagulate. Black and white shapes intersect and snap together – something complex and geometric is bootstrapping itself from the literal chaos – it is a room. A bedroom made from bits of letters, from blocks of light and shadow. A bedroom in dazzle paint.

The windows are opening in Jimmy's head – images of the things in the room assault his ruined eyes; they bloom and complexify, diagrammatically expressing their specifications, their geometrical relationship to the room's other objects, and suddenly Jimmy's head does not feel like an enclosed space at all, but a curved surface, utterly exposed, a gateway folded back on itself, a place that is no place.

There are bombs everywhere.

Tina's is not the only team attempting to penetrate Embankment. Control reports two dead and one injured by a blast in the tunnel between Temple and Embankment. The Waterloo stretch is clear, but the tunnel mouth has enough gear around it to breach the river bed if it goes up.

Finn drives up the steps connecting Northern to District & Circle West. She tops the rise and sees Levy and Perloff on the opposite platform, giving her cover.

'"It warms my heart to see such a pretty girl done up so daintily on a Sunday morning," – device deactivated on Eastbound exit – says the vicar and the little girl blushes. "Where did you get such a beautiful dress?" "Mummy made it for me," says the girl, proudly.'– Shit we've got another. – "Oh, how delightful," says the vicar, "and what a beautiful little dog!"'

Tina rides down the tunnel to join Levy and Perloff; when she arrives they clamber over to the Westbound platform. Lights either end of the tunnel blink on – other SWAT units, ready to advance.

Finn's bike is parked by the service door leading to the Man's warren. She's crouched behind it, head cocked to one side, listening to her rifle.

'"Mummy and I gave it an ickle bath this morning," says the girl. The vicar chuckles. The bright summer sunlight plays in the little girl's hair, and in the rusty pelt of the dog. The vicar pats the girl, then bends down and pats the dog.'

On the wall behind Finn's bike there's a damp-streaked poster advertising an arcade chain.

It says BOMB THE BASTARDS.

A living room blinks into existence around him. Bright, vibrant, unreal colour. Super-realist precision. He can see the table, and the trousers, flung over a tubular chair, and the Gilbert and George mounted on the wall above the table. He can count dust particles in the far corner of the room. He can see the door, and he can see that the door is locked and he can picture the numeric code for it, and he unlocks it.

But when he goes to push open the door, he finds that he cannot.

This is because he is not there. (His buttocks spasm with pain and he rubs his cheek feverishly against Dexter's shoulder.)

Jimmy is an aerial spirit gifted with second sight, wheeling about in a strange room; but at the same time he remains inside his own body – and his body is trapped in a car heading for an unknown destination.

PATIENCE, exhorts the voice that is not a voice.

Someone presses the buttons to unlock the already open door and the Flyer walks into the room. He looks straight at Jimmy.

Jimmy flinches. (Back in the car, some vestige of the gesture must have communicated itself to his body. Dexter takes Jimmy's hand in his own and squeezes – the doctor's hand is shaking, and for a dizzying second Jimmy is unsure whether he is being comforted, or whether in fact Dexter is seeking comfort from him.) The room again: the Flyer walks right through Jimmy – through the place where Jimmy had pictured himself standing – and goes up to the cupboard in the corner (MAHOGANY c.1991).

Jimmy tentatively identifies the room: it is part of the Man's apartment.

Jimmy watches the Flyer arm himself from the cache in the cupboard. He is whistling.

Jimmy studies the weapons one by one. The Flyer arms and readies them, peering now and again at their LCD readouts.

Then he reaches into the cupboard and takes out a police helmet. He puts it on and cocks his head at an odd angle, as if he is listening to something.

Back in the car, Jimmy swallows painfully. He does not understand what the Flyer is preparing for, but he knows he does not want to watch it when it happens. He closes his eyes – but he has no eyes to close.

His sight is trapped inside Josephine's apartment as surely as his body is trapped between Dexter and Barr.

Levy and Perloff have joined Finn by the door. Perloff checks the jambs and finds photosensors. They retreat to the far end of the platform. Finn mounts her rifle on her bike's firing rack and plays with the bike's e-comm panel. Tina jumps from the Eastbound platform onto the line. The power-rail is dead but she doesn't trust it, steps over gingerly, lifts herself up onto the Westbound platform and talks to Control.

Still no word from Rowley, Topor or the others.

A second team gun their bikes up the steps from Northern. Gloria covers them from the Eastbound platform as they take up positions. Then he aims his gun at the door and as he aims he says, '*So the vicar, quite enchanted by the pair, says, "Little girl, what is your delightful, well-groomed little dog called?" And the girl says –* '

Gloria fires, takes out the hinges and the locks. The door explodes. Finn puts her hands to her helmet, an autonomic gesture as she handshakes the bike, and she guns it towards the dust-clouded breach.

The bike wobbles until its own gyros mesh, and it burns rubber all the way to the door. Then it stops, wheels round, and guns back down the platform towards them.

Finn screams a warning – the bike's not in her control any more and they can all guess who's hi-jacked the uplink.

'*Porky*,' says Gloria, and takes aim at the bike. His gun refuses to fire.

The rifle mounted on the bike opens up.

Bullets lift Levy and Finn off their feet. Perloff leaps for the rail track and meets a third S WAT team bowling through the station mouth. He lies across the rails, screaming a lot. It sounds as if he'll never stop. Control cuts off his e-comm.

The bike swerves and heads for Tina. Gloria snaps the Zeiss cartridge out of the chamber of his rifle, presses the reset button and aims again.

The bike speeds up, stabilises and aims itself at Tina.

Gloria fires and blows its front wheel off. It falls forward, its forks mash the tiling for a couple of yards then dig into the cement beneath. The bike bounces high, hits the station roof, falls side-up on the platform and slides to a stop three feet away from where Tina is standing.

Far away, down the corridor, there is a shout, an inarticulate garble of noise culminating in the flat crackle of automatic weapons.

The Flyer moves to the door, fast and silent, opens it and goes out. Jimmy's eyes follow him unwillingly into the corridor.

Blue bike-lights penetrate the gloom of the unlit passage; the police have broken into the apartment.

The Flyer reaches into his jacket and in one motion he bowls two small metal devices down the corridor, and flattens himself against the door of the room opposite.

Explosions bloom like stop-motion roses and a helmeted head comes rolling along the floor towards him. The helmet comes off

and in the light of a burning painting Jimmy sees there's something caught between the head's teeth, kicking and struggling – a tongue.

There's one bike still rolling down the corridor, out of control, its driver howling and kicking about as though the bike has somehow ensnared him. Jimmy flings himself out of its way – and remains exactly where he is. (Back in the car, he mashes his head against the roof and something hard and small punches in his ribs to the left of his solar plexus, winding him. 'Control him, Doctor!' Josephine's voice is as vicious as her fist.)

His eyes are still trapped in the corridor. Something Sweet is processing this visual simulation from video pictures transmitted by cameras set into the apartment ceiling.

The wall by Jimmy's virtual 'head' is laced with blood and scraps of flesh.

NO; JACKSON POLLOCK, Something Sweet admonishes him.

There is more gunfire, wild and misdirected. Instinctively Jimmy turns his head in the direction of the sound and *Something Sweet is satisfied with Jimmy's progress; it releases him from its consensual grip. Now Jimmy can run unhampered through every conduit and switch and bell-wire and video uplink in the apartment.*

> he is in a different place, and
> has a thousand eyes. The lights
> flicker. All of a sudden, Jimmy
> is everywhere.

'*"Porky"*, *says the girl in the pink dress. The vicar scratches his head and looks at the dog, and back at the girl. "Porky?" he says –* '

Tina's halfway down the hall, breathing fast. The walls of the corridor are streaked with blood. At the end of the hall the burning bike fills the antechamber with smoke, concealing the spaces within; when she uses IR on her head-up all she gets is a thirty-second loop of Road Runner.

Foster's wired his helmet to segue with the team's Zeiss 'ware. Every piece of equipment they carry has become a potential booby-trap. Tina's feet slip and slide on the wet rubble where Alice Browning from the Waterloo SWAT made the mistake of asking her grenade where it wanted to be thrown.

Gloria's right behind Tina. '*"That's a strange name for your pretty*

*little dog," says the vicar. "Why do you call him Porky?" And the little
girl says – '*

Through the black smoke, something bright glimmers for an instant. Gloria kicks the back of Tina's knee, Tina goes with the blow
and Gloria falls on top of her, shielding her as the auto opens up.

Jimmy bounces through the station's videocameras. The gun
battle frightens and disgusts him. With a sick twist in his stomach
(wherever it is), Jimmy realises that the police don't stand a
chance. The Flyer's too quick, he has hidden arsenals all over the
apartment and the station, and he seems to know their tactics.
Jimmy examines Foster's helmet. It's got e-comms links with one
of the Man's old computers. Jimmy takes a look. It's running
programs he can't begin to fathom. It looks like the Flyer's
directing half his battle by remote control. One of the subroutines
is crunching a graphics loop. For a while Jimmy watches the
Road Runner clip, but he can't forget the screams of the police
when the Flyer first opened up. He wonders whose side he
should be on and realises with an uncomfortable twinge that it
sure as hell can't be the Flyer's. Back in the holding area, Jimmy
recalls, the Flyer as good as said it was him took out the Man.

Gloria falls across Tina's upper back, winding her. Behind them,
other team members return fire.

'Gloria?' Tina can barely breathe with him on top of her.
'Gloria, get the fuck off!'

She stares ahead. The smoke is closer now. And through it the
glimmer of a targeting laser fluoresces the gloom.

'Gloria! Fuck off!'

She kicks and punches herself free. She pulls herself up into
the path of friendly fire. He e-comm channel howls a warning
and at the same time her hands slip in the pool of blood
spreading from Gloria's chest.

Behind the burning bike something glimmers.

The SWAT team dive for cover and the grenade brings the roof in
on top of them. Tina crouches over Gloria and takes his datagloved
hand in her own. She screams at him but she can't hear herself.
Her visor is spattered with blood from her bleeding nose.

Gloria's fingers move in odd patterns. He's typing. She turns
her visor back on.

Road Runner honks and swerves around the Coyote's rock
again; across the blood-specked sky an e-comm banner proclaims: *'cos he fucks pigs*

*

Jimmy returns to the battle. Everything is still. Jimmy, appalled, tries to comprehend what he is seeing.

There is no one left alive.

No one but Foster. And there, another shape, crawling out from beneath a corpse.

Gloria is still at last. Tina lets go of his hand. Nothing moves. The air in her helmet is foul and acrid – her filters are packing up. She shimmies over the rubble towards the entrance. Now and again through the smoke and dust she glimpses bits of bodies.

She can see the platform now. She's lost her rifle, and she reaches to her hip for the Tally-Seiko.

Foster comes up behind her, grabs her hand, twists it behind her back and pulls.

Tina screams and scrambles to her knees.

Foster leads her sobbing and scuffling to the entrance and drops her. He takes her gun and wrestles her helmet off her head. He walks to the edge of the platform and looks around.

Nothing moves.

Satisfied, he turns back to Tina. 'I'm sorry,' he says. He shrugs and laughs. 'I guess that's all. Strange: I thought this might happen. It really is difficult for me. I'm – so sorry.'

Tina can't hear him. She doesn't respond. She's seen the movies. She knows what's coming.

Jimmy watches the Tally-Seiko's cross-hairs scan the wall and settle on the policewoman. Now he knows her.

It's the policewoman who stopped Protein from buying him; who saved him, after a fashion.

Above her there is a poster.

Through his thousand eyes, Jimmy reads:

BOMB THE BASTARDS.

The words assault his eyes, as potent in their own way as 'Something Sweet' has been. Reading them, he remembers the assassination; the Man had stood no more chance that day than Tina does now.

Suddenly, it occurs to him that she doesn't have to die.

'Hey, Foster,' Tina croaks, her voice quivering because she can't hear to control it. 'Don't I get a cigarette?'

Across her visor letters from an alien alphabet blink into existence. They warp in ways her eyes cannot follow and coalesce to form:

WHAT KIND OF BIT PLAYER ARE YOU, HUSSEIN?

The Flyer aims the Tally-Seiko at Tina's face and pulls the trigger. The gun fires wide. He frowns, reads the LCD on the bridge of the gun.

Where the status line should be it says:

ACME GUN CO.

He snarls, presses the eject on the Zeiss-port and throws the cartridge behind him on to the line. He shoots again. The bullet jams in the chamber and the gun explodes, taking half his hand off. He screams and topples off the platform.

That, Jimmy thinks, *is for the Man*. He zooms the station's last intact platform camera at Tina. She's breathing hard, not moving. There's blood trickling down her neck from where her ear-drums are busted.

Foster leans up and tries to stand. Above him, from cobwebbed tannoys, an ancient voice thunders: '*Mind the Gap*.'

Foster gets to his feet, looks round him wildly and spots Tina. She's pressed herself up against the wall, hands by her sides, staring at him.

He snarls and reaches inside his jacket. He brings out a Thompson-Ramsaye .45.

All a Ramsaye does is fire bullets. There's not one damn thing Jimmy can do about that. Jimmy shouts. Jimmy screams. He flails about. Dexter gets a grip on his arm with both hands and Josephine Barr gasps and shifts away fast. 'For fuck's sake,' she mutters.

Foster aims for Tina's head. He doesn't shoot well with his left hand, and he's close to blacking out. The bullet goes in low. The dum-dum head rips her bullet-proof apart and the explosive core detonates in her stomach.

In rage and frustration Jimmy hits out. His right fist mashes itself into the headrest of the front passenger seat, his legs kick and kick again against the entangling folds of the blanket, his left arm arcs back and catches Josephine in the mouth,

and somewhere beneath the rails a circuit flips and Foster, crouched with one foot on the power rail and one on the dirty shingle rail bed, starts dancing and jiving and shedding sparks like there was a party going on inside him.

Jimmy refocuses on Tina. There is a lot of blood.

'I'm sorry,' he says. Josephine, who assumes this apology is directed at her, punches him in the mouth anyway.

'I'm not very good at this yet,' says Jimmy through broken teeth, 'and I didn't understand and it happened too quick and I – I'm so sorry.'

'Oh *shit*,' Tina says, in between screams.

Jimmy grits his teeth: from its siding, the Tube train rumbles forward. It rolls into the station. Foster's bones crackle beneath its wheels.

Jimmy blinks and the doors open.

Tina crawls towards the carriage and lifts herself over the lip of the deck. Her feet don't quite clear the doors before she passes out.

Jimmy blinks again. The doors close, gripping her calves. The train pulls out of the smoking station.

The ride is smooth now – Jimmy feels the car ascend a tollway ramp, and by the sound of the engine they're cruising near to maximum on a virtually empty private highway. It is very quiet in the car, quiet too in Jimmy's inner ear. Something Sweet has stopped talking to him; it no longer needs to.

Jimmy's eyes tighten shut as he concentrates. Silently, the car's cellphone dials Tower Control.

Five

St James's Park Underground: the police have received an anonymous tip-off, and have forced access to the disused station. Engineers assemble halogen lamps, aim them at the tarnished rail and at the far wall. The damp-rotted remains of advertising hoardings shimmer like an undersea surface. A medical team waits on the damp-streaked platform for Tina Hussein to emerge from the tunnel. They hear the train before they see it. When it clears the tunnel they race forward to the carriage from which Tina's legs dangle. They are a bloody mess. The pneumatic doors have acted like a crude tourniquet, otherwise she would already be dead from shock. Her pulse is one fifty, her blood pressure seventy over thirty-five. Her heart sounds are muddy – indecipherable. Her pupils do not respond to light.

They carry her out of the station towards the ambulance. Its sirens are already at pitch.

Police with bomb disposal gear struggle down the tunnel towards Embankment, looking for Tina's feet. They can't use bikes because this stretch of line was never modernised; there's a three-foot-deep inspection trench where the rail bed should be.

The ambulance jockeys the traffic to St Thomas's; the chief paramedic calls his crash team and tells them you could strain greens through Tina's stomach. Her spleen is ruptured, her aorta's lacerated and there's possible cardiac damage.

Tina goes straight into theatre. The surgeon administers a cardioplegic, plugs her circulation into a heat exchanger and takes her body temperature down into the low twenties.

She's on the operating table for seventeen hours.

The police recover her left foot, but they can't find the other one anywhere.

Josephine drives for the last half-hour. Rain lashes the car windows. Jimmy wonders what has happened to the driver who had taken them this far.

Jimmy knows they must be getting close to Josephine's house because the car is wobbling about and he can hear snow crunch under the tyres – what is more, there is a house-shaped carnival of electrical fields jigging about behind his eyes. The car stops and Dexter leads him gently out into a strong, fresh wind. Jimmy looks round, playing blind, but already he can tell that the house is full of the kind of toys he's suspected Josephine might own. Lots of cameras – and, on the floor above, a fragile blue line: an IBCN cable. Jacked into it (a faint greenish fuzz behind his eyes) is a telephone.

Dexter leads Jimmy through the front door. Jimmy sniffs, maps the house, handshakes Josephine's computer, connects with the nearest satellite and listens in on its telemetry, figures from this the exact latitude and longitude of his present position (somewhere forgettable in Banffshire – OS map number 29), learns the sort and access codes to every one of Josephine's bank accounts, swallows hard at the sum total of Josephine's wealth – about four billion ECUs – measures the power consumption of the teasmade alarm clock by Josephine's bed, learns what time the alarm is set for, and the station to which the alarm is tuned, catalogues the security equipment around the house, the protocols by which the surveillance cameras survey each room, and how to control them – and wonders: What's in the basement? Whatever it is, there is a lot of it; it fills his dead eyes with virtual light.

Josephine dumps Jimmy untidily in a corner and turns on the television. Driving tires her. She needs a rest.

It's Jimmy's face on the screen. He is smiling. Where his eyes should be there are black pits belching smoke (a little poetic licence on Jimmy's part). Josephine lets out a scream of shock and dismay.

Dexter comes in with a cup of coffee.

'On-line,' says Jimmy.

He drops it.

'Bad,' Jimmy admonishes him. 'Axminster.'

Josephine turns away a moment and when she turns back she has managed to force her face into a smile. 'Forgive me,' she says. 'You startled me.'

Jimmy frowns.

'Well, my boy,' says Dexter, 'this *is* wonderful news. Take a seat by the fire.' He takes Jimmy's elbow and leads him to a sofa by the empty fireplace. 'Can I get you anything? Milk? Fruit juice? I'm afraid I can't offer you alcohol or caffeine – doctor's orders!' There is something false in his chuckle, but Jimmy is too phased by this abrupt shift in the way they are treating him to care much about such niceties.

'Can you see?' Josephine asks, solicitous. 'I installed the cameras especially for you.'

Jimmy stares at her. 'But Sweet said – '

Dexter leans over and pats his knee. 'I expect Something Sweet uttered a lot of paranoid nonsense at you, Jimmy,' he says. (Dexter has an excellent bed-side manner.) 'Forget it. Something Sweet is an acquisition/retrieval system. The interpretation of data is a job for you, for *your* conscious and subconscious processes. As the two systems equilibrate, your own mind and Something Sweet, so there may be disparities, mistakes: nonsense.'

'But why – ?'

'Orange juice?' Josephine hands him a tumbler.

'Thank you,' says Jimmy, taken aback.

'The anaesthetic will wear off in about six hours,' Dexter assures him. 'Something Sweet needs time to clock and hand-shake your visual cortex; it needs to establish itself behind your eyes. That is why I turned off your sight for a while.'

'Oh.'

Jimmy wonders whether to ring the police. He decides against it. Without eyes he can't escape, and if the law take him Protein will buy him and he'll be laboratory meat within the week. And as for Dexter and Barr – people like that don't stay in jail very long.

'Cigarette?' Josephine offers him a Gauloise. Then Dexter takes him to see the basement.

The room is windowless and low-ceilinged. It is so bright Jimmy must shield his eyes against the glare. Up against the wall there is a slime-green fish-tank on a trolley. In the centre of the room is an old leather easy chair with the stuffing leaking from its seams, and a desk so old and battered it might be made of real wood. Upon the desk are a rusty in-tray, a Black & Decker circular saw and an antique Amstrad PC.

Dexter smiles when he sees Jimmy staring, then leads him to the easy chair. 'Do sit down. I want you to look at a snapshot.' He takes it out of the in-tray and hands it over.

Jimmy looks.

It is a picture of two men in a fist-fight.

While he is looking, Dexter bends and taps at his keyboard. 'This room is wired,' he says.

'I know,' Jimmy replies.

'Of course you do.'

'What's it for?' Jimmy looks round at the blank, magnolia-painted walls. His eyes have adapted to the electromagnetic glare; it no longer pains him.

Dexter taps some more. 'In a moment. How do you feel?'

'Fine,' says Jimmy.

'Uh-huh.' Dexter peers into his archaic monitor. 'The photograph – it doesn't excite you?'

'No.'

Dexter grins. 'Liar.'

'What?' Jimmy is shocked.

'Nothing so unsubtle as an intentional lie. But this gadget' – Dexter taps the side of his PC – 'knows. You are sitting at the core of a phased-array magnetic-field generator. The combined high-field ESR is capable of monitoring the output of any given neurone in your skull.'

'Really?' says Jimmy, impressed. 'Which one?'

'Josephine bought it for me. Or rather, her employers did.'

'Protein, you mean?'

Josephine comes in. She is wearing a black raincoat. Maybe she's been out parking the car.

Dexter turns to her. 'Jimmy here wants to know who he's working for.'

'Protein's main competitor, Jimmy,' Josephine says. She walks around the back of Jimmy's chair and massages his shoulders.

'Congratulations, Jimmy,' says Dexter, studying his monitor once more.

'What for?' asks Jimmy, flattered and bewildered. He stretches luxuriantly. Josephine is an excellent masseuse.

'I'm running a program which will tell us if it's safe to continue,' Dexter explains. 'It tells me you're A-Okay to undergo the second stage of our operation.'

'What's that?' Jimmy asks, intrigued.

'Installation and customisation,' says Josephine. 'Not Protein's idea, of course. Self-annealing optical implants are not their field, and that's what you need for this.'

'For what?' Jimmy insists, impatient and uneasy all of a sudden.

Dexter points at the fish tank. 'We're going to put your brain in that,' he says.

Jimmy looks at the tank and laughs; the laughter dies away. There are wires in the soup-green water: struts and lattices and spines of burnished metal. They catch the light. The water pulses with a strange, undersea rhythm.

Dexter hits the ENTER key. The fish tank bubbles and fluoresces. Migraine skewers Jimmy's brain and his eyes fill with alphanumerics. He gasps with pain. His eyes fill with tears, and through them he reads:

ACHEBE NANO-OPTICS (SYSTEMS) INC

The words blink out. Too late, Jimmy realises his mistake. The fish tank is alive.

He turns in panic, sees Josephine's black plastic raincoat; he recognises it. He looks up at her. 'Hey,' he says, 'you killed the Man's chauff – '

Josephine leans forward and slips a knife into Jimmy's carotid artery, just below the sternocleidomastoid.

Blood leaps from the puncture in arcs four foot high.

Josephine pulls him back into the chair. The fish tank parks itself nearby and gurgles happily. Dexter picks up his Black & Decker from the desk and revs it. Dizzily, Jimmy wonders what to do now.

Some of his panic must be getting through to his tumour; suddenly a terrible falsetto voice inside his head screeches:

MBTHEBASTARDSBOMBTHEBASTARDSBOMBT
HEBASTARDSBOMBTHEBASTARDSBOMBTHEBA

But Jimmy, in the few seconds of life remaining to him, has a better idea.

The End

On the day of Sergeant Tina Hussein's leaving party, Inspector Emily Lerner is called away to show Sergeant David Hirst around Tower Control. Afterwards she sits him down with a coffee in her glass-walled inner office and tells him who he's replacing.

'Gloria was one of my best men,' she says.

Sergeant Hirst nods. 'Sure.'

'So if they give you a hard time out there,' says Lerner, gesturing at the nearly empty outer office, 'it's just their way of coping. Things will get better in time. Be patient with us. We lost a lot of friends recently.'

The door to the outer office swings open and a woman enters. She walks slowly to her desk, her legs rigid.

'That her?' Hirst asks his new chief.

Lerner nods. 'That's her.'

'She's transferring?'

'Quitting. Says she's going back to college.'

Hirst swirls coffee dregs around his plastic cup. 'Is it true – I mean, I hear she got new feet.'

'Feet. Spleen. Aorta. Heart. Flown in from São Paulo specially.' Lerner thinks a moment. 'You know much about this case?'

'Some,' says Hirst. 'I was running surveillance on a dodgy share deal at London Stock Exchange that Friday. The grid reference for that Banffshire house hijacked every Reuters board in the building.'

The woman with new feet has cleared out her desk. She slides the drawers shut. She picks a pen and paper out of her jacket pocket and writes something.

'Barr still operating on this patch?' Hirst asks, turning from the window.

'We won't be seeing Barr or Dexter ever again,' Lerner replies. 'Life sentences, both.'

Hirst shakes his head, puzzled. 'You mean no one bought them? Protein? Achebe?'

'Achebe tried. They were outbid.'

'Who by?'

Lerner nods at Tina Hussein's retreating back.

Hirst frowns. 'A cop buys out a combine? With what?'

Lerner shrugs. 'Someone sent a four billion ECU credit transfer to put her back together again – and told her to keep the change.'

Tina totters out of the office, her ankles supported by the temporary exoskeleton. As she goes she drops a piece of paper onto Gloria's desk.

Tomorrow morning the new kid will find it.

Live hard, it says. *Die young.*

And leave a beautiful corpse.

FOAM

Brian W. Aldiss

'There's nothing for it when you reach the Point
of No Return – except to come back.'

E. James Carvell

Many Central and Eastern European churches
had been dismantled. The deconstruction of Chartres
Cathedral was proceeding smartly, unhindered by Operation
Total Tartary.

On the previous day, a guide had taken me around Budapest Anthropological Museum. I had wanted to see the *danse
macabre* preserved there, once part of the stonework of the
cathedral at Nagykanizsa. Although the panel was in poor
condition, it showed clearly the dead driving the living to the
grave.

The dead were represented by skeletons, frisky and grinning. The line of the living began with prelates in grand
clothes, the Pope leading. Merchants came next, men and
women, then a prostitute; a beggar brought up the rear,
these allegorical figures representing the inescapable grada-
tions of decay.

As I was making notes, measuring, and sketching in my
black notebook, the guide was shuffling about behind me,
impatient to leave. I had special permission to be in the
gallery. Jangling her keys more like a gaoler than an attendant, she went to gaze out of a narrow window at what could
be seen of the prosperous modern city, returning to peer
over my shoulder and sniff.

'A disgusting object,' she remarked, gesticulating with an
open hand towards the frieze, which stood severed and out of
context on a display bench in front of me.

'"What is beauty, saith my sufferings then?"' I quoted
abstractedly. To me the *danse macabre* was a work of art,
skilfully executed; nothing more than that. I admired the way

in which the leading Death gestured gallantly towards an open grave, his head bizarrely decked with flags. The unknown artist, I felt sure, had been to Lübeck, where similar postures were depicted. The helpful guidebook, in Hungarian and German, told me that this sportive Death was saying, 'In this doleful jeste of Life, I shew the state of Manne, and how he is called at uncertayne tymes by Me to forget all that he hath and lose All.'

For a while, silence prevailed, except for the footsteps of the guide, walking to the end of the gallery and back, sighing in her progress, jingling her keys. We were alone in the gallery. I was sketching the Death playing on a stickado or wooden psalter and goading along a high-bosomed duchess, when the guide again shuffled close.

'Much here is owed to Holbein engraving,' said the guide, to show off her knowledge. She was a small bent woman whose nose was disfigured by a permanent cold. She regarded the work with a contempt perhaps habitual to her. 'Theme of *danse macabre* is much popular in Middle Ages. In Nagykanizsa, half population is wipe out by plague only one years after building the cathedral. Now we know much better, praise be.'

I was fed up with her misery and her disapproval. I wanted only to study the frieze. It would buttress a line of thought I was pursuing.

'In what way do we know better?'

It is unwise ever to argue with a guide. She gave me a long discourse regarding the horrors of the Middle Ages, concluding by saying, 'Then was much misery in Budapest. Now everyone many money. Now we finish with Christianity and Communism, world much better place. People more enlightenment, eh?'

'You believe that?' I asked her. 'You really think people are more enlightened? On what grounds, may I ask? What about the war?'

She shot me a demonic look, emphasised by a smile of outrageous malice. 'We kill off all Russians. Then world better place. Forget all about bad thing.'

*

The grand steam baths under the Gellert Hotel were full of naked bodies, male and female. Many of the bathers had not merely the posture but the bulk of wallowing hippopotami. Fortunately the steam clothed us in a little decency.

Tiring of the crowd, I climbed from the reeking water. It was time I got to work. Churches long sealed with all their histories in them were to be opened to me this day. By a better guide.

Everyone was taking it easy. Headlines in the English-language paper that morning: STAVROPOL AIRPORT BATTLE: First Use Tactical Nukes: Crimea Blazes. The war had escalated. Everyone agreed you had to bring in the nukes eventually. Hungary was neutral. It supplied Swedish-made arms to all sides, impartially.

The Soviet War marked the recovery of Hungary as a Central European power. It was a godsend. Little I cared. I was researching churches and, in my early forties, too old for conscription.

Wrapped in a white towelling robe I was making my way back towards my room when I encountered a tall bearded man clad only in a towel. He was heading towards the baths I had just left. We looked at each other. I recognised those haggard lineaments, those eroded temples. They belonged to a distant acquaintance, one Montague Clements.

He recognised me immediately. As we shook hands I felt some embarrassment; he had been sacked from his post in the English Literature and Language Department of the University of East Anglia the previous year. I had not heard of him since.

'What are you doing in Budapest?' I asked.

'Private matter, old chum.' I remembered the dated way he had of addressing people – though he had been sacked for more serious matters. 'I'm here consulting a clever chap called Mircea Antonescu. Something rather strange has happened to me. Do you mind if I tell you? Perhaps you'd like to buy us a drink . . .'

We went up to my room, from the windows of which was a fine view of the Danube with Pest on the other side. I slipped into my jogging gear and handed him a sweater to wear.

'Fits me like a T. I suppose I couldn't keep it, could I?'

I did not like to say no. As I poured two generous Smirnoffs on the rocks from the mini-bar, he started on his problems. '"Music, when soft voices die, Vibrates in the memory . . ." So says the poet Shelley. But supposing there's no memory in which the soft voices can vibrate . . .'

He paused to raise his glass and take a deep slug of the vodka. 'I'm forty-one, old chum. So I believe. Last month, I found myself in an unknown place. No idea how I got there. Turned out I was here – in Budapest. Budapest! Never been here before in my natural. No idea how I arrived here from London.'

'You're staying here?' I remembered that Clements was a scrounger. Perhaps he was going to touch me for the air fare home. I gave him a hard look. Knowing something about his past, I was determined not to be caught easily.

'I'm attending the Antonescu Clinic. Mircea Antonescu – very clever chap, as I say. At the cutting edge of psycho-technology. Romanian, of course. I'm not staying in the Gellert. Too expensive for someone like me. I rent a cheaper place in Pest. Bit of a flophouse actually.' He laughed. 'You see, this is it, the crunch, the bottom line, as they say – I've lost ten years of my memory. Just lost them. Wiped. The last ten years, gone.'

He shone a look of absolute innocence on me. At which I uttered some condolences.

'The last thing I remember, I was thirty. Ten, almost eleven years, have passed and I have no notion as to what I was doing in all that time.'

All this he related in an old accustomed calm way. Perhaps he concealed his pain. 'How terrible for you,' I said.

'FOAM. That's what they call it. Free of All Memory. A kind of liberty in a way, I suppose. Nothing a chap can't get used to.'

It was fascinating. Other people's sorrows on the whole weigh lightly on our shoulders: a merciful provision. 'What does it feel like?'

I always remember Clements' answer. 'An ocean, old chum. A wide wide ocean with a small island here and there. No continent. The continent has gone.'

I had seen him now and again during those ten years, before his sacking. I.suggested that perhaps I could help him fill in gaps in his memory. He appeared moderately grateful. He said there was no one else he knew in Budapest. When I asked him if he had been involved in an accident, he shook his head.

'They don't know. I don't know. A car crash? No bones broken, old boy. Lucky to be alive, you might say. I have no memory of anything that happened to me in the last ten years.'

Unthinkingly, I asked, 'Isn't your wife here with you?'

Whereupon Clements struck his narrow forehead. 'Oh God, don't say I was married!'

He drank the vodka, he kept the sweater. The next day, as suggested, I went round with him to the Antonescu Clinic he had mentioned. The idea was that an expert would question me in order to construct a few more of those small islands in the middle of Clements' ocean of forgetfulness.

The clinic was situated in a little nameless square off Fo Street, wedged in next to the Ministry of Light Industry. Behind its neo-classical façade was a desperate little huddle of rooms partitioned into offices and not at all smart. In one windowless room I was introduced to a Dr Maté Jozsef. Speaking in jerky English around a thin cigar, Maté informed me we could get to work immediately. It would be best procedure if I began to answer a series of questions in a room from which Clements was excluded.

'You understand, Dr Burnell. Using proprietary method here. Dealing with brain injury cases. Exclusive . . . Special to us. Produces the good result. Satisfied customers . . .' His thick furry voice precluded the use of finite verbs.

Knowing little about medical practice, I consented to do as he demanded. Maté showed me up two flights of stairs to a windowless room where a uniformed nurse awaited us. I was unfamiliar with the equipment in the room, although I knew an operating table and anaesthetic apparatus when I saw them. It was at that point I began to grow nervous. Nosto-vision equipment was also in the room; I recognised the neat plastic skullcap.

Coughing, Maté stubbed his cigar out before starting to fiddle with the equipment. The nurse attempted to help. I stood with my back to the partition wall, watching.

'Wartime . . . Many difficulties . . . Many problems . . . For Hungarians is many trouble . . .' He was muttering as he elbowed the nurse away from a malfunctioning VDU. 'Because of great inflation rate . . . High taxes . . . Too many gypsy in town. All time . . . The Germans of course . . . The Poles . . . How we get all work done in the time? . . . Too much busy . . .'

'If you're very busy, I could come another day,' I suggested.

He squinted at me and lit another cigar. 'I am expert in all science, so many people take advantage of me. Even when I am small boy, I must carrying to school my small brother. Three kilometre to the gymnasium . . . Now is shortage of material, I must do all. This damned war . . . Many up-heaval . . . Spies and traitor . . . Everywhere same . . . Today toilet blockage and how to get repair? You cannot be nervous?'

'I have an appointment, Dr Maté. If later would be more convenient . . .'

'Is no problem. Don't worry . . . I treat many English. Get this nurse to move, I explain all.'

Maté sought to reassure me. They had developed a method of inserting memories into the brains of amnesiacs, but first those memories had to be recorded with full sensory data on to microchip, and then projected by laser into the brain. That at least was the gist of what I gathered from a long, complex explanation. While I listened, the nurse gave me an injection in the biceps of my left arm. They would need, Maté said, to append electrodes to my cranium in order to obtain full sensory data matching my answers to his questions.

'I don't really know Montagu Clements well,' I protested. But of course I could not simply refuse to co-operate, could not walk out, could not leave poor Clements without doing my best for him.

Indeed, my eyelids felt heavy. It was luxury to stretch out, to groan, to relax . . . and to fall into the deepest slumber of my life . . .

The cathedral in which we walked was almost lightless. My extended senses told me that it was vast. I asked Dr Maté what we were doing there. His answer was incoherent. I did not press him. He seemed to be smoking a cigar; a little red glow formed occasionally as he inhaled, but I could smell no smoke.

In order to keep my spirits up – I admit I was apprehensive – I talked to him as we progressed step by step. 'I suppose you read Kafka, you understand the complexities with which he found himself faced at every turn. As a psychologist, you must understand that there are people like Kafka for whom existence is an entanglement, a permanent state of war, while for others – why, at the other extreme they sail through life, seemingly unopposed. These differences are accounted for by minute biochemical changes in the brain. Neither state is more or less truthful than the other. For some truth lies in mystery, for others in clarity. Prayer is a great clarifier – or was. My belief is that old Christian churches served as clarifying machines. They helped you to think straight in "this doleful jeste of Life".'

I went on in this fashion for some while. Dr Maté laughed quite heartily, his voice echoing in the darkness.

'You're such good company,' he said. 'Is there anything I can do for you in return?'

'More oxygen,' I said. 'It's so hot in here. As a church architect, I have visited, I believe, all the cathedrals in Europe – Chartres, Burgos, Canterbury, Cologne, Saragossa, Milano, Ely, Zagreb, Gozo, Rheims – ' I continued to name them for some while as we tramped down the nave. 'But this is the first time I have ever entered a hot and stuffy cathedral.'

'There are new ways. Neural pathways. Technology is not solely about ways of conducting war. It brings blessings. Not least the new abilities by which we may see human existence anew – relativistically, that is, each person imprisoned in his own *Umwelt*, his own conceptual universe.' He let out a roar of laughter. 'Your friend Kafka – I'd have lobotomised him, speaking personally – he said that it was not only Budapest but the whole world that was tragic. He said, "All protective walls are smashed by the iron fist of technology." Complaining, of course – the fucker always complained. But it's the electronic fist of technology which is smashing the walls between human and human. I exclude the Muslims, of course. Down they go, like the Berlin Wall, if you remember that far back. In the future, we shall all be able to share common memories, understandings. All will be common property. Private thought will be a thing of the past. It's simply a matter of microtechnology.'

I started laughing. I had not realised what good company Hungarians could be.

'In that connection, I might mention that Jesus Christ was evidently pretty *au fait* with micro-technology. All that resurrection-of-the-body stuff. Depends on advanced technology, much of it developed during that lucky little war against Saddam Hussein in the Gulf. Strictly Frankenstein stuff. Robbing body-bags. Dead one day, up and running – back into the conflict – the next.'

Maté was genuinely puzzled. We halted under a memorial statue to Frederick the Great. Maté had heard of Frankenstein. It was the other great Christian myth which puzzled him. This was the first time I had ever encountered anyone walking into a cathedral who had never heard of Jesus Christ. Explaining about Jesus proved more difficult than I expected. The heat and darkness confused me. I knew Jesus was related to John the Baptist and the Virgin Mary, but could not quite remember how. Was Christ his surname or his Christian name?

My father had been a Christian. All the same, it was difficult to recall the legend exactly. I was better on 'Frankenstein'. But I ended by clarifying Jesus' role in the scheme of things by quoting, as far as I could remember, from a hymn, 'He came down on earth from Heaven, He died to save us all.'

Although I couldn't actually see Maté's sneer, I felt it in the darkness. 'Where was this Jesus when Belsen and Auschwitz and Dresden and Hiroshima happened? Having a smoke out the back?'

Somehow, I felt it was rather sacrilegious to mention Jesus' name aloud where we were. The cathedral was constructed in the form of a T, the horizontal limb being much longer than the vertical, stretching away into the endless dark. Oh, the weight of masonry! Like fossil vertebrae, great columns reared up on every side, engineered to support vast weight, as if this whole edifice was situated many miles under the earth's crust, the mass of which must somehow be borne.

So I say. So I understand it. Yet those stone vertebrae, in defiance of the dull facts of physics, writhed like the chordata, climbing lizard-tailed into the deeper darknesses of the vaulting. It was the cathedral to end all cathedrals.

Maté and I now stood at the junction of the cathedral's great T. The vertical limb of this overpowering architectural masterpiece sloped downwards. We stopped to stare down that slope, more sensed than seen. Kafka could have felt no more trepidation at that time than I, though I covered my nervousness by giggling at Maté's latest joke. He claimed he had not heard of the Virgin Mary, either.

I stood at the top of the slope. With me was another church architect, Sir Kingsley Amis.

'The font is somewhere over there,' he said, gesturing into the darkness. 'But I'd better warn you it's not drinking water. Even if it was, you wouldn't want to drink it, would you?' He gave a throaty laugh.

Both he and I were greatly diminished by Dr Maté, who now made a proclamation, reading from a box. 'We're here now, on the spot you see indicated on your map, adjacent to the *pons asinorum*. Presently a devil will appear and remove one of you. I am not permitted to say where he will remove you to. We have to keep destinations secret in wartime, but I am authorised to say that it will be somewhere fairly unpleasant. As you know, the war between humanity and the rest is still on. But Geneva rules will apply, except in so far as fire and brimstone will be permitted on a strictly controlled basis. All torture will be attended by an authorised member of the International Red Cross.'

'How long do we have to wait? Is there the chance of a drink before we go?' Sir Kingsley Amis asked.

'Devil should be here shortly. ETA 2001,' Maté said.

'Shortly' was just another of the euphemisms such as surface in wartime. It indicated an eternity, just as bombs are described as deterrents, 'This'll spoil his day' means 'We'll kill him', and 'God' means 'A ton of bricks is about to fall on you'. Myself, I prefer euphemisms.

Phew, I was so tired. Time in the building was lethargic, with every minute stretching, stretching out in companionship with the night towards infinity. Reality wore thin, bringing in illusion. At one point I almost imagined I was sitting typing while a dreadful, senseless war was waged in the Gulf. But the gulf of time I was in was much greater. Forget reality; it's one of the universe's dead ends . . .

Interest is hard to sustain, but my feeling was as much of interest as terror. Only those who enjoy life feel terror. I admired all the melancholy grandeur round me, the reptilian sense of claustrophobia. It compared favourably with the slum in which I lived.

At the bottom of the slope before us, a stage became illuminated. You must imagine this as an entirely gradual process, not easily represented in words. A. Pause. Stage. Pause. Became. Pause. Ill. Pause. You. Pause. Min. Pause. Ay. Pause. Ted. Trumpets. It was illuminated predominately in bars of intersecting blue and crimson.

Funebrial music began to play, brass and bass predominating.

The music, so kin to the lighting, was familiar to me, yet only just above audibility, as the lighting hovered just above the visible end of the spectrum.

These low levels of activity were in keeping with the enormous silences of the cathedral structure. They were shattered by the sudden incursion of a resounding bass voice which broke into song. That timbre, that mixture of threat and exultation! Unmistakable even to a layman.

'The devil!' Kingsley Amis and I exclaimed together.

'And in good voice,' said Dr Maté. 'So this is where I have to leave you.'

I was stunned by his indifference. 'What about that sewing machine?' I asked. But he was not to be deflected.

Even while speaking, he was shrinking, either in real terms or because he was being sucked into the distance; darkness made it hard to differentiate. However, I had little time to waste on Maté. Attention turned naturally to the devil. Though he had yet to appear on the dim-lit stage, I knew he was going to come for Kingsley Amis.

'I'd better make myself scarce too,' I said. 'Don't want to get in your way.'

'Hang on,' he said. 'You never know. He might be after you. Depends on whether or not he's a literary critic.'

When the devil arrived on stage, he was out of scale, far too large – ridiculously far too large, I might say, meaning no disrespect. It was hard to discern anything of him in the confused dark. He was black and gleaming, his outline as smooth as a dolphin's even down to the hint of rubber. He stepped forward and advanced slowly up the ramp, still singing in that voice which shook the rafters.

This struck me as being, all told, unlikely. It was that very feeling that all was unlikely, that anything likely was over and done with like last year's cricket match, which was most frightening. I trembled. Trembling didn't help one bit.

I turned to Kingsley Amis. He was no longer there. I was alone. The devil was coming for me.

In terror, I peered along the great wide lateral arms of the cathedral.

'Anyone there?' I called. 'Help! Help! Taxi!'

To the left was only Stygian darkness, too syrupy for me to think of penetrating, the black from which ignorance is made. As I looked towards the right, however, along the other widespread arm of the building, something materialised there like a stain: light towards the dead, dull end of the electromagnetic spectrum.

All this I took in feverishly, for the devil, still singing, was approaching me still. Perhaps I should apologise for my fears. As a rationalist, I had but to snap my rational fingers, it might be argued, and the devil would fade away in a puff of smoke. To which I might say that, rationalist or not, I had spent too many years in my capacity as church architect investigating the fossils of a dead faith not to have imbibed something of the old superstitions. But – this was more germane – I had a belief in the Jungian notion of various traits and twists of the human personality becoming drama- tised as persons or personages. This enormous devil could well be an embodiment of the dark side of my character; in which case, I was all the less likely to escape him.

Nor did I.

As I took a pace or two to my right, starting to run towards that faint dull promise of escape, a vision distantly revealed itself. Fading into being came a magnificent palladian façade, lit in a colour like blood, with doric columns and blind doorways. Nothing human was to be seen there – no man to whom I might call. If the burrow to my left represented the squalors of the subconscious, here to my right was the chill of the super-ego.

I ran for it. But was hardly into my stride when the singing devil reached me. I screamed. He snatched me up . . .

. . . and bit off my head.

To any of you with decent sensibilities, I must apologise for these horrific images. You may claim they were subjective, private to me, and should remain private, on the grounds that the world has nightmares enough. Perhaps. But what happened to me was that my head was bitten off almost literally.

My memory was wiped.

It's a curious thing suddenly to find oneself walking. Imagine yourself in a cinema. The movie begins. Its opening shot is of some character walking, walking across a featureless landscape. Photography: grainy. The shot immediately holds your interest, perhaps because our ancestors right back to the Ice Age were great walkers. Now imagine that you're not

sitting watching in your comfortable stalls seat: you are that
character. Only you're not in a movie. You're for real, or
what we call real, according to our limited sensory
equipment.

Your life has just begun and you're walking across what
turns out to be Salisbury Plain. It's cold, there's a hint of rain
in the breeze. The place looks ugly. But walking is no
trouble. It's everything else that's trouble.

Like how you got where you are. Like what happened.
Like what your name is. Like who you are. Even like –
where are you going?

Night is closing in. That much you understand.

What do you do? You go on walking.

Over to your right in the distance, half-hidden by a fold of
land, is a broken circle of stone monoliths. You kind of
recognise it, although no name comes to you. It's the ruin of
a Stone Age cathedral, taken out in the war with the Nean-
derthals, cobalt against the overpraised English countryside.

You continue as dark continues to fall. Your legs keep
working, your pace is unvarying. You become slightly afraid
of this remorseless body, asking yourself, Is it mine?

Dusk gathers about you like a coat when you climb a fence
and reach a road. There is almost no traffic on the road. You
try to thumb a lift from the cars as they approach from either
direction, sweeping you with their headlights. Past they go,
never pausing. Bastards.

The fourteenth car stops. A woman is driving. A man sits
beside her. They ask where you want to go, and you say
Anywhere. They laugh and say that is where they are going.
You climb in. You huddle on the back seat, unable to answer
any of their well-meant questions.

They think you are a loony, and drop you in the nearest
village. You are inclined to agree with their judgement. You
wander hopelessly along the road, then, frightened, back into
the village. The village is called Bishops Linctus. By now its
streets are deserted. Lights glow inside the pub, The Gun
Dog, but, with no money in your pocket, you are afraid to
enter. There are countries where you might enter and be

looked after in a hospitable way; you do not feel that could happen in England.

A young man in gumboots saunters along the road with a shotgun under his arm. He stares at you hard as he passes. He returns and addresses you. He is guarded but friendly. He seems not to believe you have lost your memory. Nevertheless, he takes you along to his house, which is one of a line of council houses on the edge of the village, just before the plain recommences its reign.

His old mother greets you. She is surprised, saying that Larry never speaks to anyone. He tells her to shut up. You stand there, back to the kitchen wall, while she fries up Larry's favourite meal, which is sausages and mashed fish fingers. You and Larry sit and eat at the table. It is good.

He has a room he calls His Room. It is locked. The old woman interrupts to say it is full of guns. He says to shut up. He tells you he is a farm labourer or sometimes a brickie. At present he is out of work. He lets you doss on the floor of his bedroom. The place is full of gun magazines, and there is a Kalashnikov in Larry's bed. He sleeps with it.

You express your gratitude.

'I like helping people,' Larry replies. He puts out the light.

You lie there on the floor. Despite all your worries, you feel pleasure and comfort in those words of his, 'I like helping people. Words of Jesus.' And so you sleep.

Only you're not in this movie. This is my movie. I'm for real – or what I call real, according to my limited sensory equipment.

Morning. When I woke, Larry was already up and about. I could hear his mother shouting at him. For a few seconds, I was living with this present situation. Then the edge of the abyss reappeared. I could remember nothing further back than the time I was walking over that miserable plain.

When I got up, the old woman gave me a cup of thin instant coffee. I stood with her against the sink. She had a canary in a cage.

'It's Kevin. We call it Kevin. I think it's a girl. One of the family, aren't you? Keeps me company. Say hello to Kevin. I wash it every Saturday, under the hot tap. It likes that. Don't you, Kevin? You like a nice wash under the hot tap. It's one of the family. Sing for your mummy, then. Who's a good Kevin?'

I was watching through the window, as Larry loaded boxes of ammunition into the back of an old battered Land-Rover.

His mother caught my glance. 'He's going into Swindon to try and get a job. You stay here with me. He's a dangerous driver, is Larry. We'll go down and see Dr Roberts. She's a sympathetic woman – trained in London, she was – and she'll help you.'

Larry was looking preoccupied. His movements were slow, his gaze abstracted, as if he were composing a poem in his head. Without glancing back at the house, he climbed into the cab of the Land-Rover. Nothing happened. I went to the window to watch, obscurely thinking something was wrong. The back of his head could be seen. Motionless. Not trying to start the vehicle. Just sitting there in the driver's seat.

The council houses followed the curve of the road, which wound up a slight incline. Beyond the houses was open agricultural land, the plain. The village lay in the opposite direction. From the last house, three hundred yards distant, a woman emerged, wearing an old blue raincoat and pushing a baby's push-chair. She had a scarf tied over her head and was evidently going into the village to shop.

Larry moved as she drew nearer. The window of the vehicle wound down. A rifle muzzle protruded from it. A shot sounded.

The woman in the blue raincoat fell to her knees, still clinging with one hand to the push-chair.

As three more shots rang out, the push-chair blew apart. The woman's face was covered with shreds of baby as she fell on the road.

Larry's mother had seen at least part of this. She was drying a plate on a tea towel. She dropped the plate, ran from the kitchen, and opened the front door.

'No, no, Larry! Stop it, you fool. Whatever do you think you're doing?'

Larry had descended from the Land-Rover after firing the four shots. He moved slowly, with a sleep-walker's lethargy. With that same lethargy, he snugged the butt of the rifle into his shoulder and fired at his mother. She was blown from the porch back into the passage. He fired two more shots into the house. I ran to the bedroom and heaved myself under the bed, fighting blindly with the magazines. I was sure he was after me.

There the police discovered me, four hours later, lying in a pool of my own urine.

So it was that eventually I found myself in a hospital in Swindon close to other victims of Larry Foot. After shooting the woman from the council house and her baby, and his mother, Larry had walked into Bishops Linctus and shot dead the first three people he met, wounding several others. BISHOPS BLOODBATH screamed the tabloid headlines. The quiet little affair roused much more excitement than the Soviet War (in which British troops were involved) then reaching one of its many climaxes outside Tiblisi. Why had Larry done it? The explanation given was that he had always been keen on guns. Presumably the same explanation would cover the Soviet War.

Armed police from Bishops Magnum and Salisbury shot Larry down behind the Shell garage. He had liked to help people, poor Larry. At least he gave a little pleasure to the bloodthirsty readers of the *Sun*.

This incident got me swiftly – in an ambulance – into the realm of professional medical scrutiny. Within a few days, I again had an identity. I was Roy Edward Burnell, a university lecturer and specialist in church architecture. I had written a learned book, *Architrave and Archetype*, a thesis linking human aspiration with human-designed structures, cathedrals in particular.

The chief medico in charge of my case, a Dr Rosemary Kepepwe, entered my hospital room smiling, bringing with her a copy of my book. 'We're getting somewhere, Roy,' she said. 'We'll contact your wife next.'

I smote my forehead. 'My God, don't say I'm married.'

She laughed. 'I'm afraid so. At least, you were married.

We'll soon have her tracked down – and other people in your past. What is the last thing you remember before the white-out?'

Even to me, her attitude seemed amateurish. When I said something of the sort, Dr Kepepwe explained that most of the original staff of the hospital were serving with British troops in Operation Total Tartary, in Murmansk, Usbekistan, the front in the Caucasus, and the new revolutionary area opening up round Lake Baikal. The disintegration of the Soviet Union had created a tremendous demand for medication.

'My husband was a brain surgeon,' Kepepwe said. 'The best husband a woman could have. David won the Isle of Wight Sea-Fishing Trophy two years in succession. Everyone respected him. We have three children, one of them at Eton and one now working as a waiter in a Little Chef off the M25 at the South Mimms Service Area. But David volunteered to serve with Total Tartary. I had picked up a bit of surgery from him, of course, so here I am.

'You were quite lucky to get here. Salisbury Plain is all mined these days.'

'Lucky me,' I said. But it appeared I did not know how lucky. I had marvelled that it was such a quiet hospital, and ascribed this to efficiency. Not so, Dr Kepepwe explained. I was the only patient in there. All the other wards were empty. Civilian patients had been turned out three days earlier, as the hospital prepared to receive wounded from the Eastern theatre of war.

'Anyhow, I'd better take your details,' Dr Kepepwe said, reluctantly. 'Then I'll bring you a cup of tea. What did you say was the last thing you remembered?'

I told her. I had gone to South America to view some of the ecclesiastical architecture there. I arrived in Buenos Aires and checked into my hotel. I remembered going up in a gilt elevator. And then – white-out. The fear of standing on the edge of a great abyss overtook me.

Dr Kepepwe saw the expression on my face. 'Don't worry – you're not alone, Roy. How does it feel?'

'An ocean. A wide ocean with a small island here and there. No continent. The continent has gone.'

As I spoke the words, some strange thing struggled in my mind. A name almost came back to me, then died.

So I waited. Waited to be restored. To pass the time I had access to the hospital library on VDU, together with TV and video. Also the new media craze, the NV, or nostovision. Laser projectors could beam whole programmes into the mind, where the programmes became like your own lived memories, though they faded in a few days. In view of my deficiencies, I avoided the NV and stuck to the library; but little I read remained in my mind.

What sins, what meannesses, what grave errors I had committed in the previous ten years had been forgiven me. I waited in calm, without apprehension.

Dr Kepepwe assured me active steps were being taken to trace those who had been intimate with me during the ten blank years: my parents, my academic colleagues. The confusions of war, the tight security covering the country, made communication difficult.

When she left in the evening, I wandered through the great empty building. In the dark of the long antiseptic corridors, green LEDs glowed, accompanied often by hums or growls. It was like being in the entrails of a glacier.

On the desk in Rosemary Kepepwe's office stood a photograph of her husband David, very black, smiling genially with a large fish on a scale by his side. I wondered about their lives; but there was nothing on which to speculate. She was little more to me than an embodiment of kindness.

Only my slippered footsteps on the stairs, the tiles. I was a ghost among the ghosts of multitudinous lives whose CVs, like mine, had been lost. Who had lived, died, survived? A phrase came back uncomfortably from the white-out, 'the sorry jeste of Life'.

But, I told myself as I took a service elevator up to the roof, I should not think in the past tense. Any day now and the hospital would be filled again with the living – the military living, harpooned by their wounds, poised on the brink of a final white-out. They would survive or not, to accumulate more memories, happy or sad as the case might be.

On the roof, the habitations of air-conditioning plants painted black by a city's grime lived and breathed. I stood on the parapet, looking out over the town of Swindon, willing myself to feel less disembodied. The stars shone overhead, remote but always with promise of something better than the brief rush of biological existence. As I drank them in, a roar of engines sounded.

Three B-52 Stratofortresses flew overhead, from the west towards the eastern stars.

I went downstairs again, to my ward, my nest in the glacier. I must wait. Waiting did not require too much fortitude. One day soon, Dr Kepepwe would do the trick – with luck before the war-damaged moved in to supplant me in her attentions.

The days would pass. Help would come.

Indeed, the days did pass.

And then Stephanie arrived.

Stephanie was a vision of delight, tall, fine-boned, aesthetic of countenance, walking easy and free inside a fawn linen suit. Hair tawny, neat, almost shoulder-length. I admired the way she strolled into the ward, doing quite determinedly something not to her taste. With a cautious smile on her face. And this lady had been my wife. I could have forgotten that? I could have forgotten all the times we had enjoyed together, where we'd been, what we'd done? So it seemed. My head had been bitten off.

Like most gusts of pleasure, this one brought its pain. She sat facing me: calm, sympathetic, but at a distance I had no way of negotiating, as I listened dismayed to what she revealed of those islands, that lost continent.

Stephanie and I had married eight years ago, only four weeks after meeting in Los Angeles for the first time. We were divorced five years later. Here indeed, I thought, must lie some of those sins, meannesses, and grave errors. She broke this news to me gently, casting her clear gaze towards the window in preference to seeing my hurt. The hospital authorities had tracked her down in California, where she was enjoying success as a fabric designer and living with a famous composer of film music.

'You don't owe me anything,' she said. And, after a pause, 'I don't owe you anything.'

'It's good of you to come and see me. The war and everything, and that jumbo blown out of the skies over the Atlantic . . .'

A small laugh. 'I was interested, of course. You're a bit of medical history.'

'We had no children?'

She shook her head. 'That whole business was the reason for our falling out.'

'Shit,' I said. A long silence fell between us. I could have crossed the Sahara in it. 'Did I ever – I mean, since we split up – did I ever – did we communicate at all?'

'It was final,' she said. 'I didn't want to know. I like my new life in the States. What you did was up to you, wasn't it? But you did send me postcards. Generally of draughty old churches here and there – of the kind you used to drag me into when we were together.'

'You can't beat a good old draughty old church,' I said, smiling.

She did not return the smile. Perhaps the woman lacked humour.

'I brought a couple of your cards along in my purse,' she said. I noted the Americanism as she dipped into her hand-bag. She pulled out one card and handed it over, extending it between two outstretched fingers – as if amnesia was catching.

'Huh, just one card. I tore the others up, I'm afraid.' That, I thought was a little unnecessary pain she had no reason to inflict . . .

The card, crudely coloured, showed a picture of a church labelled as St Stephen's Basilica, although I saw immediately that architecturally it was not a basilica. I turned it over, glanced at the Hungarian stamp, and read the few words I had scribbled to Stephanie, only three weeks earlier.

'Budapest. Brief visit here. Making notes for lectures as usual. Need some florid Hungarian architecture. Trust you're

well. Have met strange old friend – just going round to
Antonescu's Clinic with him. Love, Roy.'

I went back to the Gellert. There, not entirely surprisingly,
was Montagu Clements, still wearing my sweater.

He raised his hands in mock-surrender. 'Pax. No offence
meant, honest, old chum. Since I lost my job I've worked as
a decoy for Antonescu, luring on innocent foreigners who
come here to take advantage of low Hungarian prices. Econ-
omic necessity and all that.'

'You had your hand in the till – now you've had it in my
mind. Stealing a memory is like murder, you miserable
slob.'

'Yes, and no doubt it will be legislated against when
nostovision becomes something less than a seven-day
wonder. Till then, Antonescu earns a modest dollar from his
bootleg memory bullets. They're short of hard currency, the
Hungarians. Let me buy you a drink.'

I almost threw myself on him. 'You've poisoned my life,
you bastard, you'd probably poison my drink.'

He was very cool. 'Let's not fall out. You have a contempt
for me. Think how I might feel about you. I've had to edit
ten years of your memories, a lot of which weren't edifying.
You should be happy to be rid of them.'

'I see, Clements – the FOAM Theory of History . . .
Never learn anything. Just bloody forget. Haven't you ever
heard that saying about those who forget history being
doomed to repeat it? Why do you think the world's in such a
fucking mess?'

He remained unmoved. 'I have no idea, old boy. Nor, I
suspect, do you, for all your academic posturing. Without
wishing to hurt your feelings, your last ten years were full
of crap. But there – everyone's last ten years were full of
crap . . .'

We were standing in the baroque foyer of the hotel, which
had been built in the great European hotel age during the
peaceful years preceding the First World War. I gestured
through the doors, through the glass of which traffic could be
seen crossing the Szabadsag Bridge. Beyond lay the dense

Magyar thoroughfares, the grandiose piles of masonry, where fat profiteers sweated over their calculators.

'I was already on my way to the police, Clements, *old boy*. Don't pretend we're friends. You had me dumped on Salisbury Plain, don't forget.'

Clements turned on one of his innocent smiles. 'Just think, it could have been the Gobi . . . I interceded on your behalf. Be British, old chap – let's compromise. Let's do a deal.'

'What deal?'

He said, 'We could discuss business better in the bar. You want your memory back, eh? Don't go to the police and I'll bring you your memory this afternoon. Agree? Say three-thirty, after I've taken my customary nap. OK?'

So I agreed on it. I agreed, thinking I would go to the police later. Clements turned up at three fifty-five.

We sat at the upstairs bar with two tall glasses of iced white Eger wine, for which I paid. He produced in the palm of his right hand two slender plastic spools, which I recognised as nostovision bullets, ready to be inserted into the head-laser.

'I had some trouble getting these, old chap. How about fifty dollars each?'

'Maybe you really have lost your memory or you'd know I wouldn't fall for that. Hand them over. Why two bullets?'

He took a reflective sip of his wine. 'Antonescu's at the cutting edge of psycho-technology. We have to know our customers. They're mainly in America and the Arab World. It's a specialised market. We boiled your memory banks down into two categories – the rest we threw away, sorry to say. There's your speciality, church architecture and all that. That spool has a limited but steady sale to academics – a tribute to all the knowledge you had packed away. I suppose you'll be glad to get that back. Surely it's worth fifty dollars to you?'

'Come on, Clements, what's the other bullet?'

'A hundred dollars, old chum? It's all your life and activities with a woman called Stephanie. Very erotic stuff, believe me. Very popular in Saudi Arabia.'

I threw my wine in his face and grabbed the two bullets. I leave it to you to decide which bullet I played first.

The Soviet War continues. Heavy fighting in the Caucasus despite bad weather conditions. Radio reports said that Alliance forces used chemical and bacteriological weapons in the Kutaisi area. Questioned, American General 'Gus' Stalinbrass said, 'What the heck else do we do? These assholes don't give up easy.'

Last night, four Georgian soldiers crossed the Tiblisi lines, found their way through a minefield, and gave themselves up to a British journalist, Dicky Bowden. One of the soldiers was a boy of fourteen.

Bowden said, 'Starved and disaffected troops like these are all that stand between our advance and the Caspian Sea.'

He was confident that the war would be over in a week or two. Say a month. Maximum two months.

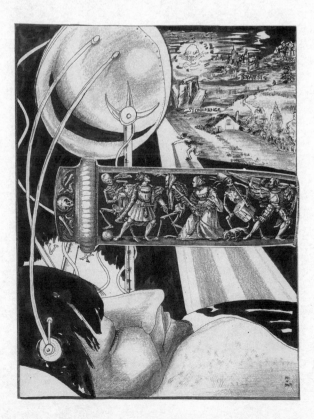

SF Novels of the Year

John Clute

Someone must have been telling lies about O., for without having done anything wrong he was cancelled one fine morning. He had, it cannot be gainsaid, noticed a growing silence in the world outside his window, but had dismissed the tightness in his chest as catarrh, for he had done nothing wrong, and *he had been well reviewed*; so he was unprepared for the knock upon the door, or for the strange men in the closely fitting black suits that marked them as Samurai of the Robust Accountancy. 'Who are you?' asked O., though he must have known, for their eyes slid off the living. 'Are you *Orbit Science Fiction Yearbook*?' asked the first Samurai. 'I am that paraclete,' said O. 'Then you are no more,' murmured the second, 'for you are cancelled.' 'Ah,' said O. In his heart, it may be, he had long suspected his own guilt or *redundancy*, and so, after a pause, he asked only, 'Will there be a trial?' The Samurai shrugged. 'If you insist,' said the first, from the side of his mouth. 'It would change nothing,' said the second, for the hands of the first were already at O.'s throat, while the second thrust the knife into his thudding heart and turned it there twice. 'Like a dog!' said O.; it was as if he meant the shame of his *cancelling* to outlive him. But of course it never does. It was a good year for science fiction.

That is, if any good science fiction was being written, it was a good year for good science fiction to be written in. Samuel R. Delany had been saying recently that sf — which was 'a critique of the object rather than a critique of the subject' — could be distinguished from the mimetic novel by the fact that it paid attention to the objective world, which was not merely a show whose variables were tied to human consciousness. In that sense certainly, 1990 was a good year for sf. Good sf needs a foregrounded world, needs the compost of history to feed on — the simplest definition of science fiction being *free history* — and there was plenty of history in 1990, just as there was in 1989, for provender. Three decades after Sputnik spoiled John W. Campbell's white wedding with the future, two decades after the first augurs of nanotechnologies to come began to shrivel the knobs and diodes of the old sf, less than a decade after William Gibson's heroes began to surf Odysseus-like down the data seas in quest of Ithaca-wombs for one, the genre might still continue to emit replicants of the Golden Age like some vast incontinent egg-spewing factory-farm Gold-style Goose; but 1990 was a good year all the same for those sf writers not owned by farmers or otherwise obsessed with the past. (The world is never past. It is only our memories which cloak the eye with similitudes, our memories which sharecrop the stone that refutes Berkeley.) History on show, then: it will be interesting to see if anything good came of it.

One of the year-monitors has, of course, been disappeared. The cancellation after three years of David Garnett's *Orbit Science Fiction Yearbook*, in which this reviewer's annual sf novel roundup had previously appeared, leaves the UK without an anthology forum of assessment. But we can still get a sense of things. *Locus*, the California-based 'newspaper of the science fiction field' which continues to represent the sound of sf talking to itself, continues to present its bibliographical statistics according to its own strangely unique criteria. Charles N. Brown and William G. Contento's *Science Fiction, Fantasy, & Horror: a Comprehensive Bibliography of Books and Short Fiction Published in the English Language*, an annual series of bound volumes recast from data first made available in issues of the magazine, continues strangely (despite the subtitle) to list only sf books that *Locus* received free for review (which is a truly odd test of legitimacy to apply in a reference book designed for general use) *during the year in question* (which is, if anything, even odder), so that more appositely the subtitle should read: *A Comprehensive Bibliography of Books and Short Fiction Received by* Locus *for Review in 1989, including Books and Short Fiction from 1988 That Got Lost in the Mail until Early 1989, or Maybe the Publisher Hadn't Heard of Us Till Somebody Told Him Though That's Really Kinda Hard to Believe, and some Very Early Copies of a Bunch of 1990 Books Somebody Sent One of Our Reviewers.* All of which means that anyone using the *Locus* annuals to research any one calendar year must not restrict themselves to the volume ostensibly covering that year. They must in fact obtain — or find together, at the same time, in some library — not one but three volumes: that for the year in question, that for the year preceding the year in question, and that for the year to come.

The *Locus* yearbooks are not, therefore, in the end, true bibliographies at all; they are, in fact, *diaries* of the postal experiences of one small magazine. Which is something of an embarrassment in the matured world of sf 1991, especially given the enormous usefulness — and astonishing accuracy — of Brown/Contento's treatment of the data actually admitted into their fold. By notating only those books which they have seen (which is no real excuse for not going out and finding those books they have not been given), and by saying exactly when they first touched the flesh of each book, the editors have avoided innumerable ascription errors, and manage to stay clear of ghost titles (except for listing advance copies of books which may never get published). The annuals are accurate and information-packed, talking bibliography of the most enjoyable sort; and Hal W. Hall's 'Research Index' is as comprehensive as any index of non-fiction could possibly be that excludes reviews (and therefore much of the best critical work done in the field, but who can cover everything?). And the 'Book Summary' for the forthcoming *1990* volume, a draft of which appears in *Locus* 361, tells us that 1188 new books were published (or, as we've seen, received by *Locus*) in 1990, which returns us to the heights of 1988. Of this 1188, 281 were sf novels, 204 were fantasies, 168 were horror, 90 were collections of whatever ilk, and 73 were novelisations (other categories filled up the total). Our remit – the 281 sf novels – is, therefore, lighter than it might initially have seemed, though still too huge to manage without dynamiting the pool. Of the 281, an unknown number were sharecrops, most of which bite the hand of novel, and which will very soon (rumour has it) be published on edible paper; they still, for the most part, don't pass our lips. On the other hand, this reviewer may have seen a counterbalancing slough of books that failed to qualify for *Locus*'s *Comprehensive Bibliography of Books and Short Fiction Published in the English Language* – like, for instance, the six titles Gene Wolfe has published since 1983 with Cheap Street, a Fine Press which does not solicit reviews, and does not therefore send off free copies to magazines, so that not one of these books has ever been mentioned by *Locus*, and might just as well not really exist at all, right? So it's swings and roundabouts. So we plunge.

Typical of the kind of book that might well escape the *Locus* remit – though Phil Stephensen-Payne, who seems to assemble British listings on a more comprehensive Books Noted basis, may have entered it into the forthcoming 1990 volume – was Christine Brooke-Rose's *Verbivore* (Carcanet), a surly bristling assault on data-noise that reads, like so many devout expressions of cutting-edge postmodernism, strangely medieval: a hedgehog Canute drowning in the language sea, the century tide. Bruce Sterling might designate *Verbivore* as an example of slipstreaming – of feeding like a dolphin on icon scraps tossed into the wake of the ship of genre – but Brooke-Rose is stranger than that, and perhaps a harbinger. The secret chambers of the book, like the pomegranate-hearted futures we're falling into, are a maze of options drenched in sf; it is the telling of the thing which claws back dead dignities of the autonomous word.

There were other books in the slipstream, too, some of whose authors might not have welcomed the knowledge that they were officially in tow. *Hayduke Lives!* (Little, Brown) by Edward Abbey (1927–89) brought back the members of *The Monkey-Wrench Gang* (1975) to attempt, one final time, to save the West from the catastrophic engines — literally depicted — of Late Late Capitalism. In *The King* (Harper & Row), Donald Barthelme (1933–89) rein-serted King Arthur into the jaws of the current (i.e. 1940) world, which gnashed; but the Matter proved undegradable, and Bar-thelme's last fling at 'flippancy' seemed, as always, like a washing of the sense of here and now. It was hardly a new book, or a novel, but *Toward the Radical Center: a Karel Capek Reader* (Catbird Press) presented a number of newly rendered excerpts from familiar plays and longer texts which cleaned up the old translatorese and evoked something of the quicksilver urgency (the Nazis are coming the Nazis are coming) of the original garrotte-tonguing tales. Alex Comfort, who was a very gloomy teenage prodigy in 1937, and who later moved through ferocious pacifism into sex and gerontology, returned to the glooms in *The Comforters* (Duck-worth), set in a gloomy near-future Britain (this may be tautological), and it was gloomy. *The Emperor of America* (Simon & Schuster) by Richard Condon shot off fireworks into the mouth of darkness of his native land, mapping Kronos's teeth, avoiding like the plague the Matter of Reagan (see below) by setting his alternate-history plot just after old death-rattle rode west in 1988.

In *McGrotty and Ludmilla: or, the Harbinger Report* (Dog & Bone: Glasgow), Alasdair Gray applied the pissed *récit* style of Scottish satire to a few near-future English targets, fairly mildly for him. Patrick Harpur's *Mercurius: or, The Marriage of Heaven and Earth* (Macmillan) is gaga if Yeats was: if 'Sailing to Byzantium' is a ferry ad, then *Mercurius* is orthodox astrology. *Fires' Astonishment* (Secker) is Geraldine McCaughrean's second attempt to novelise a folksong — 'The Laily Worm and Machrel of the Sea' in this case — and duly inserts a genuine stained unstalwart dragon into medieval England, where it pouts steam. Wolf Mankowitz, in *Exquisite Cadaver* (André Deutsch), writes a traditional posthumous fantasy, but by setting it in a surreal American West opens the revolving gates of dream, so that what is real and what is waiting become one. Milorad Pavic's *Landscape Painted with Tea* (Knopf) proved you could repeat a fluke, because this gallimaufry, like a dwarf crab-apple sprout gone godzilla, is a solipsism no less self-fertilising than *Dictionary of the Khazars*; the translation, by Christina Pribicevic-Zoric, is again superb. Leo Perutz's 1933 novel, *St Peter's Snow*, was finally translated (Harvill): the eponymous virus had, during the Middle Ages, infected Europeans with the disease of Christianity; and now, in 1933, hundreds of years later, once again virulent, it has begun to create Nazis everywhere. In *The Quiet Woman* (Bloomsbury), which is also a kind of Plague Journal, Christopher Priest anatomises the Thatcher Years with a savagery all the greater for its absolute failure to shout; it was the neatest exercise in devastation published this year. *Vineland* (Little, Brown) by Thomas Pynchon, a 400-page scherzo whose panache mocked the seventeen-year gap since *Gravity's Rainbow*, teetered at the edge of the Reagan Years, but refused to carry its protagonists into the new world, like a wise lungfish spying out the terrain and seeing it was the beach at Bikini; it seemed all the more civilised for this. *Haroun and the Sea of Stories* (Granta) by Salman Rushdie could attract no reviewer who did not know the real story: perhaps someday we will be able to read this one, which at first glance seemed a fossil in ice, with liquid eyes. With *The Ice-Shirt* (André Deutsch), in which berserkers shapechange into the first explorers of Vinland, William T. Vollmann began to publish a grandiose mythos of America in a projected seven volumes, but can Deutsch survive the next six, can anyone teach the endlessly logorrhoeic Vollmann how to stop: something his mentor, Laurence Sterne, never learned in time. And Kurt Vonnegut cast an extremely cold eye: *Hocus Pocus: or, What's the Hurry, Son?* (Putnam), set at the end of the century, views an America owned but already abandoned as a rotten investment by Japan, in a prose icy with despite. It is the story of a man — soldier, teacher, hypocrite, jailbird of the planet home — who has been worn past frazzle into permafrost. As he talks to us, he continues to cough himself to death: because, like the planet, he cannot stop smoking.

It was a quiet year for dinosaurs, those writers we have defined in previous years as Cargo from the Golden Age, though some of them continued to issue shares (non-voting, non-preferred). Isaac Asimov and Arthur C. Clarke both 'collaborated' in the production of novels both of which — though neither outcome was technically a sharecrop, neither younger partner being sufficiently junior or impoverished to have to work for hire — had all the *seeming* of the sharecrop title: the clone gaze inwards of each book at the altar of the past; the enervating belatedness of plot and discourse; the medusa chill of the sealed and finished texts. In *Nightfall* (Gollancz),

Robert Silverberg, using every ounce of his enormous skill, managed to sound just as Asimov might have sounded if Asimov had been dumb as well as lacking in metaphor: which (as Asimov and Silverberg are among the most *intelligent* writers of the century) only underlines the terrible penalties of flirting with death. The original short story from 1941, though written in a style less clean than Asimov later mastered, conveyed its great notion in a flash: the intoxication of which can still keep the reader from wondering about camera obscuras, or cellars, or the slow onset of star-revealing dusk, or indeed the vast eclipse-defeating roundness of your typical planet. In the novel, which was told with beggaring clarity, there was no flash of revelation; nothing but a slow benumbing bathetic club-bore *drone*, like some Pentagon colonel with a pointer after the Gulf War, the very antithesis of a smart weapon. Arthur C. Clarke, on the other hand, granted Gregory Benford more or less free scope to sequel *Against the Fall of Night* (1953); Benford's effort, to which he gave the revealingly Whiggish title of *Beyond the Fall of Night*, and which appeared with Clarke's original in one large volume (Ace/Putnam), reads intermittently like a singleton, though always the pallor of displaced ontology frails out the bones of the thing. In the end the Janus-face profile of *Beyond the Fall of Night* is a trick of the shadows, for one face is stone and the other bulges with unshed tears. Ask Paul· Preuss.

By himself, Clarke wrote *The Ghost from the Grand Banks* (Gollancz); it seemed slim and sketchy, like a whole tale half-seen in North Atlantic fog. For page after page *The World at the End of Time* (Ballantine) and *Outnumbering the Dead* (Century), both by Frederik Pohl, read like more snoozes from the owl of Futuria, but then you saw the eyes were open, watching. The first book is dense with numeracy, swift in the telling, full of jokes and deft new sailor's knots of narrative, but bleaker in the gaps than a cracker-barrel at the end of time; and *Outnumbering the Dead*, a short tale about a lone mortal genetically barred from the immortality of his fellows, read like a meniscus over depths of pain. There was nothing new from L. Sprague de Camp, A. E. (Greatest Living ex-Canadian) Van Vogt or Jack Williamson, though next year will be different; but the grave of Robert A. Heinlein gave birth to something of a revelation: the uncut *Stranger in a Strange Land* (Ace/Putnam) might have restored a few too many passages of insufferably bent polemic, the sort of shadow-boxing solipsism alpha males tend to get up to when they think they're talking politics, but the telling throughout was significantly less choppy: double-cream pulp, which is nothing to sneeze at. And finally, by dying, Donald A. Wollheim (1914–90) proved likely to generate better stories in years to come, if one may judge by the obituaries beginning to waft gingerly heavenwards, than a lot of those he managed to publish in his lifetime as the genius of Ace and DAW.

It was a good year for science fiction, if you could only get the old rogue males – those writers, mostly not women, who began their careers in the aftermath of World War Two, just when history began to ice over – to stop flossing in the mirror. Poul Anderson, whose worn incisors decreasingly reave the gist of things, though his gloom hastens, provided in *The Shield of Time* (Tor), which is a loose fixup, another meditative time-cops foray into the past, where the gang played pattycake once again with history in order to save some awful new era. Ancient-Mariner-like, Gordon R. Dickson failed once again to weaken, or relent: *The Dragon Knight* (Tor) and *Wolf and Iron* (Tor) both said everything they were going to more than thrice, with glittering eye; but the latter, set in the usual depopulated post-holocaust America, did parlay its garrulousness into a long, devoted, surprisingly pacific, detail-obsessed paean to survival, though not eftsoons. Philip José Farmer closed down the teetering architectonic of his Dayworld-Dystopia sequence with *Dayworld Breakup* (Tor), many pages of which were spent at the abacus working out how many totally interchangeable identities the protagonists had accumulated, in a prose crammed with narrative bald spots, gaping blank *non sequiturs*, daft hypnopompic caesuras, and pyramids (or hierarchies), pyramids (or phalluses), pyramids (pyramids) everywhere. Yes! it was like spelunking the inside of a dead skull. Yes! it was like reading A. E. Van Vogt: Gosseyn with a penis. Charles L. Harness also slid pastwards, in *Lurid Dreams* (Avon), halting at the *locus classicus* of all American alternate history tales – the Civil War – and using, as has become *de rigueur*, the undead Edgar Allan Poe to carry the burden of the underside of the Dream. Showing some grasp of the art of hara-kiri, Harry Harrison *seemed* bent (but we cannot pretend to have read the contract) on franchising *himself*, in a packaged continuation of his own *Bill, the Galactic Hero* from 1965: *Bill, the Galactic Hero on the Planet of Bottled Brains* (Avon), which he wrote with Robert Sheckley, economically conveyed a sense of terminal exhaustion through the quality of its many jokes. Backseat-writing in Oz, R. A. Lafferty composed, or published, a small cornucopia of little books, of which *Dotty* (United Mythologies Press) was maybe the best: but they were all weirdly side-of-the-mouth, disengaged from the illiberal hidden agendas that stove them in like rocks of faith, and from the baroque inscapes they foundered to espouse. And

Kate Wilhelm, in *Cambio Bay* (St Martin's), could not manage to hold her breath until she got the thing told: *whooshing*, as usual, all over the second half: but wait for next year.

Tiptoe, we enter the world of the primes, writers at the peak of their careers. Though it is dangerous terrain, one thing is going to save us, something we know which they do not, for they are conditioned not to perceive certain facts of life at this stage of their metamorphosis into dinosaurs. As we can see, the jungle is full of large dens, each occupied by one of these figures of great ego who, though better-armed than samurai, seems at the same time far more delicate. Each den is furnished with memorabilia and kudos, which cannot be told apart. Oscars or Nebulas, which cannot be told apart, burden each mantel. Each writer sits with his or her back to the lamp. As we enter one of these dens, we must prepare to begin a 'conversation' with the writer whose task or 'rapture' we have visibly interrupted. In this 'conversation', we will pretend to talk about almost anything under the sun, but we *must not persevere* in this stage of the 'conversation' after the writer himself has begun to speak, for it is now that the real 'conversation' begins. It is now that we become privy to the writer's most secret thoughts: the significance of the Quest for Greatness in her early work, the extraordinary size of his last advance, the great affection evinced towards her by the population at large, the unique curvature of space whereby he occupies in perpetuity the very centre of the world. Several hours will pass. Our attention must not be permitted to flag. Fortunately, it is during this period that we will remember the one thing we know which he cannot, because his condition – Oliver Sacks has called it anosognosia – can be defined precisely as an inability to perceive his condition. The one thing we know *which he cannot know* is that there are other people in the world. That the jungles of the world are full of them. That the aisles of the jungles of the world echo with identical bellows of territoriality and triumph, day and night. That the anosognosia of the writer in his prime is universal, a Universal prank of the Anarch.

We exaggerate. We're all just folks down here in the brier patch. Piers Anthony, for instance, did nothing but write more books (list available on request). Iain (Middlename) Banks fisticuffed his way through another Culture tale in *Use of Weapons* (Orbit), the best of the lot so far, though barnacled with the same baroque jaw-jaw that sank *Consider Phlebas*. But this time the plot — two chronologies (one reverse) snapping together like a heat of steel into scissors — worked very hard indeed, and in the end the book *took*. It held. Greg Bear's *Queen of Angels* (Warner) transformed its eponymous

Los Angeles into a beehive of significant furore: with nanotechnology come biotransforms, cops and robbers, AIs pregnant with selfhood, voodoo shenanigans à la mode, and a writer the awfulness of whose work Bear seemed insufficiently to recognize. *Heads* (Century), set in the same universe some decades further on, tested out as equally complex within its long-novella compass: lacing together cryogenics, researches into absolute zero, Moon culture stuff, and a rebirth threat from icy death of a California guru whose manipulative fake religion totally failed to resemble (said the lawyers) any twentieth-century Son-of-Edisonade claptrap we might have experienced here on Earth. Gregory Benford we have already descried, toughing out the anxiety of influence in the aisles of Arthur C. Clarke. Terry Bisson made like Terry Southern in *Voyage to the Red Planet* (William Morrow), appearing to spoof everything from Hollywood film 'culture' to the Nixon-death of NASA to Edgar Rice Burroughs's Mars: but within the tale everything worked, the science, the technologies, the protagonists, Mars herself. And we went along. In *Time and Chance* (Tor), Alan Brennert formidably recast an old *idée fixe* — changing lives with an alternate self from an alternate world — and transformed the gimmick into a genuine exploration of the roots of character, which turned out to be a fibrous nurture/nature maze, as in the vale of sorrows. David Brin took *Earth* (Bantam Spectra) into the palm of his hand, and saved it: though not without the help of some magnificent entrepreneurs, the Three Crones, and Gaia herself. And Lois McMaster Bujold carved a tiny prequel niche for Miles Vorkosigan to stuff in *The Vor Game* (Baen) while waiting to conquer the galaxy by 2000 or so (our time) with nothing going for him but wit, money, luck, knuckle-headed adversaries, mercenary cadres who love him half to death, a supernaturally powerful and devoted Pa, a plethora of space-opera clichés longing to be of assistance, and one quite exceptionally sympathetic author. There's Bs for you.

Jonathan Carroll (next letter) juggled so many balls in *Black Cocktail* (Century) that you just knew he'd step on one, and Tilt, and the game would end in tears: and it did. Michael Crichton did a lot of dinosaur research for *Jurassic Park* (Knopf), a novel which turns dinosaur research into fast food for browsers, with Dreadful Warnings on the package about those unbridled scientists who brought you the plots of *The Andromeda Strain* and *Coma*, but at least the book was biodegradable: it digested in a flash. Stephen R. Donaldson brought his massive countenance to bear on the frail vessel of space opera in *The Gap into Conflict: the Real Story* (Collins), and holed it, in a style more Hun than Gothic. Mary Gentle, having tied her shoelaces together with Writing Hooks, duly tripped headfirst into *Rats and Gargoyles* (Bantam Press), grade-school tics and gimmicks sprNewnging from her grab-bag; but once inured to all this stuff, the reader began to witness something complex and fine take shape, a through-composed Neoplatonist memory-theatre fabulation woven from holy dung. *The Difference Engine* (Gollancz), by William Gibson and Bruce Sterling, grows in hindsight, like a time-bomb, a terrifying alternate-universe depiction of 1855 Britain transformed into a satanic slum by Babbage's eponymous computer; but the fact remains that Dickens — whose fever-dreams Gibson and Sterling have, perhaps not unconsciously, ransacked — is conspicuously absent from a book otherwise stuffed with real authors, and that absence shuts the book's mouth. Colin Greenland won the Arthur C. Clarke Award for *Take Back Plenty* (Unwin), a space opera whose exuberance is perhaps a touch lucubrated, but whose intelligence and tact shine constantly through. Joe Haldeman's *The Hemingway Hoax: a Short Comic Novel of Existential Terror* (William Morrow) also grows in the mind's eye, a revision not harmed by acquaintance with the subtitle (omitted from the British edition), as the book is everything claimed for it: funny, horrific, short, about Hemingway, and (like any good tale of parallel worlds) the tale it tells fucks essence. In restored form, *The Stand* (Hodder) by Stephen King is even more like a new novel than *Stranger in a Strange Land* (Putnam) having been reassembled, recast, rewritten, refurnaced into a thousand pages of flow and gush and slag and gem, a book Paul Bunyan might have written had he managed to outstare W. H. Auden, whose libretto for Benjamin Britten's *Paul Bunyan* transmogrifies into culture hero the axe-wielding Caliban of Maine. Nancy Kress (in her alpha person novitiate) gave us *Brain Rose* (William Morrow), getting a few more tropes under her belt (each book improving, traversing larger snatches of the territory), exploring (this time) the narrative possibilities of the human brain, Previous Life Access Surgery into the hinterlands, diseases in the world which wipe the maps of memory and blind the cast: memory and perception, as we have begun to learn, being one. After quite a few books which failed to gain the high ground, Michael Kube-McDowell finally wrote, in *The Quiet Pools* (Ace), a tale whose premise was strong enough to catch the mind. Humanity is genetically divided into two unequal segments: those billions of us compelled to remain upon the home planet, and those few capable of departing, like butterflies escaping a sewer.

It was good to see something like the return of Ursula K. LeGuin, though *Tehanu* (Atheneum), an ostensible sequel to *The Earthsea Trilogy*, was less a reunion than an imposition of *curfew*. It was like a cop in the treehouse. The grown woman at the narrative heart of

Tehanu lives in a different world than the lads who played at Eden in bramble archipelagos, incarnadining like berries the world-sea of the garden of longing, but to say so was not to tell us what we did not know: it was to blindfold us with rectitude. Farewell Ged. *Only Begotten Daughter* (William Morrow) continued to test – as only James Morrow can – the tensile limits of whimsy, so that the brilliant segments of this novel, just as in his previous books, overdosed on *wry*, overdosed on *worldly-wise-owl*, overdosed on *conceit*. Bill Ransom's *Jaguar* (Ace) also wore its virtue, though not upon its mutton sleeve, as its Vietnam-vet protagonist accumulated, slowly, in dream world after dream world, bad karma: and paid. Kim Newman, not for the first time, married *film noir* and the subconscious in *Bad Dreams* (Simon & Schuster UK). Mike Resnick's *Second Contact* (Tor) beetled through old genre crap like salts, but why. With *Pacific Edge* (Unwin), Kim Stanley Robinson concluded his Orange County sequence, three novels which stack vertically to make a palimpsest, each volume expressing a different calculus of the future in the same place. This time it was utopia, or as close to the pale fires of utopia as we might wish to earn: planet-maintenance; softball; enforced miniaturisation of corporate life; softball; the centrality of the polis; softball. *The Hollow Earth* (William Morrow) by Rudy Rucker took on board a much younger Edgar Allan Poe than sf novelists in 1990 *usually* give space to, sending him down a Symmesian polar hole into a hollow Earth, making the book a kind of sequel to *The Narrative of Arthur Gordon Pym* (1838), which text the incorrigible Panshin Gang claims, in *The World Beyond the Hill* (1989), Poe 'broke off short, unable to nerve himself to enter and stay': poor, feeble, hidebound, pre-Doc-Smith Edgar Allan Poe, born too soon to dare to dream the big dream and *stay* there like a man, like we do.

In *Orbitsville Judgement* (Gollancz), Bob Shaw keeps something of the scale of his Dyson Sphere world, while dinkytoying the plot into melancholy doodle; but Charles Sheffield plunges into the gigantic artefact universe of *Summertide* (Ballantine) with swelling glee, makes a meal of the hugeness. Lucius Shepard's *Kalimantan* (Century) is set in a 1980s Borneo iridescent with belatedness, for the book is a parody-with-love of the scientific romance and Joseph Conrad, horripilating with that genre's anxieties about toppling off the thin plate of the illuminated world into the Universal Anarch swallowing All. *Hyperion Cantos* (SFBC for the omnibus), a title Dan Simmons seems to have selected to comprehend *Hyperion* (1989) and *The Fall of Hyperion* (Foundation Doubleday), makes almost seamlessly one novel, though the second volume, which bases itself on Keats's second poem about coup d'étating the gods, imitates at times its model's spasms of failed rapprochement with the great subject: but in the end Simmons's extraordinary concentration on the job of juggling his immensely complicated plot does pay off, and the book emerges phoenix-like from the dross and Sevagram of sf's space-opera tradition. *Hyperion Cantos* may be the first full-grown space opera ever written (this reviewer has called it an entelechy opera, but that's another tack). Rising like Excalibur from a slurry of sharecrops and series-fillers, Brian Stableford's *The Werewolves of London* (Simon & Schuster UK) utterly transformed the werewolves-are-our-elder-cousins-from-the-dawn-of-time novel into a discourse on the nature of the Victorian world-view. This discourse — being genuine — sucked the blood right out of the poor werewolves, who were fake: good. Nothing exceptional had seemed likely to come from John E. Stith, a part-time author of several mildly virtuous novels, until this year, with *Redshift Rendezvous* (Ace), a hard-sf romp into a hyperspace whose fundamental laws differ from ours: the plot wambled, ideas turned the pages: good.

Raising the Stones (Foundation Doubleday) by Sheri S. Tepper, set in the same unforgiving universe as *Grass* (1989), continued to raise the ante on reading her without fail-safes: when she tosses off crap, the intelligence is too sharp for the text and the language too canny, and the stuff goes rogue in the mind: and a book like this one, a complex, booby-trapped assault on the integrity of 'man', utterly fails to absent itself. So you can never get away from it. Ian Watson's *The Flies of Memory* (Gollancz), a mere bagatelle from the gadfly of the Western world, did manage to pack into relatively few pages half a dozen protagonists, eight cosmologies, ten gods a-leaping, and a few laughs; the book was brilliant but fidgety, skating over the ocean of story like a goosed waterbug. In *The Divide* (Foundation Doubleday), Robert Charles Wilson anatomised split minds, staying strictly on the slicks of the surface of these things. The death on page one of a character who may have been King Arthur initiates a musical-chairs guignol of recruitment in Gene Wolfe's *Castleview* (Tor), set in the far west of modern Illinois, and a final Arthur re-enacts the primal drama in jig time: to touch the book with the mind's eye was to stumble from the shock: but the book climaxes with such bravura speed that all aesthetics of ending are scorched: and the shock finds no ground. The closet-drama Vertigo Baroque of *Heathern* (Unwin) chilled some readers of Jack Womack's third novel, which is set in the near-future Manhattan of the previous two, but a small moral allegory did peep through the cinders, saying listen. It was possible to.

There were some newer writers. Relevance to the times did not seem generally to overcome them. In *The Land Beyond; a Fable* (Unwin), Gill Alderman submitted her planet Guna to some dry-deluge plotting that sucked the moisture from the very soil; Terry Dowling's *Rynosseros* (Aphelion: Adelaide) knuckled under to Cordwainer Smith's vision of Norstrilia, without the plot line or the potty poetry; Scott Edelman's *The Gift* (Space and Time) was a gay vampire novel, gandy dancing for AIDS; Gregory Feeley's *The Oxygen Barons* (Ace Specials) applied a dry-ice virus to the tropes of hard sf, more than becoming its model; *The Hour of Blue* (North Country Press) by Robert Froese did, with some energy, address the condition of the Earth; Elizabeth Hand's *Winterlong* (Bantam), though something of a wallow, seemed slim and supple and muscular if you did a mental edit: and the writing was both shadowy and exuberant; Lisa Mason's *Arachne* (William Morrow) was almost too expert in its renewal of cyberpunk turns; Judith Moffett, in *The Ragged World: a Novel of the Hefna on Earth* (St Martin's), yanked Zenna Henderson into the big city; Allen Steele set *Clarke County, Space* (Ace) in Clarke County, Space, and seemed content to settle there.

And that was the year we had, a better year in which to write sf than to read it. But we're century migrants, the lip of time is sucking fast, wait for next year, some revelation is at hand. In the 25 years since this reviewer – since I – first published in *New Worlds*, whole logjams of books have passed downstream to the sea, which bought them all. In 1966 it seemed urgent to read on, because the next book might well contain some code for seeing things in the light, exposing the morrow; enfranchisement now for mortals! But the books turned out fictional, as one had thought they might, and sank waterlogged downwards: holed like the years. And if I continue to read now, 220,000 hours later, it is not to gain wisdom (I failed) but to taste the mind of the makers. Grasping is what seems to count, a posture that dances the time jig: not answers. If it's only shadows on the walls of the cave we see, let their loins be girded. This year shadows were cast once or twice, in novels by Thomas Pynchon, Dan Simmons, Brian Stableford, Sheri Tepper, Kurt Vonnegut: not necessarily the best books read, but the ones most pugnacious to shape. And the year turned, and the shadows dance. I may awake one morning from uneasy dreams and find myself transformed.

ROBERTS & VINTER LTD.
Publishers

Very promising
Keep trying

MANAGING EDITOR: 42-44 DOCK STREET, LONDON E.1
EDITOR, NEW WORLDS SCIENCE FICTION:
17, LAKE HOUSE, SCOVELL ROAD, LONDON S.E.1
EDITOR, SCIENCE FANTASY: 18, NORHAM GARDENS, OXFORD.

The Editor thanks you for submitting the enclosed material, but is
returning it as he regrets there is no immediate prospect of making
use of it in our publications.

Past, Present and *Future*

David Garnett

The first issue of *New Worlds* was published in
1946, although it developed from an amateur magazine called
Novae Terrae which originally appeared in 1937. *New Worlds*
was edited by E. J. Carnell until 1964, when Michael Moorcock
became editor.

Science fiction was never the same again.

What Moorcock did with *New Worlds* has become the stuff of
legend – and a doctoral thesis. *NW* was the inspiration for a whole
generation of sf writers, in Britain, the USA and around the world,
and its name still causes many authors to say: 'I always wanted to
be published in *New Worlds*.'

As well as editing *NW*, Moorcock later took over as publisher
and financed the magazine by writing sword and sorcery novels.
Brian Aldiss was influential in securing an Arts Council grant for
New Worlds – and questions were asked in Parliament. In the early
seventies, ten volumes of *NW* appeared in paperback, published
first by Sphere, then by Corgi. Six of these were also published in
the USA, by Berkley and Avon. It was these volumes which probably reached the widest readership. The last of these came out in
1976, when *New Worlds* returned to magazine format and a very
irregular schedule. Only five issues appeared over three years, until
September 1979.

That was the last time *New Worlds* was published.

And now, twelve years later, this is the new *New Worlds*.

'Short stories are the very heart of science fiction. Magazines and
original anthologies such as this one produce the very best in
science fiction: new stories by the genre's most famous authors, and
new stories by the latest talent in the field.'

That was what I wrote as part of my introduction to *Zenith*, the
first anthology of new sf stories which I edited. Published in
1989, the book was intended as the first in an annual series of
original stories. *Zenith 2* appeared the following year, but by then
the publisher had been bought by another company – one con-

glomerate selling out to another international corporation – and the series was cancelled.

As he has already mentioned in his introduction, Michael Moorcock then asked me if I would like to edit *New Worlds* – and this, the first volume in a new series, is my answer.

The sixties is history, but it was without doubt the time when the world's most imaginative and innovative sf was published in Britain – and that meant it was published in *New Worlds*. This was what became known as 'the New Wave', and many of its foremost exponents were American.

And, again without any doubt, for the first time in two decades, it is Britiain which is producing the most exciting contemporary science fiction. There are more good new writers than ever before.

Part of the credit for this must go to *Interzone*, and to its editor David Pringle. The magazine made its debut in 1982, and the fiftieth issue was published a month or two before this volume. Authors need a magazine which appears regularly in their own country, a place where manuscripts can be sent. The very existence of *Interzone* has encouraged the development of new talent, even if authors find print elsewhere.

The story of British science fiction during the eighties, however, is more than the story of *Interzone*. The first author in this volume, Storm Constantine, began her career in 1987 with the publication of a novel, and she already had three books in print before her first short story appeared. ('The Pleasure Giver Taken' in *Zenith*; and she also had a story in *Zenith 2*.)

Ian McDonald is the only other writer to appear in this *New Worlds* who was also in both volumes of *Zenith*. (Brian Aldiss was in *Zenith*, Michael Moorcock and Simon Ings in *Zenith 2*.) McDonald lives in Belfast, and his first story was published in *Extro*, a short-lived magazine published in Northern Ireland, in 1982. His next stories appeared in the USA, in *Isaac Asimov's Sf Magazine*, and it was in America that his first two books were published, a novel and a collection of short stories; his next two novels also first appeared in the USA.

New Worlds, even when edited by Carnell, always published American authors as well as British. And this *NW* includes a story by the American writer Paul Di Filippo. His first story was published in 1977, and he has appeared in a wide variety of publications. More American authors will appear in future volumes, and possibly there will be contributions from non-Anglophone writers.

J. D. Gresham is making only her second appearance in print

with her *New Worlds* story, and she should soon be one of the many new authors with a novel due for publication.

No matter how many short stories a writer has sold, it is book publication which is regarded as the first major success, and at least seven British authors will be having first novels published during 1991 and 1992 — an unprecedented number. These include Eric Brown and Stephen Baxter, both of whom appeared in *Zenith 2*. Brown's first book has already been published, a collection of short stories. Simon Ings, also from *Zenith 2*, is another of the seven. Before too long the co-writer of his story in this volume, Charles Stross, will join the ranks of those who have sold their first novel.

Kim Newman, meanwhile, has probably sold as many books as all of these combined. His first story appeared in 1984, and featured a character named Jack Yeovil. Yeovil has since become Newman's alter ego, the name under which his 'young adult sex and violence fiction' is published.

Jay Summers becomes the latest author to have his first story published in *NW*, joining an impressive list which includes Robert Holdstock, Ian Watson and Geoff Ryman. The story included here is not only the first time Summers has been published, it is the first story he ever submitted for publication. He was born the same year that the 'New Writers' issue of *New Worlds* (which included Hold-stock's first story) appeared.

And Matthew Dickens was born the year that Moorcock's second Jerry Cornelius novel, *A Cure for Cancer*, was serialised in *New Worlds*: the final year of the sixties.

Before very long, *NW* will be publishing authors born in the seventies.

Michael Moorcock, Brian Aldiss and John Clute, however, go back a little further than that. (As indeed do I. My first-ever story was rejected by Moorcock in 1965. Like so many others, it was always my ambition to be published in *New Worlds*. My name appeared in the 'New Writers' issue — just my name, which was included in a list of writers 'we expect to publish in the near future' by Graham Hall, who edited that particular issue. But I suppose that editing *New Worlds* is almost as good as having a story published in it.)

Moorcock first appeared in *NW* in the last month of the fifties, with a story written in collaboration with Barrington Bayley. Two more stories, another collaboration with Bayley, and one guest editorial later, and Moorcock had become the editor. He occasionally relinquished this role over the next fifteen years, as with the paperback 'quarterlies', the last five of which were edited by Moorcock and Charles Platt, then Hilary Bailey and Charles Platt, and then by Hilary Bailey alone.

Brian Aldiss's association with *NW* goes back even longer, to 1955. 'I always wrote my best for *New Worlds*,' he said recently, as is confirmed by his story in this volume. Writing about him in *Zenith*, I said: 'Brian Aldiss is the godfather of British science fiction: author, critic, editor, essayist, historian, reviewer, actor . . .' To this can now be added 'artist' – he illustrated his own story here.

John Clute first appeared in *New Worlds* with a short story, in 1966, and he is now acknowledged as science fiction's premier critic. William Gibson has referred to him as 'an urban literary wit whose grasp of the genre, and of its place in the wider world of letters, is very likely unequalled in our time and language.' His essays on 'science fiction novels of the year' previously appeared in another anthology series which I also edited, *The Orbit Science Fiction Yearbook*, and were acclaimed by publications as diverse as *Analog* ('marvellously and acerbically opinionated') and *Science Fiction Eye* ('required reading for anyone serious about sf as a literature'). When the *Yearbook* was cancelled after three volumes, Clute agreed to continue his series of articles for *New Worlds*.

There were two volumes of *Zenith*, three volumes of *The Orbit Sf Yearbook* – but there will be at least four new *New Worlds* . . .

These volumes will be published by Gollancz over the next two years. As it says on the title page, I am the editor, while Michael Moorcock is consultant editor.

This is the place where I should be publishing my manifesto, an editorial rallying cry, proclaiming that *New Worlds* will be publishing the best new sf that can be found anywhere.

It will.

But probably the best statement which can be made is to be found in the contents of this first volume: these are the kind of science fiction stories I like, and these are the kind I shall be including in future volumes. The rest of the series will also be carrying the occasional non-fiction piece, such as the Clute essay, but the emphasis will be on good fiction.

Much of what is included here goes far beyond the traditional limits of sf, but the best science fiction is always on the edge of becoming something else, transcending the genre.

As yet, I cannot say for certain exactly what I will be including in future volumes because editors can only select from what they are sent, and we always need new stories, new authors.

What I can promise about this new series of *New Worlds* is that, whoever the author, every story will be a true original.

I look forward to it all.

The Authors

STORM CONSTANTINE shares her birthday with Aleister Crowley and her home with two cats and a hidden variable. She is the author of the Wraeththu trilogy (*The Enchantments of Flesh and Spirit*, *The Bewitchments of Love and Hate* and *The Fulfilments of Fate and Desire*) and the novels *The Monstrous Regiment*, *Hermetech* and *Aleph*; her next book will be *Bury the Shadow*.

PAUL DI FILIPPO was born thirteen days after Elvis Presley's television début, and he lives in Providence, Rhode Island. His short stories have been published in magazines such as *Fantasy and Science Fiction* and *Amazing*, and anthologies such as *Synergy* and *Universe*. He writes book reviews for *The Washington Post* and ass-kicking non-fiction for magazines such as *Science Fiction Eye* and *New Pathways*. His first novel, *Ciphers*, was published in America in 1991; the second, *Joe's Liver*, will appear in 1992.

J. D. GRESHAM was born in 1952 in the Midlands and spent her early life there. She has been working in education in Britain and Italy for sixteen years and is currently based in London. Her first published story was in *Other Edens III*. A novel is in progress.

IAN McDONALD lives in Belfast with his wife and two cats. His first story was published in 1982. He is the author of the novels *Desolation Road*, *Out on Blue Six* and *King of Morning, Queen of Day* and the collection *Empire Dreams*. His next book will be a graphic novel, illustrated by David Lyttleton, called *Kling Klang Klatch*. 1992 will see publication of his fourth novel *The Inarticulate Speech of the Heart* and a second collection of short stories. Following that will be *Necroville*, to be published as both a novel and a graphic novel.

KIM NEWMAN was born the day that Republic Pictures went into bankruptcy, brought up in the West Country and educated at Sussex University. He has had nine novels published since 1989: *The Night Mayor*, *Bad Dreams* and *Jago*; the others have appeared under the pseudonym Jack Yeovil. More books are forthcoming, under both names.

Newman has also written non-fiction books such as *Nightmare Movies* and *Wild West Movies*, published short stories and articles in numerous magazines and reference books, appeared on a variety of television programmes, and is the film reviewer for Channel 4 daily. In 1991 he won the British Science Fiction Award for his story 'The Original Dr Shade'. With Paul J. McAuley, he is currently editing an anthology called *In Dreams*.

JAY SUMMERS was born on the 23rd anniversary of a military test on Nagasaki. He lives, as an experiment, in the UK, and works as an artist and writer. 'Indeterminacy' is his first published story.

MICHAEL MOORCOCK became editor of *New Worlds* in 1964 at the age of 24. Excerpts from the first Jerry Cornelius novel began to appear in *New Worlds* in 1965; the novella 'Behold the Man' was published there in 1966, and won the Nebula Award. The first Elric stories were published in *Science Fantasy*, the companion magazine to *New Worlds*; the latest Elric novel is *Revenge of the Rose*. Moorcock's next book will be the third Pyat novel, *Jerusalem Commands*; the fourth and final Pyat book will be *The Vengeance of Rome*. He has two cats.

MATTHEW DICKENS was born six days after the first manned lunar landing. His first story was published in *Interzone* in 1990, and he is now one of that magazine's assistant editors; he has also had several stories published in small press magazines. He read English at Southampton University and in 1991 was awarded an MA in Renaissance Literature from Sussex University.

SIMON INGS lives in London and is the author of two forthcoming novels: *Hot Head*, a thriller set in a unified Europe, will be published in 1992; *In the City of the Iron Fish*, a literary fantasy, has yet to be scheduled — or finished. His short fiction has been published in the anthologies *Other Edens III*, *Zenith 2*, and the magazines *Interzone* and *Omni*. He is a founder member of 'The Unlimited Sex Company', a theatre group which includes sf writers Colin Greenland and Geoff Ryman. The photograph of Mr Ings was taken shortly after Charles Stross described to him the workings of his new computer.

CHARLES STROSS was born in Leeds in 1964. An ex-pharmacist turned technical author, he works part-time as a freelance journalist and writer of short stories (*Interzone, There Won't Be War*) and novels (which have yet to sell).

BRIAN W. ALDISS lives in Oxford. His novels *Report on Probability A, An Age* (now titled *Cryptozoic!*) and most of *Barefoot in the Head* were originally published in *New Worlds*; his most recent novel is *Dracula Unbound*. He is currently writing *Remembrance Day*, a companion novel to *Forgotten Life*. His next book will be a collection of poems, *Home Life with Cats*.

JOHN CLUTE is currently editing, with Peter Nicholls, a new edition of *The Encyclopedia of Science Fiction*, to be published in 1992. His articles covering sf novels published during 1987, 1988 and 1989 were published in *The Orbit Science Fiction Yearbook*, 1–3.

DAVID GARNETT's first novel *Mirror in the Sky*, was published in the USA in 1969.

New Worlds,
c/o Victor Gollancz Ltd,
14 Henrietta Street,
London WC2E 8QJ.

Telephone 01-836 2006 · *Vigollan London WC2* · *Trade & Deliveries*, 30 Maiden Lane WC2

DIRECTORS
LIVIA GOLLANCZ (Governing Director and Joint Managing Director)
JOHN BUSH (Chairman and Joint Managing Director)
ALICK BARTHOLOMEW · MARY BRASH · LADY GOLLANCZ · GILES GORDON

VICTOR GOLLANCZ, LTD
14 Henrietta Street, Covent Garden, W.C.2

LONDON

12th December 1967

David S. Garnett Esq.
22 Tudor Road
Hunts Cross
Liverpool 25

Dear Mr. Garnett,

I have read your manuscript, MIRROR IN THE SKY but I am afraid I don't feel it is up to the high standard that we try to keep in our science fiction list.

I am, therefore, with regret, returning your manuscript to you.

Yours sincerely,

John Bush
Director

The BSFA takes you beyond your imagination

The British Science Fiction Association is your key to the many worlds of Science Fiction. You will discover everything you always wanted to know about SF in Britain — and more. Six times a year *Vector* brings you interviews, book reviews, and incisive articles in one of the leading critical magazines on SF. Six times a year *Matrix* brings you right up to date with all the news, plus film and magazine reviews. Six times a year *Paperback Inferno* gives you a searing overview of paperbacks in the UK. And three times a year *Focus* provides a unique forum for every SF writer in the country.

All this for just £12 a year. If you enjoy science fiction, join the BSFA. Write to Joanne Raine, Membership Secretary, 29 Thornville Road, Hartlepool, Cleveland TS26 8EW. In North America: Cy Chauvin, 14248 Wilfred St, Detroit. MI 48213, USA. Rates $25 sea/$40 air.

1971–1991
20th Anniversary Year

SCIENCE FICTION · FANTASY · HORROR

84 SUFFOLK STREET, BIRMINGHAM, B1 1TA
Tel: 021-643 1999 Fax: 021-643 2001